The Psychiatrist

Conscript, Prisoner, Interpreter, Healer

John West

AUTHOR'S NOTE

This story is set between 1985 and 1990 and the framework is factual. Eric West rarely spoke about his wartime experience but once he had retired as a psychiatrist in 1985, he suggested that the two of us, father and son, make a pilgrimage to his old battlefield sites in Flanders. Regrettably, we never made that trip. To compensate, many years later I undertook the research that forms the basis of this novel. I knew very little about my father's military service or his time in captivity, apart from the fact that he had worked as an interpreter. Most of the snippets of information were told to me by my mother. I knew less about my Uncle Geoffrey.

The events described affecting the brothers Eric and Geoffrey West in wartime and during Eric West's medical career are as accurate as they reasonably can be, including the descriptions of the officers and men of his artillery regiment, his German guards and fellow prisoners of war at Stalag VIIIB Lamsdorf.

However, this is a novel. During the research for this book, I made contact with as many survivors of this story and their descendants as I could. I found that, even when I was successful, memories were vague and sometimes contradictory. A constant emerged, all too often 'they didn't really talk about it.' For this reason, some of the characters described during the 1980s and their stories are imaginary, although in the course of my father's career, I am sure there was a 'Mary' character, as well as a fiercely patriotic teenager in Polish Silesia anxious to put the world to rights and more than one German ex-POW rehabilitated through his work at Camp 167 in Stoughton near Leicester.

For those readers who would like to know more about deep sleep treatment, IS9, the Special Allied Airborne Reconnaissance Force (SAARF), the 140 (5th London) Field Regiment Royal Artillery, the British Expeditionary Force's rear-guard action at Cassel in May 1940, the Queen Victoria's Own Madras Miner & Sappers Regiment, Stalag VIIIB Lamsdorf, the history of German Upper Silesia and the British post-war Denazification Programme, I have added a list of sources in the acknowledgements.

John West, October 2021

FOREWORD

When John West asked me if I would consider writing the foreword for this book based on his father's wartime story, I didn't hesitate to say yes.

As a military author specialising in stories of elite forces and special agents, I am no stranger to the remarkable endurance that can be summoned in the face of truly soul-breaking circumstances. The epic missions and escapes behind enemy lines which I have written about reveal extraordinary levels of bravery, resolve and resilience. Perhaps what is not so well written about is the psychological toll taken on those who served and especially those captured as prisoners of war. When all hope of escape has been extinguished, surrounded by traumatic scenes of human suffering, the battle then lies between surviving the brutality of your captors and fighting the demons in your own mind. For many, even years later, the ghosts of the past never leave.

As a doctor himself, John's attention to detail and his understanding of the human psyche are wonderful skills, especially when combined with the talent of a writer ...

The Psychiatrist is an exceptional book which unfolds in the manner of a good thriller. Told through the eyes of John's father, psychiatrist Dr Eric West, it takes the reader on several profound journeys, with Eric recounting and reliving his own engrossing experiences during the Second World War, first as a young soldier and later as a POW.

Initially stationed in Cassel, France in 1940 as part of the 140th (5th London) Field Regiment, Royal Artillery, Eric was part of the unit that was assigned to defend the British Expeditionary Force's heroic and miraculous evacuation from Dunkirk. Their efforts enabled three hundred thousand troops to make it back to England. Despite this, the unit never received official recognition or commemoration for their actions. Witnessing the full horror of the carnage following the heavy ground and air attacks by German forces, many of Eric's colleagues and friends were killed or captured. Eric survived but was taken prisoner and transported to the German-Polish border town of Lamsdorf, Silesia, before being transferred to Beuthen work camp, Arbeitskommando E72, a coal mine supplying the German war machine. It was here that Eric and his colleagues would spend the remainder of the war until January 1945 when the camp was evacuated.

The opening of Eric's story begins through his work as a psychiatrist forty years after the war, when he encounters an intriguing case of a patient who he discovers has her own secret war story to share. After years of providing talking therapy for his patients, Eric suddenly finds himself on the receiving end. Realising he needs closure and a chance to lay his own ghosts to rest, he sets off on an epic journey with his younger brother, Geoff, to revisit the scenes where he and his colleagues made their last stand in Cassel before being captured. Knowing that his real test remains in Poland where he was imprisoned, Eric summons up the courage to confront his demons once and for all as he makes the ambitious trip with his brother, retracing his footsteps and memories of life in captivity and the reality of his imprisonment for five long years.

Reliving all the memories and nightmares he had locked away for decades, Eric begins his own cathartic process. But as his trip ends he realises he has learnt very little about his brother's own wartime experiences in India; in fact, there's a great deal about his brother that he has no knowledge of at all.

I won't spoil the rest of the book or the twist at the end, for obvious reasons, but I commend this heartfelt and illuminating story to all who may read it.

Damien Lewis
Dorset, December 2021

To my parents

Eric West (1919-1992) and Joy West (1926-1979)

their grandchildren,

Joe, Rachel, Felicity, Holly, Emilia,

and their great-granddaughter,

Grace.

ACKNOWLEDGEMENTS

This book would not have been possible without the hard work, intuition and original thinking of my ghost-writer and book coach Ken Scott, to whom I am eternally grateful. Scotty (**www.kenscottbooks.com**) is passionate about World War II history and has written or co-written five books on this subject. With thanks also to my editor Joan Elliott at Fortis Publishing for her patience, encouragement and support.

I published much of the historical material about my father's wartime service in the Royal Artillery and his captivity in Stalag VIIIB Lamsdorf on this website: http://140th-field-regiment-ra-1940.co.uk/. Since the publication of the website, a plethora of new information about the regiment has emerged. This includes the diary of Lieutenant Graham Somerwill (with thanks to Martin Felstead), the private papers of Captain Sirkett (with thanks to his widow Sally), the diary of Brigadier the Honourable Nigel Fitzroy Somerset (with thanks to his grandson Henry Somerset), the private papers of Major Nevill Christopherson (with thanks to his grandson Tom Christopherson), the diary of Captain Cecil Hood (with thanks to his granddaughter-in-law Helen Hood). I'm also indebted to the following descendants of the men of the 140 Field Regiment: Richard Johnson for his recollections about his father Gunner Eric Johnson; Barry Ross for his original research into his uncle Bombardier Arthur Ross that culminated in the book *The Missing Son of Silvertown — Reported Missing for 15 Months* (2021) ISBN 978-1527265066); John and Alvin Bradbury, sons of Gunner Ernest Bradbury; Martin Felstead, son of Sergeant Frank Felstead and to Simon Conant, grandson of Sergeant Alfred Sheppard.

Additional material about the life of Lieutenant Colonel Cedric Odling TD was kindly provided by the Downhill Only Club based at Wengen Switzerland, and by Duncan Reynolds, Chairman of Odlings Ltd, Hull. Major David Clarke's articles about the Nazi occupation of Europe are available in the archive of the Daily and Sunday Express newspapers.

Lieutenant Colonel Graham Brooks, one of the commanding officers of my father's 140 Field Regiment wrote a book about the formation of the regiment in 1939 and its experiences in the British Expeditionary Force called *Grand Party* (1941) Fleet Street Press (now out of print). Captain Ronald Baxter, one of the regiment's officers captured at Cassel, donated his wartime diaries to the Imperial War Museum, **www.iwm.org.uk/collec**

tions/item/object/1030018252.

Information about the last stand of the 145 Brigade at Cassel during the final week of May 1940 is available in the books *Fight to the Last Man* by Simon Sebag-Montefiore (2006) Penguin ISBN 13:9780670910823 and *Cassel and Hazebrouck 1940* by Jerry Murland (2017) Pen & Sword Military ISBN 9781473852655. A German perspective on the fighting is outlined in *Dunkirk. German Operations in France 1940 by* Hans-Adolf Jacobsen (2019) Casemate ISBN 978-1-161200-659-8. I am grateful to Sergeant David Hineson who has conducted much original research on the fighting at Cassel, Mr Ian McCorquodale, nephew of Major J.R.H. Cartland MP and Paul Hunt, son-in-law of Bombardier Harry Munn and author of the website *'Dunkirk — the Untold Story'* **www.mgb-stuff.org.uk/harry/**. There is a file in the National Archives on mistreatment of soldiers marched into captivity in 1940, TS 26/214 *Brutality to prisoners on route of march from Cassel-Hazebrouck.*

A full archive of the career, media appearances and writings of Dr William Sargant are kept in the Wellcome Museum, and I am grateful to Lord Owen for his insight and memories of working alongside Sargant as a junior doctor at St Thomas' Hospital.

Information on Intelligence School-9 (IS9) and the Special Allied Airborne Reconnaissance Force (SAARF) is available in the National Archives; I am grateful to the historian Helen Fry for her help in sourcing material about IS9 and POW communication and to Diane Garside, Nelson College, New Zealand for sharing her research into her great-uncle John Ledgerwood who worked for MI9 from captivity. Further information about SAARF is available in the book *Some Talk of Private Armies* by Len Whittaker ISBN 0 9509694 0 0 and *The Last Escape* by John Nicholl and Tony Rennell ISBN 0-670-910946. The National Archives have a file on the Eichstätt tragedy, TS 26/533 *Eichstätt murder by exposure to allied air attack.*

The Lamsdorf website **https://www.prisonersofwarmuseum.com/** set up by Philip Baker has an active community of POW descendants. It is a rich source of information for relatives of POWs at Stalag VIIIB. Conditions at E72 Arbeitskommando and its infamous commandant Arthur Engelskircher have been described in the POW biographies *Boldness be my Friend* (1953) by Richard Pape ISBN 0755316266 and *Greece Crete Stalag Dachau* (2014) by Jack Elworthy ISBN 1927249120. I am also deeply indebted to Roger Hawkins and Christine Parry (son and daughter of Private George Hawkins) who have conducted extensive personal research on their father's captivity at E72 and his Long March. Their original research helped unlock the key to my father's previously missing years during his captivity. I am also grateful to John Glover, son of Private Ray Glover, a POW at E72 1940-45. I've received much helpful information and local knowledge from Dr Anna Wickiewicz, Manager, Department of Education and Exhibitions, Central Museum Prisoners of War, Łambinowice, Poland and Dr Joanna Lusek, Head of History Department, Upper Silesian Museum in Bytom, Poland. Norman Gibbs' wartime diary resides in the museum, donated by his family and resulting in Dr Lusek's book (in Polish): *Norman Gibbs, Prisoner of War number 16349, Retrospective Diary* (2018) ISBN 97883-931223-1-8.

The National Archives in Kew have documentation about mistreatment of British and Palestinian POWs at the E72 work camp: TS 26/555 *Beuthen: general*; TS 26/194 WO 309/307 *Hohenzollern Mine, Beuthen, Germany: ill-treatment of British POWs*; TS26/194 *Stalag VIII B: murder of Guardsman D. Blythin;* TS 26/305 Stalag VIII B: *murder of Privates Krauze and Eisenberg.*

The post war trial of Gerhard Spaniol is documented in the following National Archive files: WO 235/729 DJAG No 685. *Defendant: Gerhard Spaniol. Case No 270. Defendant: Fritz Pantke. Case No 249*; WO 235/394 *Beuthen case. Defendant: Gerhard Spaniol. Place of Trial: Hamburg*; WO 309/1093 *Hohenzollern Mine, Beuthen, Germany: alleged ill-treatment of British POWs* 309/820 *Beuthen, Germany: ill-treatment of British POWs by Gerhard Spaniol.*

The rehabilitation of German POWs in British hands and the Denazification Programme is described in *German Prisoners of War 1940-48. Policy and Performance.* 2006 Thesis. University of Swansea by Gillian S Clarke and *Enemies Become Friends: A True Story of German Prisoners of War* 1998. Pamela Howell Taylor ISBN 9781857761894.

The Queen Victoria's Own Madras Miners & Sappers Regiment is now called the Madras Engineers Group. They have a regimental museum at Bengaluru (Bangalore) and archive material is available at the Imperial War Museum, **www.iwm.org.uk/collections/item/object/1500009888**.

I am grateful to my two 'beta readers' for their insight and guidance.

Finally, I'd like to thank my partner Sara Walker for her unflinching support through the many long hours spent researching this story.

PROLOGUE

ST HELIER HOSPITAL, SURREY 1990

I accidentally pricked my finger some weeks ago.

I'd set myself a project to tidy the vegetable patch; it was shamefully overgrown. Not long before, I had received a letter from the council. It said that my allotment agreement was being rescinded due to the 'obvious lack of any activity'. I was clearing weeds, alone, and I picked up a thorn that dug into my finger as I pushed some rubbish into a dustbin.

That's funny, I thought as it started bleeding. *That blood looks mighty anaemic.*

I made a note to myself to visit my doctor so that I could arrange to have a blood test, wrapped my handkerchief around my thumb and carried on with the job in hand.

Within a couple of weeks, I'd been diagnosed with colon cancer. I was listed to go under the knife in one of the hospitals I had spent so many years working in.

I wrote a memo and handed it to my son together with a notebook containing a list of all my saving accounts… just in case. He was a doctor too and so he would understand and deal with it practically, I reasoned to myself.

The instruments were over noisy that day in the operating theatre. Clattering, banging, crashing all around me. I wanted to close my eyes, I wanted the anaesthetist to do her job as quickly as possible and send me into an involuntary, unconscious world. I looked to my left and then to my right, a fully fitted theatre for major surgery, so why were they being so damned noisy?

The staff were talking among themselves; someone lifted my arm without even asking my permission then read out my name and number from the plastic band on my wrist. The anaesthetist had placed an oxygen and anaesthetic mask over my face and, within a few short seconds, I began to recognise the beginnings of my recurring bad dream.

It's been years since I was last there, I thought to myself.

I was losing control despite my instinct to fight it. I closed my eyes; my destiny was in the hands of others now. "Count to ten, Mr West."

She didn't even call me 'Dr West' I noticed silently to myself.

"Count, Mr West."

"One, two, three, four, fi... fi... five..."

Damn... another background noise, a clattering banging noise, steel on steel. Where am I, what was it?

"Sechs, Sieben..."

Someone was counting us into the crowded cage. I didn't want to go in. Although at the point of a gun, I had no choice.

"Acht." He slapped me on the back.

Sweating, fearful men, some Polish, a Frenchman but mostly British boys like me, good boys... my friends... all of us prisoners of the Third Reich.

We are crammed in; I can hardly draw breath and the steel cage door slams shut.

Someone shouts, "Abfahrbereit!"

It is dark, and we begin the jerky descent into the dark abyss, down one thousand five hundred feet into one of the deepest coal mines in Silesia. I can feel the pressure changing in my ears. I close my eyes. "Gunner, jump out of the car and help dig us out of here, would you?"

"What! Where am I?"

"The Brunig Pass of course."

"What?"

"The cage, I'm in the cage."

"What bloody cage?"

The unmistakable, aristocratic voice of my commanding officer bellows in my ears.

"Where are we?" I repeat, totally bewildered.

"Switzerland man! Bloody Switzerland."

"Colonel Odling, is that you?"

"Of course it's me. West, get your arse out here and help dig us out. We'll have to fit those snow chains after all."

Snow... a blizzard. But it's a mine. There's no snow in a mine.

"We're going to miss the Olympics if you don't get yourself into gear.

Olympics…?

We dig the car out of a large snowdrift, and we're on our way again.

"Sleep, West, you deserve a rest, we'll wake you up when we get to Bavaria."

My eyes close.

There are thousands of people there, families with skis tied onto their cars, thousands of skis, skis everywhere you look. And we are there. We're at the Winter Olympics of 1936. More shouts, screams, cheering. We are standing by the finishing post; someone has crashed and medical men are attending to them. Their faces are blank, no features, no eyes, no mouth. Just a blur. And on their upper arms, those sinister red bands. I tremble with fear. Not the colonel. He isn't even watching the sport. Just those bloody Nazis. "Just look at those remarkable military men, West. The Germans have picked the finest specimens in Europe for this new Nazi army."

"Don't trust the bastards," a different voice chips in.

A faint cockney accent, no trace of Odling's clipped, public school tones. I can't place who he is, but he seems familiar; he is ranting and sounds angry.

The cage. I'm back in the cage but it's still. No movement at all. It's lying on its side in the snow. Odling has gone, the car has gone, the skiers have disappeared and so have the Nazis. "Get out of that bloody cage, Gunner West!" he shouts.

I do as I am told.

As I do, I step into an elegant café. The voice hands me a beer. "Don't you go listening to Odling, West. Look at him; it's not normal the way he looks at those pretty Nazi boys. I'm telling you; those bastards mean trouble."

I gaze across the room and there's Odling and a table full of Nazi soldiers with the red arm bands and now they have faces; they are handsome, smiling, white teeth, beautiful blond hair. And then the voice registers. It's 2nd Lieutenant Clarke, of course it is. He continues, "I saw what they did to those poor Jews here."

"Here?"

"Vienna lad."

"We are in Vienna?"

"Yes."

But we were in Switzerland, and then Bavaria and in a cage in Silesia. How are we in Vienna? This sort of makes sense, but at the same time it's nonsense. And 2nd Lieutenant Clarke, he was a journalist; he was there in Vienna when it all kicked off.

Hitler. Shouting and screaming. The devil reincarnated. He is demanding a union between Austria and threatening to invade them if his demands are not met. "He means trouble that bastard," Clarke says. "I did warn them. I was there, I wrote about it, but they ignored me. All I got was a bullet in my hat for my troubles."

He points over to the far side of the café and Hitler is still gesticulating on his lectern but although he is animated and his lips move, I hear no words. And then I can hear a different accent. A Scottish accent and I recognise it immediately. I am conscious of smiling to myself. It's Captain MacDougall. "Run for it, Eric!" he screams. "Follow me."

I jump up and run from the café into the fields outside. I follow the captain as he dives into a water-filled ditch. The water is cold and those Nazis with the armbands are there. I look behind me, they are running so fast, getting closer and firing at us. Their bullets are whizzing over our heads. MacDougall shouts, "Get up, Lance Bombardier, make a run for it!"

I try to get out of the ditch, but something is weighing me down. "Wake up, West, for God's sake!" MacDougall shouts at me. "Get a grip man!"

I feel the dull thud of a bullet in my back. It doesn't hurt but I feel paralysed. I just want to sleep. No more bullets, I hope, that wouldn't be good. I'm drifting away. "Bloody well wake up, West!"

"Wake up, Mr West."

A different voice. Not Scottish. Not a man. I looked up into bright fluorescent lights. A young nurse. Pretty.

"The operation is over. Mr West. Everything is finished and you're in recovery."

She adjusted the oxygen mask over my face. I breathed a sigh of relief. I'd made it.

There was no Colonel Odling, no Clarke, no MacDougall, and definitely no Nazis. Not here in the recovery room.

Chapter 1

The nurse had called her 'Mute Mary' and the name had stuck. It hadn't been the nurse's fault; despite her psychiatric training, she had lost her temper when Mary had consistently refused to talk. Occasionally the nurses had not even bothered with her name and just shortened it to 'The Mute.'

It had not been the worst thing that had happened to Mary during her sixty-odd years. After years of getting nowhere, she had learnt to take a path of least resistance. She waited in the day room and flicked through some old newspapers. She never usually bothered with the newspapers, preferring to lose herself in the pages of a book, but an article written a few weeks back had caught her eye. The article was headlined 'The Pat O'Leary Network', the coincidence of that surname amused her and took her straight back to her wartime days.

The O'Leary line was one of the many escape networks that operated during the war and one of her jobs had been to facilitate contact between Allied Prisoners of War and the various safe houses and couriers by sending coded letters to the camps. Although at the time, living through the Blitz and hearing the terrible stories from the occupied countries was scary, there was also something about her work that had satisfied her, using her extraordinary brain to outwit the enemy.

Before the war, Mary had lost touch with her father. She was told that he'd run off with an actress and any mention of him at home was banned. Her mother had family connections with the army and, in 1940, she had joined the Auxiliary Territorial Service, she was a junior commander at the age of twenty. It wasn't long before she came to the attention of her superior officers; one of them commented that she bordered on genius. Early on, her officers had spotted her mathematical skill and application.

1

With good reason, a couple of her officers felt her personality wasn't best suited to conventional military life, she was seen sometimes as a disruptive influence and not one to mix. Mary was recruited into Intelligence School 9 (IS9), a branch of MI9 at Wilton Park, Beaconsfield, just outside London.

She was not one for taking direct orders without at first analysing those orders. She had a habit of taking everything very literally. That was her personality. If she could see a logical conclusion to the instructions she had been given, she would carry them out unfailingly.

Mary was in Camp 20. The main house was famously used to bug captured German officers. They were treated like house guests in the hope that, in unguarded moments, they'd give away important information to the interpreters, some of whom were refugees from Nazi Germany, working silently in the basement listening into the conversations with headphones. Meanwhile, Mary had found her calling, processing coded letters. Her main role was in steganography, the art of hiding one message inside another using 'noise' words. They would create hidden information in a seemingly innocent letter. At Camp 20, Mary was undoubtedly the star of the show, able to decipher messages quicker than the others, some of them veterans of the Great War, with decades more experience.

By the summer of 1940, after the capture of a significant portion of the British Expeditionary Force at Dunkirk, MI9 had established that it needed to smuggle maps, currency, and escape aids into the Prisoner of War (POW) camps. Not only were some of the best officers and tactical brains of the British Army holed up in these POW camps, but also ordinary men hell-bent on escape. MI9 reasoned that there was no greater wastage of German armed forces manpower than to be chasing escapees. But more than that, given the right information, the escapees could also create havoc and mayhem, striking at the heart of the Reich. And even the men incarcerated could play a part. The machinery and equipment, particularly in the mines and at factories, were forever breaking down. Thanks to the ingenuity of the men working there who were constantly throwing a spanner in the works... literally.

MI9 invented fictitious cover organisations to 'donate' relief parcels for the camps. Organisations like the Prisoners' Leisure Hour Fund and the Ladies Knitting Circle sent packages to selected prisoners and there were general communal packs with playing cards, dominoes, and magazines. Mary had a particular pride in her personal invention, the Jigsaw Puzzle

Club. At first, there were no coded messages in there, only unmodified games and puzzles. After several months of seemingly 'innocent' packages, MI9 tested the water, hiding silk maps in John Waddington & Co board games and even using actual currency hidden within the Monopoly money to assist the escapees. Coded letters were written by Mary and some of her team in the form of love notes to individual prisoners.

By the beginning of 1942, MI9 had more than nine hundred coded letter writers regularly writing to POWs in the camps. As the war progressed, Mary was involved in compiling reports from escaped and repatriated non-combatant or injured POWs. They were all asked to fill in IS9 Liberation Questionnaires. She had studied the camps encyclopaedically and had locked herself away, sometimes for sixteen hours a day, reading every single questionnaire and the many heart-breaking stories from the POWs themselves. Mary had a photographic memory, she absorbed everything, and it was generally accepted that nobody knew more about the camps and POWs than she.

As the war progressed and by late 1944, there was great concern about the POWs at the highest levels of government and within Mary's department at IS9. The Allies were completely in the dark about Hitler's intentions regarding the quarter of a million Allied POWs he held. Plans were under way for a massive Allied invasion of the Lower Rhine region. One of the main factors in deciding when the operation went ahead was what the Germans intended to do with those prisoners incarcerated in camps in Poland and Czechoslovakia. There had been intelligence reports that Hitler planned to march every prisoner into the heart of Germany to use as a bargaining tool. Others believed they would simply be executed. There were rumours of a crazy last stand deep in a 'Fuhrer Redoubt' in the mountains of Bavaria. By now it was becoming clear that the rumours about extermination camps might be horribly true. It was imperative that the right people were on the ground very quickly to monitor every move the Germans made with their prisoners.

For those reasons, Mary had been considered for recruitment into the Special Operations Executive (SOE). She attended her first screening interview for a potential position within SOE as a front-line female agent.

Her grasp of languages was improving all the time. They had brought in a native-speaking German, a Czech, and a Pole to work with her night and day for nearly six months. At the end of that time, she spoke as though she'd been born in Munich to a Polish mother and Czechoslovakian father. Mary found herself in front of the renowned SOE chief, Vera Atkins. Almost as soon as the interview started, Vera Atkins asked, "Now, do you like heights, Miss O'Leary?"

A strange question, but Atkins explained that they would need to parachute Mary into German-occupied territory. Her fluency in German, and the fact that she was female, would mean her movements would attract less suspicion. Her task would be to establish contact with escaped POWs and certain individuals in the camps; to be a body on the ground to keep tabs on what the Germans' movements were. She would be the wireless operator, responsible for sending and receiving messages from London. It would be a dangerous job, Atkins explained that the wireless operators were highly vulnerable to detection and would have to be constantly on the move.

The parachute course lasted six weeks. Mary completed a series of jumps with the Parachute Regiment at RAF Ringway near Manchester; she hated the training. She misheard the instructor's shouting and the first jump resulted in a twisted ankle, the second jarred her back. She was on the point of resignation right there on the parachute training field; the more this course went on the more she felt her place was not in the front line. She might end up as more of a liability. In the end, the decision was made for her as, at the next interview stage, taking account of her overall performance, the SOE delivered its verdict. Although she'd passed the unarmed combat course in Scotland, they had concerns about her aptitude. And, of course, there was the parachute problem. As things stood, they said, there wasn't a place for her within the organisation. "There is someone we'd like to send you to see, however," they told her at the interview. "He'll be based at the Wentworth Golf Club; it'll be an interesting day out for you."

As the new year of 1945 beckoned, London had become as dangerous as it had been during the Blitz, or possibly more so, as Hitler's Vergeltungswaffen 1 (V1) and later V2, 'Vengeance Weapons' were raining down on the capital. However, in Europe, although people barely dared to say it, the war had turned in the Allies favour. The first signs of a London spring were emerging and, in the parks, snowdrops had appeared. The Allied invasion of mainland Germany was imminent after four hard years of conflict.

Finding Wentworth was a challenge. There was no public transport from Virginia Water train station, and no signage for the mile and a half walk towards the golf club. However, the prosperous tree-lined roads of Christchurch Road and Wellington Avenue, illuminated by dappled spring sunlight, were delightful as compensation.

The golf club at Wentworth was surreal. The clubhouse that used to belong to the Duke of Wellington's brother-in-law was a white, castellated, two-storey building. A Union Jack was flying from the mast and armed sentries stood at the front door.

After showing her identity papers and appointment card, Mary was escorted by a guard away from the main house and towards a steep flight of steps leading underground towards a steel, blast-proof door. Mary passed a comment to the guard, "It feels like the entrance to a tube station."

"Funny you should say that," he said. "This is a section of underground tunnel, we've had it buried here and adapted for our own purposes."

The guard knocked on the door.

"Come in."

Inside this bizarre subterranean world, Mary got a surprise. The room was full of people, not the normal two- or three-person panel she was expecting. "You're just the person we need, Miss O'Leary," she was told within a few minutes of entering the room.

It wasn't really an interview as such; they had obviously made up their minds before she had even arrived. She found the whole experience of this strange environment, surrounded by men and women in uniform speaking in various European languages, quite unsettling. "You are now a member of the Special Allied Airborne Reconnaissance Force (SAARF), and you should prepare to leave at short notice," she was told.

Within the hour she was on her way back home.

After the Allied crossing of the Rhine, news came through that an air bridge to Germany had been created and membership of SAARF no longer required a parachute certificate. Mary was put on immediate standby; her team of three were to be flown deep into southern Germany, a journey not without considerable danger but, at least for Mary, the parachute obstacle had been removed. The destination was to be an airstrip in southern Germany. There, the team would collect a canvas-roofed Willys MB Jeep that was to be their mobile office. There was a trailer for the all-important radio equipment. The Jeeps would have a protective steel pole bolted vertically on the front bumper. This was to counter the lethal wire booby traps, commonplace across the roads of occupied Germany.

They flew in on a full moon in a C47 Douglas Dakota from RAF Broadwell in Oxfordshire. SAARF had requested an RAF Transport Command plane; it was captained by a pilot from Melbourne, Australia. Mary sat in silence, alone with her thoughts, near the front of the plane. She could see the wing and one of the two radial engines. The Dakota vibrated with the power of its twin propellers and rumbled down the runway. She noticed a stream of oil running down the top of the wing. She wasn't sure if that was supposed to happen, or a sign that the engine might cut out. No one else inside this multi-nationality aeroplane seemed concerned. The Dakota's fuselage levelled as the tail wheel lifted and the entire shaking structure started to rise into the night air.

Too late to change my mind now, she thought as the patchwork quilt of Cotswold fields disappeared under the silvery haze of the moonlight.

The other two SAARF members, both seasoned soldiers, one of whom was Polish, sat nearer to the rear of the plane, looking out of their windows in contemplation of what lay ahead. She watched the oil running along the wing for the rest of the flight. They were all nervous, Mary had been told by one of the instructors that the life expectancy for agents in the field had been only six weeks. Hopefully, her mission with the SAARF was less risky than that, but she knew that if they hadn't been returned safely to Blighty in six weeks they would be living on borrowed time.

Two-and-a-half hours later, after they had crossed the German border with France, the pilot throttled back and brought the Dakota in low. The rough grass airfield, surrounded by parked transport aircraft, tanks and trucks came into view. The plane circled a couple of times giving the passengers time to observe the wreckage of the Luftwaffe aeroplanes lying forlornly on either side of the main airstrip. Mary watched out of her window while the main wheels lowered and the stream of oil she had been watching throughout the flight started breaking up as the air flowing over the wing slowed. She saw the rush of German soil as the Dakota made contact, bounced back into free air, and then lodged itself more definitely onto the airstrip before taxiing to a halt. At last, the hours of dreadful noise and vibration came to a stop and the side door was opened onto a cool dawn in Allied-occupied Germany.

Chapter 2

THE WIND CRIED MARY

Mary's mother, Roslin O'Leary, had pulmonary tuberculosis. She had been losing weight rapidly. She tried to convince Mary that it was the stress of the war and related to her father leaving, but Mary had insisted that she saw a doctor. They argued, as usual. Mary was bloody-minded, but eventually her mother caved in and agreed with her daughter that it would do no harm to get it checked out. She got an appointment for her chest x-ray and, once the film had been prepared, she saw the chest specialist at St Bartholomew's Hospital, a nice elderly man in a starched white coat and thick bifocal glasses. The calendar on his desk showed it was Thursday, 8th March 1945.

Roslin couldn't wait to tell her daughter the good news, it was at bay, no more treatment was needed, just another x-ray appointment in six months (or when the war was over, whichever came sooner, the doctor had cheerfully suggested). Hopefully, Mary would be home soon to hear this news. Roslin almost skipped out of the hospital, at least this was one less thing for her to worry about.

She decided to celebrate and splash out her ration cards for once, perhaps with a decent cut of meat from Smithfield Market. There were rumours that a fresh consignment of rabbit was available. She was last seen walking out of the outpatient building into the spring sunshine. As Roslin approached the market, it's possible that for a fraction of a second she felt a rush of air moving ahead of the pressure wave.

Along with one hundred and ten other souls, her body was never found. The V2 rocket struck just a few yards away from where she stood. Roslin was only identified by the remains of a watch, engraved with the date of her wedding, Valentine's Day, 14th February 1919.

Mary never forgave herself for not being with her mother at the appointment as they had previously arranged. She, of course, was engaged in her secret war work in SAARF at the time and knew nothing about the attack. Many of the V2 impacts in London were being censored in the press or passed off as gas explosions. The V2, the second of Hitler's three Vergeltungswaffen weapons, was close to achieving its objective of destroying civilian morale in the capital. The joke doing the rounds was, 'Have you heard about Hitler's new secret weapon, the flying *GAS* main?'

Mary didn't even get home for the funeral; a token service but no burial as such because there was nothing to bury. It had been more than a month before she even found out about her mother's death.

For Mary, life went rapidly downhill after the war. Her time in SAARF had been the most fulfilling of her life, but the unit was disbanded in July 1945, and its work was so secret that Mary could confide in no one. She missed her mother terribly and the guilt of sending her to that hospital gnawed away at her like a hungry dog on a bone. But she also missed the excitement of the war years. She felt restless and unsettled, possibly even unwanted; effectively now an orphan, she got in with a wrong crowd.

Despite her instincts, Mary had no option but to make friends with her flatmates, bumping into them several times a day. She started to smile a little and enjoyed nights out at the local pub with her fellow tenant, Mr Evans. Evans had a bedroom on the second floor. It was the early 1950s and London was just recovering from the war years.

Mary had never touched a drop of alcohol until she moved into that flat. Now she enjoyed the place it took her. It allowed her to drift away and forget about the horrors she had witnessed in wartime. It dulled the pain. She had no recollection of when her drinking converted to alcoholism. Soon, she realised that she needed to drink every day and the quantities needed to take her to that special place were eating into her wages. She started to skip meals, replacing them with cider and some nights were so heavy she slept right through her early morning shift. Although Mary had found a part-time job as a clerk at the local school, it was only a matter of time before she lost that job. Only a matter of time before she was unable to pay her rent and ended up out on the streets, sleeping rough in a local park.

Thank goodness for Evans. He looked after her when she had turned up at their local pub, even bought her drinks right up until closing time. It seemed like a good idea when Evans had suggested he sneak her back into the flat. It was a cold night. "You'll freeze to death out here," Evans had said as he draped his big coat around her shoulders and steadied her sway as she staggered back along Torbay Road, holding onto him as if her life depended on it.

She could not recall entering through the old Victorian door or the journey up the stairs to the second floor. She had a vague recollection of being helped to undress as he guided her into his bed, but she remembered every bit of the nightmare when she awoke with a start, to find Evans lying on top of her.

There were two, four-inch needles made from bone that held her long hair in a bun on the back of her head. Mary hadn't thought about the consequences as she removed them, only that it would be the quickest way to get him away from her so she tried to poke them into his back. Suddenly, her self-defence training in SAARF had taken over; her actions became automatic and free of mercy. "Survive at all costs have no qualms about any body part, gouge out their eyes or pull off their balls," the instructors had screamed at her. "Preferably both!" One of the needles struck home, no more than half an inch into his flesh but he leapt from the bed screaming like a man possessed.

He reached for the nearest weapon he could put his hands on, a kitchen knife from the drainer on the sink. He called her a cock-teasing bitch and said something about carving her face up so that no man would ever look at her again. He rushed her, the knife held up high and Mary pushed the two bone needles in front of her to try and protect herself. He crashed into her and they fell back onto the mattress. She waited for the blows, waited for the pain, waited for squeals and shouts of anger.

But he was stone still and she lay for a while wondering why. She eventually rolled him away and, to her horror, noticed that one of the bone needles had lodged deep into his right eye socket. His mouth lolled open, his tongue flopped from the side of his mouth and a bloody red gore oozed from the hole in his face where his eye had once been.

Mary heard the commotion from the rest of the flats. Someone was on their feet in the bedroom above her and there were more footsteps outside Evans' door. She was frantic with panic but remembered to pick up her rucksack and unlock the door before she ran out into the corridor. "It's Mr Evans," she said to the man who blocked her way, "he's had an accident."

"An accident... what happened?"

She pointed into the bedroom. "Go and take a look."

As the man rushed in, Mary ran down the stairs and into the London night.

She had been on the run for a month before they caught up with her. She was charged with murder. She had tried to explain the attempted rape but because she had waited so long the police couldn't conclude that a sexual assault had even taken place. She was convicted of manslaughter and sentenced to fifteen years imprisonment.

It was five months into her sentence when she attacked the assistant governor. He needed more than thirty stitches when she plunged a broken cup into his face several times. They had been alone in her cell; he claimed to have heard her in a distressed state when on night shift and went to investigate. After that attack, a Home Office Psychiatrist diagnosed personality disorder. She was sectioned under the Mental Health Act, transferred from prison and, as an acknowledged difficult case, was sent for a more detailed assessment to the Royal Waterloo Hospital, part of the St Thomas' group of hospitals.

There, Mary encountered Dr William Sargant and had several sessions with him and his team. She flatly refused to talk to any of them. She was particularly fearful of Dr Sargant; he carried a certain aura. There was no doubt that he was well-respected. He instilled a combination of fear and devotion in the members of his medical and nursing team. Mary underwent three courses of electro-convulsive therapy (ECT) and, yes, there was a difference, her memory had been dulled.

Sargant had at least identified the stresses that might have precipitated Mary's illness but then he told her that more treatment was needed to 'reset her brain' to the time before it had been 'overloaded' with 'distress signals'. It would mean getting the nurses to fit a catheter; she would be woken only to eat, with bowel actions induced once a week by enemas. More courses of ECT would apparently 'need' be given, two or three times a week. Mary did her best to resist and protested violently against it. No one had asked her for permission. She sensed that the so-called treatment was abuse, but she felt she was fighting a losing battle, and the more violent she became, the more they increased her medication.

On one occasion, when she awoke, a doctor was bending over her, discussing with his minions the necessity for the enema the nurse was inserting into her anus. Mary was naked from the waist down and he talked about her like she was a dead slab of meat. She summoned all of her energy reserves, ripped out the enema and tried to get dressed. The

10

psychiatrist simply called in the heavies, the orderlies. They restrained her and injected another cocktail of drugs into her. As she drifted back into her semi-permanent narcotic state, she heard the doctor speaking to his students. "Mary's lack of cooperation means she isn't as well as she claimed to be. At this rate, she'll never get out of here."

And so, Mary spent the next decade or more being passed from pillar to post in various secure locations, and now, here in Somerset, she had ended up detained in Tone Vale Hospital, where she had been for the last eighteen months.

Chapter 3

GRAND PARTY

I had finished my final clinic, packed up my desk, and closed the office door for the last time. My colleagues had organised a 'surprise' retirement do with speeches, although it wasn't so much of a surprise as it happened to everybody who retired with a decent amount of service under their belt.

There were the usual crumpled NHS sandwiches supplemented by a few slightly stale biscuits. It was all compensated for by a beautiful homemade cake brought in by the ever-reliable Mrs Hilda Knight, my loyal secretary who had supported me through thick and thin. She had piped 'Dr West' in white icing, even though she always knew me as Eric. In private I called her 'Mouse'. Over the years we had quietly developed a complete understanding of each other and there were times I wondered what I would ever do if she left my employment. We were both married so that was as far as it went, but there were days where I felt that it was only Mouse who truly 'got me.'

One of my colleagues stood up and gave a speech about me; to my surprise, he deviated from the jollity and referred to the 'hard time' that 'they had all known about' at Dunkirk. That gave me quite a jolt. After all, it had been forty-five years since I had been at Dunkirk or, more correctly, about twenty miles south of the place. "And on that subject," he went on, leaning forward towards Mrs Knight, "we've managed to find this old book in the second-hand bookstore we know you love to visit."

He pulled out a small package wrapped in plain brown paper and handed it to me.

Perhaps the glass of wine I had enjoyed had affected me, as for a moment I felt quite moved. Something stirred inside me.

Hopefully, nobody noticed, I thought as I stood to a round of applause,

I did my duty and steered my speech back into the usual in-jokes about the hospital and gave what I hoped was a witty speech, then it was time to head back home.

I wasn't looking forward to the unheated, empty house. I certainly didn't break any speed limits that night. Something was bothering me and it was on my mind for most of the duration of the drive. It was with me constantly over the next few weeks, so much so that I knew I had to do something about it or I would carry the nagging feeling to the grave.

When I was home, I unwrapped the present and found a slightly tatty book, published in wartime. The date, 1943, was pencilled in the front cover. It was entitled, The Grand Party by Graham Brooks.

Oh, my goodness, I thought. *The clever buggers have managed to find the book written by one of the commanding officers in my old Artillery Regiment.*

Major Brooks, as he was then, commanded the battery of my regiment that had escaped at Dunkirk. The men of the battery had been less fortunate – we had been trapped there.

On the front cover was the comment, 'In what happened to these men you can see clearly what happened to the British Army. And more important why it happened.'

What a fabulous gift. I remembered hearing years before that poor old Brooks had died just after the war had ended. He'd been invalided out of the army with complications from having seawater inhalation whilst getting his men off the beach.

It was still early, just after nine o'clock, but I couldn't think of anything better than retiring to bed and starting my new book that very night. I believe I fell asleep in the early hours.

* * *

I had agreed to a part-time retirement post and had been assured that the hospital visits would be sporadic and by mutual agreement. I was to be an assessor for the Mental Health Act. But it was on my terms. If I didn't want to work on a particular day, then I didn't work; it was as simple as that. They were under no illusion that my fishing and gardening would always come first. One of the first Mental Health Reviews I was requested to attend was a long drive to Somerset. Fortunately, my son had been one step ahead of me and suggested I'd need a decent car for these visits.

"A perfect retirement present to yourself," he'd said.

He had brought round the brochures for a Mercedes saloon, roomy enough for all the provisions I always liked to carry with me and a whole new experience compared to my trusty but aging old Vauxhall rust bucket. It was a bit of a wrench buying a foreign car, particularly a German one, but that feeling soon passed as it hummed comfortably on the 'A' roads that I preferred to take.

Great, I thought. *I'll kill two birds with one stone and take the fishing tackle. I'll look up a good hotel in my AA book, it never lets me down.*

There were plenty of well-stocked lakes in that area.

It was early afternoon when I checked into the hotel. I thought about a few hours fishing before dinner but it was spitting with rain and I didn't really fancy it, so I read a few more chapters of Major Brooks' book. I turned to a chapter entitled Bugle Party and found a list of my old officers set out in the manner of a schoolboy adventure that characterised Brooks. He had been a short man, slightly hunched and with a baby face that reminded us of Winston Churchill. At times, when reading maps, he wore a monocle. In civilian life, I remembered that he had worked as a lawyer for the Daily Express newspaper. The chapter read:

In the early days, the regiment comprised Colonel Cedric Odling, Wykehamist, champion skier, connoisseur of wines, who was the first commanding officer. Neville Christopherson, of the cricketing dynasty, member of Lloyd's, was second-in-command, schoolmaster Major Edward Milton commanded one battery, I the other. The first two are prisoners-of-war, recovering from wounds; the third died of wounds after being captured at Cassel; I have been invalided out as the result of a hangover from Dunkirk.

We were thus made up of undergraduates, a solicitor, barrister, stockbroker, journalist, architect, surveyor, civil servant, bank manager, research chemist, three members of Lloyd's and several businessmen: a fairly representative body of London Territorials.

In building up our battery, I had imported two Fleet Street friends as subalterns. Dennis Clarke (son of Tom Clarke, distinguished editor and journalist), who had already been under fire, getting a Nazi bullet through his hat while representing the Daily Express in Vienna during the pre-Anschluss riots; and Tony Philpotts, assistant general manager of the Evening Standard. Dennis Clarke, a major now, was mentioned in dispatches after Dunkirk and has recently been gravely wounded in

Tunisia. With his grasp of languages and intimate knowledge of the enemy and occupied countries, he could have had a cushy intelligence appointment, but maintained that a man of his age should be doing a job of fighting – and has done it.

So, there is the cast. The curtain is up. As Stanley Holloway says: "Let battle commence."

As I read through the names, all sorts of memories came flooding back. I lowered the book and stared out of the window. I watched the rain pattering against the glass. It had been forty-five long years ago, but at that moment it was as if it had all just happened yesterday.

The Mental Health Review wasn't until four o'clock the following day which would give me time for a good morning's fishing, a quick wash back at the hotel followed by a short drive along the A38 to the hospital.

The fishing was pleasant enough, the lake was in a beautiful, serene setting and thankfully, the rain held off. As for the fishing expedition, there was no joy. Not a single fish, not even a nibble, nevertheless it was a calm, enjoyable morning.

One of my old colleagues once told me, "It's called fishing, not catching. Get used to it."

To be honest, I probably didn't have the patience for fishing. I wondered if the hobby might have better suited my old friend Jack Portas, I recalled that he always had much more perseverance than me.

That afternoon, I left the hotel and drove to the secure hospital. Those old asylums were always built-in splendid, magnificent grounds, like old stately homes. The gardens were well looked after, the lawns manicured like a billiard table and always a gardener or two working diligently if you looked for them hard enough.

I climbed out of the car and stretched. I was as stiff as a board. I had sat for too many hours in the car the previous day and by that cold lake on a small camping stool that maybe was ill-suited to a man of my age, a pensioner indeed.

The hundred-yard stroll to the entrance through the gardens and the walk-through reception had cheered me up. I noticed a border of bright delphiniums just outside the main entrance and wondered whether anyone would notice if I took a cutting for my own garden.

Perhaps on the way back, I thought to myself as I fiddled with the penknife in my jacket pocket.

They were expecting me and, after a long wait, a male nurse appeared to greet me. I followed on behind him as he led me through two secure doors with a massive set of jangling keys at his hip. He ushered me into a small office and, with a mighty crash, he heaved a six-inch tome of papers onto the desk. "Dates right back to the 1950s, Doctor, quite a history, but a total blank before 1945."

"The war years," I said. "We don't know where she was or what happened?"

"Nothing, Doctor."

"And she's never told anyone where she was?"

"Not a soul."

I put my glasses on, ready to take a look.

"Would you like a cup of tea or coffee, Doctor?'

I shook my head, reached across the desk and pulled the first of the files towards me.

"Not at the moment," I said. "Perhaps in a few hours when I've had a good look through these."

I started sifting through the mounds of fading, yellowed paper and immediately noticed the 'St Thomas Hospital' headed pages.

Nostalgically, early in the file, I found entries by my old boss Dr William Sargant. He had listed his potential diagnoses, personality disorder, repressed memories and endogenous depression. His subsequent letters had prescribed a course of electro-convulsive therapy, abbreviated throughout his notes as ECT. I even recognised the anaesthetist's handwriting. I shook my head, as even then I knew ECT was being used for all the wrong indications in those days. With a somewhat sinking heart, I noted the next entries recorded in the file and saw that deep sleep treatment had been prescribed but, after that, the notes abruptly finished.

Have they been removed like so many of the deep sleep patients? I wondered.

William Sargant was always a quixotic character. He had attracted me to the profession because he was an obvious leader; he had quick humour and seemed to offer certainty and confidence. His optimism was a tonic for the depressed. He would say, "I will get you better – do not doubt this; together we will end your depression."

He reminded me of my officers in the war, who I had learnt to follow unquestioningly. One of his best quotes was, 'Jesus Christ might simply have returned to his carpentry if he'd had modern psychiatric treatment.' That always gave me a belly laugh.

I knew from my own experience how some of the physical treatments he expounded, such as ECT, could be lifesaving. Sargant had a stock line for his medical students. He'd ask them how many patients they thought committed suicide even when in severe pain. "Very few," he would say, "yet many psychiatric patients do take their life. Why? Because they are experiencing something worse than pain."

To him, the side effects of psychiatric treatments were something to be lived with or overcome by getting the individual dosage right. However, as I became a fully-fledged psychiatrist in my own right, I started to realise his flaws. Like many visionaries, he was stone-cold wrong about some things.

Four years before, my paper about the efficacy of ECT had been published in the British Medical Journal. It was entitled 'ECT in Depression – a Double-Blind Controlled Trial' and I was the sole author. I had done the statistical analysis myself. Mrs Knight had typed up the manuscript for me, and I had acknowledged her at the end. I was quite proud of the work; it had proven scientifically that ECT, in the right setting, could reverse depression more quickly than drugs or psychotherapy and help steer patients away from self-harm or worse. The reputation of ECT, I always felt, had been damaged by inappropriate use outside good indications. Maybe there was no greater evidence than the case before me, this woman with a criminal record, as far as I could tell, had no clear evidence of an actual depressive illness.

Mary didn't want to talk. She had refused to talk to over a dozen psychiatrists during her long detentions over the years, so why would this one be any different? It was always the same. They'd want her to talk about the trauma she had suffered in the past, to retrieve locked away memories as if that would miraculously unlock the key to her troubled mind.

What did they know about trauma, how could they even begin to understand what she had been through, and more importantly, why would she want to relive those horrors all over again? Given all that had happened after the war, she knew she was unlikely to gain a release from a life in hospital and so why didn't they just leave her alone? "Mary."

The nurse calling her name brought her back to the present. She looked over.

17

"The doctor is here to see you, Mary."

Mary nodded and stood up. The nurse walked over to her.

"See if you can at least manage to say hello this time."

Mary said nothing.

"Would you like one of us to chaperone you, Doctor, or would you like us to wait outside the door?"

I shook my head. "That won't be necessary, you can go back to the ward, I'm sure you've plenty of work to do."

I sat down at the desk and waited for her. Five minutes later she shuffled reluctantly towards me. She looked straight down at the table and let out a long deep sigh.

Hmm, poor eye contact, I thought. *A mesomorph in build.*

"Hello, Miss O'Leary, how are you?" I waited then I continued. "I've come here as an independent psychiatrist to review your care and the plans we should be making for your future."

I hardly got a word from Mary during that first meeting. In fact, her eyes never left the table for just under an hour. There were long periods of silence. I tried to probe gently into her past, asked her about which treatments she felt had helped her over the years. I tried small talk, asked what she had been doing that day, what book she had been reading. (Her notes indicated that she was seldom without a book in her hand.)

I asked about her feelings of injustice, of anger, of regret. She said nothing. I suggested a break and told her that, before our next meeting, I needed to speak with the doctors who were looking after her. Only then did she speak, but they were not the words I wanted to hear, they were scathing and hurtful. She stood and slammed her cup of tea into the saucer spilling the dregs all over the desk. How would I understand about loss of liberty, she'd screamed at me, how could I possibly know what she'd gone through?

As she stormed out of the room, she continued with her tirade, right up until the point where she slammed the door behind her. Her final outburst was that the last person she was going to trust was another psychiatrist; yet another doctor who had been born with a silver spoon in his mouth and didn't know anything about the evils of the real world.

The nurse who had been standing outside the door was smiling. "That went well," she said.

I thought she was joking and started to laugh.

"No, I mean it," she said. "That's never happened before."

18

I looked at her confused.

"What's never happened before?"

"She spoke to you. She's never spoken to a doctor before, let alone during the first meeting."

"But she didn't speak, nurse, she shouted. She shouted and screamed like a banshee."

"She spoke to you, Doctor," the nurse repeated. "You need to come back here as soon as you can."

Chapter 4

MISSING YEARS

It was less than a fortnight later when I returned to see my patient, Mary O'Leary.

The nurse had suggested a more informal meeting place; in the day lounge. To my amazement, Mary hadn't taken any real persuasion to see me again. The staff had been surprised too; after her outburst we thought I'd be the last person she would want to see. I wondered if it was because we were from the same generation, veterans of 1919. I was led down the corridor and, as we approached the locked lounge door, I noticed that this time the male charge nurse was smiling. I wondered if he knew something I didn't. He located a key from his collection. "There's nobody else in there, Doctor, just you and her."

He unlocked the door and guided me in. I took a deep breath. After nearly forty years as a psychiatrist, I prided myself on my ability to find access into some very shattered minds. I sensed Mary had seen things that nobody should ever have to see.

My approach was to cut out the drama and take a logical step-by-step analysis of each part of the brain. I would assess her calculation, memory and language then try to re-assemble those parts that functioned and those that were in disarray. But above all, I would talk and I would listen.

The room was more informal than the previous one and, on the wall, hung a rather innocuous watercolour painting.

"Just take it slowly, I meant what I said last week, this is a real breakthrough."

I straightened my tie, cleared my throat.

"Thank you, nurse. Hello, Miss O'Leary," I called over.

She stared out of the window, didn't acknowledge my presence. I sat down in the seat beside her.

Our first meeting had ended rather abruptly. I decided to take it easy and start with some things about me. I was curious as to why there were no records about Mary O'Leary during the war years. I had treated a few ex-soldiers over the years and their notes from the War Office were always concise and complete; slap dash was one thing the War Office could never be accused of.

But for Miss O'Leary... nothing. Were the records there? Had someone just not bothered to request them?

I'd looked at her school records from the thirties, a very intelligent girl, great marks, not a blemish as a student but, during the war and then post-war, it all started to unravel.

'No father,' I had read in her notes, 'her mother killed by a bomb.'

Could her problems have started from that? Was she caught up in the Blitz?

I decided to try and find some common ground.

"You're the same age as me, Miss O'Leary, we went to school just a few miles from each other." I cleared my throat. "May I call you Mary?"

She said nothing. I took it as silent approval.

I talked about my school years, my friends, our qualifications, told Mary she was a lot brighter than I was and I think I saw a glimmer of a smile, though I could have been wrong. I got nothing from her.

"Can you remember where you were when the war broke out?"

She looked bored.

I tried for a good half hour. I talked about Chamberlain's radio address and the declaration of war in September 1939. I even tried to impersonate him in his plummy tones saying, 'I have to tell you now that no such undertaking has been received and consequently, this country is at war with Germany.' I told her that by the following month, October 1939, I had joined up with the artillery. I even skipped right through to the end of the war and talked about VE day and what we got up to during the celebrations.

Not a murmur.

Was making the cardinal mistake here talking about myself rather than concentrating on the assessment? And how could I criticise? I had never talked about the war years either. My family... why couldn't I tell them? That was the biggest part of the guilt for me, that I hadn't told them anything.

"Tell me what you did during the war, Doctor."

Mary took me completely by surprise.

"I beg your pardon?"

"Tell me about your war years, Doctor."

We took a break. I think I needed it more than she did. I paced the corridor. I went in to see the charge nurse and he was astounded. Not in over twenty-five years had she ever been remotely interested in anybody else's life, not the past, or the future, or the present.

"You have to tell her," the nurse said.

"But…"

Am I ready for this, I asked myself.

There was a jumble of mixed memories, long suppressed, that seem to have found their way into the forefront of my mind.

One memory haunted me at that moment. It was during the escape from Cassel, Flanders… can I even begin to describe the look in his eyes? He was, like me, twenty-one years old, just a boy really. I held him as blood gushed from a bullet wound in his neck. I looked at him and told him everything was going to be fine, he stared back at me. He knew I was lying. I'd have to leave him to take his chances with the field dressing I'd got him to hold over the wound. *Hopefully, some German medics will find him*, I had thought as I resumed my escape.

The notes I had read referred to mutism. Mary talked to who she wanted to talk to. I smiled inwardly. A little like myself I supposed, and there was nothing wrong with that. She had talked to a cleaner, two of the other patients and an elderly female nurse. That was it. There was no husband or any family that anyone knew anything about. There were so many gaps in that file.

I walked out of the nurse's office and back into the day lounge. She hadn't moved. I sat back down and reached subconsciously for the pen that lay on the table separating us. I didn't even know I had picked it up until I focussed on the nib as I twirled it between my forefinger and thumb. It was a sign of nervousness, fear of the unknown. I took a deep breath, moistened my lips with the tip of my tongue.

"You want me to tell you about what happened to me during the war?"

"Yes."

"Okay, if that's what you want, I can tell you, but… " I tried to begin. I loosened my tie. I wasn't comfortable then repeated, "But… "

"It's not so easy is it?" she interrupted, "talking about shit that happened to you."

She knew. She knew I had suffered.

She laughed at me, told me that for twenty years or more the doctors had wanted her to talk to them and now she had reversed the roles.

"Tell me," she repeated. "I have all of the time in the world, I'm not going anywhere."

She was trying to force my hand; she held all the aces because I was retired. She knew I wasn't going anywhere either.

I stood up. I told her the meeting was finished for the day.

"But you'll come back?" she asked.

"Yes," I said, "I will. I'll come back tomorrow."

Chapter 5

A SOLDIER'S DEMONS

My plan was a simple one. I had demons; I was wracked with inner anguish too... more than anyone knew and somehow Mary had sensed that.

Mary had challenged me. I felt she had done this for a reason. Like me, and perhaps for Mary, it was time. In all the years she had been locked up in institutions, at the meetings and the interviews, had anyone really opened up to her? Had anyone laid their feelings bare? Surely it was a two-way street? This was what I was hoping for. Mary was going to hear my story and perhaps that way I would eventually hear hers.

I turned to the painting on the wall. It was a still-life of a fruit bowl with a pineapple dead centre. I smiled to myself. We had a family tradition that whenever I saw a pineapple I would stand to attention and salute. I often joked it was my 'Pavlov' response; it was something about the plume of feathers at the top of the fruit that reminded me of the formal flourishes on the officers' dress-uniform hats. On impulse, I turned in my seat and keeping a solemn, straight face, saluted the pineapple. "To the pineapple and the regiment."

She looked at me as if I had taken leave of my senses.

I had to laugh. I may have even detected a smile on my patient's lips too. She would certainly be wondering if there was perhaps a room in here for her crazy psychiatrist.

I told her about the plumes on the officers' hats and how a pineapple reminded me of one, my commanding officer, the colonel. Lieutenant Colonel Cedric Odling. "Many of our officers fought in the First World War and were very grand in their formal uniforms," I said quietly. "My story starts at the beginning of the Second World War."

24

I paused. I looked at her for a sign, a sign that she was listening to me. There was nothing. Her eyes were vacant. I could have been talking to the wall. That was fine. "But I have to start a little earlier, give you some background, and then hopefully you'll understand. It's a long story, Mary O'Leary, a really long story."

She spoke. "I'm not going anywhere."

A good start to the day.

"Our officers were a lot older than the men they commanded, that's what I was trying to explain, and to understand the Second World War, where my story begins, you need to know a little about the First World War too. It was the biggest mobilisation of manpower ever seen. Nothing could have come anywhere near the scale of loss of life in Europe at the beginning of the 20th Century. My commanding officer talked about it regularly, he said that when he returned home, they dubbed it the war to end all wars. He always called it by its traditional name The Great War to reflect that. He gave us history lessons as we drank our tea together in the mess tents."

She turned away from me and looked back through the window. Even so, I knew she was still with me. I turned to my assessment notes and made a brief entry that so far, there wasn't much evidence of psychiatric disease in this case. Whatever this was, perhaps it had run its course and burnt out?

I turned to face her, wondered if I was perhaps going into too much detail. "I'm not boring you, Mary, am I?"

Silence.

"The colonel was an odd one for sure; his surname – Odling – was even pronounced ODD-ling. I couldn't have imagined him stomping around the muddy trenches with the rest of the boys when I first met him, but he was there with us and, although he was rich and from a very privileged background, there wasn't any question of him giving his orders by field telephone while he sat in a French chateau with a well-stocked wine cellar."

I laughed out loud. I couldn't help myself when I thought about Colonel Odling and his obsession with fine wines. Wine, bloody wine, he never stopped talking about wine, no matter where we were. Even in the heat of battle or in a muddy field by the side of the road, he'd tell you about some fine bottle he had in his cellar back home that he was going to open and enjoy during a more serene moment. We chaps had never tasted wine before. It just wasn't the done thing for lads raised in working-class

25

districts of London. Wine was for the Toffs. The colonel tried to educate us, said that when the war was over, we'd meet up again and he'd adjust our palettes. There'd be a big reunion and he'd prepare a table of the best wines he could get his hands on.

I returned to the story. Suddenly it was flowing, those memories coming back to me as a clear picture of the colonel permeated my mind.

"We had another officer who knew what the Germans were all about too, a bloke called Clarke. Clarke was an educated man but, like me, he was very proud of his Cockney roots, and he worked for the Daily Express before the war. I think his first name was Dennis. He was known as Second Lieutenant to us gunners. He had married a Belgian lady and had been posted to Vienna in 1937. Clarke had sent reports about day-to-day life in Austria before the union with Germany, and the annexation of Czechoslovakia later that year. He was a fine journalist and before anyone had even heard of the intimidation of the Jews in Germany, Clarke had filled the Express newspaper with the details. I think it's fair to say that my regiment was more versed than most about what those bloody Nazis were all about."

There was a reaction.

Nazi. I had said Nazi and, as soon as I had mentioned that word, Mary stiffened up. Her breathing had grown a little heavier, I was sure of it. She was grinding her teeth; I was losing her. I tried to inject a little humour, told her that during one of the riots, Clarke had returned to his hotel to find he had a bullet hole in his hat, he had missed death by less than an inch.

We were interrupted. It was perfectly timed. One of the junior nurses strolled across the open lounge with a tray. Tea always helped. A nice strong pot and a plate of biscuits. The nurse poured the tea into the two cups and added some milk. I reached for the sugar bowl and heaped a teaspoon into the cup nearest to me and started to stir. "Sugar, Mary?" I asked.

"She takes two," the nurse answered for her.

I pushed the sugar bowl across the table.

"Help yourself. I want to tell you about another officer, a Captain. MacDougall he was called, he was a Scotsman from Peru."

She sat motionless while the nurse put two sugars into her cup and started to stir with the spoon.

Then an incredible thing happened. Mary swung her legs around her seat and turned to face me. "A Peruvian Scotsman," she said. "This should be good."

You could have knocked me over with a feather.

Chapter 6

LET'S STICK TOGETHER

I didn't know what to expect as I first reported to the drill hall. I was with my best mate Jack Portas. As twenty-year-old lads, we knew we couldn't avoid conscription in 1939. It was Jack who suggested we join the Territorials, and specifically the Royal Artillery, together. He and I had been friends since we had met at our local school; we both had a love of the outdoors, the mountains, that sort of thing, and we had taken a couple of walking holidays back in 1938 and early 1939.

After the war had finally ended, Jack wrote to me and reflected, 'How lucky we were, Eric, that we didn't know what was about to hit us.'

Those days were so peaceful, I thought to myself.

Long, tough days walking up the fells and my personal favourite, Helvellyn. That long, steep start where Jack and I used to almost race each other, and then, as it levelled out, those views and the exhilarating experience on Striding Edge with sheer drops into the valley below; not a walk for the faint-hearted. Four or five people lost their lives every year on Striding Edge. And then, as tradition would have it, we'd drop down into one of those quaint tea shops in Borrowdale and eat like starving men. I smiled involuntarily.

One year we had gone climbing in Snowdonia and hiked into a village pub where no one spoke English. It was a Welsh-speaking area, and to this day I can't remember the name of the place. In fact, I recently wrote on my Christmas card to Jack in his new home in Western Australia to ask him if he could remember. He replied that he couldn't. Jack loved nature, he used to sketch birds at any given opportunity, much to my frustration at times. He had a collection of moths and insects; he was such a gentle soul and I'd often wondered why he had ever joined the army. "We'd made a pact to stick together, Jack and me," I said. "We told ourselves that if this thing really did blow up into proper fighting, we'd get through the damned war no matter what. It wouldn't last long anyway and we'd soon be back home, walking those fells."

As it turned out, after the war, neither of us would ever have much of an appetite for walking again.

The Sergeant Major barked at us both, "You two stand in line, Portas, John – 139 Regiment, you, West, Eric – 140 Regiment."

"Sergeant Major Goddard was his name and, with a sense of relief, we realised our plan had partially worked. We'd been assigned to different regiments but Goddard had reassured us that both regiments would train together and, if it ever came to fighting a war, they would be supporting each other too. I looked over towards Jack and flicked him a sly wink, Mary. We were absolutely dumbfounded when that first day ended and we discussed it over our first ever pint at the Red Lion in Cheam. The landlord had only just started allowing us teenagers in."

I remembered that he had thought we were underage a few weeks before and refused to serve us. "Now that we had enlisted, it appeared all sorts of doors were opening up for us. We were afforded a certain respect."

Mary glanced casually at me.

"As recruits, we had both been assigned the lowest rank of gunner. Jack was making the most of it. I think he was quite proud of our new formal titles."

Mary coughed and looked at me. "You said you were going to tell me about the Peruvian Scotsman."

"Ah yes," I replied. "Lorne MacDougall, he was a character indeed."

She smoothed down the material on her dress, took a breath and said, "Tell me about him."

I nodded, eager to press on and quite astonished with the way this was going. She had spoken no more than a couple of dozen words, but it was a couple of dozen words more than any professional had managed to extract from her in over twenty years. And there was something else I noticed as I prepared to continue. I looked into her eyes. There was something there… something I couldn't quite pinpoint, but there was something there. Interest. That was it. She was interested in the story I was telling her. I made some more entries in my notes.

"Jack and I didn't quite know what to expect from the Territorial Army Officers. They were a different breed; they spoke eloquently and were clearly from money. We expected an 'us and them' scenario, we had heard the horrendous tales from the Great War. After all, I was the son of a lowly pipe factory manager, our officers were from another world altogether." I grinned. "Especially MacDougall, because nobody had even heard of a place called Peru, it was a month away by boat."

She avoided eye contact and I gathered my composure, told myself to get on with the plan to recount my tale. Mary's story was for another day altogether.

"It wasn't until we started our training that we began to get to know our officers better. We were sent to Totteridge Army Training Camp."

"Where was that?"

"It was in Hertfordshire during the war, it's not far from Barnet in North London."

"I see."

"We were enthusiastic and there were a lot of new skills to learn. Trigonometry, sine tables, signalling and wireless communication. We met a lot more officers there, Captain Tom Hood and Major Graham Brooks, men who I'd like to tell you about if we get an opportunity later on. During those early weeks when it seemed to rain forever, we bonded; we built up a sort of inevitable camaraderie. I couldn't quite believe it as I realised that, despite the rain, the hours and hours of drill, the route marches, and the sleep deprivation exercises during the night, I was enjoying myself for God's sake."

And I was. I loved being pushed to my limits and then collapsing in my bunk at lights out, barely able to summon the energy to say goodnight to the rest of the lads.

Not that Mary O'Leary would be interested in any of that side of the story. I wasn't going to tell her about the thrill of firing those bloody eighteen-pounder field guns either. That was one of the highlights of the training for me. It's difficult to describe those days on Salisbury Plain, the noise and the smells of cordite, the smoke and the recoil as the gun jumped back at least a foot. The clatter as each spent shell case fell, smoking, to the ground. No, she wouldn't understand that either.

"The war in Poland was over and it was fast approaching Christmas. We were all looking forward to spending a day or two with our parents but little did we know that wasn't going to happen. rumours swirled about where we might get sent. France was top of the list, but Palestine and Egypt were mentioned. But still, we sincerely believed we would be enjoying the festivities on Christmas Day, 1939. That all changed when

30

just before Christmas we were moved again, this time to Gloucestershire. A place called Dursley."

"And you spent Christmas there?" Mary asked.

"Yes, we were camped in an old carpet factory. We were all missing our families but funnily enough, the grub was good. We had a full Christmas dinner with plum pudding and mince pies. We even managed to pull a few crackers and the officers did a grand job supplying us with beer."

Two nurses stood outside. They were by the door, quite deliberately, one either side of the wooden frame. They didn't want to be seen, as if somehow that would ruin what was taking place inside the lounge.

During a pause and when the door was slightly ajar, I heard them whisper.

"She spoke again."

"I noticed."

"I've never seen her like this before."

"Me neither."

"What is he talking about?"

"I don't know, but he's bloody well talking for England, you can't shut the bugger up."

"But Mary is listening."

"That she is."

There was a pause as they stood in silence with a mixture of awe and amazement.

"Fancy a cuppa?"

"For sure. I think Mary and the doctor deserve one too."

Chapter 7

COTSWOLD ADVENTURE

I was there; I was in the moment, talking to Mary in a Somerset hospital but very much pitched back in time in the Cotswolds, back with my mates.

For the first time in forty-five years, my mind was cast back to those days spent in training.

It was a strange Christmas in 1939. For one thing, it was picture-postcard perfect, one of the coldest winters on record. There was deep snow that made it impossible for our gun tractors to climb out of the steep Cotswold Hills. The ice froze solid on telegraph wires, the weight of it pulled the poles over at crazy angles and both power and communication were getting cut off.

There had been a flu epidemic that winter, many of the men had had to go back home on sick leave and our training was disrupted. To me, it seemed quite bizarre to think we were at war, and at times, easy to forget. Everything was frozen solid, and nothing could move. The gun tractors couldn't climb up the hill out of Dursley.

It felt like a big, Boy Scout adventure. Here we were, living this surreal experience huddled together in an empty carpet factory and surrounded by snow drifts. We often remarked it was just as well no German aircraft ever flew over us. If they'd found the factory, we'd surely all have been killed.

I said to Mary, "Colonel Odling turned up on Boxing Day with a case of wine and made sure that every man enjoyed at least a glass each to toast our new regiment. 'Here's to the One Forty!' we all cheered. As we sat on box crates at crudely constructed wooden tables, little did we know what we were heading into. On one of the days when we were snowed in, we had lectures on what to expect if the Germans ever did try to invade France. The colonel had met many of the high-ranking Nazis when he was treasurer to the British squad at the Winter Olympics in 1936. I can still remember Colonel Odling telling us that the wintry weather reminded him of his visit to the Bavarian Alps. Everything in the Cotswolds had ground to a halt, and the colonel said that that would never happen in Germany because they knew how to cope with snow."

I noticed a little movement by the door and I heard the rattle of keys. It was tea break time again. I was almost disappointed that I had to stop for a while. I felt that I was only just getting going. The next bit was going to be harder for me, I knew that for sure. After tea, it would be time to take Mary O'Leary on a journey to Flanders.

I told her how there was a period of limbo between Christmas and New Year. We were granted embarkation leave, a little time with our families before we left England. "It was early March 1940 when it eventually started to happen and the feeling among the men was, 'about bloody time.' We were all primed, fully fit and we believed we were well trained, well equipped and we wanted to get amongst it, give Jerry a bloody nose, send him back to Germany with his tail between his legs. After all, we reasoned, Hitler had only been in power for seven years. He was a mere corporal and Germany had insufficient time to rebuild any kind of military capability after the Armistice.

Before we left Dursley, we were paraded along the main road for a Royal Visit by King George VI. We were standing in the freezing cold; I can remember the Queen's bright blue dress contrasting with our sea of khaki uniforms. After the Royal Party had left, we were all assembled for troop photographs, like a school photo parade. One of the photos had a gunner in the front row with a big grin on his face holding our mascot, Alice the goose, in his lap. Alice followed us everywhere and guarded us jealously."

I recalled the day we left the Cotswolds. Winter had finally receded and daffodils were starting to appear. "Although there was a strong feeling of camaraderie as we waited at the docks, for me there was sadness as I'd left Jack Portas and his regiment behind. Those boys were still waiting to complete their training and get kitted out. In fact, we took quite a lot of their equipment with us that day. As we prepared to leave Dursley for the last time I don't think I'd ever seen so many trucks, lorries and armoured vehicles in one place. Our regiment's BEF identity number 'ten' was newly painted on all our vehicles. We were brimming with confidence. The German Army was mainly horse-drawn, we British were fully mechanised," I said proudly.

"The order to leave for France had been abrupt, no time for leave and so I wasn't able to say goodbye to Mum and Dad or my brother Peter and kid brother Geoff. I was particularly annoyed that I wasn't able to say goodbye to Geoff, he was only fifteen at the time and really interested in his big brother's progress in the army."

Not to worry, I'll write to them all, I'd thought, *and anyway, common sense will prevail and we'll get sent home again.*

"We sailed through the night heading towards Le Havre. The whole ship was in darkness, every light turned off. I felt vulnerable out there in the middle of the English Channel. For the first time, I felt real anxiety. It finally seemed as though we were committing to something and, in addition, I couldn't swim. We knew there might be Germans out there and, once we were a couple of miles out into the sea, I knew that we'd have no chance if they caught up with us and sent our ship to the bottom."

Mary had finished the last of her tea. She placed her cup on the saucer and sat back as if to say, 'Tell me more.'

I was happy to oblige. I stood up, stretched and took a deep breath with my back arched. Mary remained in the same position looking up at me, wondering what the hell I was doing.

"When I first set foot on French soil, it hit me straight away. This was for real. It was the faces of the French port men and the dock workers that gave the game away. There were no smiles, no casual joviality and, like us, they knew that the German invasion of their country was imminent. What did they have to smile about? Some of our men thought they were communist sympathisers. At this stage of the war, of course, Stalin had formed a pact with Hitler; the two dictators had only just carved up Poland between themselves. French soldiers were patrolling the docks as our trucks and equipment were unloaded.

The other boys had noticed too, the grim faces had become infectious. It seemed everybody was wearing a frown as we loaded up. We were assigned to four-ton troop trucks and pulled out of the docks. We were heading to our first camp, a place called..."

What was the place called? It wouldn't come to me. I had left this too bloody long. It began with a 'B' it was on the tip of my tongue, but I couldn't remember. It didn't matter.

"We camped there for a few days, Mary, to be honest, I can't remember an awful lot about it, we may have been there for longer."

I squeezed my temples between my thumb and forefinger and rotated them around in circles as if the memory would miraculously return.

"A few days after we arrived in…"

It came to me. It was mentioned in Brooks' book; Bolbec. That's what the town was called.

"We'd managed to smuggle Alice into a gun tractor, but she ran away at Bolbec. I think she'd found other geese and perhaps didn't much fancy life on the move with us. That night, when Alice was nowhere to be seen, somebody said it was a bad omen. A few days after we arrived in Bolbec, we were on the move again, on the way towards the Belgian border. It took about two weeks to arrive at our destination, progress was slow.

As soon as we arrived, we started digging. We dug pits for the guns and trenches, we even dug drainage trenches. We spent all day and every day digging, digging, digging for weeks on end. It was clear that we were in a defensive position; we were trying to protect France from the German onslaught that, as time wore on, looked more and more likely.

That's what they said, they told us that we needed to be ready. It was another two months before Hitler invaded Belgium. We were on tenterhooks for nearly two bloody months expecting an imminent attack at any time."

I went to the table and flopped into my seat.

"Can you imagine that, Mary?" I loosened my tie. "It was enough to send a man insane."

Mary pushed her teacup to one side and stood.

"I think I want to go back to my room now."

Before I could reply she had walked over to the lounge door and tapped gently on the glass.

Chapter 8

A ROAD POOLED WITH BLOOD

I wondered all weekend whether I had managed to upset my very first Mental Health Review patient. I cursed myself for that slip of the tongue. It had seemed rather innocuous at the time but using the word 'insane' in such an environment maybe wasn't the best choice.

I had been surprised when I received the phone call early Monday morning and bloody astounded when the nurse said that Mary O'Leary had asked when the 'nice' doctor was coming back. All of the staff were talking about the change in Mary. It was not that she had started to talk to others but the fact she had been happy just to sit with me for several hours. They had noticed an occasional smile, something that hadn't been seen in a long time. As she sat with me, she appeared genuinely interested in what I had to say. Normally, all she'd bothered with was books and puzzles. She had gone through most of the battered old paperback classics that she found in the hospital. So, was it any real surprise that she wanted me back? Now she had her personal storyteller, yours truly, and unlike the books that she immersed herself in, this one was for real.

They had made another appointment for the end of the week and, as I drove into the grounds of the hospital, the strange feeling of calmness that had come over me during the pleasant drive, remained. I was no longer wary, no longer filled with a sense of foreboding, of concern. I was no longer the strange doctor trying to reach into the inner recesses of a patient's mind. I was just a storyteller with an untold tale.

"Good morning, Mary." She sat in the same seat at the same table looking out of the same window. She turned her head as I spoke. "It's a beautiful morning, the sun is shining and I'm off fishing at the weekend," I continued.

I suppose it was what salespeople called the preamble, the ice breaker. I spent five or ten minutes talking about my retirement, about fishing, how I would always throw them back.

I sensed she somehow approved of that and eventually I resumed my story.

"We travelled over the old Somme battlefields. One of the officers, Major Brooks I think, gave us a history lesson on the Great War. He'd managed to find the spot where gun pits had been dug when he was a young artillery officer, twenty-four years previously. Our battery made camp at a place near Lille. I was happy because, by that time, my friend Jack's 139 Regiment had joined us in France. They were stationed closer to the Belgian frontier. If I remember right, it was no more than a mile from the border."

I felt rather pleased with myself. How on earth had I remembered all this detail? I hadn't spoken about any of it for the past forty-five years.

"We were all told to dig in again, this would be our defensive position, we would not allow the Germans into France. If memory serves me right, we were there for nearly a fortnight, but it felt more like two months."

I recalled the sheer boredom of it all but decided not to burden Mary with the details. That was a side of the story that would not interest her in the slightest.

"Digging in had been a waste of time and energy and morale wasn't great when we were ordered to abandon our camp. The plan was now to intercept the German Army in Belgium. We had to travel through the night to Brussels. It was the 10th of May 1940 and now, at last, Hitler was advancing towards us. He had invaded Holland and Belgium. We knew at that point that we were going to be in a real battle. We could hear the bombers and heavy guns in the distance.

As we drove into Belgium through the night, the poor civilian population were on the move in the opposite direction. It was a pathetic sight to behold. The richer ones came first in their Mercedes and Citroens, often with mattresses on the roof; I think this was a vain attempt to protect the occupants inside. They were followed by a procession of handcarts, horses and donkeys. I spotted babes in arms, Great War cripples and the elderly, old men and women who looked as if they would collapse on the spot at any moment. But they dared not. The Germans were coming, and they wanted to get as far away as possible. It was clear to me that they were terrified of them. Did they know something we didn't?

We reached the suburbs of Brussels early the next morning and set up our guns on a ridge two miles behind the River Dyle. We were in a village called Huldenberg. The Belgians had flooded the river valley below. I remember one of our first targets was a crossroads in the valley that our guns had been registered on. We'd put our artillery training into practice and set the gun on the target in advance, taking account of the temperature and wind direction. We set up a Forward Observation Post which would be able to call for corrections if the shells fell short.

Once we had positioned our guns, I was ordered to join the Observation Post, to report back at the precise moment the crossroads were hit. We found a slightly elevated position less than half a mile away. We settled in and waited for the fireworks to begin.

We didn't have long to wait. As we trained binoculars on the crossroads, we noticed a German cycle corps approaching from the east. Slightly ridiculous, I thought, our first contact with the mighty German advance was a squadron of teenagers riding squeaky old bicycles. There were six bicycles, two runners, and eight German soldiers in all. It was an immediate adrenaline rush because we didn't know if they were heading our way and if so, it would have resulted in an inevitable firefight. There were only four of us armed with two rifles; I was conscious that we didn't have much ammunition between us.

We needn't have worried because, within just a few seconds of the team reaching the crossroads, our lads scored a series of direct hits. There was the screech of the shells arriving, followed by a flash of bright orange colours, and then came the thud, thud, thud as the percussion waves hit us in the chest and pushed our breath away. Our stomachs had compressed. It was a strange feeling, and I felt a slight wave of nausea that was to become familiar over the next few weeks. Finally, there was an almost gentle, tinkling sound as dust and debris settled all around us. We were elated at first. All our training had come good."

I gauged Mary's reaction. Stone-faced. She gave nothing away.

As I spoke I realised my recall of those events was alarmingly vivid. The target had been hit without the need for any ranging shots, but I remembered that, within a short time, our elation turned to despair. In the distance, we could make out the dead and dying bodies of the young men, the arms and legs, and even a head that had been detached in the explosion. Even though it meant we were safe, I could not draw an ounce of satisfaction from what I had just witnessed. The road was pooled with

38

blood and the pool was growing by the second. One young German, no more than twenty years old, lay twitching on the ground. I could hear his screams as I noticed his left leg, detached from the hip, three feet away from him. As I drew breath, I felt the perspiration break out on my brow as he arched his back upwards in a final death throw and fell back to the ground, perfectly still. I had just witnessed my first casualty of war.

Another two shells hit the middle of the crossroads; I was stunned by the accuracy and power of our guns. The German bicycles were gone, now a mass of barely recognisable twisted metal and, while I trained my binoculars on the ground looking for the Germans, I saw nothing that resembled the human form.

I had been blooded, so to speak.

"It was sheer carnage, Mary, and as we reported back on a successful operation and prepared to move out, I fully expected an element of excitement or satisfaction from my mates. There was nothing. We returned in silence; we were all in shock at the power we had witnessed first-hand. One of my companions, I can't recall his name now, but he was a conscripted October 1939 gunner, like me. He was shaking and sweating profusely as we scrambled back to our battery position. I'd never seen a reaction like this, he was deathly white, said nothing and when we were safely back, he withdrew into a foetal position with his hands covering his head."

Mary nodded knowingly.

"The officers stepped in; I could see immediately that they knew what to do. 'That'll be all, gunner,' one of them said to me. It was my cue to make myself scarce. I craved a brew. Later we learned that despite our apparent success in holding our line, the battery was already making plans to relocate.

As luck would have it, our supply depot about four miles behind our position, was on the grounds of a large cigar warehouse. The Belgian owner, along with most of the local population, had decided to run for their lives. He told our men to help ourselves to as many boxes of cigars as we could carry. With the commanding officer's approval, our supplies men had looted his factory before we put a single gun in position. The CO was a shrewd one. He knew that our morale had taken a battering in recent months and that an unlimited supply of high-quality cigars would be the perfect tonic.

As we started a supply link to one of the trucks and passed the boxes down the human chain, I saw more smiles that morning than I'd seen since we had left England. I didn't smoke, but I kept a box as a gift for my father. I'd keep it safe for him until all this nonsense was over."

I told Mary how we then encountered the brutality of the German Luftwaffe for the first time. "An hour or two later, and for the life of me it took me some time to realise what their intentions were, their aircraft came in from the east, from beautiful clear blue skies and you could hear them before you could see them. The road was congested, we had nowhere to go, civilians desperately moving as quickly as they could, pushing carts with their worldly possessions loaded onto them.

A wave of Stukas swooped in. As they came nearer, the civilians started to panic, running and diving into ditches. We prepared for the worst; we were in no man's land and out in the open. There were about half a dozen of them, our lads were firing wildly into the air. But they left us alone, Mary, it's as if they weren't interested in us."

It was the most horrific and callous thing I had ever seen. The Germans were targeting the fleeing refugees on the roads. They were waging war by creating traffic jams, thereby holding up their opposing forces which couldn't make progress through the carnage on these congested roads.

"Then I knew why the civilians we had seen through the night were in so much fear of the Germans. The first wave roared overhead, bursts of machine-gun fire from accompanying Messerschmitt fighters powdered the road. The hedgerows and the surrounding fields and carts were abandoned where they stood while the owners ran for cover."

I gulped in some air, let it drift into my throat.

"A girl… " I began.

"A girl?" Mary questioned.

"No more than twelve years old."

I struggled to speak. I would never shake that image as long as I lived.

"She was holding a doll, bewildered by it all and, by the look on her face, wondering why everybody was running away from her. Such innocence."

She had been looking from side to side, no doubt wondering where her parents had gone. I wondered too. I wondered why they had abandoned her in the middle of it all.

"The third plane straightened up and came in parallel to the road behind her. It happened in slow motion and there was nothing anyone could do. A

40

woman jumped up from behind a hedge and started screaming at her, but she just froze and looked up into the sky. I watched as the line of bullets exploded fifty metres behind her, getting closer, the woman screaming ever louder and... "

I struggled to find the words.

"They cut through her, Mary, the bullets cut through her and the child's doll catapulted up into the air. I watched the doll fly high up into the sky as the wind caught it and it floated eerily back to the ground. It fell where the poor girl lay. It settled by her side, in a pool of her blood."

I took some time to compose myself. I didn't think it was necessary to paint the full picture to Mary. This was going to be harder than I thought. There were good reasons why I hadn't ever told a soul about that poor dead child.

Chapter 9

A VISIT TO BROADMOOR

I'll write up the report in my own time, I thought to myself.

I needed more time to mull it over, to decide whether her Mental Health Act Section was warranted. Looking at it honestly, I didn't think she gave me enough to make that sort of decision. I had done most of the talking after all. I hadn't managed anything that resembled a psychiatric examination. But, having said that, I had definitely seen reactions. There were moments when I gauged that reaction from her body language alone or the look in her eyes. When dealing with a troubled mind, it wasn't always about the words.

I watched her reaction as I had told her about the little Belgian girl and the woman, probably her mother. It seemed a normal response to me. No disordered thinking that I could detect. She asked me about God, and where He was when that happened, and wasn't He supposed to protect little children?

I sighed and I was honest with her. Perhaps too honest. I'm not one to ever defend religious claptrap. I said that the faith of the most religious person on the planet would be tested if they had witnessed such an incident.

And then she had asked me to continue my story. I said I would. I had made my mind up. She'd be the first human being, but maybe not the last, to hear my story.

Was there even enough for a book? I had wondered to myself.

But I had been exhausted and called the meeting to a close prematurely that day.

On the way back home, I thought I'd call on my daughter Susan. She had set up home in the Cotswolds and, by coincidence, the new house was not too far from the old Dursley base.

More bloody memories, I thought.

I wondered if it was worth taking a small detour to see if I could find the old Champion & Sons' carpet factory where we had all billeted in that bitter winter of 1939. I had fond memories of that place; out in the Cotswolds countryside and, as it was to turn out, the calm before the storm. "To what do we owe this unexpected pleasure?" she asked.

"I've come to see my daughter." I grinned.

She slid a cup of tea over the table.

"I know you too well, Dad. I've no doubt you are dying to see us but only because you have been doing something close by. What have you been up to?"

She definitely knew me too well.

"You're right. I've been doing a Mental Health Act visit; I can't stay that long and I've got to get the report written when I get home," I said, as she handed me some homemade cake.

How I missed home cooking. In truth, I wasn't in a great rush to get back to the empty house, but I wanted to avoid giving the impression of being a needy widower. Retirement is a funny thing when you have been busy most of your working life. That was me all over, no time, always busy, even in retirement.

She flicked her hair back with her hand and let out a deliberate sigh. She'd seen and heard it all before. She stood up and walked towards the door. "I have a little surprise for you," she said. "Stay there."

I finished the last of the cake and she returned after a few minutes with a large box. I recognised it immediately, she had removed it from my back office some months before. Unfortunately, after my wife died, I'd become a bit of a hoarder and everything at home had become somewhat disorganised. The box of family photographs was very special to me. There were letters in there too, letters from my brother during his time in India. Now and again I would take them out and read them and wonder to myself if it could have panned out differently. "I've managed to get most of Uncle Geoffrey's photos and letters into this little box file," she said, lifting it out from within the box and placing the file onto the table.

There was a photo of me aged around twelve years old and my younger brothers Peter and Geoffrey aged about six taken in… it must have been 1930. There was a photo of the graduation class of officers in Queen Victoria's Own Madras Sappers and Miners taken in May 1946. She handed me another picture. "Where was that, Dad?"

I knew exactly where that was. It was Geoff on the tourist trail, in Bangalore and Mysore, another one at the hill station at Ooty with the steam train named Sapper. His Royal Engineers' unit was tasked with maintaining the rack-and-pinion mountain railway line that climbed nearly thirty miles up into the Nilgiri Hills. He was in uniform but looked every inch a tourist, smiling and relaxed. He was obviously enjoying the experience of being away from home for the first time.

"I'll try to get this all into an album in date order, Dad. Most of the photos have dates on so it shouldn't be that hard."

I felt a little guilty. This is something I should have done years ago. There was no excuse, especially now with all the time I had on my hands.

"I'm sorry," I said to her. "I really should have completed this myself. I shouldn't be leaving it to you."

"Don't be daft, Dad, it'll be good for me, it's been a long time since I've flicked through these photos. I've had a real laugh at some of them."

"Wait," I said, "I'd like to take some of these photos now."

"Really?"

"Yes... I... "

"What, Dad, what is it?"

I didn't want to tell her about the idea for a book, after all, it only just occurred to me and I needed to give it a lot more thought. I stalled while she waited for my reply; a little white lie.

"Oh, I don't know, guess I'm getting sentimental in my old age and I love that photo of your uncle on the steam train."

She picked it up. Studied it under the light. "It's brilliant isn't it and he looks so full of life... so young."

She handed it over and I pulled out another three.

"I'll get going then," I said as I stood and tucked them into my pocket.

"So early?"

"Yes, you're busy and I need to be heading off, you know how I don't like driving in the dark. Besides, Dallas is on TV tonight, I need to be up to date with it for when your sister calls me to discuss the plot! Who shot JR?" I said with a knowing wink.

She hugged me. Unusual, as we were never a demonstrative family. As I walked out to the car, I told her the Mental Health Tribunal wanted me to go to Broadmoor Hospital in December.

"What? Dad! You are kidding me?"

Her shock wasn't unexpected.

Broadmoor was the notorious high-security psychiatric hospital that housed England's bad boys, those with the worst personality disorders imaginable. Serial killers, sexual deviants, rapists who represented the highest degree of risk to society; most would never see the light of day again.

"But, Dad, you're a pensioner; they can't possibly expect you to—"

I held up a hand to stop her.

"Sue, I only told you because it's a couple of hours away, I was going to call in and visit you again. That's all."

"That's all well and good, Dad, but I just don't think you should be going to a place like that."

I let out a long sigh as she continued.

"The Yorkshire Ripper, Sutcliffe, he's in there isn't he?"

"Yes."

"And that Charlie Bronson, he tried to strangle someone in there not so long ago, didn't he?"

I managed to placate her a little. I assured her I wasn't going to sit at the same table as the Yorkshire Ripper or Charlie Bronson. She tried to fish a little, asked me who I was going to see. I couldn't tell her. Patient confidentiality. The big secret.

Maybe I can finally catch up with Ronnie Kray, I thought.

It was 1969. Ronnie was in big trouble along with his brother, Reggie. As the swinging sixties came to an end, justice had finally caught up with the notorious Kray twins. They were on trial at the Old Bailey for the murder of Jack McVitie and George Cornell. Huge crowds lined the streets outside the Old Bailey when the twins were brought every day from Wormwood Scrubs.

I'd read up on the case prior to the meeting. The murder of McVitie was particularly brutal. The prosecution alleged that the Krays had paid McVitie to assassinate an associate and business partner, Leslie Payne. The Krays were worried that Payne was about to turn informer. McVitie and his friend, Billy Exley, set off to shoot Payne, but they couldn't find him. Instead of repaying the money, McVitie kept it.

A big mistake that hadn't gone down too well with the Krays. They intended to shoot McVitie but Reggie's gun jammed. So Reggie picked up a knife and fatally stabbed McVitie in the face, chest, and stomach.

The trial was dramatically interrupted when the defence barrister insisted on last-minute psychological reports; he was trying to avoid his unpredictable client Ronnie taking the stand. The barrister knew he would incriminate himself straightaway. I had been due to meet him as part of a psychiatric assessment. But he hadn't turned up.

I'd sat for over an hour staring at the tropical fish tank that Mrs Knight and I had installed in the waiting room. My favourite fish of our collection was the colourful male cherry barb. Two burly policemen sat with us and a fleet of police cars was parked outside the hospital in anticipation of the infamous twins' visit. And then someone telephoned the office. Mrs Knight reported that Ronnie had had a change of mind. He was going to testify. He didn't want to see no shrink.

But my daughter didn't know that. Nobody did.

As I climbed into the car, I wondered what she would say if I told her I was finally going to meet Ronnie Kray.

I pulled the car into the drive. It had started to rain a few miles from home, it was raining hard by the time I arrived. I ran from the car with a newspaper over my head in a vain attempt to protect myself from the rain. And it's unexplainable, but when it's raining, the key never seems to slip into the lock the first time as it does on a sunny day.

I threw my wet jacket onto the kitchen chair, put the kettle on, and made myself a cup of tea. There wasn't anything interesting to watch on television that evening and so I telephoned Mrs Knight. I cheekily asked whether she'd be willing to type up my Mental Health Report on Miss O'Leary so that it looked neat and professional. "It won't be a problem, Eric," she said.

And then, after a slight pause, I added half-jokingly, "I've got another retirement project lined up for you."

"Tell me."

"I'm thinking of writing my wartime biography."

"Are you serious?" she questioned.

"Well, Jack Portas always said there was a good book in me."

That weekend my son telephoned to say he was planning to drop by to pay a visit. He was a doctor. It was always interesting to hear about the cut and thrust of hospital medicine from his perspective. It had been a couple of months since we'd caught up.

I stopped off at the local supermarket and picked up some supplies. I bought a cooked chicken and chips from the local takeaway on the high street. I was a hopeless bloody cook, and I certainly wasn't going to take up cookery as a new retirement hobby. I was looking forward to the night in. It would be nice to have a little company, my son's company, someone who would actively engage in a conversation with me.

The conversation inevitably wound its way round to what I was going to get up to in my retirement. I knew that he was concerned about me rattling around in the big house on my own. It wasn't easy for him either, working long hours in the Midlands, a four-hour round trip on a good day.

He had his head in the refrigerator when he spoke. He was looking at the sell-by dates of the few items I had in there. "So, Dad, any travel plans for the next year or two? New York, India or China? What about a Mediterranean cruise?"

He was joking, he knew I wasn't one for long-haul travel or exotic holidays.

"No," I said, "not at the minute, no real plans as such."

"Come on, Dad, you're a free man, there must be somewhere that you've always wanted to go."

I didn't answer at first. Mary O'Leary's psychiatric report was unwritten and still fresh in my mind, my head was full of the details I had disclosed to her.

"Come on, Dad," he prompted me, "there must be somewhere."

"Well, as a matter of fact… "

"Yes."

"I've been thinking about it a lot lately."

"Spill the beans then man, the Pyramids, the Taj Mahal, where?"

I shook my head, "Not that far actually."

"Well… "

"I'm thinking of planning a little trip to Flanders to revisit the battlefields and if possible, I'd like to retrace the place I was captured in Belgium."

"You're kidding me?"

I wasn't.

"But surely you'd like to do something more adventurous than that? And anyway, you don't like driving on the other side of the road."

He was right. I hated driving on the other side of the road, and he knew it. I would have wanted John to come but it was asking too much, I knew how busy he was. There was an awkward silence before the penny dropped.

"You want me to come with you, Dad, don't you?"

"I would like someone to come with me, a bit of a chaps' weekend away would be great."

He let out a deep sigh. I could tell he wasn't overly impressed with my choice of destination, probably even more so because I wanted him to come with me. There was a reason for that. It wasn't just a driver I needed.

"Ah, it's going to be really difficult at the moment. You see we're one man down on our rota just now – maybe next year?" he suggested. "And then, if I can get the time off, we'll take your Merc and I can do the driving."

"That would be great."

I could sense that it was probably the last thing John would want to do on his holiday.

* * *

I slept on it overnight and it came to me in the strangest dream. Geoffrey. The more I thought about it, my younger brother was the obvious choice because he'd suffered in the war too and he would understand. Of course he would. The perfect companion. My brother had a terrible time out in India. He was only fifteen when I left for France, nineteen when he left for his own war. While it was all over in Europe, those bloody Japanese were still causing trouble in the Pacific and Indian Oceans despite the Americans bombing the hell out of their biggest cities. There were stories that the Japanese warrior would never surrender. That's why my brother and his comrades were posted to India.

I laughed to myself. I was nearly posted to India too! The cheek of it, I had returned from my time in the POW camp, six stone wet through and the officer who had debriefed me on my return had said they were going to build me back up so that I could re-join my regiment. Or whatever was left of it. He was bloody well kidding, right?

No, he wasn't.

I told him the war was over, what was he talking about? He said that the war was only over in Europe and that those bloody Japs were still in Burma and Malaya. We were going to be sent over to liberate those countries, all the way down to Singapore. I made a pledge to myself that day. Even though the officer rambled on about a potential posting in India, I swore that my spindly, wasted legs and my malnourished body wouldn't leave the shores of England again, at least until the fighting was over.

Unfortunately, Geoff had no choice and he'd been sent on his way soon after I returned home. Almost as soon as he arrived at Bangalore, victory against Japan had happened. On the 6th August 1945, atomic bombs were dropped on Hiroshima and then, a few days later, on Nagasaki.

I think Geoff expected an early return home, but it wasn't to be. He was an officer cadet in the Madras Sappers and due to qualify as a second lieutenant in May 1946. I don't think he was anywhere near combat. Unfortunately for Geoff, he had to stay in India regardless. India was in a state of turmoil as independence beckoned and the country needed policing. Plus, it was a good landing stage to recover Burma in case pockets of Japs refused to surrender despite their Emperor's instruction.

Chapter 10

BROTHERS AT CASSEL

It was the late May Bank Holiday of 1985 and I drove to the port just after midday. Geoff joined me halfway down the motorway and I tried to cast my mind back to the last time when we had taken off, just the two of us. I couldn't recall, it must have been when he was a teenager. It's a sad fact of life, but when your kid brother discovers girls, cars, and motorbikes and there's a little independence money in their pockets, the hero worship relationship with their older brother tends to level off a little. Not that I was complaining, it was just nice to be doing what we were doing. It was great being together again. It had been so long.

I asked Geoff if he wanted to take over the driving, but he was non-committal. Geoff could jump into any machine and within minutes he'd master it; he had served in the Royal Engineers in India where he had been in charge of bulldozers, heavy lorries, and even steam trains.

It was a rough crossing, not unlike the crossing in 1940, only now it was daylight and I could see the swell of the English Channel under the grey, cloud-covered sky. It brightened up a little as we approached France and the announcement was made over the tannoy to return to our vehicles.

After the ferry docked, I waited patiently in line and watched the huge doors open onto a landing ramp. We were ushered out onto the dock and waived through passport control before we headed southeast on a 'D' road signposted towards Saint Omer.

"We'll take the country roads there," I said. "It's only twenty-five miles or so, and you can let me know if I start drifting over to the wrong side of the road."

Suddenly, the name Saint Omer stirred a long-suppressed memory. I remembered hearing that some of my battery had been taken there by the Germans. They had been treated in the Field Hospital. Some had been buried in the Commonwealth War Cemetery at Saint Omer. Major Milton was one of them. I wondered whether it would be possible to find his grave and pay my respects.

I mentioned it to Geoff. He said there were thousands of graves in and around Saint Omer, but if we passed the war cemetery, we could certainly take a look. I kept an eye out for it, but we didn't pass it. I wasn't about to make a fuss at this stage. Continental driving seemed stressful enough without adding unexpected detours.

The irony wasn't lost on me that the last time I was on these roads we were desperately avoiding German vehicles yet here I was, forty years down the line, the owner of a German manufactured car, sitting behind the three-pointed star, prominent at the end of the bonnet.

We tuned the car radio into Radio 4 on longwave and listened to Alistair Cooke's 'Letter from America'. His clipped, beautifully spoken English reminded me that I wasn't far from home and somehow made this unfamiliar environment less daunting. Despite my nerves dealing with French traffic and their road behaviour as another French driver loomed in my mirrors and tried to bully the car out of the way, Geoff seemed entirely comfortable. Within the hour we were heading south on the D26 road leading into Cassel.

Soon after, the twin mounds of Cassel and Mont des Recollets came into view on the horizon. My mind raced back forty years to the last time I was here. Shelling, mortaring and air attacks coming from all sides, an unholy shambles, while behind us, the big plume of smoke from the coastline at Dunkirk had become clearly visible.

I felt myself getting tenser as we approached the roundabout before the left turn onto the D933 that led up the steep hill into Cassel. The road became cobbled, slowing us down a little. The cobbles... they were familiar to me for some reason. The Mercedes made light work of the undulations, but the rapid thrumming sound transmitted through its suspension reminded me of machine-gun fire. I'll admit to the fact I was finding it difficult to breathe, my shirt collar a little tighter than I would have liked. But Geoff said something and, even though I can't recall what it was, his voice soothed me, I was glad to have him with me.

"I remember you were a handsome tyke when you went to war in 1940." He laughed. "In those days you had a full head of black hair and that natty moustache."

The cheeky bugger, but how could I argue with him? He still looked so young and, unlike me, hadn't lost a single hair on his head.

Higher and higher we climbed until, on the right, I spotted the town cemetery. Attached was a small Commonwealth War Grave cemetery. "Let's just stop here," I said and I pulled up at Dead Horse Corner.

This was a name we had given the road after the gruesome sight of two shelled horses still attached to a French artillery gun carriage, one of which had its teeth bared in a disgusting grin. I kept that memory to myself as we stepped down into the cemetery.

It was quiet, really quite peaceful and after we'd wandered around for ten minutes, I found Gunner Harry Woolston's and Charlie Williams' graves. The stark loneliness of those names inscribed on the immaculate Portland stone threatened to overwhelm me. Luckily, I kept it together. Just.

Geoff indicated that it was getting late, and we needed to get to the hotel. I reluctantly agreed; part of me didn't want to leave those boys on their own. Two fine lads who never made it back home to their loved ones.

We walked out of the cemetery and I climbed back into the car. I had adopted my normal policy of throwing money at the problem. I had booked the most expensive hotel in Cassel. It was called the Hotel Schoebeque; a typical Flemish brick-built building, very elegant with modern sun canopies on either side of a huge entrance doorway. It was clearly the best hotel in town and, in broken French with a receptionist speaking fairly good English, I booked in and she handed me the key. "Your room is on the second floor, sir."

"Thank you."

The girl asked me if I was taking dinner in the hotel. I said we were and we agreed on an eight o'clock sitting. Geoff had drifted away into another part of the hotel. He would no doubt turn up in the bar before dinner.

I went down a little earlier and noticed a German couple were struggling to make themselves understood at reception. They looked to be about my age. I wandered over and asked the receptionist if she needed any help. "I would love some help," she said. "They don't speak one word of French. Do you speak German?"

"Yes," I said.

It had been some time since I had spoken any German, but I was pleasantly surprised how it all came flooding back to me. I managed to explain to the receptionist that they didn't have a booking and wished to stay one night or perhaps even two. "Sie sprechen ausgezeichnetes Deutsch Wo haben Sie gelernt, so gut zu sprechen," the gentlemen said. I smiled. He had complimented me on my German and asked where I had learnt it. I wasn't about to go into that at a reception desk. There was an uncomfortable second or two of silence as we looked at each other. His wife said something I didn't pick up. Instead, I waved my hand in the air, told him I had picked it up over the years and we left it at that. I asked him if they were on holiday.

He introduced himself as Helmut. They had been to the west coast of France and were en-route back home across Holland to Northern Germany. Helmut said he hadn't been there for forty years. I told the couple the price of the room and they nodded enthusiastically. I also booked them into the restaurant for nine o'clock, said my goodbyes, and wandered through to the bar.

Geoff appeared not long after and we made our way to the restaurant. Unfortunately, the waiter spoke no English and I had to struggle through in French. He presented us with a fairly substantial carte de vins but the French-sounding names meant very little to me.

"Honestly, it's embarrassing how bad we are at languages. It's the bloody island mentality for sure. I dare say you are pretty good at Urdu though," I said to my brother.

After dinner, we went back through to the bar and, as I nursed a gin and tonic, I spotted the German couple I'd met earlier. They were walking towards our table, grinning and telling me how pleased they were to have found this hotel, almost at random. They spoke quickly but I managed to pick it all up. They wanted to buy me a drink by way of a thank-you. I whispered to Geoff, "They want to buy me a drink."

He looked at me rather confused. "And why would they want to do that?"

"I speak German."

"No, you don't Eric."

"I helped them check in to the hotel."

Before Geoff could say anything else, I turned towards them. "Vielen dank, wir werden zwei gin tonic haben."

Geoff looked shocked.

"I told them I would have a gin and tonic."

He was lost for words.

"I speak German, I spent five years as a German POW, remember, I sent you all letters?"

I turned to my new-found friends and thanked them for their generosity. I asked where home was.

"Meppen," he said. "In Lower Saxony."

He told me they lived in a house on the banks of a pretty river. I asked them if they'd enjoyed their vacation. They said it had been fine but seemed reluctant to expand further. I spoke to them in fluent German for at least five minutes as I tried to calculate in my head the significance of the forty-year gap between their visits.

Helmut asked me what I was doing in Cassel. I didn't want to go into detail, said it was just a few days away with my brother. At that moment, I think there was a flash of mutual understanding between us. My new friend walked away when the drinks arrived.

I looked at Geoff, who was shaking his head. "I never knew."

"You didn't ask me."

That was a little unfair, of course Geoff didn't know I spoke German as I had never had reason to ever use it in front of him. "But you sounded fluent."

"I am fluent, I was an interpreter at the coal mine, I took over from a man called Gibbs. I spoke to you about it just before you headed off to India."

"I'd forgotten, I'm sorry."

For the first time since I had returned from my time as a POW, I told my brother about a coal mine in Eastern Europe.

"Norman Gibbs wasn't in my regiment; he was in another part of the British Expeditionary Force. He was injured and captured by a German Panzer division about fifty miles from here. After that Gibbs was marched to Lamsdorf."

"Wait a minute," Geoff said, "wasn't that one of the camps you were in?"

"Yes."

"But wasn't that in the far east of Germany?"

"Yes."

"But...," Geoff looked astounded, "that's nearly a thousand miles."

"Yes, some of the journeys were made on trains; they were packed into cattle trucks like sardines. When they arrived at Lamsdorf they were told that they were working prisoners of the Third Reich. When Gibbs was declared fit enough to work, he was transferred to E72 Arbeitskommando at Beuthen, Silesia where he was put to work as a coal miner."

My brother was in another world.

"They transferred Gibbs to a coal mine. He and I were in that bloody mine together for over four years. Gibbs was the Dolmetscher."

"What's that?"

"German for the interpreter and I took over from him."

"He died?"

"No, they just relieved him from his duties."

"Why?"

I took a deep breath.

"I'm tired, Geoff."

"Sure, I understand."

I told Geoff it had been a long trip and tomorrow was another day. I finished my drink and opened up a small tourist map of Cassel. I pointed to Mont des Recollets.

"Tomorrow morning, we can start there. I'll tell you all about it."

At our table, we had been using the Michelin Road Atlas of Benelux and France Nord. I had placed it on my brother's seat, and we used it to navigate our way here. We were going to plan our tour over the dinner table but somehow hadn't got round to it. We had had too much to catch up on. I took the atlas upstairs with me as I tried to remember my route into Cassel forty-five years previously.

As I stood in the darkness of my bedroom, the large window gave me a splendid view across the plain to the south and, as we were on a hill, I could see the twinkling of houses and streetlights for miles. In the distance, there was an accumulation of lights, a large town, possibly Hazebrouck.

I opened the window as the cool night air seeped into the room and took a deep breath. I whispered to myself, "So many memories but so many ghosts out there too."

Chapter 11

FIRST CASUALTIES

I found myself falling asleep almost straight away which surprised me. I expected more demons to come and haunt me that night but they stayed away and I slept well. It was strange how even that short journey had made me so physically tired. Then I realised this was my first trip away from England for several years, my first trip since my wife died six years ago.

I woke with a start in the early hours of the morning. The bedroom digital clock read 05.15. Something compelled me to get out of bed and look outside. I peered out of the bedroom window into the darkness of a Flanders night. I could make out twinkling lights in the far distance to the south, the few cars or vans of early morning workers and delivery men making their way to work along the deserted roads.

It was cool in the room, and I was eager to get back into bed. I cursed the French hotel owners for lack of a kettle and some tea bags. They hadn't quite cottoned on to the fact that an Englishman needs a cup of tea the minute he opens his eyes in the morning.

I put the bedside lamp on and thumbed through the road atlas. I traced my finger along a marked road and the details started to come back to me. I remembered the journey we had taken back towards the Belgian border. It was 16th May 1940, forty-five years ago almost to the day. We were making a 'strategic withdrawal' we had been told; it felt like we were simply retracing our steps back to where we'd started. Near Brussels, the entire regiment had taken a wrong turn and ended up in a cul-de-sac. We spent hours in total darkness unhitching the guns and turning the trucks around to get back to the main route. It was a complete farce; it would have been funny if the Luftwaffe hadn't been a constant threat and those early summer nights weren't so short. Eventually, we got to the Belgian town of Tournai. It had been reduced to rubble by German bombing.

I remembered that we had come across dozens of men wandering aimlessly through the ruins in pyjamas, slippers, and dressing gowns. We couldn't figure it out at first and asked them what they were doing. Their lack of response and vacant looks gave it away. We were outside the ruins of a bombed-out mental asylum. The doctors and nurses had let the patients out and then ran for the hills. It was every man for himself by then. Rather than leave them in a locked up secure unit at the mercy of German bombs, they had unlocked the doors and set them free.

We had set up a defensive position in a tiny hamlet just outside Tournai and there it was marked on the map. I thumbed through the bookmarked pages of the Grand Party book my colleagues had bought me as my retirement present and looked up the names of the little hamlets where we had positioned the regiment. The book stated that we were between Ere and Saint Maur. It took a few seconds, but I found those on the map too. I took a complementary hotel pen from the bedside cabinet and marked a cross beside Saint Maur. Also on the map, the Escaut River looked like a substantial river obstacle but it confirmed to me how much Belgian territory we had been forced to concede.

We had been told to defend the Escaut, the same river that our regiment had crossed the previous day. We had almost been driven back into France by this stage. The fighting had been fierce; we had been pitched into a real war. There was the sound of boom, boom, boom as bridges were destroyed by the Royal Engineers. Down at the riverside, we heard that there was desperate hand-to-hand fighting taking place. A couple of times, we had to fire our guns to support the boys fighting down there. They'd sent SOS messages, red and green flares. I remembered the Germans had put up an observation balloon on their side of the river. The cheeky thing was there for three days, it was like a scene from the Great War. Our boys never shot it down. Unlike the Germans, we had no air cover out there. In fact, the only British aircraft we saw were occasional Lysander spotter planes. They were no match for the German Messerschmitts.

I recalled with a shiver how the Germans had spotted our position and gave us a real pounding. Some of the lads from 366 Battery suffered a direct hit. Three of their guns were put out of action. The gunners were really shaken up; I spied a spray of blood on one of their tunics. It was carnage. Bombardier Thomas Bennett, a Londoner like most of us, had been killed, and many of his mates, including Sergeant Swindle, had been injured. I had put a bookmark at the page where this incident was described. It was my regiment's first combat casualty; we'd got away from the Dyle unscathed up till then.

I pondered the places on the map for at least an hour as I wrote on a notepad the things that were coming back to me. Now I was here, in the very place where this had all happened, someone had mysteriously opened a key to my mind. I remembered a small burial ceremony where a padre performed a service with an honour guard. And... another name that jumped into my head... Slogger, Sergeant Slogger Slines, but I don't think Slogger was killed... no, just badly injured.

I climbed out of the bed. I was looking forward to sharing a little breakfast with Geoff.

Thankfully, the hotel served some English tea, but there wasn't a sausage, an egg or a piece of bacon anywhere to be seen. They brought crusty French bread and jam. It was so hard I could hardly bite into it. I admitted defeat and they brought me a soft croissant. The five years in a POW camp had played havoc with my teeth and while I still retained a few of my own, most were dentures. "It's okay for you to laugh," I said looking at Geoff's perfectly white teeth, "you've still got all of your own, wait until you're dropping them in a glass by the side of the bed."

I finished breakfast off with strong coffee and small patisseries then I unfolded the map onto the table.

It was important to me that Geoff should understand how and why we had got here. Our time was limited and so, as we finished breakfast, I retraced the route. I had spotted another familiar place on the map, just outside Lille, a village in the suburbs of the city called Sainghin en Melantois. My book didn't name the place, but Brooks' description of the Battery HQ at the farmhouse there, then called Ferme de la Coeur, brought the memories flooding back.

After the shelling incident, we had withdrawn there across the fortified Belgian border and so we were now back in France, near to where we had been in training a few weeks previously.

"The main significance of Sainghin to me, Geoff, apart from the fact I was never able to pronounce it properly," I said, "is that it was where the two batteries were ordered to separate. My battery, 367, were sent here to Cassel, our other battery, 366, were sent back into Belgium. Most of the

366 lads managed to get away to Dunkirk. Our sister regiment, 139, were sent in that direction too. Jack Portas, you remember him?"

"Yes, I do, the chap from school that you used to go walking with."

"Yes, that's him, he was in 139 Regiment and we wouldn't see each other for another five bloody years."

"But he was your best pal, didn't you sign up together?"

"Yes, but after the Dyle fighting, Jack and his regiment had been sent to Courtrai, further to the north in Belgium. They were the lucky ones because most of those buggers escaped from Dunkirk. My lot were posted here, to Cassel, and the rest, as they say, is history."

I drained the last of the ridiculously strong coffee. I pointed to the map and drew an imaginary line to Cassel.

"You realise we probably haven't got time to go there, don't you? We have to catch the ferry tomorrow so we can't do much more than just stay around Cassel."

"I know."

"So where are we going today?" he asked.

"Well, most of the Cassel sites are walkable from the hotel in town so I think it will be a good idea if I take you to my old gun position on the Mont des Recollets."

"Sounds like a plan, Eric."

We left the hotel just after ten in the morning. It was a clear, sunny day and I had a spring in my step for a change. Even Geoff remarked that I had an enthusiasm that he hadn't seen for a long time, and he was right.

I explained that Mont des Recollets, literally translated, meant wooded hill. These French boys weren't very imaginative when it came to names.

We drove back down the cobbled road to a roundabout and then picked up the D948. I pulled my notebook out of my pocket and cleared my throat. "The 29th May 1940."

Geoff looked at me.

"What about it?"

"The 29th May 1940, that was the last time I did this journey."

"No way."

"Yes. At that point, we were on the backfoot, and we were trying to get back to Dunkirk." As the wooded hill loomed up in front of us, I continued. "We had destroyed all of our guns so that they wouldn't fall into enemy hands."

59

This was where poor Arthur was shot by a sniper, the bullet had gone right through his neck. I tried to explain but the words wouldn't come. The memory was as fresh that day as it had been all those years ago and the lump in my throat was growing ever larger as we climbed up the gentle slope through the woods. We drove to a tiny hamlet and stopped the car. "Here, this is familiar. If I'm not mistaken, I think our HQ was around here somewhere."

"Really?"

"Yes."

We climbed out of the car after we had parked up. I was first out with my map and my notebook.

"We believed it was the perfect place to set up our guns because any shells would be caught up in the canopy of the forest. It protected us a little; anybody caught in the middle of Cassel was a sitting duck. They blasted the hell out of Cassel that day."

We trekked through the woods and occasionally I stared up into the canopy of the forest. It was bizarre, it all looked the same as it had back then, and it appeared that the trees hadn't aged a day.

I wondered, *How could that be, had they been taken down and replanted at some time?*

On our way back towards the car, we passed Colonel Odling's gun position that faced north of the woods. A little further on I stopped and stamped my right foot. "And this was our initial gun position, my troop was commanded by Captain MacDougall. We were told to expect a German attack at any time; that our guns were to fire at their tanks from short range. It was called firing on open sights. The guns were more suited to firing from two or three miles away, so you can imagine what sort of mess they made of a tank and whoever was inside."

"I can, Eric, I imagine they were blown to bits."

My tongue had gone dry; I moved it around the inside of my bottom lip looking for a little moisture. "We… "

Geoff looked at me.

"Did you hit any tanks?"

I nodded my head slowly, pointed along a clearing in the woods. "There… we scored a direct hit at their lead tank."

Geoff sensed what was coming.

"We split the tank in two. And I mean in two. We carved it open like a tin of beans."

And like back then, there was no euphoria, no sense of victory that one might expect. I was one of the first men on the scene, I was ordered to clear the enemy out, to make sure there were none left, and if there were, to make sure they were of no danger to my section. A fireball had erupted inside the broken tank and what was left of the German flesh that remained was slowly but surely being burned beyond recognition. I saw a severed arm and leg, a blackened head with the helmet still attached and what I assumed were little pieces of flaming human fat were dripping onto the floor of the tank. The hair of the German soldier was on fire, but a thick acrid smoke quickly clouded my view. One of them was still screaming. I'll never forget the sound till my dying day. Thankfully his screams died away in seconds.

"Everyone inside killed I assume."

"Nothing left of them, Geoff."

"We were hemmed in by Germans on both sides at this point and to make matters worse there was a friendly fire incident too," I said.

"A what?"

"A British unit had trundled up the hill in three or four light armoured vehicles and started spraying our position with machine-gun fire. There was a lot of smoke around and it was an easy mistake to make. They thought we were the enemy; we thought the same and returned fire. Several of our lads were badly injured and one of our officers was killed."

"Jesus, you never told me any of this in 1945."

I hadn't. By the time we were reunited this was a long-forgotten memory. When I returned home after the war, Geoff and I had had a few weeks together, perhaps a month, before Geoff headed off to his own personal Hell. My time as a POW, the Long March, the brutality of Cassel, and the coal mine were fresh in my memory. It was so painful that I had never breathed a word of it to him. I was grateful for the opportunity to do that now, to clear my head of more than forty-five years of torment.

"And 2nd Lt. Waterman had jumped down from his position with a Bren gun and started firing at the vehicles. The poor bugger was cut to pieces by our own bullets."

"My dear Eric, this is really bad – you've been through some rough shit, brother."

He didn't know the half of it.

Chapter 12

MONT DES RECOLLETS

We spent some time in the woods. It was nice just being together after so long. I sensed he didn't want to rush me but I told him more about my battle at Cassel as well as one or two funny stories. In times of desperation, there was always a little black humour.

While it was difficult standing in those woods, it was also a little cathartic, a type of closure. At times I couldn't talk; I choked up more than once. I wiped a tear from the corner of my eye but I also stood with my brother in the middle of a peaceful everglade as the sun pierced the roof of the forest, and we laughed. We laughed and joked.

We left the forest and continued walking around the perimeter to the south. We walked along a track and reached the grounds of a grand three-storey building that wouldn't have looked out of place as a golf clubhouse back home in Surrey. It was Chateau Masson. "This is where our HQ was, I remember it now."

I turned and pointed to the flat fields, due south. "That's where the Panzers were coming from, a dozen that I could see at least, and we knew our position was hopeless. They gave us orders to fall back; the guns were to be relocated in Cassel itself. I didn't like the fact that we had lost the cover of the forest or the look of those bloody German tanks."

"You took a few casualties in these woods then?"

"Too many."

The names were coming back to me as Geoff spoke; men whose names I hadn't mentioned for forty-five years. Men like Bombardier Beth, Goodrum and Swindle, I had known them at Dursley. One of those men was buried at the scene and must have been lying there to that day although I couldn't remember who it was.

We were now out in the open, on the D916 road between Cassel and Mont des Recollets when Geoff suggested I should take a break and a little lunch.

It sounded like a good idea; I was feeling a little drained. I ambled back to the car and on the way, I told Geoff how we had been notified that HQ and F Troop were in dire straits; we had trained with those lads, and I knew we wouldn't be seeing a lot of them ever again.

As we drove along the road from the Mont des Recollets, I recognised the copse of trees where E Troop had been positioned to the north of the main woods. The German Panzers had been attacking us from all directions and E Troop had received a few direct hits. Colonel Odling had been injured by a shell fragment and our vehicle was requisitioned to take him up to the Field Hospital in Cassel. Suddenly the poor man, his usually immaculate uniform dusty and bloodied, was lying in pain with a broken leg across the back seats.

I turned to Geoff and pointed to the roadside.

"That's where Colonel Odling was hit. They bundled him into a vehicle, and I was ordered in with him. I did my best to comfort him and realised there was really no divide between us, we had been part of a team all doing the tasks we had trained for. At that moment, I realised he was no different to us, flesh and blood, as simple as that."

"He was a good bloke?" Geoff asked.

"Yes. I always had a lot of time for the colonel."

We walked a little further.

"No one who sat with me in the back of that vehicle that day with our badly injured commander could accuse our officers of not getting their hands dirty. Odling had been injured because he was right there in the thick of the action with his men."

"I get it, Eric."

"We had taken him to the Field Hospital in the town square and met with Brigadier Somerset, and our regiment's medic, Captain Lacey."

I grabbed Geoff's arm to try to stop him from walking.

"Oh, by the way, around this time I had been awarded a stripe and promoted to Lance Bombardier. It was all a bit of a blur, to be honest."

We drove back to Cassel and decided to take a late lunch in the main square. Even though it was a Saturday, some of the places looked closed, typical of the bloody French we both agreed.

63

Eventually, I found a restaurant. Geoff had suggested some French ham and cheese and I had made the mistake of asking for it in a sandwich. Geoff was laughing as I picked it all out of the crusty bread and ate it. It was another light-hearted moment and I found myself realising how much I was enjoying quality time with my brother. It had been way too long. "Bloody French bread," I remarked.

Geoff said the bread looked delicious.

If I had ever been in the position of standing in front of the French ead of State just after the war, and he had thanked me for the role I'd played in helping rid his country of the Nazis and if he had said, 'Mr West, I thank you from the bottom of my heart, what can I do to make your next visit to France as enjoyable as possible?' I would have had no hesitation, 'Monsieur De Gaulle," I would have said, 'that's an easy one, sir, just give me some soft bread.'

Chapter 13

SOMERSET'S MEMORIAL

Over lunch, Geoff was curious to know more about some of our officers. I told him that all three of my senior officers were either killed or injured. Odling was captured here in the town, my Battery Commander, Major Edward Milton, was so severely injured that he died a day after we had tried to break out from Cassel. "Poor Milton, he was another fine chap, a schoolteacher from Essex and very proper; he commanded our 367 Battery. His driver was a fellow called John Martin."

"Really?"

"Yes, remind me when we've got a little more time to tell you about him."

I was keen to press on with my version of events, very much aware that our time together was precious; we didn't have much of it left. Perhaps I was being a little selfish, but this was very much a brothers' break and something we should have done years ago. "As I was saying, Major Milton was injured not far out from Cassel, but I heard later that Martin was unscathed. The Jerries took the Major to Saint Omer, to their hospital, but sadly I learned after the war that he died of his injuries."

I had a tear in my eye as I uttered that last sentence and surprised myself how emotional it still was after all those years. "And Major Christopherson, he was injured too, he was knocked unconscious while directing fire here at Cassel. His driver bundled him into a car, realising how serious his injuries were, determined to get him to Dunkirk as soon as he could. The loyal gunner flew up the road with no concern for his own safety but unfortunately, they ran slap-bang into a German patrol. They were both captured. Christopherson was still unconscious, and his driver was unarmed; they had no chance to fight their way out. The Major was taken to the same German Field Hospital at Saint Omer. Luckily, he survived and when he was well enough, he was transferred to one of the Oflags in Bavaria."

"A question, Eric?"

"Fire away."

"What was the difference between a Stalag and an Oflag?"

I smiled. "That's an easy one, Geoff, German is a very logical language, Oflag is simply a shortened version of Offizierslager, meaning prison camp for officers and Stalag is short for Kriegsgefangenen-Mannschafts-Stammlager, for us peasant classes. That's why we POWs were called Kreigies. For five long years, I was a nobody, no future, a bloody Kreigie."

He nodded, "I see, bit of a bloody mouthful, no wonder they shorten it."

After lunch and another glass of beer, we set off around the town on foot. We meandered into the two town squares as I tried to remember where we had positioned the guns. At the Grand Place, we found the memorial plaque to Brigadier Somerset and his Gloucester Regiment.

There was one thing that jumped out at both of us that day as we stood together solemnly and read the writing on the plaque. It read:

'In proud memory of Brigadier, the Honourable N F Somerset C.B.E., D.S.O., M.C., and the 228 officers and men of 2nd & 5th Battalions, the Gloucestershire Regiment, who fought and died covering the evacuation of the British and French forces at Dunkirk 24-29th May 1940'

My brother asked me why the Royal Artillery wasn't mentioned.

"It was the infantry who were charged with defending the town, we were just territorials and regarded as being there as support."

"That's terrible," Geoff said. "So there's nothing to commemorate your regiment?"

"Not that I'm aware of. I think they forgot about us in the chaos of it all."

I climbed the steps to the statue of Marchal Foch at the summit with the stunning views towards the coast and as I studied the map again, realised that the view looked towards Winnezeele and Watou, the breakout route.

"I'd like to drive along that road," I said.

"No problem," my brother said. "We can go tomorrow morning if you like; it only looks about ten miles away."

"I'd like that a lot."

66

"Tell me about what happened here, Eric, here in Cassel."

Without hesitation, I started to tell him.

"We were to defend Cassel and when we arrived, we were assigned to Brigadier Somerset's command, it was a hotchpotch of different regiments. We had become part of 145 Brigade or what they called, *SOMERFORCE*."

"Sounds a bit complicated, Eric, sounds like there were a lot of chiefs."

"Not really. One thing I can honestly say is that we knew what we were doing; we felt we had been well trained and we all knew our roles. I had confidence in all of our officers and even though the Germans seemed determined coming at us from the southwest, we were still confident of repelling them and holding onto the town. We were told to expect a counterattack by either the French or British, or both, and that we would be relieved."

"But that didn't happen."

"No." I took a deep breath. "The town was heavily shelled but miraculously we didn't suffer any serious casualties. From this position where we are now, you could see the amount of damage we were inflicting on the Germans. There were abandoned Panzer tanks strewn all around. We had more trouble hitting targets accurately from here though, our guns hadn't been registered and the buildings got in the way. I remember in one of the positions we had to knock a hole in the brick wall."

Geoff shook his head. "It must have been horrendous."

I had to remind myself that my brother had been in the services but of course, by the time he had completed his officer cadet training, the war was over. Poor Geoff's main enemies were the heat, the boredom and the dreadful homesickness.

"You could say that. We didn't know that at the time of course and nor did we know that we were almost being sacrificed."

We were still in the town square as I explained that Cassel was on the road to Dunkirk.

"To our east, the BEF were desperately trying to get to the beaches about fifteen miles away. We were beaten and the only option was to get back home, regroup and live to fight another day."

"I know all about Dunkirk," Geoff said, "don't forget I was following the war at school. So, your lot were keeping the Germans busy while the BEF fled and made it onto the boats at Dunkirk?"

"Yes. That's it in a nutshell."

"You drew the short straw?"

"You could say that. Anyway, Somerset made the decision to evacuate the remaining civilian population. There was no food and they were milling around with no real purpose as sporadic shells fell onto the town. Getting rid of the civilians was the only way we could establish decent defensive positions. We took over their houses, tried to make the town tank-proof. We strengthened the houses, blocked the windows, barricaded the roads, and dug trenches."

The first day was relatively quiet. I didn't want to bore my brother with the details but if my memory served me right, we were digging in and making sure the civilians left.

I took out my notebook, flicked through it until I found my notes from the 26th May. That was quiet too. My God, if we'd only known what was about to hit us. The next day, the evacuation of Dunkirk started and the Germans were trying to cut off all the roads to the port. It was our job to stall them at Cassel. There were continuous air attacks and mortar fire throughout the morning and then the Germans attacked. "The Germans attacked us on the twenty-seventh of May, so that's almost forty-five years ago to the day. They sent in their Panzers but although we suffered heavy casualties, we managed to drive them back. The houses were all in ruins."

I looked at Geoff who was gazing at the elegant French houses in the clear, late spring air as we walked around the town. They had all been rebuilt of course but Geoff wasn't seeing what I was seeing. Those houses and hotels and business premises, shops and bars would always look the same to me as they had forty-five years ago.

"Round about us, the Germans were overrunning the lower-lying towns, but it was the height of Cassel that made it so difficult to take. There were some fierce scraps at the station and some of the villages down on the plain with stories of bayonet charges and hand-to-hand fighting. For a while, some of the Royal Horse Artillery joined our troop at Recollets and told some blood-curdling accounts of their escape from Hondeghem, a village about a couple of miles to the south of here. The Germans had focussed on our HQ Company at Chateau Masson and we'd put the damaged heavy guns on the road to stop the tanks; our battery took out five of their Panzers."

I remembered it like it was yesterday and referred a lot to the notes I had made on the ferry coming across. I was also adding to them on an hourly basis.

After I had left Mary O'Leary, I stocked up on some more exercise books from the newsagent at home and started a new notebook. The Eric West book was definitely taking shape, there was enough material and I was always a stickler for the details. I'd had a habit of writing myself notes sometimes, even from radio broadcasts. At home, my constant companion, particularly since my wife died, was BBC Radio 4; their scientific documentaries being my favourite for note-taking. Perhaps there was an author lurking inside me.

The boys from F Troop at Chateau Masson had joined us in the town after they had been overrun by the Germans. We welcomed the additional manpower but I remember looking at their faces and they were not the faces of victorious men, one or two of the younger boys looked haggard and distraught. One lad's cheeks were streaked with tears. Tragically, several of their casualties had occurred when one of their shells exploded prematurely as it left the gun.

Geoff's words brought me back from my thoughts.

"You were on a hiding to nothing by the sounds of it, Eric."

"We were. The enemy got within fifty yards of the town walls that day but we drove them back."

For the first time that I could remember, my chest actually swelled with pride when I said that to my brother. We could see them at the bottom of the hill, and we were massively outnumbered, but we gave them everything we had and to my sheer amazement the buggers turned around and left us alone. We knew it wasn't over, not by a long shot, but we had scored a victory of sorts. For a while, there was a strange, eerie silence.

"They started shelling us the next morning and their aircraft dropped leaflets in English telling us to surrender."

"They what?"

I laughed.

"That's right, the bastards told us it was all over. The leaflet had a small map drawn and they pointed out that the German forces were all around us. 'Stop fighting,' it read, 'lay down your arms.'"

"But you didn't."

"Did we hell! We were British! All we needed was a strong cup of tea and we were good to go again."

Geoff looked at me strangely.

"It wasn't like that though, was it?"

I shook my head.

"No, it was Hell on earth, but I'm not kidding you, we weren't able to make any tea as the percussion blasts from exploding shells kept blowing out our petrol stoves."

I laughed.

"The bastards wouldn't even leave us in peace when we were brewing up."

Most of the buildings we were holed up in were nothing more than ruins. We were mostly operating from the cellars as it was too dangerous to stay at ground level. My brother didn't need to know that all the plumbing had been destroyed, that the place was swimming in shit; there were unburied corpses of civilians and soldiers everywhere you looked. A lot of dead dogs and horses too. The rats ran around the cellar panicking, taking a bite out of anyone who got too near.

Geoff had his own horror stories about the aftermath of the war in India; he touched on them in some of his letters back home. Geoff had demons too… more than anyone would ever know until it was too late. We'd both been through our own personal Hell.

"Talking of tea," Geoff said. "Would you like a cup back at the hotel or another beer?" He glanced at his watch. "It's getting on, I don't know about you but I feel like I have been on these legs all day."

I looked at my watch too. It was after six, where had the day gone? I was physically fine but emotionally drained. My brother was right; it was time to call it a day.

"Let's get one of those Flanders beers," I said. "I'm developing a bit of a taste for the stuff."

Chapter 14

WINNEZEELE CEMETERY

We enjoyed another calm Saturday evening; the late spring air was delightful. There were hints of perfume from the blossom trees that reminded me of my liberation forty years ago. From the restaurant terrace, we both took in the incredible view across the Flanders plain. As dusk fell, I turned in for an early night. We took a break from the war for a few hours. We talked about Mum and Dad, and for the first time, a few words about Joy, my late wife. I felt that my brother hadn't known her at all.

Geoff asked whether Joy would have joined me on the trip if she had still been alive. The truth was I wasn't sure. It occurred to me that perhaps I wouldn't have been able to make this trip with anyone else.

On Sunday morning, I decided to check out of the hotel early and loaded my bags in the car, making sure we were leaving enough time to catch the ferry. We had another quick breakfast and headed out towards the car park to plan our route.

I decided it was the right time to pick up the story of my last day of freedom – the breakout from Cassel. I was feeling refreshed, raring to go and I was looking forward to divulging the story of how I got to the Belgian border and Watou. How could that be? How could I look forward to visiting the scene of one of the worst periods of my life? Life is a funny thing; humans are complicated beasts.

As we sat in the car, planning our route, I began.

"Cassel was a mess, Geoff, and we realised there wasn't going to be any counterattack to relieve us. Our food was non-existent; we hadn't eaten a normal hot meal for at least a week and could only snack on army rations of biscuits and tins of bully beef. We were on our last few rounds of ammunition and even if we'd wanted to stay and fight, there was nothing much left to hit the Germans with.

We had artillery shells of course; the order was to continue firing the guns all through the day and evening of the twenty-ninth of May but at the same time, we were preparing to break out too. One of the officers told us that any equipment we were not using had to be destroyed. That's when we knew it was over, that the Germans had us surrounded, just as their propaganda leaflets had said. We couldn't risk working guns falling into their hands. At the very last moment, we started incapacitating the big guns. We smashed the sights and removed the firing pins. We punctured the tyres and smashed the radiators of the trucks.

We were ready to go, to break out of Cassel during the hours of darkness. There were Germans everywhere. There was hardly enough food to go round, nothing substantial, just army ration packs, biscuits and some chocolate. We were told not to worry as the Belgian border was only about ten miles away. We were to join the BEF there and then make our way to Dunkirk where boats would be waiting to take us back to England."

"As simple as that," Geoff said somewhat sarcastically.

He asked me if we were truly hopeful of getting away from Cassel and making it to Dunkirk. "Well, we had no option really, we had to hope. There was nothing else left."

We had never been in that situation before, not even our officers from the First World War because nobody had ever surrendered to the enemy. It was the great unknown. We had heard the stories of massacres and rumours were rife about just how savage these Nazis could be. I brought my thoughts back to that last night in Cassel.

"There weren't even enough small arms to go around Geoff, men were sharing rifles and I had been given two grenades."

"You didn't even have a rifle, Eric?"

I laughed it off. "No, but I was relieved because rifles were bloody heavy, and I wasn't much of a shot. Mind you, I had never been trained to use a grenade."

"You're kidding me."

"No, I knew you had to pull the pin out and they had about a five- or six-second delay, but even at Dursley, I'd never actually thrown one."

Geoff was fairly upset about that, but I explained to him that, at the time, we weren't worried about rifles and grenades and ammunition because we didn't want to use them anyway. There were so many Germans around that to engage in any sort of firefight would have been tantamount to suicide.

"We were on the run; with a mission to make it back to Dunkirk and the fewer Germans we encountered the better."

Geoff had climbed out of the car. "You can tell me about it when we're on the road."

I gave him a thumbs up. I walked across the small car park, said my goodbyes to the hotel staff, settled the bill and said farewell to Helmut and his wife who were loitering in the reception area.

"Helmut, kannich deine adresse nehem?" I said as I asked him for his address and jotted it down in my notebook. I told him it would be nice to speak or write occasionally, to practice my German. He nodded in agreement, took my address and said he'd forgotten a lot of the English he'd learned many years ago. We even exchanged telephone numbers. As we shook hands, there was what I can only describe as a hard stare from Helmut.

"What is it?" I asked. "Are you okay?"

His brows came together as he paused before he spoke.

Helmut smiled, slapped me on the shoulder. "Off you go, Eric, I'm sure we will meet again one day."

"Perhaps," I lied.

The reality was that neither of us would probably even pick up the phone let alone make arrangements to meet up.

"Safe trip," he called out as I walked away."

"And you too," I shouted back over my shoulder in German.

We set off in the car, back down the cobbled street where we picked up the signposts on country roads to Winnezeele. After a few minutes, Geoff asked me what route we had followed to get to Dunkirk.

"I'm not sure of the exact route, it was pitch bloody black! Somerset said we were heading for Watou, just inside the Belgian border, along the D137 road that headed northeast towards Winnezeele. He'd also ordered the lads from the East Riding Yeomanry to protect the rear of the breakout. I remember thinking at the time that those poor bastards had drawn the short straw because the only thing that would be happening to that lot was that they'd be killed or captured."

Geoff was shaking his head. "I can't even contemplate it, Eric; I can't even put myself in that situation. I mean… how can you obey an order when you know there are only two outcomes, death or captivity at the hands of the enemy?"

"I was holding on to the man in front," I said. "The columns of men were kept together, I was with the men of D Troop, with Sergeant Major Goddard, Captain MacDougall, Sergeant Mears and a few others, but I confess I can't remember their names."

Geoff laughed. "Jesus, Eric, your memory is incredible; I can't believe how much information is up there in that big, bloody thick skull of yours."

He was right. I surprised myself at times; I was quoting men's names that hadn't passed my lips for more than forty years.

I cleared my throat. "The officers had compasses and maps; we had nothing and relied on them. I thought we were making good progress initially, but as soon as the Germans realised we were making a run for it, there were searchlights looking for us, they even started burning farmhouses to illuminate the night sky."

"That's what really pisses me off about war, Eric, the poor bloody civilians. I saw it in India too, nobody gives a shit about the civilians, the poor French and Belgian farmers hadn't harmed a soul."

Geoff was quite animated as he ranted on about the Germans destroying their livelihoods, razing buildings to the ground that had stood for generations. My kid brother and I were singing from the same hymn sheet. As we drove on, we stopped at the hamlet of Ryveld and got out of the car. There was an old sign on one of the house walls, looking the same as it was in 1940; it read, 'Cassel 5.2 km, Watou 8.9 km.'

"It was still pitch dark when we were around here, I think. Judging by that sign we'd only made three miles progress, it felt like we'd been walking half the night."

We walked a few hundred yards down the road and in the distance, surrounded by lush green meadows, I could see the church steeple at Winnezeele. "That church steeple." I pointed.

"What about it?"

"Our officers used it as our aiming point, but we wanted to stay off the roads to avoid running into German patrols. As you can see, the land is flat and featureless; we were crawling through the ditches by the side of the road. We could hear bursts of machine-gun fire all around us, but we didn't know whether they were our lads' bullets or the Jerries. We walked until dawn and, as my eyes grew accustomed to the surroundings, I remember it was misty and wet underfoot. As first light broke, I recall a distinct feeling of vulnerability. There was no doubt about it, we were more exposed."

"And where were you when dawn broke?"

"I'm not a hundred percent sure, probably somewhere between the two towns. As the crow flies, we were probably no more than twenty-five miles from Dunkirk. We could see the faint glow from the fires in the distance. Dunkirk was burning and we got occasional drifts of the powerful acrid smoke as the wind blew in from the north."

We returned to the car and drove a bit further on across the D18 crossroads and here it came flooding back. "It must have been around here that we first heard the screeching noise of tank tracks."

That sound still haunts me to this day.

"We'd learnt to recognise that sound and knew we were in trouble. We were just approaching a signpost that told us we were one kilometre from Winnezeele. And yes, yes, it was light here, I remember now; it was definitely light when we got to Winnezeele. We heard shelling and machine-gun fire very close by. As the explosions burst over our heads, we all scattered. Someone screamed that we had to keep low, which was a ridiculous thing to say." I smiled. "Nobody needed to tell us to keep our heads down."

I wish it hadn't been light, I wish it had still been in the pitch black, dead of night because I saw things that morning that no man should have to see. I saw the dead and injured, my friends writhing in agony and heard grown men dying, calling for their mothers. I was in a ditch and I dared to raise my head an inch or two above it. It was carnage; there is no other word to describe it. "Some of the lads started to surrender around here. I saw them being marched away at gunpoint."

"But not you, Eric."

"No. We didn't trust the Germans, surrendering to them was the last thing on my mind. The place was like a battlefield from the Great War, only the uniforms slightly different but the blood and screaming were the same."

"Carry on, Eric."

"What?"

"You keep stopping just when you get to an interesting bit."

"I do, don't I?"

Geoff smiled. "To be expected. Tell me what happened next?"

We were just coming into Winnezeele. I eased the car over to the right and pulled on the handbrake. "We knew at this point that Winnezeele was in Jerry's hands. I remember we made for one of the farmhouses over there," I told him as I pointed, "praying that it wasn't being used as a machine-gun nest by the Germans. Our officers tried to keep us calm as we planned our next move. Captain Coll Lorne MacDougall was leading us."

"Coll Lorne, that's a bit of a mouthful, isn't it?" Geoff said.

I nodded. It was. Most of the other officers just called him Lorne.

I continued, "As much as we all trusted him there was panic in his eyes as he ordered us to break cover. We had just made it into open ground when there was a burst of machine-gun fire. He ran on while we all scrambled back into the ditch for cover. I didn't see the Captain after that."

"What happened to him?"

"Well, to be honest nobody really knows, but I heard he evaded capture for nearly two months."

"They got him eventually then?"

"Yes, he was taken prisoner and sent to one of the officer camps down in Bavaria. It was all a bit of a mystery how he escaped; he either lived off the land or got a bit of French Resistance help. He was mentioned in dispatches after the war."

"Really, what for?"

"Again, that was a bit of a mystery. Apparently, he was communicating while in captivity. We don't know how but there was talk of secret coded messages and communicating with MI9 by secret means, whatever that means."

"So, a bit of a mystery man?"

"You could say that."

As I looked out of the car window, I spotted the signpost to the Commonwealth War Cemetery and the church. "Look, Geoff."

He checked his watch. "We've plenty of time before our ferry, if you want to take a look it's not a problem."

"I'd like that a lot, even though it's a 'house of error'."

Geoff smiled; he knew me too well. I called churches of all denominations, houses of error for obvious reasons to us committed atheists. Even as a youngster, when Geoff was growing up, I questioned religion and everything it stood for.

We drove on and parked in the small car park next to the church. I was apprehensive as we stepped from the car. I knew why; I was going to visit some old pals and I hadn't seen them for forty-five years. I knew most of the graves were unmarked and I wasn't stupid enough to accept that every grave was marked with the correct body, but they were here all right, or at least bits of them.

I walked through the entrance to the cemetery, I could feel their presence, those boys who had been cut to pieces or blown to bits by the enemy, some who had drowned in the ditches by the side of the road, who didn't have the strength to lift their broken heads from the dirty water. It could have so easily been me.

I had carried that guilt for forty-five years. Why did I survive and those good men didn't?

The nightmares had been frequent, I guessed that most POWs felt the same and had the same nightmares as I did. The guilt came in a huge, gift-wrapped box with many compartments. There was the survival guilt of course but there was also the guilt about the inactivity. I had heard the odd comment over the years, not normally to my face, but I had heard them. Some people thought we had it easy, a cushy number in a German POW camp with three square meals a day. We played football and had boxing matches and staged concerts and pantomimes at Christmas. There was no action and no danger. That's what our letters home had said.

People back home had lost husbands and wives, brothers and sisters. I understood, I truly did. And in the pub when Frank the Spitfire pilot from Basingstoke was describing his dog fight with a German Messerschmitt and how he'd taken him out with a burst of machine-gun fire that had ripped through his cockpit, what could I say? Even Frank's ground crew had better stories than I had.

We called them the boys 'out there'; the men fighting for our liberty, I remember a sergeant major giving a Christmas toast one year.

"For the King," he said, "and the Empire and the boys out there."

The boys out there called us the lucky ones. If only they knew. Frank's war ended in 1945, mine was still ongoing. I lived it every minute of every day. A Kreigie's war is the longest bloody war in history.

The gravestones were immaculately kept, the sword of honour stood tall and proud in the centre of the small graveyard. We walked around the stones reading some of the descriptions and even though they were nearly all religious in meaning, I still found it quite moving. Before I had time to say anything to Geoff, he came back with exactly what I was thinking.

"There's a lot of religious claptrap around here, Eric, but I can't help feeling a little emotional."

I wanted to place my arm around his shoulder. I couldn't recall the last time we had physical contact. Before he'd gone off to the war, I recalled pulling him in tightly towards me and on the brink of tears, prayed to a

God I didn't believe in that he wouldn't have to go through anything like I had.

We walked on. Sure enough, we found many gravestones marked, 'A Soldier of the 1939-45 War. Known unto God.'

"Known unto God," Geoff said. "What on earth does that mean?"

"Rudyard Kipling?" I said.

"What?"

"Rudyard Kipling, he worked for the Imperial War Graves Commission that set up these cemeteries after the Great War."

"What, the Jungle Book author?"

That's him," I said. "His son Jack was killed in Loos in 1915."

"Really?"

We walked towards the remembrance stone inscribed with another of Kipling's suggestions to the commission, 'Their name liveth for ever more.'

"Yes. The story goes that he pushed his son into the Great War. The poor kid had an eye defect, he could easily have avoided the front line, but Kipling pulled a favour and his son was accepted into the Irish Guards."

"Jesus!"

"Yes, can you imagine that? And then the reports say that during his first battle, he went missing in action and a few days later they found his dead body."

What must Kipling have gone through? I thought.

Through words, he had managed to express his combination of grief and guilt about the complicity he must have felt in his son's death. I fancied myself as an amateur poet and many of my attempts were scribbled down in my various notebooks. Some of them were decent enough, but somehow, I had never managed to define the emotions I was searching for.

I remembered Kipling's poem My Boy Jack and also his short story, The Gardener, about a woman searching for her illegitimate son who had been killed somewhere near to where we were now standing. He had been buried in a Flanders cemetery just like this one. When it came to pulling out the emotion, Kipling beat me hands down. I made a mental note to read through my Kipling anthology again, but I still remembered that first stanza.

"Have you news of my boy Jack?"
Not this tide.

78

"When d'you think that he'll come back?"
Not with this wind blowing, and this tide.

We walked back to the car in silence.

My brother broke the ice. "Where next?" he said.

"We're on the Belgian border," I replied. "Let's hope they'll accept French francs as I haven't brought any Belgian currency with me."

I climbed into the Mercedes, turned the key in the ignition, and eased the vehicle into gear as I drove towards the Belgian town of Watou. A cold, sweaty sheen enveloped my body. I tried to remember the details of Rudyard Kipling's The Gardener.

Chapter 15

WATOU

The border was non-descript, not a soul there, not a policeman or a border guard to be seen. I slipped my passport back into my pocket. The last time I was here, the border was clearly marked by anti-tank obstacles, barbed wire and half-built pillboxes, all remnants of the Gort Line that we'd help build before the German invasion at the beginning of May.

"It was a bit of a blur how we'd made it to here, Geoff, but I know that I was one of only a few hundred who did. We'd had to negotiate the barbed wire obstacles in the semi-darkness, but we were getting nearer to British-held territory. Or so we thought.

It wasn't to be, the entire area was awash with Germans. There was no sign of our lads or, for that matter, the French army. The evacuation of the Dunkirk perimeter had been completed a day or so previously. We had been defending that retreat and were now stranded in no man's land."

I turned to my brother. "Watou was in German hands. We were still in mortal danger. I was with Sergeant Major Goddard and a few other lads. Goddard told us to stay put, there was no point trying to advance in daylight."

It felt right, it was time to tell him. It was an old, family rumour which started after I'd told Joy the story, but I'd not gone into any detail. Good, old, mild-mannered Eric had disabled a Panzer tank. The reality was it was true; I had killed two men in the heat of battle.

"When it was dark, we followed the ditches and skirted southwesterly along the town. By then we were in complete disarray, I was moving with men from several regiments, some of whom I hardly knew. As it was the end of May, the daylight came quite quickly, it was decided that we'd wait for first light to see the lie of the land."

I paused. I struggled for the words.

"Go on, Eric."

I think my brother sensed that I was about to disclose something dramatic.

"You've heard of Barbara Cartland?"

"No, who's she?" said Geoff.

"The novelist," I went on. "You must have heard of her?"

Geoff laughed, shrugged his shoulders. "No, but what has she got to do with any of this?"

"Her brother was in the artillery like me. Major Ronald Cartland, one of the bravest men I knew. He was a Member of Parliament, a Churchill ally, and so he didn't even need to be there. He was leading a column behind us. We were hunkered down in a ditch, slightly further to the east, maybe three hundred yards away, waiting for first light. As it was the end of May, it was getting light quite quickly, about four-thirty in the morning, there was a freezing mist and nobody dared move. Major Cartland had reached the road behind us; Goddard, Mears, me and our group of lads had managed to make slightly better progress, following our compass bearing towards Dunkirk. Major Cartland was leading a mixture of men of his own regiment and maybe about twenty-five of our boys from the 140 Regiment. Like us, they were hiding in a drainage ditch beside the road. Then three German tanks rumbled along the road and came into view."

"Jesus, Eric!"

My heart was in my mouth. "The Germans skirted past our position; they hadn't spotted us, but they were heading directly towards Cartland's men. As the mist started to lift, they were completely exposed."

"What happened?"

"The poor bastards had no option but to surrender, Cartland was on his feet determined to save his men and it looked like he was surrendering. He was probably shouting to the tanks, 'Wir geben auf, wir geben auf.' The lads were pouring out of the ditch with their hands in the air when the lead tank's turret opened, and it looked like Major Cartland repeated that they were surrendering."

I felt the tears well up in my eyes as I faced Geoff. I was overcome with emotion.

"From where I was looking, they had their hands in the air, they did, I swear they did."

Geoff gripped me by the elbow as I continued; the memories of those broken bodies lying in that field in their final death throws were as fresh to me today as they had been all those years ago.

"There were war crimes committed that day, Geoff. The Germans were all fired up. Of course, we had given them a hard time at Cassel and they had lost mates too. The Panzer tank rolled forward and a split second later its machine guns opened up. Major Cartland was hit, I saw him fall to the ground and the men around him were mowed down without mercy. Eight chaps from my regiment, one officer and seven men lay there, dead or dying."

I paused for breath and to my amazement, I reeled some of the names off.

"Lieutenant Cook, Jimmy Hardy, Horace Nicholls, Sid Vangrosky, Alfie Thorpe, Billy Davies, Ed Strahan and John Duffield."

"My God, you still remember their names."

"I'll never forget them, Geoff. Sid was an east-ender and Jewish, always trying to check whether our rations were kosher."

Memory. That was the key factor when you get to my age, that's the first tell-tale sign that the wheels are beginning to fall off. Lost memory is the bogeyman that haunts us all. We start forgetting to turn off the TV, can't think what we've had for lunch or what the neighbour at the end of the street is called despite the fact she's lived there for thirty-five years.

My notes help me, but I also test myself regularly too. I note specific dates, VE Day, VJ Day, Dunkirk, Operation Barbarossa, the A-Bombs, liberation of the camps and the Long March – I have the specific dates all written down. Once a week I do it. Write it all out again and then check each date fastidiously with my notes. I pride myself that I get most of them spot on. After the memory goes, then it's the fantasising that breezes in like an arctic gale.

I was in my early fifties when I stood with an elderly patient gazing out over the fields from his bedroom window. He was talking about his mother, the route he took to her house each day, and how he had visited her just that morning. I thought it was unusual because he was in his late seventies and by definition, she would be pushing for her century. He was also in a secure unit. But he said how she had baked him an apple pie on Sunday and that he was looking forward to her birthday at the end of the month. I wondered if he was somehow going out on an accompanied visit. Bob Sinton, my patient, waxed lyrical about his mum and it was the happiest I had seen him in a long while. When I eventually left him and walked down the long corridor, I bumped into one of the nurses. "I didn't know Mr Sinton's mum was still alive," I said. "There's nothing about her in my notes."

"That's because she's dead," she said rather bluntly.

"What?"

"Yes, Doctor, she died forty years ago."

It took some time to conclude the story. My brother stood alongside me patiently, giving me the time I needed.

"Having witnessed that scene we decided to stay low in our ditch for the day. But then an hour or so later, we also had an encounter with a tank, this time a light one that sounded as if it was going to cross over our ditch. Maybe we'd be safe but maybe it would find us. If it did, would they accept our surrender? Then I remembered my two grenades... "

"No, Eric, you didn't?"

"Something welled up inside me, something I'd never felt before. It was rage sure enough but tempered with some cold calculation of the decreasing number of options we had. When the tank was less than thirty yards away, instinct took over and I sprinted across the open field. I kept behind the tank, so they didn't see me. Before I knew it, I was scrambling over the back of the tank desperately trying to get to the open turret."

It was all so easy. One grenade.

"I pulled out the pin and counted to three, dropped it down the hatch, and ran back to our ditch for my life. Sergeant Major Goddard grabbed my arm halfway across that field and steered me towards a dense forest. I remember Sergeant Mears was with us too. I heard the explosion almost straight away and then everything went quiet. As we paused for breath, Mears told me that most of the chaps had been caught and it was just the three of us. Goddard said a few more of our lads had got away but they were nowhere to be seen."

We passed the signpost that told us we were now in Watou, I could feel a cold sheen of sweat creeping down my back.

I told my brother how we'd hid in ditches until darkness fell. We did everything in that ditch; the indignity of it all, but there was no choice. The Germans knew we had escaped, and they were after us for blowing up their tank. Standing up to take a pee up against the nearest tree guaranteed a bullet in the back.

"We just couldn't move."

"There was nowhere to run?"

"No. And we'd seen what the Germans had done to Cartland and his men, so we couldn't surrender."

"I can't imagine, Eric."

Of course he couldn't imagine, he couldn't imagine because he wasn't there.

"But you were caught the next day?"

"Yes, I think it was early morning. We'd had nothing to eat and had no rations left. We were cold and dirty; we could hear Germans shouting nearby. Goddard said we had to make a break for it through the woods, but we still needed to keep to the ditches. We had to crawl on our hands and bloody knees and slid on our stomachs for the best part of a mile."

I'll never forget that night, the longest of my life and every minute of that night, thoughts of death were never far away.

"It was almost a relief when we were caught. I heard the patrol before I ever saw them. There was a thwack of a bullet next to my right thigh and then an angry German voice shouting something indecipherable. Goddard told us that the game was up, we had to climb out of the ditch and take our chances."

"And you didn't even have a gun, Eric?"

"No, and yet I even thought about lobbing my remaining grenade into their midst. We thought it was certain death. This angry young German was screaming at us with his rifle poised and ready. They were around Goddard too, stripping his revolver from his holster. They punched and kicked him a few times just to let us know who was in charge. It threatened to get out of hand, it was escalating quite quickly and their voices grew angrier and louder; they hit Goddard again and again. I felt for the grenade in my pocket. If they were going to kill us, I was determined to take a few of them with us."

It's a strange feeling, not wanting to die, and yet planning your death at the same time. Suicide by grenade; exactly what I was planning as I located the ring of the grenade with my finger. I'd pull it out in my pocket; nobody would know and then I'd simply walk over to them with my arms held high. I had no sympathy, there would be no regrets. But then a strange thing happened. Another voice, a calm soothing voice, a German officer with his Luger pistol pointed at us. He was talking to his men, and it was clear that he was giving the orders. Gradually the tension evaporated. I couldn't understand a word of what he was saying.

"What happened then, Eric?"

I had been lost in my thoughts again.

"In perfect English, the officer told us that we were POWs and that we would be looked after well. They marched us back to Watou, and into the main square."

"The main square?" Geoff questioned.

"Yes."

"Great... then let's take a look."

I drove into the centre of Watou, found a parking space by the side of the road and we walked up towards the main square. We strolled just once around the square at a glacial pace. It was not where I wanted to be, I fought the urge to turn around and run away as fast as my old legs could carry me.

"Fancy a beer?" Geoff pointed at a bar in the far corner. "Or perhaps you need a whisky?"

It was a pleasant day; the sun had just poked through the clouds. Geoff suggested we sit outside at one of the small tables. It sounded like a good idea; I relaxed a little more, trying to tell myself over and over again that it was 1985. It was as if I had two little Gremlins lodged within my head fighting with each other. One wanted the 1940 view of the square, the devastation and destruction, those bloody machine-gun nests trained on the assembled prisoners; the other, today's pretty little scene with whitewashed buildings, grey slate roofs, not a tile out of place and a few townsfolk milling around minding their own business.

I looked out onto a scene of serenity, thirty or so parked cars squeezed neatly into the small spaces, a Great War monument standing elegantly on a small patch of well-manicured lawn.

The man who served my drink was slightly older than me. I wished that I could have spoken Flemish because he had the look that he had lived here all his life. Years of nicotine abuse had bunched wrinkles around his eyes and his mouth. I wanted to tell him we tried our best; we really did, but the boys 'out there' had come good in the end. They had returned four years later to deliver their freedom eventually. I'd played my part too; keeping the Germans at bay and ensuring that three hundred thousand troops made it safely back to Blighty to fight another day.

The local Belgian beer sealed the argument. I was drifting back into 1940. I didn't hold back; I told my brother how it was. As I looked out over the square it was all so clear.

"They made us sit down in the square, perhaps two hundred of us. There, there, there and there." I pointed. "German machine gunners in position."

"It must have been terrifying, Eric?"

"It was. When we had first started to walk at the end of a rifle through the forest, I remember being relieved that they hadn't shot us on the spot. That particular German officer had probably saved our lives. Strangely enough, I had trusted him when he said we were his prisoners and that we'd be taken care of. I suppose we had no choice."

I was aware that I struggled to speak. My brother prompted me.

"And?"

"... when we arrived here it was different, the air was filled with tension again. We were scared and desperate; the Germans were angry and quiet. There was very little conversation around. I think we were afraid to draw attention to ourselves, anxious that the Germans were waiting for an excuse to open fire on us."

I glanced at my watch, aware that there was a ferry to catch.

"Go on."

"There were rumours of massacres, that's why we were so scared. One of the lads close by was whispering to his mate that the SS had slaughtered British soldiers in a barn several miles to the north. I didn't want to believe what he was saying at the time but, yes... it turned out to be true."

I pulled my notebook out of my pocket.

"Wormhout," I said. "I researched the incident some years ago, although he got a lot of the facts wrong. He claimed there were over two hundred killed when in actual fact there was only eighty."

Geoff nearly choked. "Only eighty!"

I smiled. "I didn't mean it like that, I meant there wasn't as many as two hundred."

"I knew what you meant, Eric. We knew nothing about this at the time; it was all happening when we were at school."

It was another nice moment, despite where we were sitting, in a place where it could have gone so wrong. I looked into the eyes of my brother; a pleasant feeling enveloped me. It was good that we had found a little black humour from somewhere. I guess crying and laughing were the only options available. I suppose I was grateful that my schoolboy brother didn't have any idea what was taking place less than twenty-five miles across the sea.

I continued. "The SS soldiers marched their prisoners along a road, they were shooting the stragglers and those too wounded to stand. It was brutal and eventually, the remaining one hundred prisoners reached the barn at Wormhout, just about ten miles north of here. They herded the prisoners into the barn and closed the door. The chaps inside clearly thought it was a routine security measure, perhaps they'd be holed up for a few days while transport arrived to take them on to POW camps. But no, soldiers from the SS started throwing stick grenades into the building."

I took another mouthful of beer, wiped the froth from my top lip and faced Geoff.

"It must have been horrendous in there, but the grenades didn't kill everyone. When the SS opened the barn, the men who were still in one piece staggered blindly towards the entrance. The SS lined them up and shot them and then they went into the barn and finished off the wounded. Incredibly a few men escaped, I don't know how, but they did."

I looked out across the square and then back to my brother. "I was one of the lucky ones I think."

I noticed a slight sag of his shoulders as a frown crept across his face, but he said nothing.

All the while, I had noticed the barman who had been hovering in the doorway. He eventually came out to the table to clear the glasses. To my amazement, he spoke good English and asked me if I had been here before.

"Yes," I said, "in 1940."

He gave me a knowing nod of the head. "You have that old soldier look about you Monsieur. I remember the Germans being here in 1940 and I remember you poor English soldiers getting assembled in this square and inside the church over there." He nodded towards the church opposite. "This town had two German air raids and we had many bodies to bury. We buried them at the church just here," he said pointing across the square. "And then in 1941, the mayor decided to rebury the British soldiers I remember helping carry some of them to the field just out on the Hootkerkestraat about five hundred metres north of here. There were at least fifty of them. I helped with those burials too. One of them was a British Member of Parliament, Monsieur Cartland. His brother was also killed in the fighting around here and is buried at Zuidschote. That's only about twenty kilometres away. To lose two brothers in the same battle — it must have been so sad for their families."

He took a beer mat from the table and started to draw a sketch map.

"You may wish to pay your respects; the soldiers were buried in a temporary graveyard." He laid the beermat down beside me. "You will find it quite easily. It's in a small copse of trees and although there are no bodies there now, we maintain it like we would maintain our own fathers' graves."

He introduced himself as Jan and shook my hand warmly. He thanked me and then turned quickly on his heels.

He called back over his shoulder, "There will be no charge for your drink."

Chapter 16

BEHIND THE IRON CURTAIN

We made it to Calais in silence. As the ship crossed the Channel, I looked out onto the gentle swell of the waves. I watched the French mainland disappear and felt a sense of relief. Perhaps some of the guilt that I had carried for so many years had lifted. I felt that my brother knew me a little better.

Once again, Geoff's words brought me back to the present. "We didn't get very far, did we?" he said.

"I beg your pardon."

"Your story, Eric. We didn't get very far, you didn't even tell me where they took you after Watou."

His words took me a little by surprise. I felt that I'd done nothing but talk for two days but, on reflection, he was right. There was still so much to tell.

What he said next nearly shook me from my seat. "Why don't we go to Poland, Eric, to the camps where you were held?"

"What?"

"There are museums there, monuments to some of the prisoners, a big Russian monument apparently. I've heard they are all very well kept, and that coal mine you once told me about, let's see if it's still there."

To say I was astounded by what he had said would be an understatement. Where had that come from? I was speechless.

"I'd like to go," he said, "and, to be honest, I've never told you about India either."

"But… "

"Eric… "

"Yes?"

"I'm so glad you called me. It's been good getting to know each other again."

I slept better after the Flanders trip. I could mark it as another triumph for talking therapy, the psychotherapy that I'd prescribed over the years for countless patients. But Poland was an altogether different proposition.

As I had gotten older, I had become more and more of a nervous traveller. Getting to Poland posed a whole series of insuperable problems. It was behind the Iron Curtain for a start, a Communist State. I'd witnessed the scenes on the television news, the ugly scenes of the rioting at the shipyards at Gdansk and martial law. The Solidarity movement and its leader, Lech Walesa, were always on the news.

We talked for some time and at first, I had said point-blank that I wasn't going. Eventually, however, he persuaded me that we needed another brothers' trip away. After another trip to my travel agent, tickets and money were sorted. They recommended hard currency as they said travellers' cheques might not be recognised out there. On their advice, I ordered Deutschmarks, Dollars and Polish Zlotys. I made sure that there was a cancellation clause on my tickets, just in case I changed my mind. There was a British Airways flight from Heathrow, the travel agent explained, air travel to Poland had recently resumed. I was nervous.

I hadn't always been this unadventurous. I remembered when the children were very small, my wife Joy and I had visited the USSR in the mid-1960s. We went by boat from Tilbury to Leningrad and then took a train to Moscow. It was at the height of the Cold War; I remember we both wrote our wills before we left. I had always wanted to visit since nearly being liberated by the Red Army in 1945.

The sound of the Red Army advancing behind us was never far away, and the obvious fear that their advance made on the faces of our guards was palpable. There was something almost majestic about the might of that advance that had fascinated me.

But, there was one fear I couldn't shake and part of me said that I needed to face that fear head-on.

The Germans had forced me down a coal mine. I believe I'd joked to Geoff just once that I had been a coal miner but hadn't told the rest of my family anything about it. As far as they were concerned, I'd spent the entire war incarcerated in wooden barracks playing cards and generally whiling away the time.

How would this trip affect me?

In Flanders, I had been with comrades from the regiment. I knew Jack Portas wasn't far away either. It was terrifying but it was all over in four weeks. Out there in Silesia, the loneliness was all-pervasive and I was stuck out there for five long years; those were the worst years of my life. Could I really face going back?

Chapter 17

A SECRET REVEALED

I wasn't entirely happy with myself after that recent Mental Health Act visit. I'd spent most of the time talking about myself and my war experiences. I worried I was making a mess of my first-ever review. Not a good start, I reflected. Mrs Knight had typed up the first part of her report for me, a summary of the thirty years of medical records and reports.

Something was pulling me towards another meeting with this patient, Mary O'Leary. Strictly speaking, it wasn't necessary, as I had pretty much prepared my report and I thought it best not to put in a travel and expenses claim this time. When I had sat in front of the woman, I told her things that I'd never whispered, even to my late wife Joy or, for that matter, to any other living soul. I sincerely believed that I owed her a small thank-you for listening. The meetings were no doubt the catalyst to my visit to Flanders for the first time since 1940.

To my complete surprise, when I stopped at a phone box to arrange the visit, Mary immediately agreed to the meeting. I walked into the same room, she sat in the same seat and, as she heard the door open, turned her head and smiled. To my utter astonishment, she dispensed with the formalities and spoke first.

"How was your trip?"

I stopped short of the table. What had she said?

"My trip?" I questioned. How on earth did she know, I hadn't told anyone.

"Last time," she answered, "you told me so much about your time in the war, I figured you were itching to get back there and see how it all looked. Now you're retired, there's nothing to stop you. It's been some weeks since your last visit so I put two and two together and guessed you may have been on a trip."

I pulled out a chair. "Well, Mary, you guessed right, I've been to the places I told you about. I've been paying my respects to some of my friends who never made it."

The two nurses stood outside the glass door.

"I was going to bring you a coffee," the oldest one said as she popped her head in, "but I'll leave it for now."

"We don't want to stop you in mid-flow," her colleague added smiling directly at Mary.

I'd asked about her war records and once again she was quite talkative. She took me by surprise, said that her war records had been secret; she'd been an agent specializing in radio communications.

I fell back into my seat. "My word, you're a dark horse, Mary O'Leary."

She told me that she had been recruited into the Women's Auxiliary Airforce (WAAF) where, early on, her officers had spotted her talents. She was wasted where she was, she should transfer to Military Intelligence, they had said. It was difficult to take it all in at first, but the more Mary spoke, the more I was beginning to form the same opinion as those officers. I asked her about the puzzles she still enjoyed, the crosswords. I had noticed a few newspapers in the day room, all open at the crossword page, all crosswords duly completed.

I pointed at one. "Your work?"

She nodded.

I reached across for the newspaper. It was the Guardian. There was a big old crossword puzzle, completed in blue biro, some forty plus clues.

"And how long did it take you to complete this?"

She shrugged her shoulders. "I'm not sure, I don't time myself."

"Approximately?"

She looked around the room at the scattered newspapers. "The staff bring me all the newspapers every morning, they know I won't be long and that they'll be free in time for their first tea break."

"I see." I counted the newspapers I could see, about six of them. "So, these newspapers, you do all of the crosswords before the staff's first break of the morning, so what… about an hour, perhaps a bit more?"

Mary let out a little squeal of derision, "Hah, not that long."

"So how long?"

"About twenty minutes."

"Impressive, twenty minutes a crossword," I said.

Another laugh. Short but telling.

"Twenty minutes for the lot," she said.

I nearly fell off my seat as the enormity of what she'd just said sank in. How could that be? I was stunned into silence.

What a waste of a life, I thought to myself.

There are moments in a psychiatrist's career when one truly wonders about the system. Where had it all started to go wrong for this genius that I now found myself sitting opposite? But more than that, why had the wrong never been corrected? How had my colleagues who had preceded me, men like the great Doctor Sargant, messed it up so badly? I'd read her history of violence and there was more than a suggestion that Mary had only reacted so badly when she had been threatened. I had researched the case. Evans, the man she had attacked, had form; two previous sexual misdemeanours. The governor of the prison she had attacked had resigned a few years before retirement after a serious accusation from a female inmate. What had we done to this poor woman? Now I understood why she had screamed at me about loss of liberty.

To be honest with myself, I wasn't convinced that we psychiatrists had properly protected this patient when she was at her most vulnerable. Was it time to tell her that I understood; that I'd been in the same boat too? Could I tell her that I'd been deprived of my liberty for five long years, had been brutalised more than she could ever have imagined, and forced to work as slave labour? "You shouldn't be in here, Mary, should you?" I asked.

"It's all I know."

"But you shouldn't be in here," I repeated.

She seemed to hesitate for a second or two before she spoke.

"You go through every emotion, Doctor. Injustice is the first one and then regret, wishing you could have turned back the clock and done something different. I have spent months... possibly years replaying the incidents over and over in my mind."

I recalled the notes. "The incident when you attacked the man?"

"Yes. I made a serious error of judgement; I thought he was a nice man, quiet and shy. But they say those types are the worst." Mary leaned back in her seat. "I was extremely drunk; I wasn't thinking straight, and I'd always had a temper. I just lost control." A tear rolled gently down her face. "It was as simple as that; I panicked and ran. That was my downfall, my one big mistake and if I'd stayed and just explained myself, perhaps they may have sympathised. They may have listened but, because I ran away, I was guilty. They found me guilty and I found myself incarcerated."

I gave her time. I listened, I knew there was more to come, this had been my task right from the beginning, to get Mary O'Leary to talk. All the while I tried to work out what psychiatric disorder I was confronting. Was this a personality disorder? Were her thoughts so disordered to be described as psychotic? Was she depressed? Was there post-traumatic stress as William Sargant had documented all those years ago?

"And then the days blend into each other. You tell yourself that there's no point looking back and trying to change things because it's impossible... you can't. Then you become bitter and resentful, you want revenge, you want to hurt those people who keep you under lock and key. When they sent me to the hospital from prison, I told myself it was all part of the process, to prepare me for release. But then..."

"But what, Mary?"

She picked up a glass of water and raised it to her lips. It hovered in front of her face for a few seconds and then she looked over the top of the glass.

"I'm still here, Doctor... I'm still bloody well here and no one can tell me why."

We were interrupted by the nurses who decided it was time for tea. Much to my surprise they sat down and joined us. Even more surprising was that Mary didn't seem to mind. But I minded. Mary had really started to open up and I wanted her to keep going.

Let it go, I said to myself. *Be patient. Mary isn't going anywhere.*

I sat back and took stock... studied Mary's interaction and pretended to write a few notes. I allowed myself an imaginary pat on the back. To be honest, I felt good about what I had achieved so far as Mary, the so-called mute, swapped pleasantries with the two nurses for a full quarter of an hour, glancing occasionally at me, almost as if asking telepathically, 'When are we continuing?'

The nurses made their excuses and before we knew it, we were alone once again, chatting like two friends catching up on old news. We talked a little about the weather and the food in the hospital. Mary said the tea had been too strong and then I was keen to pick up where we left off.

"I know what it means to lose your liberty, Mary."

She frowned. Let out a sigh.

"I do, Mary, the war... I was a prisoner of the Nazis for five years, out in one of their coal mines in Silesia."

I watched as the colour drained from Mary's cheeks.

"You were a POW?" she said slowly.

"For five years. I know what it's like to be told you can't go home when it's what you want to do more than anything else in the world. I know five years is nothing compared to your time under lock and key, but you have to believe me that I know what it's like."

"Yes," she said quietly.

"And I could also say that you have a warm bed, decent food, and the staff respect you and treat you well, which was something I never had."

She stared at me for a long time.

I continued. "Nobody knows what we went through. We were the forgotten ones, out on a limb thousands of miles from home, starved and tortured, some of my friends executed in cold blood. Nobody knew anything about what we were going through."

I thought I saw a slight shake of her head before Mary reached across and stroked the back of my hand. "My dear Doctor, I know more about POWs than you could possibly imagine. Of course, I shouldn't tell you too much, what with the Official Secrets Act we both signed."

I swear I caught Mary giving me a sly wink.

To my astonishment, notwithstanding the Official Secrets Act, she told me all about her role at MI9. She told me that she specialised in communication channels with prisoners and interviewing the few who were liberated prior to 1945. She spoke about the time and effort her team dedicated to POWs in covert operations. I had heard an odd rumour about silk maps, radios and even some theories about secret messages hidden in Red Cross parcels coming from home. I was flabbergasted when Mary confirmed it was all true.

I thought about those countless days of despondency, days where we felt we had been abandoned, days where we believed that we were permanent slave workers of the Third Reich, days where hope was non-existent. But they did care.

This lady sitting opposite me cared. Even forty years later I could see that she cared, she spoke with a passion about the fate of hum-drum old Kreigies like me. She wanted to know everything that had happened to me, I told her about my capture at Watou and the hellish journey to Lamsdorf. She sat patiently while I told her about the mine at Beuthen and John the

96

Bastard, how they starved us and how eventually I had ended up as an interpreter. She had changed. She laughed a little, I noticed that her body language wasn't quite so defensive, no folded arms. She even edged her chair a little closer.

"The POWs," she said, "that March, my God that Long March, I can't believe how long that went on for."

Very few people knew about that March. It just wasn't something you talked about.

"The March, Mary," I said, "I was on it too."

She nodded her head, spoke in barely a whisper, "I thought so. You have that look in your eyes, the look of a man who has suffered."

She leaned forward and reached for my hand again, gripped it hard. I felt uncomfortable but before I could pull away or offer any objections she started to speak. Once she started, I sensed wild horses weren't going to stop her.

"Doctor West, I think I'm allowed to tell you that I was part of an organisation called SAARF, the Special Allied Airborne Reconnaissance Force. I was flown into southern Germany as the war was ending in 1945, SAARF was put together in a hurry by a brigadier, oh what was his name now?"

I laughed. "You have a memory like mine."

"I do, it's called old age, I think. We used to call him Crasher. Oh, I remember now, it was Nicholls and I was part of Operation… oh what was it called again?"

Mary looked to the skies for a moment or two and then began again, "Vicarage, that was it, Operation Vicarage." She looked up. "Doctor West, I still have my old SAARF wings in a tobacco tin in my locker. Wait there," she said, getting up and disappearing through the door.

A few moments later she reappeared brandishing an Old Holborn tobacco tin. Ironically, I noticed it had an artillery gun depicted on the lid. She opened it and inside was a black lapel badge embroidered with the letters SAARF in white. There was a second badge which, to my eye, looked like a decapitated swan in flight, white on blue, with the swan's head replaced by a red arrow, the arrowhead cutting through a chain of small red circles. I could sense her pride at those badges that I suspected had been kept secret until this moment.

"I understand, Mary, sometimes it's hard to let go of certain memories."

"Yes. We knew all about the prisoners and we knew how you were all starving. We knew that Hitler had one last throw of the dice, his prisoners were a bargaining chip or worse a sacrifice he was prepared to make. We had to try and figure out his plans before he even knew what they were himself. We feared mass executions and we were determined to stop them. We had a few men in the camps with radios they'd built from smuggled parts. One by one, the communications dried up as the Nazis evacuated the camps and the radios were left behind. All we could do was monitor the Marches and convey their positions to London. We didn't want any of the Allied aircraft mistaking them for Germans, though it happened more often than you would think."

I had heard about a lot of Allied aircraft mistakes, poor men who had survived five years of Nazi torment only to be slaughtered by their own side.

"I covered German administration Area VII," Mary said, "and once we'd occupied it, I was flown there to make contact with the camps. Luckily, I avoided the parachute drop. Knowing my luck, my radio would have broken upon impact. I wasn't the most elegant when it came to hitting the ground, I never mastered the timing; a broken leg was always a real possibility. Later we established contact with one of the officers from Oflag VIIB in Eichstätt. The Americans were closing in on region VII and he told us that the commandant was preparing to evacuate the camp. They were getting ready to march somewhere, though they didn't know where."

I interrupted. "We were in the same boat; there were all sorts of stories about where they were taking us."

Mary was nodding. "We feared for you chaps in the camps down there in Silesia. There were terrible rumours about the Nazi death camps. At first, we couldn't believe what we were hearing, it didn't seem to make any sense but then we started seeing the proof."

She said, "Did you know anything about the death camps at the time?"

"Yes, we knew that the Jews were disappearing, and we'd seen and smelled the transport trains. It was the stink that still haunts me even now. Our camp was only a few hundred yards from the main railway line between German Silesia and Krakow. The Poles and the Russian prisoners were telling tales so awful that we sensed there was some truth in them, but nobody ever realised the scale of it."

"This was why we were so desperate to monitor the Long Marches," she said. "You lot were on the move quite early if I remember, it was late

98

January 1945 when you left and at first you seemed to be going around in circles but then you eventually headed west into Germany. We breathed a big sigh of relief; you were marching away from the death camps."

"How?" I asked.

"By wireless. My God, I dragged that bloody wireless right through Europe, it was the size of a small horse and even the aerial was forty feet high."

"Forty feet high!" I exclaimed.

"That's right," she said. "We needed all the power we could get as we knew you were using homemade crystal sets, sometimes the signal would only get to us if the atmospheric conditions were right. We looked for churches across the country, holed up in them for a day or two. The churches were perfect because they all had spires and I could rig up the aerials without them being seen. Most of the priests were quite accommodating bringing us food and water as soon as they realised what we were up to, although we had to be careful because there was still a lot of Nazi sympathizers around and, although we were behind Allied lines in occupied Germany, there was still a lot of sabotage going on."

I shook my head. "I had no idea you could be in touch with London from so far away."

"It wasn't easy, sometimes we were live for five or six minutes before our signals were picked up. We used morse code, it was one of my fortes. I could bash out almost thirty words a minute. But we had to be careful because they told us that to be on the wireless for more than twelve minutes meant that the Germans could be onto us and trace where the signal was coming from. We used codes and ciphers so that the Germans didn't know what we were saying but they could still locate where we were. By then, we were much safer and behind Allied lines, but we had to keep an eye out for renegade German patrols. It was the Hitler Youth kids who were especially dangerous. On one occasion I heard them searching the church. I heard their voices which carried to me on the still night air. They found nothing. One of them said their signalman had got it wrong and they left after no more than twenty minutes."

"So, you were safe?"

"Yes. I caught up with my team in the forest and told them what had happened. We were never on the wireless more than eleven minutes after that. One of them always stood over me with a watch and indicated when the time was up."

Mary told me how she had read the riot act to her two colleagues that night in the forest and because they'd been so nearly caught, they all knuckled down and became more cautious.

"We never ventured out much during daylight hours after that, then, several weeks later we got the call to move a little nearer Eichstätt. Our officer said they were on the move. He couldn't take his radio with him of course; it was much too big to smuggle out. Imagine our horror when they started to walk east. And this was only three weeks before the end of the war, middle of April 1945."

I was puzzled. "They were walking east?"

"Yes, we expected them to head west towards Munich. It made sense that Hitler took the prisoners into the heart of German cities, where he could use them as human shields so the Allies couldn't bomb them. Munich was just a short march away, but the officers were walking in the opposite direction, towards Czechoslovakia and Poland."

"Towards the death camps."

"Yes. We'd had intelligence reports of a death camp called Theresienstadt in Czechoslovakia, the Nazis looked like they were gearing up for more arrivals as it was only two hundred and fifty miles away. We estimated that the march from Oflag VII could reach Theresienstadt easily in two to three weeks. I reported all the information back to London."

"My God, you thought they were sending the officers to their deaths?"

"London wasn't sure, but there were some of the best brains in the British Army in Oflag VII and I was told to stick as near as possible to them without being caught, report on every single mile they marched. I was just a few miles away when the Germans marched them out of the camp on 14th April. I was trying to get a signal to London to tell them what was happening but wasn't having a lot of joy. No one in London was picking up."

I watched as Mary's face changed.

"I was too late, Doctor. I heard the American planes from some distance."

"My God, no!"

"Yes, I'm afraid so.

"They swooped in from the north. They were American air force P-47 Thunderbolts with fifty-millimetre cannons, rockets and bombs fitted to them. Oh, Dr West, those planes were nothing like the Spitfires and Hurricanes you had seen in 1940. They weighed eight tons and once they started firing at the ground the roads would turn red as they destroyed everything in their path. The men were resting by the side of the main road awaiting orders. Despite objections by the Senior British Officer, they were being marched in broad daylight and the camp commandant, Oberst Bessinger, had forbidden the use of any identifying flags or red crosses. Failing to use recognition symbols at this late stage of the war, with the air swarming with our aircraft, was a war crime. There were Hungarian SS troops nearby, they wore green khaki uniforms and that's how the mistake was made."

Mary stopped for a while. She sobbed a little before continuing.

"Fourteen of them were killed and dozens badly injured. Who could blame the crews? After all, we were in the heart of Germany. The prisoners regrouped; the Germans ferried the injured off to hospital but those who could walk were sent on their way again."

"And the officer?"

"He survived and as far as we could tell the column was continuing to move eastwards."

I sat in cold contemplative thought. Poor bastard, watching his mates shot to pieces literally days before the end of the war in Europe. What must that do to a man's mind?

"And, Eric, sorry, Dr West," she went on, "there's one thing that happened after this. I haven't told anyone about it before. My team were getting ready to load the Jeep with our equipment and a US airman walked past whistling to himself smoking a cigarette. I couldn't help myself. Something inside me snapped. I ran up to him and slapped him hard across the face. He got such a fright he slipped and fell to the ground. I was amazed at my own strength and then I started to kick him, even though I could see he had a pistol in his holster. My boys pulled me off and apologised to the American, who dusted himself off and gave me the dirtiest of dirty looks, calling me a madwoman and a crazy bitch. But, Dr West, I felt so mad about what had happened at Eichstätt."

Mary explained that throughout those long winter months from January to April 1945 where we had marched on near-empty stomachs, we had been monitored the whole way.

"Oh yes, we knew about you poor men. The camps had gone quiet on us since late January. Churchill had negotiated safe passage to Odessa for POWs that fell into Soviet hands. We did our best; unfortunately, there wasn't much we could do for you out there."

I was genuinely surprised to hear this. I wished I had known at the time that we were being tracked. After five years stuck in my coal mine, I had assumed I had been completely forgotten. It might have made it a little more bearable.

As Mary continued, she described how they had moved with the Eichstätt prisoners, following, as best they could, the intelligence they were getting from the ground nearby. Eventually, towards the end of April, Patton's Army had overtaken the column and they were liberated at Moosburg. "Our task was done, they were safe," she said.

I remembered my own first contact with Patton's Army — a poorly aimed rifle shot in my direction as they mistook our gaggle of men for German soldiers.

"Eventually we found our contact from Eichstätt amongst the Moosburg POWs. Captain MacDougall's signals were weak at times but… "

"What did you say?" I interrupted.

"Captain MacDougall's signals were weak," she repeated.

"The officer, he was a captain?"

"Yes."

"Was he called Lorne?"

"No. I don't think so."

My heart skipped a beat for a second. I remember that Mary had mentioned an Officer MacDougall during one of our first meetings and I had thought nothing of it. After all, how many MacDougall's are in the British Army? But when she had said Captain… well that narrowed it down a little bit.

"He definitely wasn't called Lorne?" I asked.

She hesitated, scratched her head and then the light bulb ignited in her head. "I've got it, no it wasn't Lorne. No, he was called Coll."

It was a thunderbolt moment. We had talked about my war, Cassel and the officers. Latterly we had talked about Mary and her role in the war. I had felt quite proud of how much she had disclosed. But now, in one brief sentence, in a few words, we were connected; we had been on the same team. I felt closer to Mary because she knew what I had been through. She had lived every inch of that Long March, and in many respects suffered as a result. She had suffered because she had been aware of exactly what was happening, of the men dying in the freezing snow. Her hands had been tied. There was nothing she could have done about it.

I was aware that she was staring hard at me. "What is it, Doctor, you look like you've seen a ghost?"

"I don't believe it," I said. "Coll Lorne MacDougall, my God, so that's why he was mentioned in dispatches."

"I don't understand."

"Coll Lorne MacDougall of 140 Regiment. Mary... you were working with my battery officer. I last saw him escaping in a hail of bullets from a ditch on the Belgian border."

Mary was astounded.

"Did you ever meet him?" I asked.

"No, but I did feel that I somehow knew him. We had picked up signals from him back in 1940 when he was on the run in France. Later I had communicated with him for several weeks at Eichstätt, Oflag VII. I followed him, and the other Eichstätt officers, all the way back to the Czechoslovakian border."

There was no doubt about it. Mary had seen the Death Marches at first hand too. I sat with her for another hour or so. She told me about the skeletal thin dead bodies, the corpses along the route, the stench from the ditches at the side of the roads, and the dead eyes of the prisoners, civilians, Jews and Soviet POWs as they passed a few feet from her in her hiding places in forests or roadside buildings.

A nurse came in and told us the time. A gentle hint that we had rabbited on for hours. I looked at my watch, couldn't believe I'd been there that long. We said goodbye, she held out a hand and I shook it gently. As I drove away, I knew that Mary O'Leary was ready.

Chapter 18

POLAND

It turned out I didn't have an option. My brother was as stubborn as they come and wouldn't relent until I had made all the arrangements. Just as well because without his insistence I would never have got around to it. And after all, I had made a promise to him in 1945, that we'd travel and share our war experiences when this bloody war was over. It had been way too long. It transpired that visitors to Poland had to undergo an interview at the Polish Embassy in order to secure visas.

"Is it worth the hassle?" I asked in a conversation with him one night.

"You tell me," he bounced back at me. "It's not like you have to visit Timbuktu to get a visa, it's a day out in London, that's all. If they don't issue the visa then bugger them, but at least you gave it a try."

Poland was very much a satellite state of the USSR; however, the Polish Embassy was still in its historic building in Marylebone. I was under no illusion that a visa was guaranteed, it was very much up to the man in uniform who now sat opposite me. I had submitted details and dates of my proposal and, with a stern face, he sat and studied the paperwork. He asked me why I wanted to go to Poland and couldn't quite grasp it when I stated it was for a historical visit. I explained that I had been a POW during the war and this was a kind of pilgrimage.

"Why?" he said.

"I haven't a clue," I replied. "It was my brother's idea."

The man looked puzzled and then grinned. With a flourish, he thumped his rubber stamp on the blank visa page of my open passport. He told me that it was my honest reply that had convinced him. As I was leaving, he reached across the table and shook my hand.

Several times he said, "Thank you, sir,"

He told me he had lost a lot of his family at the hands of the Nazis. As I left the offices in Portland Place I wondered if the Upper Silesians we would encounter on our visit would be so accommodating. I had read a book from the library that documented the history of Silesia. It said there was still a small section of the community who were very much pro-German. I couldn't wait to tell Geoff the good news.

Towards the end of the year, during the middle of November and armed with the correct documentation, I confirmed the flights with my travel agent and paid the balance. That was it, no going back. I was booked to fly out at the year-end, 1985.

I immersed myself in a series of books. Now I had a mission. I was hungry for knowledge; I wanted to know why we had been sacrificed, why I had spent five of the best years of my young life as a prisoner. I wanted to know if the politicians or the generals could have done anything differently.

I picked up a copy of Dunkirk — the British Evacuation, 1940, by Robert Jackson. I visited the library regularly over the next couple of months and tried to get a hold of POW books, books on Polish and Silesian history. I filled four or five exercise books with notes of my memories that were slowly filtering into my head, filling voids that had been left for decades.

I knew this wasn't going to be a normal holiday. Warsaw would be an unknown entity; we'd have to put the trip together once we arrived. The travel agent had no information about trains or local transportation that operated out there. She had booked just one night in a Warsaw hotel and that was as far as she had got. I had a taxi booked to collect me early morning for the flight to Warsaw.

I couldn't sleep; I finished the last few chapters of Jackson's book at four in the morning. It didn't really tell me anything I didn't know. Dunkirk, Jackson wrote, was organised chaos. It seemed I was one of nearly 40,000 troops who had to be abandoned there.

The taxi driver rang the doorbell a little after six in the morning. As I opened the door, the cold hit me. I couldn't help thinking about those freezing days and nights during what historians were now calling the Long March at the end of the war. And here we were, heading back there amid an Eastern European winter, where long-repressed memories were about to be rekindled.

As the taxi driver stood on the doorstep he reached for my suitcase and asked me where I was flying to.

"Poland," I said.

"You must be bloody mad visiting Poland this time of year, guv'. It'll be bloody freezing."

I couldn't have agreed more, and yet this trip had to be completed in the harshest of conditions. I couldn't explain to the taxi driver why. He wouldn't have understood.

It was only an hour's run to Heathrow. As soon as I got to the airport, Geoff was keen to pick up the story where we had left it, the town square at Watou on the last day of May 1940.

We had sat in that square for hours, or so it felt, and I remember it had started to rain. The Germans took shelter in the buildings surrounding the square. They had machine-gun nests strategically placed, so the entire square was covered. We wondered if they would open fire and that would be the end of it all. They took a perverse pleasure as they watched us getting soaked to the skin, laughing at us. As nightfall drew in, we were ordered to our feet and began to pull out.

"We marched, Geoff, we marched for days and there was little or no food. I remember being annoyed because they'd split me up from Sergeant Mears and Sergeant Major Goddard. They were taken on a separate march because of their rank. We lowly ordinary ranks were herded towards the far end of the square, kicked and punched into a line of twos and threes. We were left under no illusion that if we didn't keep up a strong pace we'd be in for more of that sort of treatment."

"Where did you march to?"

"They marched us right through to Holland."

"Bloody Holland, Eric!"

"Yes, just over the border into Germany. Belgium first and then into Holland."

I took out one of my notebooks from my pocket and flicked through the pages.

"They marched us nearly three hundred miles to a place just inside the German border called Versen. That's where Stalag VIB was."

My brother was shaking his head.

"I don't suppose the march was too pleasant, was it?"

I laughed. "Not the best hike I've ever had brother."

I really didn't enjoy the take-off. I sat tense in my seat as we entered the cloud cover after about a minute of ascent. Once the buffeting calmed down, I was able to give Geoff a few more details. I looked around, couldn't see him at first, and couldn't understand why we hadn't been allocated seats next to each other.

Eventually, he appeared.

"The worst bit was losing your mates. I was now marching with strangers; those familiar faces around me had been killed, captured or sent on a different route.

On the second day, as men fell behind, the Germans started the executions. We were weak, some weaker than others and some of the men had been wounded. They had no chance of making it. I'd heard the shots from towards the back of the long line, two or three hundred in our march. Word slowly filtered down that the stragglers, those who couldn't keep up with the pace, were being shot and thrown into ditches. They were doing it to terrorise us and the locals. What better way for a conquering power to demonstrate total control than parading their captives and mistreating them in this way.

I didn't believe it at first until I saw it with my own eyes. The lad was no more than twenty years old and the line had been allowed ten minutes rest. When we were told to stand, he didn't. He had a horrific head wound; a white, blood-stained bandage wrapped around his skull covering one eye. He had two mates urging him up to his feet, but he was shaking his head and asking to be left where he sat. Two guards came to see what was happening and one of them ordered him up. He spoke in broken English, told the boy to get to his feet. His mates stepped forward to help him up, but the Germans wouldn't let them, they said he had to stand up on his own. They told us to start marching and the young lad stayed where he was. I kept looking back. I knew what was going to happen and sure enough, the German started shouting something at him. As we walked away, I looked over my shoulder and I saw the German cock his rifle. He pushed the barrel against the boy's head and pulled the trigger. His head jerked backwards, and he fell into the ditch stone dead. Some of the lads rushed towards the Germans, but their mates held them back. One fellow said the young lad was going to a better place."

The air hostesses were in the aisle serving drinks.

"There was no food for days, not until we reached a place called Kortrijk, where there was a small soup kitchen set up and we all got a mug of watery, vegetable soup."

"And you hadn't eaten for some time before that?"

"No. I can't recall exactly, but we definitely hadn't had a hot dinner since Cassel. It was just biscuits and the odd tin of bully beef. I was walking beside a fellow called Jim, and I noticed he kept pulling something from his pocket and sticking it in his mouth. I asked him what he was eating; he thrust a handful of green stuff into my hand. 'Dandelion leaves,' he said, 'look out for the dandelion leaves by the side of the road, they're full of nourishment.' I'd to grab a handful whenever I could. If there was a slug attached to the leaves, well, that was a protein bonus. It was good advice and I did just that."

"Slugs! Eric, I bet they didn't taste very nice."

"You got used to them, they weren't so bad. You had to look out for water too because the Germans were only looking after their own. Most evenings there was a field kitchen set up and their troops were fed well."

"But not the prisoners?"

"No, a bowl of thin cabbage soup every few days that was our lot."

I couldn't quite describe to my brother, the feeling of sheer hopelessness and nor did I want to. I remembered the long hikes with Jack Portas in the Lake District and how it had been a sheer joy to stride out and push yourself to what you thought was your limit.

"We were literally running on fumes; it was the fear of being shot and slugs on those dandelion leaves that kept me going. We were drinking dirty water too and the dysentery started after about five days."

I told Geoff that the Germans were determined to maintain up to twenty miles a day. They hadn't said where we were heading or how we were going to get there, but it didn't take a genius to figure out that we were heading towards Germany. Because of the dysentery, they allowed men to wander to the side of the road and drop their trousers into the ditch, but if they took too long they were at risk of being dispatched with a bullet to the head.

"There were always rumours that trucks or trains would be waiting for us in the next town, but I think that was just wishful thinking because the trains and the trucks never materialised. The Germans taunted us, said that we were walking as payback because the RAF had destroyed the bridges and rail tracks."

I referred to my notes and the route I'd drawn up during my research. I had an old leather satchel with me; it was filled with my exercise books. I didn't know for sure of course, but some of the places rang a bell, places like Ghent and Antwerp.

"We got a hot meal outside Antwerp, a vegetable and sausage stew with some bread. I swear it was the best thing that had ever passed my lips."

As a POW who had experienced five years of near starvation, you somehow learn never to say no to food. You know your next meal is never far away but… you can't take that chance.

I had sketched the route of that march in my notepad. We travelled through Belgium, crossed the Dutch border, across the river De Lek towards Utrecht, and then onwards towards Germany.

"By now we knew there were no trucks or trains coming. Some of the men had totally given up hope. They shuffled on, by now it couldn't be described as a march, the men had been pushed beyond endurance. As the road signs told us we were getting nearer to Germany and walking towards the unknown, some of them made suicidal runs into the fields."

"They were shot?"

I nodded. "… the lads could hardly walk, never mind run. The Germans took their time. It was like a sport to them, a human duck hunt. The Germans were laughing as they were hit. I watched the first few and willed them to escape, but it was never going to happen. After that, I looked the other way as soon as someone made a break for it and just heard the rifle crack. I buried my face into the collar of my uniform."

We didn't speak for some time after that revelation. Despite telling myself otherwise, I knew it had taken a lot out of me. I fought the urge to clam up. We were flying into Warsaw with a distinct purpose, I needed to get a grip.

The jet engines throttled back and the captain announced that we were about to start our descent into Warsaw.

More unpleasant bumps to endure, I thought to myself as a tightened my seatbelt.

Geoff asked, "Do you remember much about the first camp?"

"Stalag VIB? Not really, I think most of it has gone from my memory. I remember briefly meeting Eric Johnson there. He asked me if I had any food and I handed him some of my dandelion leaves. Johnson was in the Chateau Masson fighting at Cassel. He was in F Troop, the next time I would see him would be in the coal mine. He was there for a year or so."

I was aware that Geoff had gone somewhat quiet at that point.

I turned to face him. "What is it?"

He seemed to pause before he spoke, "I remember that time well, Eric."

"You do?"

"Yes. It would be around the time we received the dreaded telegram. I was fifteen and had just got home from school."

"Ah right... the 'missing in action' telegram."

"That's it."

"I can't imagine what it did to Mum."

"She was in pieces; she was never the same again and wandered around in a daze for days. She wouldn't let me out of her sight and carried that telegram round in her apron pocket, taking it out and reading it every hour as if somehow the words would change into something that would give her some hope."

I fastened my seatbelt.

"We were there a week, possibly a day or two longer. Thank God the food was regular, we got a little coffee and bread each morning and, in the evenings, a mug of cabbage soup. I could feel my strength returning and it was just as well for what we were about to go through.

They put us on a train."

I took out my second exercise book. It was the route across Germany to a place called Lamsdorf.

"This wasn't a passenger train; we were herded into cattle trucks. It was difficult to sit down. They kicked and punched and struck the last dozen or so men into each carriage with their rifle butts, maybe as many as two hundred to a wagon. They locked the doors behind us. God help the lads who were the slightest bit claustrophobic."

I didn't know which way we travelled down to Lamsdorf because most of it was done in the dark. I remember we stopped at Hanover station and there we were allowed onto the station platform. It was all stop and start, ten miles here, twenty miles there and then pushed into a siding for hours at a time.

"At Hanover, a Red Cross delegation was waiting. The guard's behaviour improved under their watchful eye, we were given soup and we were even allowed to use the station toilets."

"There were no toilets on the train, Eric?"

I didn't want to go into the details of how we had to defecate in a corner of the truck we had earmarked as the toilet area or how the shit swilled around the carriage whenever we went around a bend or when the train braked. I didn't want to tell Geoff how we permanently held a handkerchief over our faces because of the stench.

Several of the lads had escaped, squeezing out of the small windows, and jumping into the countryside under the cover of darkness. Some of them jumped out at speed. I'm sure most were killed. I liked to think of myself as a mentally strong man but even I was pushed to a place that I'd never been to.

"No, Geoff, no toilets, we peed where we stood."

That was all he needed to know.

I traced the route to Lamsdorf in my exercise book with my finger while he looked on. "Potsdam or possibly Leipzig," I said, "Wrocław and eventually our destination."

"How long were you on the train, Eric?"

Three weeks.

"Fucking hell, Eric!"

Chapter 19

WARSAW

The biting cold hit as soon as we stepped from the plane. The pilot informed us that it was ten degrees below freezing. The wind made it feel much colder.

I had once enjoyed those cold, frosty walks in Borrowdale and had even hired some crampons one day as Jack Portas and I tackled a fell under two feet of snow. Jack said there was no such thing as bad weather, only bad clothing. He was right; we were well equipped and as we walked above the thick cloud line, the sun poked through at the top. We looked out onto a carpet of cotton wool as far as the eye could see as a bird of prey swooped towards us, its head scanning left and right wondering what we were doing invading his territory without invitation. It was a stunning experience, an incredible day's walking. I told Jack that it was winter hikes from now on. I had never enjoyed a day in the hills so much. But that all changed after the winter of 1944.

I hailed a taxi into Warsaw. The taxi driver spoke no English, but I started to converse in German with him. Although he wasn't fluent, we understood each other. I managed to get across to him where I was staying in the city. He said something about being rich, I gathered from that comment that my travel agent had pushed the boat out again. The taxi driver said that the Raffles Hotel was one of the best in Warsaw.

I shrugged it off; it was cheap in comparison, a fraction of the price of a London hotel.

"Far less than the hotel in Cassel, I expect," I mumbled to Geoff.

It was nearly dark. The flight time had been less than three hours and it had just turned three o'clock in the afternoon. It was grey with patches of snow on the ground. It was classic communist, exactly how the western

112

governments and the media portrayed Eastern Bloc countries. It was difficult to find anything attractive as we sped towards the city.

There were miles of blocks of grey granite, depressing, tenement-type buildings, flats and apartments, an occasional office block and an odd shop lit up the gloom. There were streetlights but I noticed that they weren't lit, a testament to the desperate economic situation and the strikes that had almost crippled the country.

I muttered to myself on more than one occasion, "What the hell are we doing here?"

That all changed as we drove into the heart of the city and as if by magic, the buildings turned into elegant facades of a different era. The straight lines and precision of the architecture gave away the fact that the buildings had all been painstakingly recreated after the destruction of Warsaw in 1944. I think the taxi driver was taking us on an impromptu tour before we reached the hotel, racking up a few more zlotys on the metre. He pointed out the Royal Castle, the Chopin Museum and the Museum of the Warsaw Uprising. I knew about the Warsaw Uprising of 1944 but didn't really know the details. I spoke to the taxi driver; I said that was a place I would like to visit. "Are you sure?" he said.

"Yes, I knew some of the men from the Uprising."

"What?"

I explained that I had been in a POW camp for five years. Towards the end of the war, I had learnt all about the events in Warsaw. After the Uprising, the Nazis rounded up the survivors and the Polish Home Army.

The Wehrmacht, realising the war had turned against them, and with an eye to future war crime investigations, promised to treat Polish Home Army soldiers in accordance with the Geneva Convention. Over the next few days, they started sending them to POW camps in various parts of Germany. Some of them ended up in Lamsdorf, and a handful came to our coal mine because they had been miners or electricians in civilian life.

I felt a lump in my throat. The rest were shipped off to the death camps.

Geoff had understood why I wanted to go to the museum. I'd try and get some tickets from the hotel reception. He said he didn't know nearly enough of what I had been through, that he was keen to learn. I could have said the same thing; I knew very little of what Geoff had been through in India, apart from his occasional letter.

I suppose this was what the trip was all about. Two brothers, two very different stories.

The Raffles Hotel was splendid. A notice board in several languages told of one hundred and sixty years of history. I checked in and booked dinner in the restaurant for eight o'clock. Geoff was keen to drop our bags and do a little of the 'tourism trail' before eating. We could talk again. It sounded like the perfect plan though we didn't have much time. We had a coffee in the main square. The café owner had about half a dozen strategically placed old black and white photographs (usually in dark corners) of the destruction the Nazis had caused.

Chapter 20

KATOWICE

The following morning, in the Warsaw Uprising Museum, I watched a blurry video in English which said the Nazis destroyed eighty-five percent of the city. It seemed to gloss over the fact that the Red Army stood by while Warsaw was destroyed under its nose. According to German plans, Warsaw was to be levelled and turned into a military transit station. Demolition squads had used flamethrowers and explosives, destroying houses and businesses. They had concentrated particularly on historical monuments to wipe the culture of Poland from the face of the earth. Libraries, schools and churches were razed to the ground.

We had decided to walk to the Central Train Station in Warsaw; it was less than a mile from the hotel. Within ten minutes, the imposing shape of the station, a washed, concrete structure, loomed up in front of us.

"Not my idea of elegant architecture," Geoff laughed.

"I don't know," I said. "I think it could grow on you."

We didn't hang around long enough for it to grow on us and wandered into the station to purchase the tickets for Katowice.

Geoff was in a trance as his eyes fell on two steam trains, one of which stood stationary at a platform, the other, slowly pulling out of the station, huge plumes of steam billowing out behind. The noises were from a different era.

"My God," he said transfixed, "I love trains so much, I'm going to really enjoy this bit of the journey."

I figured that Katowice was about three hours away by train, a good base for our visit to Lamsdorf and, of course, the coal mine at Beuthen. According to an old, pre-war map I had secured from my library, Beuthen was no more than ten miles from Katowice Station and the Lamsdorf Camp about another eighty miles from there. Beuthen was, in fact, no more, as it was now renamed Bytom. Along with much of the old German Upper Silesia, it had been incorporated into the new post-war Poland. The last time I was there, forty years ago, I had been marched out of a proud German border town.

Once we arrived at Katowice, a guest in the hotel suggested I could probably hire a taxi driver for the day; it would be a fraction of the cost of a labourer's day wage back in England. Once again, I think I surprised Geoff by ordering our tickets in perfect German. I felt more than proud of myself as I walked to the platform for the journey to Katowice, which according to the timetable, was two hours and fifty-five minutes.

As we approached the train, I shook my head. "It's donkey's years since I saw one of those."

I had naturally assumed that European rail was all diesel-powered.

I don't think Geoff even heard me above all the noise because he was like an excited schoolboy and almost sprinting along the bloody platform to get on the train. I climbed the steel steps to the carriage, settled down in my seat.

The train made its way slowly through the drab industrial buildings and tenement blocks of the southwestern suburbs of Warsaw. The city gradually faded away and we were rolling through the snowy and surprisingly beautiful Polish countryside.

I'd drawn up a sketch map back in London. I traced the route in pencil and ticked off the station place names. The tenement blocks were back as the train pulled into a station called Częstochowa, but after twenty minutes we were back into forests, now with hills visible in the distance.

We didn't have a lot of conversation on the three-hour journey into Katowice. I sat staring out of the window, giving a running commentary of each station we pulled into, but Geoff was in his own little bubble. As we got nearer to our destination, it hit me that, over the next couple of days, I was about to confront my worst nightmares. Here I would have to relive the horrors and brutality that I'd encountered during my worst days.

Why am I doing this? I thought to myself.

I knew that, in truth, it was now or never — something I had to face up to.

I had noticed what I assumed to be the ticket inspector walking up and down the train several times. He had given us a wide berth, inspecting other passenger's tickets but leaving us alone. Now he was back and with someone else, a serious-looking chap in a suit and tie. They were making a beeline straight for us.

They stood over us for a second and then the suit questioned, "English?"

"Yes, sir," I smiled politely.

My smile wasn't that infectious as he started to speak in Polish. Geoff looked at me and then we both looked at the ticket inspector and his accomplice.

"I don't speak Polish, sir," I said.

The suit frowned and said something undecipherable in Polish.

"My brother speaks German," Geoff offered, as quick as a flash.

The man appeared to look straight through my brother.

I'd almost forgotten. "Ich spreche Deutsch."

That seemed to work as the suit asked me what the purpose of my visit to Katowice was.

Here we go again, I thought.

I'd been through all of this in the Embassy.

Geoff whispered between his clenched teeth like a ventriloquist, "He's SB, Polish secret police, I'd heard they are quite common out here."

Thankfully neither the ticket inspector nor the suit noticed. They didn't speak or understand much English. Nevertheless, I smiled nicely and told our new friends about my time in the POW camps during the war and how I wanted to return to Poland to pay my respects to some of my comrades who hadn't returned home. I used the German word for comrade, Genosse, figuring it might buy me a few brownie points behind the Iron Curtain.

"Wir werden Sie beobachten," he said before walking away.

What did he say?" Geoff asked.

"He said he'll be watching us."

"Jesus Christ, talk about being friendly."

The ticket inspector checked the tickets and told me in not so good German that we'd be arriving in Katowice in half an hour. The suit didn't go very far during that last half hour, I noticed him several times behind the glass carriage door and, true to his word, he kept a beady eye on where we sat.

As the train pulled into Katowice Railway Station, I collected my suitcase and made my way onto the platform. I glanced casually behind me and noticed that the suit had climbed from the train too. I decided to have a little joke, about turned and walked directly up to him, asking in perfect German, where I could secure the services of a taxi driver.

He growled and pointed towards a far corner of the platform.

"Follow the exit signs," he said.

Poor Geoff was mortified as I sniggered and walked away from the suit.

"I don't know what you said to him, but I guess it was your idea of a joke."

"Not at all, Geoff," I said. "Just asking him where we could get a taxi."

As soon as we left the drab station concourse, the dust and the taste of coal dust hit us immediately. It was like something from Dickensian London, and I reached into my pocket for a handkerchief to cover my nose and mouth. Geoff made a comment about getting out of this place as quick as we could and we set about looking for a man with a car.

It didn't take us long. The car was a hideous, white, rusty Polenz. I swear I had faced Panzer tanks more aerodynamic but, nevertheless, the driver smiled at us, and he spoke some German. I said that I wanted to secure his services for a few hours. He looked around suspiciously, leaned in towards me, checked no one was within earshot, and quietly asked if I had any US Dollars. I did and, after a very rapid negotiation all in whispers, for a very reasonable twenty US dollars, I owned him and his cab for the day.

He asked where I wanted to go first and although I knew Beuthen was nearer, I wasn't quite in the frame of mind to visit the mine just yet. I didn't even know if I wanted to.

"Lamsdorf," I said.

Antoni, (he had introduced himself) said he had never heard of the place. He asked whether I had pronounced it right. I explained that Lamsdorf was a POW camp but he was still none the wiser. When I took out the sketch of my map and pointed out exactly where Lamsdorf was, his eyes lit up and he nodded his head.

"Łambinowice, Łambinowice," he repeated. Then he said in German."I will take you, not a problem."

He walked around to the back of his car and opened the boot as I gazed inside. It was full of jerry cans and stank of petrol fumes. Antoni took one look at how clean my bag was, took it from me, and laid it on the front passenger seat. He opened the back door and I climbed in as he started the engine, clunked it into gear, and sped off, explaining that diesel and petrol were unfortunately still rationed, as were many food products.

"Bloody Russians," he muttered under his breath.

Katowice city was bleak, I couldn't quite believe how industrial the city was. I counted three power stations and mines that reared up in front of us before we had gone no more than a mile. It looked like the architects and the planners of Katowice were under pressure to cram as much dirty grey brick into the city as they possibly could.

We passed the standard grotty tenement building; the square blocks of flats and I watched the inhabitants of the city shuffle about their business. Antoni pointed out the queues at the shops and laughed out loud as he said the city was the worst place in the world to live. I wasn't going to doubt him for a second.

As we drove out of the city limits and we'd been in the car for around twenty minutes, Antoni pointed out what looked like a large radio mast.

In perfect English, he said, "Gliwice Incident."

A shiver ran the length of my spine. I realised we had just passed the place where the second world war had started, and incidentally where my war had nearly ended.

I whispered to Geoff, "Do you know where we are?"

"No," he said.

"That radio mast we've just passed was the staged incident, where Germany justified their invasion into Poland."

"I'm not with you."

Of course he wasn't, he was a fifteen-year-old kid at the time and, to paraphrase Chamberlain talking about Czechoslovakia in 1938, this part of Europe truly was a 'faraway land of which we knew nothing.'

"It was the night of the thirty-first of August 1939," I said, "when a group of German agents dressed in Polish uniforms attacked and seized the Gliwice Radio Station. They gave an anti-German broadcast in Polish. It was made to look like they were saboteurs."

"I see," said Geoff, "because Gliwice was in Germany at the time, it was spelt differently in those days."

"Exactly, right on the border. There were other incidents too; all making it look like Polish aggression against Germany. Adolf Hitler used them to set the stage for war."

I looked back over my shoulder as gradually the mast disappeared.

Chapter 21

GLIWICE

It was as familiar to me then, as it was in January 1945. It was at the beginning of that bloody Long March. The Russians were so close we could hear their guns, feel the percussions, smell the cordite. "Stop," I said to Antoni. "Halt! Halt!"

I think I took him by surprise; he must have thought there was something wrong. He slammed on the brakes and the car shuddered to a stop. I apologised to him in German, said that I needed to get out of the car for a minute or two. I had already opened the door. It had started to snow but luckily it wasn't lying on the ground.

"It's bloody freezing," he said. "Are you mad?"

"Not mad, Antoni, I just need to see this."

I walked away from the car.

"Come, dear brother," I said. "I'm going to show you where I was nearly shot."

We walked across the road as I pulled my coat collar up and rubbed my hands together to keep warm. As we got to the other side of the road and I looked over my brother's shoulder, I could still make out the shape of the top of the mast at Gliwice, but it was the gravestones that had caught my eye. There was a lot more of them than there were in 1945, but the low, stone surrounding wall hadn't changed. "Over there, Geoff," I pointed.

He followed my finger.

"Do you see that large cross by the road?"

"Yep."

"Well, we had all been marching along the road when we were told to take a break."

"At the end of the war?"

"Yes," I said. "There were a lot of rumours and whispers among the prisoners. It was said that they were going to march us deep into Germany so that we could be used as hostages."

"Because the Nazis knew it was all over at that point."

"Yes. It was January 1945 and we were cold and starving but we sensed it was all at an end."

I pulled out my notebook. Jesus, it was so cold I could hardly turn the pages but, eventually, I found the dates I was looking for. I had made what I thought were significant notes from November 1944 to January 1945. I watched Geoff's face as I spoke.

"It was over, we knew it was and it was around the autumn of 1944 when the stories started to surface."

"What sort of stories?"

"We were hearing about mass extermination and genocide, they were incomprehensible. I'd experienced the Nazi brutality first-hand, and... "

"Really?" Geoff questioned. "To be honest, Eric, you haven't told me that much about that side of things."

I nodded. He was right. "In time, Geoff, it's coming I promise you. You may find this hard to believe, but hour by hour it's lifting."

"What's lifting?"

"Everything. Being here and seeing it's returned to civilisation. Well, civilisation of a sort anyway. I'm staring my worst nightmare straight between the eyes, Geoff, and it's working."

"I'm glad to hear it."

I swallowed. My throat was dry because I knew the litmus test would come at the E72 coal mine. As of now, I wasn't even sure if I could make that final journey. I told him what we were hearing about Auschwitz, how Himmler had ordered the gas chambers destroyed.

I looked at him. "You've heard about Auschwitz I assume?"

"Yes, you've mentioned it before, but to be honest the communications in India were pretty dire."

"Auschwitz, Geoff," I said, exasperated. "The mass extermination camp, Auschwitz Birkenau, the Jews, the Gypsies, the Slavs, surely you know all about Auschwitz?"

"Tell me about your escape, Eric, Auschwitz isn't really relevant."

"Of course it is, I'm trying to paint the picture of how desperate we all were.

"I get that."

"We wondered if we were on our way to the Allied version of Auschwitz. We'd heard what had happened to the Jews, the Russians and many of the Poles. Some lads said they were marching us to extermination camps."

"And you suspected it might be true."

"I did. I'd witnessed some terrible things at that bloody mine."

Geoff held his hands out in front of him. "You keep saying but you never tell me, and you haven't told me anything about the mine either."

I gripped him by the elbow. "No, Geoff, but I will… just give me a little time."

I walked over to the wall, passed a wooden sign that read, 'Cmentarz sw. Wojciecha' and crouched down. "We were sitting here Geoff and I noticed that our German guards didn't seem particularly bothered about watching us too carefully. They were standing in groups by themselves, just talking."

"So you decided to make a run for it?"

I smiled. "Yes… the shortest escape attempt in history."

Geoff laughed. "Tell me, brother. I'm all ears."

I told Geoff how easy it was, how I had never said a word to anyone and just slipped over the low wall into the graveyard. I had a theory that I could hide behind the gravestones, where they wouldn't be able to see me. If I made it to the far end of the graveyard, there was a forest where I reckoned I could hide out. My plan was to eventually make my way back to the Russian lines. We could hear their artillery behind us; they couldn't have been more than ten miles away.

"It seemed like a good idea at the time?" Geoff laughed.

"It was a good idea," I said. "I had it all figured out. I reckoned I would find some berries in the forest and the trees would give me some shelter. There was no problem with water because there was snow on the ground. I knew I just needed to find some food to build me up enough to get over to the Russians."

"So what happened?"

"Well," I pointed. "There were a lot fewer gravestones back then, maybe no more than a few hundred. I took my time and crawled along on all fours. My head never came above the level of the shortest headstone. 'Patience. Don't run,' I kept telling myself."

"Where did you get to?"

122

"Right to the end. It took me about twenty minutes, I was so bloody well proud of myself when the forest opened up in front of me. It was about a hundred yards of no man's land, but I knew that if I went for the dash across the ploughed field, there was a chance I would get spotted and shot."

I told Geoff that I was prepared to wait, to stick it out until darkness came in or until the rest of the guards and prisoners left.

"A wise move," Geoff said.

"I thought so, but I'd been spotted. I'd been behind that last gravestone no more than two minutes, I was reading the name on it when I heard a rifle cock and a German voice telling me that I'd been a very stupid man."

Geoff had located a gate and walked through it.

"Come on," he shouted, "see if we can find the grave that nearly had my big brother's name on it."

It wasn't difficult to find. The cemetery had been sectioned into three or four parts, one section ended with gravestones of burials up to 1945 and there was a small monument, in Polish, which we assumed was a memorial to the victims of the war. I knew roughly where I had been hiding and checked two or three of the gravestones. I found it. A man called Jakub Kosecki, he'd died on the day of my birthday, 1941. How ironic.

The grave was in a state of disrepair, no surprise really; probably most of his family had been wiped out long ago.

"I was sitting here, prepared to wait it out when the Feldwebel appeared over the top of the headstone. I think the fact that I spoke German probably saved my life because bizarrely we engaged in conversation for some time. He was quite aggressive at first and I feared the worst — that I'd be shot where I sat. I told him that didn't worry me, what was the difference in being shot where I was or murdered in the death camp they were marching us to."

I explained to Geoff how the Feldwebel uncocked his rifle and sat down beside me. He was a reasonable man, and he knew the war was over. He even gave me a biscuit to eat. He said that he wouldn't shoot me but I had to make my way back through the graveyard and return to my mates from E72.

"And you did?"

"I had no choice, Geoff, it was that or a bullet. When I climbed back over the wall though, I had another trigger-happy Nazi threatening me with another bullet and asking where I'd been. I answered him in perfect

German that I had been answering the call of nature and would he prefer that I expose my bare arse to him. It drew a few laughs from his mates and diffused the situation; he gave me a kick and pushed me back in the line."

We heard a horn blasting and, as the road was very quiet, assumed it was Antoni. We walked back through the cemetery and sure enough, he was standing by the car, waving his arms and beckoning us towards him. He told me we had to get going because there weren't many daylight hours left. He asked what it was I wanted to see in Łambinowice. I said the POW camp, or what was left of it. He shook his head, said there was no POW camp that he knew of. I assured him that there was and if he could take me to Łambinowice train station, I'd show him where the camp was from there. He was shaking his head.

As we got back into the car, he was muttering under his breath that I was wasting my time.

"He's not so sure," said Geoff. "Are you sure there's something there? It would be a horrendous waste of time if there was nothing to see."

I assured Geoff that I'd definitely read somewhere that there was something to commemorate where the old Lamsdorf Camp had been, and it was no surprise that Antoni didn't know about it, after all, he was a taxi man from Katowice. What would he know about a town way outside his normal working circle? Geoff agreed, he reminded me how bloody difficult it was to get here in the first place, and how many tourists did I think would be making this sort of trip? He was right, of course. I hoped that what I had read about Lamsdorf was true, that there'd be something to see.

Chapter 22

ŁAMBINOWICE

The station at Łambinowice was as bleak and desolate when we arrived as I remembered it from 1940. Apart from the name change from the German Lamsdorf to Polish Łambinowice, it was every bit as cold and uninviting. The wind had picked up, it felt around twenty below and Antoni's car heating system was non-existent. We were wrapped up with scarfs and gloves, including our driver, who looked like he was ready to take on a downhill ski run.

Antoni pointed at the station façade and told me to take a look. He said I was mistaken, there was no camp around here, I clearly had the wrong place. But I wasn't mistaken, I was slap bang in the middle of my forty-five year nightmare.

"Recognise it?" Geoff asked.

I nodded. There were no words. Geoff drifted on ahead and I wanted to follow him, but my legs had other ideas, they were rooted to the spot. Only as Geoff disappeared was I able to put one foot in front of the other and follow him.

I joined him on the platform as the wind whistled down the tracks. There were no people there and the grass looked like it had grown over the tracks. It wasn't well maintained at all, and one could have been forgiven for thinking it may have been derelict, the station possibly moved to another location. But no, in the distance I heard the rumbling of a train and within a few minutes, a small locomotive trundled through the station. It didn't stop and we were left with our thoughts. Eventually, I managed to string a few sentences together for Geoff.

"This was where they brought us in 1940, on that train journey from Hell."

I pointed to a part of the building that looked as if it had been added to the main structure at one point.

"They loaded the dead bodies over there, men who had given up on life during the trip. They piled them up like dead pheasants on a country shoot. We stood in silence. I might be wrong, but I think the Red Cross were here and we got a little soup before we set off on the mile or so march to the camp."

I felt the tear roll down my cheek. Geoff noticed.

"Let's get you out of here, brother," he said.

"Yes," I replied, "but just give me a minute."

"I'll see you in the car," he said as he walked away.

As he disappeared from view, I broke down and the tears rolled freely down my cheeks. Those poor men. My comrades.

I stayed in that bleak station at the mercy of the elements for a full ten minutes and I sobbed like a baby. Afterwards, I felt that a weight had somehow been lifted. It's what I had to do. When our hearts break, we cry and there is nothing wrong with that. My arrival here, in June, or it might have been July, 1940, was the first time in my life that my heart had been broken. I was just twenty-one years of age. Sadly, it wouldn't be the last time either.

I stepped back out of the station, turned around, and stared at the dirty red brick frontage. I confined it to memory, took a deep breath, and then headed towards the car. I had exorcised one or two demons. I congratulated myself that I'd had the courage to return here. Whether I could make it to the mine was a different matter.

I leaned over towards Antoni.

"Okay, sir," I pointed up the road. "That direction, that's where the camp was."

"No camp," Antoni repeated.

I assured him that I was one hundred percent sure. There was no doubt about it. Wouldn't you know that Antoni was right? I was aware that we had only marched a mile or so from the station in 1940 but, after five miles, I hadn't spotted anything resembling a camp or what was left of one.

"Bugger," I said "There's no bloody camp or memorial."

At the mention of the word memorial, Antoni sparked into life.

"Yes, memorial, memorial, denkmal," he said, "denkmal."

He was pointing up the road. Denkmal, that's German for a monument or a memorial. Antoni said there was a POW memorial a mile up the road.

126

As we stepped from the car I was struck by the total lack of familiarity and wondered if perhaps I had to accept that my memory had become clouded over the years, that somehow my brain had foreclosed on my less pleasant memories. However, as we walked towards the white marble monument and the writing became visible it clicked with me. I knew exactly where we were.

"This was the Russian camp, Geoff."

"Ya, Russen," Antoni barked out enthusiastically.

"And your camp was around here too, Eric?"

"Yes."

I turned around slowly, 180 degrees and I knew. The Lamsdorf main camp was about a mile away from the Russian camp. I looked over the top of the trees to my right.

"Over there, Geoff." I pointed.

I looked up ahead, Antoni appeared strangely interested in the Russian memorial and we walked over to join him. He was unusually animated, rabbiting away in Polish, forgetting for a moment that I didn't understand a word he was saying. He stood near a stone plaque inset into the ground. On it was written in Polish were the words, 'Chwała Ofiarom Barbarzyństwa Hitlera'.

"What does it say?" asked Geoff.

Antoni was still jabbering away in Polish, pointing to the plaque.

"In German, Antoni, what does it say in German? I don't understand a bloody word you are saying."

He stopped in mid-sentence and the penny dropped. At last, he spoke in German, just one sentence and I understood.

I turned to Geoff. "It says, 'Glory to the victims of Hitler's barbarism.'"

Antoni nodded, I nodded back to him. Geoff took a deep breath and let out a sigh.

I knew all about the Russian camp and how the Germans treated them. There were stories filtering through, stories that seemed too wicked to be true. At the time we told ourselves that the Russian chaps were perhaps exaggerating a little because no men could be so cruel. But after the war, I made a point of reading and then re-reading what the Germans did to the Russians. I compiled my own dossier, which ran to over two thousand words. I even attempted to write a poem but, in the end, gave up, screwed up the paper and threw it out.

Adolf Hitler had made no provision for the hundreds of thousands of Russian POWs he had in captivity. In the middle of atrocious winters, there wasn't enough shelter and scores of them froze to death.

Geoff noticed me rummaging in my satchel for my notes.

"What is it, Eric?"

"This place," I said. "You wouldn't believe how the Germans treated the poor Russians. They were just like us, young conscripts, most of them, who'd had no choice but to fight for their country and then had the misfortune to get caught. The Germans had signed up to the Geneva Convention, but they used the excuse that because the USSR hadn't signed the treaty, the bloody convention went out of the window."

Geoff looked like he wanted to say something but sensing what this place meant to me, he decided to keep his counsel.

I recalled those Soviet miners who worked with me and how they were always last in the queue when the food was dished out. Sometimes there was no food for them at all. When they were too weak to work, they were shipped back here to Lamsdorf. Sometimes we just noticed that the Russians we had been working with suddenly weren't there anymore. Eventually, we came to realise exactly what had happened to them.

I had located the page I was looking for. "Nearly half a million Soviet POWs died in captivity."

He shook his head. "And I thought India was bad."

We couldn't hang around too long as it was bitterly cold at this point, but now I knew for sure the exact location of the Allied POW camp at Lamsdorf. As we walked back to the car, I noticed another part of the camp, literally thousands of old gravestones shaped in Christian crosses and dozens of trees that had sprouted up over the years. We ambled over. I was aware that my teeth had begun to chatter and wanted to get away to somewhere warm, but something drew me towards them.

"We'll need to take a look," I said to Geoff.

Antoni followed on behind as I wondered if perhaps some of the victims of the war had, in fact, been given a decent individual burial instead of being heaped in mass graves, as the Germans seemed to favour. No such luck. The gravestones were victims of the Franco-Prussian War, all dated 1870 to 1871. Incredibly, an odd name could still be read, mostly French names. I had read that Lamsdorf had once been a training camp for the Prussian Army but then became a POW camp for French prisoners. It all made sense. After that it became a POW camp for the British and French during the Great War.

"What a fucking nightmare," Geoff said. "No wonder the people look so bloody miserable."

I couldn't help laughing. He didn't use the F word very often, but I knew exactly what he meant.

"Ghosts," I said as I looked around. "Ghosts everywhere you look, ghosts of every nationality you can think of."

We didn't stay long as Antoni kept pointing at his watch and then the sky, indicating that it would be dark soon. Before we left, I was keen to find the Allied part of the camp, now I knew where it was. I gave Antoni the directions and told him where to go.

Sure enough, as we'd been driving no more than a few minutes the terrain started to look a little familiar.

"Over here, Antoni," I said. "Pull in over here."

He pulled over into a small layby cut into the overgrown forest and even though there was nothing immediately recognisable, I knew where we were. The large double gates with the barbed wire on top had disappeared completely but there were still the remains of rotting wooden posts. I remembered those posts were seven feet high with another three feet of coiled barbed wire on top.

I got out and started walking. As I walked a little further, I could see more posts that once marked out the perimeter of one of the largest POW camps in Europe. I walked on as Antoni leaned on the car and lit a cigarette. I'd noticed he'd taken a bottle from the glove compartment and had taken a drink.

He must be thirsty, I thought to myself.

As we walked a little further, I was aware that Antoni was following on behind me and, dare I say it, but he was beginning to look as if he was interested.

We wandered through a cut in the forest and stumbled upon old cement girders, the remnants of foundations and, at one point, a fair bit of a roofless building that still stood, though someone had clearly taken a sledgehammer to the brickwork and carted home a few tons of free bricks. We walked through the doorway that still stood, overgrown by foot-high grass covered in a thick frost.

"Recognise anything?" Geoff said.

"I think so."

Antoni said something and pointed. We looked towards where his arm was outstretched. We were surprised. As the forest opened, we spotted a tarmac track and a few more buildings, but this time they were far better maintained. As we got closer, I could see that there were lights on and a neat well-manicured lawn, the fencing freshly painted.

And then it came to me. I knew exactly where we were. I froze to the spot.

"What is it?" Geoff asked.

I know what that building is, it's the old commandant's office and that larger building next to it was the guard hut."

"No way."

"I'm telling you."

Antoni had kept on walking and stood in front of a large sign on two wooden posts. He looked over his shoulder.

"Museum," he shouted.

I laughed at Geoff. "Well, even you understood that, mate!" I found my feet again and started walking over. "Yes," I said to Geoff. "The same in German as in English, even you couldn't get that wrong." I grinned.

I pushed at the entrance door. The museum, it seemed, was open, although I was its only visitor, probably for the entire day by the look of things. I felt a chill run down my spine as I remembered what this place used to be. I was escorted around the museum by a lady who introduced herself as Celina. She spoke very good English. When I told her that I had been a prisoner here during the war, I swear she treated me like a Hollywood movie star. At one point she led me around holding my hand which I'm sure made my young brother quite jealous.

The museum had a display of old black and white photographs, most of those photographs were of Russian POWs, but they showed the camp as it was during the war, in its former glory, if that's the right expression.

She was clearly very proud of her museum but, to be honest, it wasn't such an emotional jolt as seeing that Lamsdorf railway station. Everything was neat and tidy, pristine, the walls had been recently white-washed and everything was in its place. My memories of the main camp at Lamsdorf were of chaos, dirty sleeping quarters, cockroach and rat-infested buildings and stinking latrines. Oh my God, those latrines.

Going to the toilet was the worst experience I can remember at the mine, especially in the winter months because the cesspit froze over. We sat on planks and did what we had to do and because it was so cold the shit froze almost immediately and grew into huge piles; it wouldn't filter into the main tanks of the cesspit. One particularly bad winter, the frozen pile of shit grew bigger and bigger. I remembered that a guard had ordered half a dozen of the lads to break up the large frozen piles and roll them back into the main cesspit with their hands. It wasn't the best job in the camp. In summer it was nearly as bad, the stench unimaginable, as millions of flies congregated around the cesspit.

I told Celina that I'd been in this place, the main camp, for only a couple of weeks. Before I left, I had been given an official Stalag VIIIB postcard which I sent to my parents. We were issued with a POW number and Stalag identity code which we had to write on the bottom. My life as a nobody, a bloody Kreigie, POW Number 12965, had begun.

"West," I announced sternly. "Kriegsgefangenennummer eins zwei neun sechs fünf."

Towards the end of our visit, Celina showed me a Red Cross parcel dated 1944. That gave me a real shock. It even had the original wrappers for the chocolate bars; the tins were original too. There were tins of spam, an apple pie, a small bag of raisins, and some biscuits.

I turned to her. "Those parcels kept us alive, they really did."

As we left, Celina took me into another small outcrop to the main museum. She took me to a glass case.

"Well, I never."

"Camp currency," Celina replied before I had a chance to explain. "Although the real camp currency was cigarettes or alcohol."

I bent down to take a closer look, the German Eagle in the bottom left corner and denominations in ones, twos, fives, and tens and written across each note in bold black type **Gutfchein Uber Reichspfennig,** literally translated, a coupon for Reichspfennig.

I said goodbye to Celina soon after. We had been there for nearly two hours. She asked me if I could come back another time.

"I'm sure I will," I lied.

As I sat in the back of the taxi, I told Antoni to take me to the nearest hotel.

He burst out laughing.

Chapter 23

WATER OF LIFE

Antoni told me there were no hotels that he knew of in Łambinowice, the nearest hotel was back in Katowice, but there was a slight problem, he didn't have enough petrol to get us there. I assumed it was a simple enough solution to stop at the nearest petrol station, but Antoni informed us that he had used up his rations for that week and he wouldn't be permitted to fill his tank for another three days. Before we had a chance to discuss the situation further, Antoni screeched to a halt beside a public telephone kiosk and jumped out of the car. We watched as he made at least two or three phone calls and then walked back to the car with a big smile on his face.

He opened the door and spoke in German. "I will get petrol tomorrow and take you wherever you want to go. Tonight, you will stay with me and my family." He climbed in and sat down and looked in the rear-view mirror. "I charge ten US dollars."

What could I say?

"Includes supper," he said.

Even better. I was feeling quite hungry by now and realised I hadn't eaten since breakfast time. Antoni reached into his glove compartment after I had agreed to the deal. I handed over one of the ten-dollar notes from my travel agent's wallet. He pulled out the glass bottle I had seen him drinking from earlier.

"We celebrate." He grinned and thrust the bottle towards me.

"Celebrating with water," I muttered softly to Geoff. "He'd be a big hit in an East London pub."

I looked at the label just as I was about to take a swig, *Vodka Stalinskaya*.

"Surely not," I mumbled. "He's been drinking from that bugger all day and I don't even like vodka."

132

I leaned forward. "It's water, Antoni, yes?"

He burst out laughing. "No water, only vodka, Antoni doesn't drink water."

I took a decent mouthful, and the bitter after-taste coated the inside of my mouth. I smiled back at Antoni.

"Good ya?"

"Yes, very good, Antoni."

It was good... until it hit the back of my oesophagus that is. It felt like someone had jabbed a thousand red hot needles into the back of the tenderest part of my throat. I gasped out loud trying to get a rush of cool air into my mouth. Antoni burst out laughing. We shared the last dregs and then set off.

Antoni lived in a place called Pyskowice, about twenty-five miles from Katowice. I was convinced that his car was running on fumes by the time we arrived there. The needle on the petrol gauge had been on the red line for what seemed like the last forty kilometres. We passed a lake on the right-hand side of the road, just visible by the light from a full moon. Before I dared to believe the town might even be picturesque, we pulled up outside the usual, non-descript, battleship grey apartment block. Antoni announced that we had arrived.

It was clear that Antoni had called ahead as the whole family were at the door to greet me. There was his wife who he introduced as Elwira, a short woman, her mousy brown hair tied up in a plain bun. She wore a flowery apron that wouldn't have looked out of place in 1940s London.

I was introduced to the three children. Manka was a little girl of around eight years of age, clearly excited to see this strange foreigner. Holleb, a little boy a couple of years older than Manka, dressed in an oversized, grey, polo neck jumper that nearly reached his knees, a hand-me-down. And finally, there was Mania, a sixteen-year-old girl who spoke almost perfect English. She became the self-appointed chairwoman of the evening's happenings. I knew from the outset that she had an intelligence and a wisdom way beyond her years.

Despite the less than salubrious surroundings, I was welcomed like royalty into Antoni's family apartment. It was clean and tidy, and perhaps, fuelled by the vodka, I had a nice warm feeling about the night ahead.

The living room was sparse, a small, black and white television playing to itself in the corner, a sofa, one tatty armchair, a large dining table, six chairs and very little else. There were a few, old, black and white photos sporadically placed on the walls and one coloured, professional portrait of the whole family taken some years ago; Manka, just a babe in arms. The flooring was worn linoleum with one threadbare rug in front of a raging, coal fire. Along with the smell of coal, the room was filled with a beautiful aroma of something that Elwira had been cooking in the kitchen.

Antoni sat me at the table and within minutes, a bottle of vodka and two glasses were placed in the middle. He poured a couple of large glasses. Despite my protests he wouldn't take no for an answer. By the time the whole family joined us, a big pot was placed in the centre, I was conscious that I was grinning innately like someone who had lost their mind. We were presented with a traditional Polish dish called Bigos, a stew with sauerkraut and homemade Polish sausage served with bread.

It was refreshing not to have to think in German, as young Mania's English was excellent. Everything I said, she translated to her family. It suited me fine. I was aware that I was quite inebriated by the time the evening meal came to an end. Mania seemed fascinated when I said that I had been a POW at the hands of the Germans, a little over sixty miles from this place.

"The Germans treated the Polish people terribly," she said. "They stole State property and industries, killed factory owners, and seized their businesses for the Third Reich. Poland was plundered and exploited." Mania turned to her father and said something in Polish.

I sat with Mania while she told of her country's struggle. She told me how the exiled Polish Government in 1941 issued a paper detailing the mass kidnapping of young women for sexual slavery. "The Polish people have suffered like no nation on earth," she said and translated to her father again.

Just after midnight, I turned in; a double bed with sparse furnishing and a thick eiderdown that had seen better days. The flat wasn't very big; I suspected that Elwira and Antoni had given up their bedroom for the night. For ten US dollars, I don't suppose they minded too much.

Chapter 24

BYTOM

I slept late. Antoni woke me just after nine o'clock and I had a blinding headache. Geoff was in the room too and he asked me how I felt. "I've felt better, brother."

As we walked through to the lounge, the breakfast table was set, with the whole family sitting patiently waiting. They had obviously broken into their rations and made a pot of coffee. There was fresh bread in the oven and eggs boiling on the stove. The coffee was a godsend. Elwira disappeared and returned with the eggs, bread and what looked like Polish jam. I tucked in like a hungry navvy.

I had secured the services of Antoni for the day again, once he convinced me that he could get hold of some petrol. I handed over twenty dollars and told him that I wanted to go to the town of Bytom, formerly Beuthen under German rule, and see the coal mine where I had spent most of my captivity.

There then ensued what looked like a fierce argument between Mania and her father. At one point he lifted his hand to her as if he was about to give her a clout. I intervened and he said it was none of my business. I told him that he'd made it my business as soon as he'd raised his hand towards her.

"What does she want?" I asked.

He let out a deep sigh. "She wants to come with us."

"That's it?"

Mania jumped in and stated her case. She said she knew the history of Bytom and wanted to come with us and be our guide.

"Splendid," I said. "I can't think of anything better."

"That's decided then." I turned to Mania and in perfect German announced that I would be delighted if she could accompany us. Her father let out a little protest grunt but, nevertheless, walked towards the front door of his apartment.

We had to drive to a secluded spot in a forest just on the edge of town where Antoni furtively met a man and handed over some money. The black marketeer went to the boot of his car and pulled out two jerry cans. Antoni poured one into his tank and put the other in his boot and then, wouldn't you know, the man handed over a bottle of vodka too. Antoni unscrewed the cap, took a swig and then offered it to the man. He also took a drink, handed it back and Antoni slipped it into the glove compartment. I glanced at my watch. It was ten-thirty in the morning.

As we approached the outskirts of Bytom, I braced myself for a day of memories. If anything, the town looked much worse than the German border town called Beuthen I had remembered from forty years previously. It was filled with drab, dilapidated buildings. Many parts were a ghost town. Mania said it was poor, very industrialised, low wages. She said that before the war, in the 1920s, Beuthen was very much a German city, seventy-five percent of the population German.

As Antoni negotiated the potholes, I attempted to explain to Geoff how Upper Silesia was shaped like the toe of Italy, kicking to the east rather than the west. At the mid-foot was the old Prussian town of Breslau, the capital of Silesia. The triad of industrial towns Beuthen, Hindenburg and Gliwice were at the toe, here on the Polish border. It was the powerhouse of Nazi Germany, dominated by coal and other heavy industries. To demonstrate its importance, Hitler had built a Reichsautobahn from Berlin to Breslau and on to Gliwice and its final destination, Beuthen.

"But there was always a Polish under-movement," Mania said, turning her head towards us from between the front seats to make her voice heard above the noise, "they knew that Bytom truly belonged to Poland and not Germany. They were singled out and persecuted, sometimes sent to prison or taken away and never seen again."

We arrived in the town square. The last time I was here it would have been under escort with guards. I remembered the main road we'd travelled down was named Adolf Hitler Platz. I had been taken to a dentist somewhere nearby. Two teeth were extracted in less than a minute, no anaesthetic and some dirty old lint to stop the bleeding. At least it was free and no waiting either but it was the beginning of my lifetime of dental woes.

Our first stop, Mania, our self-appointed guide informed us, was the synagogue in the town square. There was nothing there. Mania stared up through a gap between two ugly apartment buildings.

"Mr West, it was Kristallnacht, ninth of November 1938. This was a Jewish quarter; the Germans had a Kristallnacht right here. For two nights the local Nazis rioted and unleashed a terrible fury culminating in the burning of the Synagogue. They lined the Jewish people up on the other side of the street, beat them up, and made them watch as they burned it to the ground. Hermann Goring was here to watch the proceedings."

There was a moment of silence as we looked into a void that was clearly a huge part of history.

"Eventually, they rounded up the Jewish community of Beuthen. They found every single man, woman and child. Those who were too infirm to make the short walk to the train station were executed on the spot."

I felt my chest tighten.

"The Beuthen Jews were the first Jewish community to be liquidated during the Holocaust."

We walked slowly back to the car. I didn't know if I could even face the mine after what Mania had just told us. I had seen evil in the camp and at the mine. I had witnessed executions and brutality, seen young men lose their minds, but the more I learned about a war that I had been thrown into, and of the deranged minds of those crazy Nazis, the more I wanted to cover my ears and scream, 'No more!'

I was lost in my thoughts as the car crawled through the traffic. Nobody said anything; even our guide had lost her tongue.

"Stop!" I shouted suddenly, pointing out of the window. "That place, that place over there."

It looked a little different, but I knew exactly what it was. "It was a hospital," I said.

"It still is," Mania said.

"I've been, I've stayed here, they brought me here from the mine."

I laughed inwardly, that was the only way the Nazis would ever take you to hospital if you were too ill to stand on your own two feet.

"Why were you there?" Mania asked.

"There was an outbreak of sore throats at the mine, Mania. I coughed a lot, but like I said it wasn't possible to see the camp doctor unless you were at death's door. I ignored it for two weeks, just tried to get on with the job until I got to the point where I couldn't swallow, couldn't eat anything. I was starting to feel dizzy every time I stood, I was dehydrated beyond belief. All I wanted to do was to curl up on my straw palio and sleep. I couldn't get warm even with an army greatcoat on top of my blanket, fully clothed."

I woke one morning shaking like a leaf and burning up. Luckily that morning's guard was one of the sympathetic ones. He was an old Great War veteran, too old for active service, and he ordered a couple of the lads to run for a stretcher. I heard him tell them to, 'Hurry before it's too late.'

"I was in a bad way and, as they put me onto the stretcher, I fell in and out of consciousness. I can't remember how I even got there but I recall waking up cocooned in beautiful white sheets. There was an SS doctor in charge, I didn't hold out much hope of surviving. But how wrong could I be, the man was a real gentleman. I was bowled over by the kindness of the nuns who nursed me through the worst of it. The doctor had diagnosed rheumatic fever, I remember that distinctly, his exact words... 'Du hast rheumatisches Fieber.' He examined me with his vintage stethoscope and looked a bit glum."

Before the war, I was a public health clerk for the council. I knew all about the scourge of rheumatic fever, especially as it could quite easily develop into heart disease. One of the New Zealanders at the camp, Frank Wallace, died in this hospital, his body was swollen like hell when they brought him in, I think he may have had heart failure. They buried him just outside the mine in a grave next to one of our lads." A lump formed in my throat. "Poor Blythin." I whispered.

Blythin's execution will live with me until my dying day.

"Did Blythin die from the fever too?" Mania asked.

"No, I—"

Antoni interrupted us, said that we'd need to get going if we wanted to see the mine. It was just the distraction I needed.

"Tell your father to take us to the railway station."

"Next to the mine?"

"Yes."

I felt slightly disorientated but remembered that the camp was very close to the railway line and the station just a few hundred yards away. We'd stood and watched the trains pass through the station on a regular basis. It was the movement of the tectonic plates of war; it was on a massive scale, and it hit us hard. During the summer of 1941, in our first year at the camp, we started to see war machinery making its way across

Poland and on towards the USSR. The Germans were getting ready for the invasion of Russia.

Those trains were relentless and overloaded with new tanks, much larger and potent than the tanks we'd been firing at in Cassel just a year previously. We had even noticed reconditioned British equipment salvaged from our efforts at Dunkirk. That was hard to take.

We felt that we'd done our bit to destroy everything, but in fairness, it was all a chaotic rush and a run for our lives and some of the BEF wouldn't have had time. We had finished our shift at the mine one day and two or three guards stood examining one British tank, now emblazoned with the Wehrmacht white cross. They noticed us looking on and started to taunt us.

"Beutepanzer," they shouted, "Beutepanzer."

"What are they saying?" one of the lads asked.

"Loot tanks," I said, "stolen tanks."

We climbed back in the car. It was an enormous relief as it was bitterly cold, heavy ice covering the pavements and no sign of any attempt to salt or grit them. Apparently the council workers of Bytom were on strike. Antoni opened the glove compartment and took a long mouthful of vodka. He offered the bottle to me. I said a polite no thank you.

We were in the car no more than ten minutes. It was a slow drive and skirted the edge of a large park on the left-hand side of the road, a rare oasis of greenery in the city squalor.

And there it was, a railway line and a small station with the sidings I remembered so well. Antoni stopped the car right next to the railway line and asked us if we wanted to get out. "Yes," I answered immediately. "And Antoni..."

"Yes, my friend."

"Give me some of that vodka."

Chapter 25

RAILWAY TO HELL

Standing within sight of the massive station near to the mine in Bytom was something I hadn't thought would hit me so hard. I had thought the mine would be the hardest part of my journey today.

As I stood next to those railway tracks, I realised that most of my nightmares originated from this very spot.

I was glad my kid brother was by my side.

The German troops rolled through this station, trains full of brainwashed young Nazis. When the trains stopped, they got off to stretch their legs, the place was bloody crowded and they jeered and taunted us, some of the younger ones held their food rations up in the air, one soldier who obviously wasn't that hungry, stamped his into the platform as his mates all cheered. The irony was obvious, we were starving.

I turned to Mania. "They've dug most of the tracks up now, that's the only piece they got left." I pointed. "Four, five, six lines at the most."

We strolled over and I stood on one of the tracks.

"I recall my friend George left from here. They sent him to Berlin, to Genshagen. The Stalag III D Holiday Camp."

"A holiday camp," I don't understand Mania interjected.

"We called it the Holiday Camp," I said. "Genshagen. The Germans needed more fighting men and so they were recruiting from anywhere. They'd set up a unit called the British Free Corps."

I glanced at Mania, she was taking it all in, eager to learn and absorb anything she could.

"Then they decided to try and recruit the British. It was an experiment. George was one of the men they selected from the mine."

"When he returned, he said he'd been to Billy Butlin's for a month." I laughed. "He said it was better than Skegness. They slept on mattresses in

140

dorms, which were heated. They started feeding them three times a day. There were hot baths and showers, even a swimming pool. George said it was fabulous and then they started taking them into classrooms, showing them war reports of how well the Germans were doing and how they could all be a part of the Third Reich. George realised that they were trying to indoctrinate them after a couple of weeks, but he sat back and took the extra food and, in his own words, 'enjoyed it while I could, I knew it wasn't going to last.' He was never going to switch sides and fight for the Nazis. At the end of about four weeks, they marched them all into a storeroom and tried to make them switch their uniforms for Nazi ones."

"And did they?" asked Mania innocently.

"Like hell, Mania, they were British. Actually, the whole holiday camp project was a double-cross led by one of our Royal Artillery boys. His name was Sergeant Major John Brown. He'd been captured near us; his unit was at Cassel in 1940. It's a whole story in itself."

I paused while it crossed my mind that Brown's letters were probably being deciphered by 'my' patient Mary O'Leary.

My chest swelled with pride as I told Mania and Geoff how George relayed the tale and how they all told the Germans where to stick their Nazi uniforms. George told them he'd rather stick pins in his eyes.

Good old George, I thought to myself. *I wonder where he is now; if he's still alive?*

Mania was grinning. I think she was proud of George and the rest of the lads too. I climbed over a few more lines of track and Mania followed.

"We'd been at the mine no more than two or three weeks when we started hearing the trucks overloaded with human cattle passing through this station. It didn't matter what time of day we finished our shift at the mine, these trains were running regularly, slowly rumbling along the tracks heading eastwards in the direction of Krakow to Auschwitz. We could see the human misery through gaps in the woodwork. Old cattle trucks, just like the ones they used to transport us to Lamsdorf, but if it were humanly possible, even more overcrowded. Shockingly, we could see and hear the cries of women and children, even young babies thrust up towards the steel grill, gasping for air. As the trains headed across the border into Poland, there was a discernible, lingering stench of death. It was like the sweetish smell from decomposing deer in the Lake District. I'll remember that until the day I die.

One of the guards told us they were Jews on their way to work camps, but as the weeks and the months rolled by, it was clear that wasn't the case. We talked about the trains in the barracks at night, babies and young children being sent to work camps? It made no sense. There were upwards of twenty trucks to a train and at least half a dozen trains most weeks. It wasn't right and I remember distinctly reading chalked on one truck in German 'seventy-four persons' and yet we estimated around three hundred people packed in there. The numbers were beyond comprehension, Mania. We staged a train count one week, and in between the shifts we managed to have a man there almost twenty-four hours a day for the duration of the week. We counted eight trains that week. I worked it out in my notebook. Wherever it was the Jews were heading to, the Nazis were sending nearly fifty thousand a week."

Mania said nothing.

I've no doubt that many of those cattle trucks were full of prisoners who would be 'put to work' but our suspicions were proved right one day when a train passed and some of the guards started to laugh. I saw one of them make an unmistakable cut-throat sign, drawing his fingers across his neck.

We didn't know what it meant back then of course. But even now it freezes the blood in my veins. There were sections of the German population who knew exactly what was going on. After the war, they all denied it, claimed it was a secret Nazi operation and the public knew nothing. Perhaps. But those soldiers in the camp knew. They knew exactly where those cattle trucks were heading and what was going to happen when those poor souls arrived. I remember how some of them pointed to smoke rising from factory chimneys nearby and laughing. And if they knew, how many more knew? It's a question I often ask myself even to this day.

Antoni shouted something from over by the road. He was walking back towards the car.

"He wants us to go," Mania said.

I had no objections; I was glad to get away. It was bitter cold. A few strides in, Mania held my hand which surprised me. I stopped momentarily.

"What is it?" I asked.

She looked up at me and smiled, her eyes full of warmth.

"I have no grandfather, the Russians took him away not far from here, at Miechowice."

I shook my head. "I don't understand, where is Miechowice, what happened there?"

She tugged at my hand and pulled me towards the car.

"I will tell you all about it tonight."

We had driven no more than a mile when I caught a glimpse of the familiar winding towers as they loomed up ahead in between the buildings. I was enveloped with a cold sweat. I gripped the seat in front of me and muttered to myself, 'You can do this, you can do this.'

But there was something else.

"There it is, pull in here," I said, almost hyperventilating. "This place, I know it, where are we?"

"Szombieki," Mania said. "In your time this place would have been called Schomberg."

"Yes, please stop, over there by the cemetery, my friends are there."

I got a shock when I saw how many gravestones there were. It had been more than forty years and there were hundreds more than I could remember, but I was determined to find them.

We'd walked along seven or eight rows before Mania took my hand again.

"Tell me who you're looking for."

"My friends, David Blythin and Frank Wallace are buried here."

I felt Mania's grip tighten a little. It appeared that she had adopted me as her new grandfather.

"They are not here, Mr West."

"Yes they are, I attended their funerals."

"No," she said, shaking her head from side to side slowly. "After the war, all of the Allied prisoners' remains were moved to the Commonwealth War Cemetery in Krakow."

I was a little deflated as we got back in the car.

It's an old cliché to say somewhere hasn't changed when it's changed beyond all recognition. Although there were more houses and buildings, the fact was that Schomberg hadn't changed that much. The building was slightly cleaner and it had been extended but it stood in the middle of a large green patch of land, although now most of it was covered in snow.

There hadn't been any snow when they had moved us into the deserted old brewery building in September 1940.

"Stop," I said. "Can you stop here a minute Antoni? That's where we were billeted for the first eighteen months."

Mania had never heard the word 'billeted' but I explained and she translated without thinking as I spoke in English. Antoni pulled over. We didn't get of out the car as it had started to snow.

"We were a small, select group to begin with. That building over there," I indicated with my finger, "was an old beer hall; there were just a hundred of us in there at first, thirty beds, three men to a bunk. Later in the war, they built us a new camp inside the mine complex, but to start with we were here. We were all Dunkirk veterans and there were quite a few artillerymen like me. There were also quite a few Geordies in our group, boys from the Durham Light Infantry. I remember Sergeant Whitehead." I laughed out loud. "Poor bastard, he talked about nothing else but his beloved Newcastle United, said they were the best team in England and cursed Hitler for having the bare-faced cheek to get the football stopped in 1939. The sergeant had no teeth. He had been wading out to the boat at Dunkirk and realised he had left his teeth in his overcoat on the beach. He went back to the beach to look for them and the silly bugger was captured by the Germans."

Mania couldn't stop laughing.

"He claimed he didn't need his teeth anyway because all we got fed was cabbage soup. I billeted here with Eric Johnson and Sergeant Mears from my old regiment although I think they arrived a few weeks after me." I turned to my left. "And there, just over there was a separate camp for British Palestinians. They were Jewish, Pioneer Corps, but because they were British, Hitler hadn't decided what to do with them.

The Jews had shoulder flashes to mark them out, but they knew that if they stepped out of line that was the end of them. I'm sure the guards had been told that any excuse and they could be shipped off to Auschwitz. Those Palestinians were the bravest of the brave."

I took a moment to compose myself, I remembered so many of those lads packed into the cattle trucks never to be seen again.

Antoni started the engine. As we pulled away, I recognised another building.

"And there, another camp, the woodworkers camp, they supplied the huge pit props. They worked seven days a week felling trees and dressing the wood."

I was glad to leave Schomburg and yet I remembered a few of the good times too. There was an officer called Weise, what a character, he was always drunk. God knows where he found all the booze. He took the inspections each morning and if there was anything out of place, he'd go crazy. One day, drunk again, he took a gun out and rammed it in Norman Gibbs' ribs. Norman bravely pushed it away and told him not to 'point that silly little thing at me.' Weise went back into the guard room and promptly fell asleep. He was harmless really, just as long as he had his drink and a comfy bed to lay his head down."

It was only a matter of time before his superiors tired of his behaviour and one day he wasn't there anymore. We asked some of the guards and they said he'd been posted to the Russian front.

It was January. They had given Weise a death sentence. He never returned.

Chapter 26

ARBEITSKOMMANDO E72

We were heading for the mine, the last port of call. Antoni sensed my rising fear and reached in his glovebox for the bottle. I felt its warm glow on the lining of my throat and as the alcohol kicked in, I felt considerably better.

I hope it's strong enough to confront these darn demons, I thought.

Now I understood what Dr William Sargant's 'Excitatory Abreaction' treatment was all about. Of course, I'd assisted in some of those physical psychiatric treatments when he was my boss at St Thomas'. His aim was to recreate a stressful stimulus or memory and force his patients to confront it. But now, here I was having an abreaction all of my own. I suspect Antoni's vodka was every bit as effective as the pentobarbitone we used to use.

Antoni drove the taxi through the tunnel underneath the railway line. All of a sudden, there it was in front of us, the Hohenzollern Mine with its brick-built one hundred and fifty-metre-high winding tower, shaped like a miner's mallet standing upright on its handle. At the time it contained what was then state of the art, electrically-powered winding wheels. In a bizarre way we were all a little proud of that fact, a strange camaraderie that we were working in one of the most modern pits in Europe. But I would keep that to myself. It looked a bit dilapidated now.

We passed the pit entrance and I was intrigued as a tram ran alongside us. I stared into the windows, as for a few seconds its speed matched ours. I looked in on the occupants and caught the stare of a small boy, who waved at me. I waved back; he stuck out his tongue as his train driver increased his speed and disappeared.

"Tell us about the mine, Eric," Mania said.

I needed a minute. I needed many minutes.

"Yes... I will."

As we approached, I could hear once again the familiar buzzing and clattering noises those winding wheels made as the two-storey cages were simultaneously lowered into the dark abyss, even though they were as still as a hibernating dormouse. In my mind's eye, the mine was bursting with activity although it was as quiet as a dark night.

Antoni brought the car to a sudden stop and Mania jumped out eagerly, they had backed me into a corner. I had nowhere to go. I sat for some time, maybe a minute or more and then I gripped the handle and pushed down hard. I opened the door and tapped lightly on Antoni's driver's window.

"The vodka, more vodka," I said in German.

He frowned and I could see why as he held up the bottle and there was no more than an inch covering the bottom. I took it from him and drained every last dreg. I handed him ten dollars and told him we could get some more on the way back. It raised a smile, and he gave me a thumbs up.

"So, what were the guards like here, Mr West, would they really have shot you?" Mania asked.

"It depended, some of the older ones were okay to be fair, a lot of them were well in their fifties and many of them had served in the Kaiser's Army. They just wanted to get home and avoid the frontline. There were civilians posted to the mine too, a man called Spaniol and one nasty man called Hoppe."

"Tell me more, please."

"Gerhard Spaniol was a chubby chap. He'd been the mine foreman since the 1920s. He and his wife and three daughters lived on the site. I remember he slapped some prisoners around the face a few times. There was a rumour Spaniol had hit a British soldier on the head with an axe but I wasn't sure if that was true. I suspected it had been done by a guard. Hoppe was worse, he punched and kicked for little reason and of course, if you hit him back it was a death sentence. Hoppe had a brother who worked at the mine and helped to cover his tracks. He'd get us to do unauthorised work after shifts, clearing snow and tending to his large vegetable plot. He had a life-sized dummy in the garden, dressed in a British uniform and he'd use it for bayonet practice."

Hoppe didn't get it but, I think as the war progressed, Spaniol began to see the writing on the wall and he toned down his behaviour. I managed to get on with him.

"I could see that Spaniol was having to keep up coal production and he himself was at the mercy of the sadists around him I suppose. After the war, I was asked to testify on his behalf at his war crimes trial in Hamburg, to say I hadn't seen him abusing us POWs."

"Surely not?" Mania said.

I nodded.

"What happened?"

"I never went."

"Why not?"

I started walking away towards the pithead and she chased after me.

"Why not, Mr West?"

I kept on walking.

"Mr West!"

I stopped. "It was too soon," I said. "They had taken away five years of my life and I wasn't ready then to lend a helping hand."

"You were bitter?"

"Not bitter Mania, just not ready to talk about my experiences there and certainly not ready to offer any of them a get out of jail free card. Spaniol had helped the Germans to hold me under lock and key for five years. If it had been ten years later, who knows?"

We walked a little further.

"One guard was nicknamed the Farmer's Boy," I said, "and it stuck with him to the end. Farmer's Boy, that's a laugh, he was old enough to be our grandfather but he had a ruddy complexion and happy-looking face so that's what we called him. He treated us okay. We liked him."

"And the boss, what was he like?"

"You mean the camp commandant?"

"Yes."

A shiver ran the length of my spine. Suddenly I was aware of just how cold it was. It was late afternoon, any warmth in the sun had long gone.

"Mr West?"

"Engelskircher was his name, Unter-Feldwebel Johann Arthur Engelskircher. We just called him John the Bastard. John the Bastard of 398 Battalion, Landesschutzen, Gliwice. Served in the Kaiser's Navy. Originally from Torgau in Saxony."

I walked on. I changed the subject.

"I'd never even seen a coal mine before, Mania. I was bloody terrified. I didn't have a great head for heights. If I'd known that the shaft was over

148

one thousand feet deep, I'd have thrown myself at the electric fence or given Hoppe a good sorting and faced the firing squad."

We now stood just a few yards from the pit head. I was aware of a slip of a girl standing by my side again.

She reached for my hand again.

"The first morning was the worst. We had been woken at six o'clock and given a chunk of bread and some weak coffee. They took us to meet the civilians, the men who had worked the pit before the war. They were all elderly Polish men, skin and bones, devoid of any hope in their eyes. We were to find out that their families had been ripped apart by the Nazis. Their young sons had been either forced to fight on the Eastern Front or were taken hundreds of miles away from their homes into slave labour camps. Even their daughters had been forced to work in factories. But those miners were the lucky ones because they'd all worked the mine before the war. They were classed as experienced workers."

Those poor men, I could still remember some of their faces; the Germans treated them like dogs. They got the worst of the rations and some of them were working twelve-hour shifts, seven days a week. They stayed in the camp with us; the Germans wouldn't even allow them home to see their wives. And they died in there too.

The Germans and the overseers sent them into the most dangerous areas of the mine. Carbon monoxide poisoning was a constant threat. I lost count of the poor Polish men who were sometimes rushed up to the surface, vomiting, struggling for breath, some barely conscious and for many it was too late. They didn't make it in time.

There were roof collapses too, the poor Poles were sent into areas of the mine that were poorly maintained, where the pit props were clearly struggling to hold up the tons of rock above them. And these men were experienced, they knew as they were forced into tunnels to dig out the coal that there was a real chance that they wouldn't make it out alive. The overseers down there were mostly Volksdeutsch, Germans whose parents and grandparents had settled in Poland, where their children had been born some generations ago but were very much still considered German. There was a real hatred between them and the native Poles.

The Volksdeutsch carried pistols, which they drew on the Poles on a regular basis. They carried batons called 'pit sticks' which they beat the men with. Sometimes they were beaten just because the overseer claimed they weren't meeting their quotas.

Over the years, many of the Polish men were overcome by the fumes or killed in collapses. They were there one day, missing the next. We asked about them. They were our good friends, but the other Poles just seemed to shrug it off, it was part of life under the Nazi yoke. All they could do was concentrate on their own survival. I tried to talk to them a lot, I tried to encourage them, tell them that the war was going well and that it would soon be over. I told them that for the best part of five long years.

Mania gave my hand a tug. "Mr West, tell me what happened."

"We were taken to a clear patch of cobblestones and there, in a great dirty heap, was the pit gear and clothing. It was filthy; I could see something moving in the dirty great pile. Hoppe was there and he ordered us to dress. I pulled on a leather helmet and a light coat, trousers and a dark striped smock, rough material that made me itch. They segregated us into small groups. Terry Downs was there, the guards called him 'baby' because he was just a youngster, he had joined up at sixteen and Bill Hennessey the boxer was there too and Ray Glover from the Durham Light Infantry. They assigned us to some civvy Silesian miners, the groups were known as Abteilungs. When we were dressed, we made our way to the pit head and they herded us towards the two-storey cages, about twenty men to a cage."

I took a deep breath.

"As I said, the first time was the worst. I just closed my eyes as the cage dropped like a stone into the depths. The Silesians were laughing at us, one of them gripped me by the arm and said to me in German that we were the lucky ones; that working the pit was a grand job. I opened my eyes, he was grinning. There was something in his eyes that told me he was actually quite genuine."

Yes, the cage was a bloody nightmare. Every time I set foot in there I broke out into a cold sweat, but once we were down there it wasn't all that bad. We were safe, away from our camp commandant and the other sadistic bastards at ground level and we bonded within our own little Abteilung. The mine shafts were unusually high, almost cavern-like, so we could work without stooping. The work kept us fit and, more importantly, kept our minds occupied. We spoke a mixture of English and German; the Silesians were as keen to learn English as I was to learn German, most of them were nice chaps, a little older than us, but grand chaps. We worked a thirteen-day shift, with one Sunday off in two. On the last day, we washed our clothes in the shower."

"You had showers?" Mania asked.

"We did. There were showers and a tiled washroom on a lower level. A few weeks into the brewery camp, we were given a razor and a toothbrush from the Red Cross. We took our time down there. In a way the Silesian was right, we had it better than some of the lads in Lamsdorf."

I learned most of my German down the mine; we spoke to each other one sentence in English and one in German.

Mania gently pressured me for more information. She was keen to learn. She had an ex-POW in her midst to provide living history and she was like a dog with a bone. It was question after question.

"Everything in the mine here was enormous. The coal face was ten feet high in places and the pit props were the size of trees. We enlarged it every morning by blasting with explosives inserted into the seam. Of course, we were never allowed anywhere near the explosives."

Safety didn't come into it. We were expendable; we knew that, both the prisoners and the Silesian civilians. It was dangerous work and if a prisoner died as a result of a mining accident, then the Germans reported it as such. Miners were killed regularly, even in England. The year before the war, I remember on the radio, hearing that nearly a hundred were killed in an explosion in Derbyshire. Coal miners dying, it was no big deal, part of the job.

"We worked two shifts, morning and afternoon. On the night shift, we extended the conveyor belt another two yards deeper into the seam ready for the next day. The coal was shovelled onto the conveyor belt that ran to the wagons. It was tough work, there were a lot of rats down there, but it had electricity throughout and bright lights."

"Rats," said Mania, "how disgusting."

Chapter 27

SILENT NIGHT

"**Working** in the coal mine had its compensations when the winter weather arrived. It was so cold up top, but the mine was always quite warm. I was on the coalface for four years."

"And were there Germans down there?" asked Mania.

"Yes, but they were just overseers, they left us alone for the most part, they made sure we didn't jam up the machinery."

We were very aware that we were assisting with the German war effort and a lot of the lads, me included, tried our best to stop the production. We learned that the coal we were digging was being converted into a crude petrol substitute that was powering the Luftwaffe. Indirectly, we were enabling the bombing raids on our own families back home.

"We tried our best to derail the coal trucks by jamming steel pegs into the tracks and managed it most months. A derailed coal truck meant at least twenty-four hours lost production. The Polish Silesians were in on the act too, they hated the bloody Germans, I think they derailed the trucks more than we did."

I noticed Mania beaming when I said that. I left out the detail that some of those sabotage attempts resulted in executions at the pit head. We British soldiers fared much better because getting caught in an act of sabotage meant just a severe beating and a trip back to Lamsdorf to spend a week in the cooler, solitary confinement.

It was hard work and, at times, brutal and back-breaking, but it wasn't all bleak.

I had to explain to Mania how we got paid and how the Germans sometimes allowed us to go into town with a guard in tow. She was shocked.

"You didn't escape?"

"No."

This was a big part of my guilt, especially when I returned home and learned just how many people had attempted to escape. During the 1950s, while I was at Medical School, there were dozens of books published by escaped POWs. The truth was that most were recaptured quite quickly. How many times had I been asked this back home by work colleagues, sometimes even by my family?

Mania stood with her hands on her hips. Suddenly her newly adopted grandfather wasn't the hero she first thought.

This time it was me who reached for her hand. "Walk with me."

I took her back towards the pit head, Antoni followed on behind. We climbed up a few stone steps onto a big cement block.

I stopped and pointed west. "What country lies over there, Mania?"

"Why, the GDR, East Germany of course."

"Yes," I nodded. "So no point in escaping west, was there?"

"Of course not," she agreed.

I turned one hundred and eighty degrees. "And what about escaping to the east?"

"Perhaps... "

"Not a chance Mania, we would have to walk three hundred miles through German-occupied Poland, and even then, we would only reach Ukraine, which was also occupied by Germany and half the population sided with the Nazis."

"So impossible to escape east then?"

"I suppose so." She didn't look so convinced.

I turned around to face south. "Your knowledge of history is second to none, Mania."

"Thank you."

"And what about your geography, what countries lie due south of here?"

She faltered. I could see the cogs turning in her head. I turned to Geoff. He shrugged his shoulders too.

"I'll tell you what countries lie south shall I?"

She nodded.

"Czechoslovakia and Hungary." I turned again and faced her directly. "And who occupied Czechoslovakia in the war?"

"The Germans."

"Correct," I said, "and Hungary was in the Axis."

I turned due north. I looked out over Poland. I told her that if we walked north without stopping, we would come to the port of Gdansk.

"Heading north to Gdansk was the only possible way to escape and the Germans knew it. It was pointless heading east, west, or south so the Germans packed Poland with troops and if by a miracle, you made the three hundred mile trek to Gdansk without getting caught or shot; well done. It was crawling with Jerries and getting on board a ship heading out to somewhere neutral like Sweden, was virtually impossible."

I didn't need to tell Mania about Sweden during the war. She knew her history. Although the Scandinavian country maintained a neutral stance, they also allowed the Wehrmacht full use of their railway system and even German troops on leave were allowed free movement on the railways. The German war machine stomped unhindered through neutral Sweden for most of the war. Even if we made it by boat to Sweden, we were still only halfway home.

"You'd better believe that we thought it through, Mania. There were escape committees back in Lamsdorf. We had maps and there were civilian clothes smuggled in and fake IDs too. But every time we worked it out, we concluded that it was just bloody impossible."

"But many men escaped from Lamsdorf," she said.

"Yes, they did," I answered honestly, "but most were caught and a lot of them were shot."

But there was another reason we didn't escape.

"There were two Palestinian boys, my age." I looked them up in my notebook. "Eliahu Krauze and Berl-Dov Eisenberg were their names. They were both Polish Jews, originally from Lodz, and serving in the British Pioneer Corps. They would have been under no illusions about how much danger they were in. Three of the Palestinians made it out of the E593 billet one evening. The Germans caught Krauze and Eisenberg about seventy miles away. They'd been walking around in circles for days trying to avoid the Gestapo.

The Germans were furious. John the Bastard stepped up his sadism to a new level. The day after they'd returned to their camp, he and one of the guards, Fritz Pantke, took them into the fields, pretending to look for the other escapee. When they were out of sight of the camp, he drew his pistol and shot them both in the back. He pretended they'd tried to escape again. Krauze was killed instantly; poor Eisenberg was badly injured, but conscious. He didn't really stand a chance — the British medics did what

154

they could for him at the Lamsdorf hospital, but he died a month later. Before he died, he'd told the medics exactly what had happened; they'd both been shot in cold blood.

And then they halved our rations for two weeks, just to teach us all a lesson. Our Sundays off were cancelled for months and we were all made to work an extra hour every day.

Krauze and Eisenberg's escape attempt had cost them, and us, dearly. Although I badly wanted to try and get away, I made a pledge to the boys in E72 that I would never do that to them. I'd never forgive myself if my mates were punished because of my foolhardy actions."

"I understand," Mania said.

I think she did.

Suddenly, despite the gloomy mood, I began to remember the lighter, even funny, stories during my time here at the mine. It felt as if a cloud was lifting. With every little anecdote, I looked at the smiling faces of Mania and Antoni, occasionally Geoff.

"They called our accommodation the Bier Halle but in 1942 they moved us. They had built some wooden billets right next to the mine. They gave us a day off to move accommodation and, on the day, there was a Red Cross food parcel waiting for us in the new billet. It was a hot summer's day and they let us walk the short distance to a lake of clear water. It was a man-made lake, caused by the extraction of clay, which was baked and used as bricks for the pit. I remember that the water was crystal clear, and the lads could almost touch the brilliant red, clear bottom as we dived in after they told us we could swim. I had never learnt to swim, so I just sat on the edge dangling my legs in the water and enjoying the moment. It was a sheer joy, something we hadn't experienced for years and reminded me of happier times."

Geoff was by my side again.

We took a walk around and to my amazement, we found the exact place. It looked much smaller than I remembered and the water looked filthy.

"This is it. This is the lake."

There was a notice in Polish. Mania translated. It meant 'Danger, no swimming'. We walked a little further.

"Over there, that's where we played football. There was a guard called Potkempe. He was rumoured to be an international referee and took his job very seriously. Rooms one and two would play against rooms three and four, and he would be the ref. There were a lot of Welsh lads in three and four, so it was quite a competitive affair, there was a big rivalry between us and the Welsh lads when we took to the pitch and no quarter was given."

"Jesus," Geoff said, "I thought it was just George who got sent to a holiday camp, football, swimming… "

"And we boxed and held music sessions."

"Music sessions!" Geoff exclaimed. He was laughing. "A bloody holiday camp I tell you."

"The Germans gave you instruments?" Mania queried.

"No, we had to save our camp money and buy them ourselves. After a while, we'd gathered enough instruments to make our own E72 Orchestra. Engelskircher fancied himself as a bit of a musician and sometimes he muscled in. He played the drums, out of time of course; there was nothing we could do to stop him spoiling everything. But he did allow Colin Bissett, one of our New Zealanders, to go into town to buy a replacement bow for his violin. In fact he went with him. Later, we had a whip-round of our camp money and Colin was able to buy a beautiful antique violin from a music shop somewhere in Silesia. Colin had been a talented violinist before the war. The guards called him Bisset Immer mit seiner Geige, Bisset always with his violin. I heard later that his precious violin somehow made it home to New Zealand, somewhat battered after the Long March, but amazingly still playable.

One Christmas, we had the most magical moment. I can't remember which year, but it was the only winter there was no snow. It was a pitch-dark, clear night. We'd gathered outside with our orchestra for some carol singing. Of course, none of us knew any of the words and it soon got to the la-la-la stage. We started trying to sing Silent Night when a guard outside the wire joined in. He sang in German, and he had a wonderfully clear voice; we went silent until he finished. Colin played his violin, doing his best to keep in time with him. The guard and his prisoner were working together to create a spiritual duet. None of us wanted the moment to ever end. We raised an enormous cheer for the two of them.

Stille Nacht, Hellige Nacht, Schlaf in himmlischer ruh. Sleep in heavenly peace.

I can hear that beautiful voice now."

Chapter 28

MESS POT LETTERS

I pulled my coat collar up to my neck. Antoni and Mania were already back at the car. In the last ten minutes the wind had picked up and flurries of light snow were blowing around the pithead like mini-tornadoes.

While I really didn't want to hang around the mine too much longer, I felt there were many stories left untold. No worries. Perhaps tonight we would talk some more. Mania and Antoni had climbed into the car and Antoni turned on the engine for heat. Once again, through the misty, steamed-up windows, I noticed him lean forward for the glove compartment and his own special brand of central heating.

I waited. I wanted another few minutes here. Just me and my brother.

"Have you heard of a Dear John letter?" I asked Geoff.

"Can't say that I have."

"I'm a great people watcher, Geoff. Ever since I can remember I've looked at people and wondered what is going on in their heads." I looked up and pointed at the old derelict winding towers. "I think my career as a psychiatrist was forged here, watching men losing everything they had, I watched them lose hope and I watched them crumble. The violence and brutality took its toll, but it was the mind games that tipped some men over the edge."

"The edge?"

"Yes, that oh so thin line where sanity ends, and insanity begins. The edge… where the only people who know where it is are the ones who have gone over it."

Geoff smiled. "Very profound Einstein, and what has that got to do with your letter to John?"

"I was here five years, Geoff, letters from back home were the only thing that kept me going. The hope that someday it would all be back to normal, and I'd be home enjoying a Sunday lunch with the family or a night in the pub with some of the boys. Letters were our lifeblood, the only thing we had to hold on to. I saw men ripping themselves inside out because they hadn't received any letters when the rest of us did."

"And what about the Dear John letters?"

I stopped, placed a hand on Geoff's shoulder. "Those letters were the worst, those and the mess pot letters."

"The what?"

"Well, there were the mess pot letters; we even had a board for mess pot letters. I swear those boys had some nerve pinning their letters up so that everyone else could read them."

"Just explain, Eric!"

Geoff was getting frustrated.

"A mess pot letter was a letter from their wife or girlfriend telling them that their wretched lives in captivity had taken an almighty turn for the worse, that their dearly devoted womenfolk had, in fact, had a baby by another man."

"No... "

"Yes."

"And they pinned the letters up for everyone to see?"

"They did?"

"Why?"

"For their own sanity Geoff. It was a mechanism to cope."

I told Geoff how one wife had had the bare-faced nerve to try and tell her husband that she'd been standing in a cinema queue when a young woman had thrust a baby into her arms and ran away. The letter from the wife described how it was a cold night and she couldn't just leave the baby in the street.

"And he believed her?"

I shook my head. "Of course he didn't, but can you imagine the shame?"

"And he pinned it up on the board?"

"He did. There was another letter I recall, from a wife who worked on a farm. She'd had two babies by two different Italian POWs and had the cheek to say she'd slept with not just one enemy soldier but two!"

"My God."

We were laughing, my brother and me, because like the incarcerated men who'd been delivered a mess pot letter, we saw the funny side. It was

158

gallows humour, because if those men didn't laugh, then they'd surely cry forever.

"Words, Geoff, they were just words on a scrap of paper, but those words could tear a man's heart to pieces. These were men who were suffering from shell shock, they'd watched their best mates slaughtered at Dunkirk, lost their brothers and comrades. The only thing that they had to cling onto had been ripped away from them in the cruellest way they could possibly imagine. When I took over as interpreter, I studied those mess pot men, Geoff. It was no laughing matter. They put on a brave face, but I watched them closely."

I noticed sometimes how they started to talk to themselves.

Just a few words at first, sitting on their bunks, sometimes clutching the letter that had changed everything. Some stared into space for hours. I can't recall any who cried, but perhaps I'm just blocking that out. Then there were the men of religion. They prayed, they prayed out loud, asking their God if they were being tested, asking their God to intervene.

"There was an older man from Kent, the son of a vicar. He prayed that if he ever met up with his God in heaven, then his God would have to beg his forgiveness for what he'd been through. He'd had it particularly bad, lost a lot of mates, his battalion had taken a right hiding. I remember the first time he discovered that the Nazis worshipped the same God he did. He was in denial; he wouldn't have it. He said it was impossible, the Nazis had no God, they worshipped the Devil he said. Eventually, we got him to talk to one of the German guards who confirmed his worst nightmare, and he was never the same again."

"He got a mess pot letter too?"

"He did. His wife had been sleeping with the local vicar, a conscientious objector who managed to get out of active service. He'd spent six months in prison and then got out and comforted the wife who was struggling with her husband's absence. He comforted her while her knickers lay around her ankles."

Geoff and I had a laugh about that vicar comforting the wife, but who were we to judge? It's no wonder men lost their minds.

Most of the men in E72 were in their early twenties. They'd just discovered the pleasures of the female flesh. Their wives and girlfriends back home were no different. And then they'd been given eight weeks training, a Lee Enfield rifle and a uniform then told to go and kill Germans.

I started to laugh as I remembered another mess pot letter, one that had been sent to a bloke called Bill, from a little village way out in Herefordshire, a place that nobody had ever heard of.

"What is it?" Geoff asked.

"Bill got a letter from his missus. I watched as he sat on his bunk reading it and he wasn't too well educated so he always took an age to read his letters from home. Quite often he'd come over and ask me what a certain word was. Any word over six letters and he was snookered."

"You're kidding."

I wasn't.

"I'd read my letter several times over and pushed it under my mattress for safekeeping when Bill started leaping in the air. He announced that his wife was pregnant and that he was going to be a father again. The poor man was genuinely ecstatic, it was the happiest I'd seen him since we'd met."

Geoff threw me a puzzled look. "And so what? It's a cause for celebration, isn't it?"

"He'd been a POW for three years, Geoff."

"Aww… shit, his wife had been playing away and he didn't even know."

I shook my head slowly. "I tried to let him down gently. I asked Bill if he knew how long the gestation period of a woman was."

"And?"

"He asked me what a gestation was. He thought it was a vegetable."

Geoff put his hands over his eyes and couldn't stop laughing and yet it wasn't funny anymore.

"The lads were laughing at him too; one of them was on his back on his bunk, couldn't control himself and said it was the funniest thing he'd ever heard. I looked at Bill and knew I had to tell him. He looked around the billet at the lads laughing and just didn't get it. I stood up, told him that we should go for a little walk around the camp."

"And what happened?"

"He didn't believe me at first and then it registered… he realised that was why the lads were laughing. They were laughing at him."

"Poor bastard."

"Indeed. Bill deliberately attacked a German guard a few days later. It was a vicious assault as he took out his anger on the poor bugger. After that, he disappeared from the camp. We didn't see him again."

Chapter 29

LOVE AND AFFECTION

Husbands and wives were separated through no fault of their own, some of them for five years. They had expected loyalty from their wives; after all, they were fighting for them and their families.

They accepted the danger, the very real possibility of death, the years away in a foreign land, the not knowing when their captivity would end. It wasn't much to expect from the girls back home, they reasoned.

Those mess pot wives were ridiculed, left without a leg to stand on. Pinning those letters to the mess pot board was a sort of divorce statement; it was a way of telling your mates that you wouldn't stand for the betrayal.

"We were all human, Geoff, we all need love, we all need affection, and yes, of course, a sexual release of some sort. We had Polish and Silesian girls working at the mine; their men had been taken away too.

There were a few lads who took Polish girlfriends, it was more common than you think, one lad, Ray, he was in the Durham mob, his Polish bird Anna had a child. Everyone knew about their love affair except for the Germans. They were besotted with each other."

I looked out in the distance over a dark and dreary Bytom. "Ray and Anna's child will be around forty-five years old now. He or she is out there somewhere if they survived."

My mind drifted. Those poor Russian girls.

"We had a briquette factory on the site, a place where they made small coal bricks from the dust and debris we brought up from the mine. It was a twenty-four-hour operation and the lads on light duties would work in there too, lads recovering from injury. The Germans treated the poor Russian girls like animals. They'd been brought to the camp when their villages and towns had been torched by the Nazis, their men, their brothers, husbands, and fathers killed in front of them."

I remembered one girl who told me that they'd shot her grandparents in her back garden as they stood and made her watch. Most of the older generation were exterminated.

"The girls they brought here were all in their twenties. John the Bastard, the cockroach that he was, was never far away from them."

"He was your camp commander?"

"Yes."

"He raped them?"

"Yes, he and his minions would sneak into their barracks and visit them regularly. Sometimes they didn't even wait until they'd finished work; the guards would rape them in the factory as a punishment while everyone looked on. They'd beat and humiliate them; the younger guards would be encouraged to take part, an initiation test, a rite of passage. More than a few of those poor Russian girls never recovered from the experience. Suicide rates were high in the briquette factory."

Geoff shook his head.

I tried to get my bearings and wondered where the factory was situated but it wasn't coming back to me.

"We had to march every day past that brick factory and most of the time the poor girls were half-naked. John the Bastard warned us just to look. Any prisoner caught fraternising with the Russian girls would be shot. We'd been there about six months when some of the lads started to talk. They were thrown into close proximity with these girls and nature took its course. It was their only escape from the daily loneliness and terror they were subjected to. It was just about the only part of the lives they could control themselves."

I turned to Geoff. "Imagine that?"

"I can't."

"The girls were regularly beaten by the Germans and lived in beastly, filthy conditions. They were told when to eat and what to eat, when to shower, their working day controlled to the minute; even told what time to take a piss. The only thing that brought them a little dignity, Geoff, was when they volunteered their bodies willingly. The Germans didn't even provide them with any underwear; they were draped in sackcloth, their undernourished breasts sagging through the thin material. That was it, Geoff, that was all they had."

162

I often wondered what happened to those poor girls after the war. I looked over towards the car. Some of those girls weren't much older than Mania.

"I'm sure a few cigarettes or some food may have changed hands, but the boys all said to a man, that the girls were more than just prostitutes, they saw it as a way of defying the Germans, the only thing they could do to protest."

"And love affairs, Eric?"

"Yes, Geoff, without a doubt. Those girls had nothing; their families had been wiped from the face of the earth. They craved love and affection, both mentally and physically."

"And the Dear John letter, what was that all about, Eric?"

"My dear brother," I said, as I took a deep breath. "A Dear John letter is the worst sort of letter any prisoner can receive."

And there were scores of them during my time in the camp and more than a dozen suicides that I can recall.

"A Dear John letter is a letter from your girl, telling you that she has fallen in love with someone else and that you are surplus to requirements. It is a letter that you can do nothing about because you are incarcerated thousands of miles away with no possible way of returning home to patch things up. Those letters were a fate worse than death for a POW. A Dear John letter is worse than a mess pot letter because a Dear John letter leaves you with no dignity."

Geoff didn't reply but I noticed he'd gone very pale. Probably the cold.

"C'mon," I said and pointed. "The car."

I walked over slowly. "That's the worst thing, Geoff. There is nothing you can do about it and as you curl up at night on a thin, cold, hessian mattress, your wife or the girl you absolutely adore is probably curled up in the arms of another man. He's free, you're not."

Geoff muttered something as he ducked into the car, and I eased in beside him.

"And they start to bond, Geoff, and you know they are starting to bond while you can do nothing but complete your shift at the mine or wherever it is the Nazis have sent you. You have nothing to look forward to but that evening's cabbage soup."

Geoff grunted.

"It's enough to push a man over the edge, Geoff."

163

The Dear Johns were never put on the mess pot board. There was nothing to laugh about in the Dear John letters. They were daggers through the heart.

Chapter 30

EXECUTION

We were heading back to Antoni's flat. It had been agreed that I would stay one more evening; the dollars had been tucked away in Antoni's coat pocket. Mania was delighted of course, and I looked forward to the family dinner that I was sure Elwira was now preparing. Antoni, once again, had stopped at a phone box and called ahead. There wasn't much conversation in the car on the way back to the flat, I think my companions knew that it had taken a lot out of me.

As we drew up at the flat, Antoni appeared a little concerned. I looked up and noticed Elwira standing at the window and looking nervously through the curtains. She caught Antoni's eye and he nodded at her. A car was parked on the other side of the road. I noticed the figures of two shady-looking men inside, I thought I recognised one of them. The car door opened, they both got out and walked towards us. I don't know why but a shiver ran the length of my spine. Sure enough, one of them was familiar to me. It was the man in the suit who had challenged us on the train to Katowice. I couldn't quite believe it. Had they really been shadowing us for nearly two days?

They approached Antoni. He looked terrified as did young Mania. They questioned him, I heard him mention some of the places that he'd taken us, Szombierki and Bytom. The other man nodded as Antoni mentioned the places. I figured that they had perhaps been trying to trip him up, get him to lie about where we had been. I wasn't unduly worried because if they had tracked us, they would surely have put two and two together and reached the conclusion that I was genuine. I kept looking over, smiling at the suit.

Antoni's interrogation lasted less than five minutes and they seemed satisfied. As they turned to walk away, I held out a hand to bid them goodbye. They didn't take it, instead, in perfect English, the suit told me that they'd be watching us. At that moment, the irony struck home. We'd gone to war to liberate Poland, forty-six long years ago. Had anything changed here for the better?

Elwira had been busy again. After a worried-looking exchange of words between her and Antoni, she eventually greeted us with a big smile and I got the impression that she too, was enjoying the experience. It was a break in what must have been a bleak existence, dining with someone other than her children and an overweight, dour husband.

As we walked into the lounge Mania tilted her nose in the air and took a deep breath. "Mmm… mother has been baking fresh bread."

It was late, the other children were tucked up in bed and within ten minutes of our arrival, we were sitting at the table gossiping like old friends. Mania had taken charge and was explaining everything to her mother in Polish. Now and again I heard Pan West and picked up on the route we had taken and the visit to the cemetery at Szombierki.

Elwira listened hard; she appeared genuinely interested in everything her daughter had to say. Elwira brought in another huge bowl and plonked it into the middle of the table. Mania glowed with pride as she explained that this was a Królewski stew. In the old days, it was only served to the nobility. It was full of exotic and quite expensive spices; a special dish generally reserved for Easter and Christmas. I gathered that my dollar contributions meant that there had been a little more money to go around.

Unlike last night's fayre, there was more meat than cabbage. It was delicious and I had to admit, that the bloody vodka complemented the dinner perfectly. We ate from earthenware bowls with a spoon in one hand and a chunk of fresh bread in the other. After my six years as a widower, it felt good to be part of a family again.

Antoni disappeared quite quickly after dinner, I'm not surprised, he must have downed an entire bottle of vodka during the course of the day. God knows what state his liver was in. Nevertheless, despite his seasoned drinking, he was definitely a little unsteady on his feet. Mania and I chatted in English and Elwira listened in for some time, clearly very proud of her daughter's grasp of the English language. To be honest I was too tired to think and talk in German. Mania's eagerness to talk English made it all too easy.

Soon it was just me and Mania.

"Tell me about Mr Blythin," she said suddenly. She took me by surprise, and she poured out a small vodka. "He was killed at the mine was he not?"

"Yes."

"Did someone kill him?"

I nodded slowly. "Yes... the camp commandant, the man Engelskircher."

I explained to Mania that the commandant was not a nice man and there was a Polish civilian called Riedel, he was a nasty piece of work too.

"Sadly, Mania, war gives men power and once power has been granted, there will always be those who will abuse it. Just like the commandant of the camp. I believe Mr Riedel was a very weak man before the war started; a nobody. I can't imagine he ever achieved anything in civilian life, a labourer perhaps, maybe he even worked in the mine before the war started, nobody knew because no one would ever talk to him."

"And he mistreated the men?"

"He did," I answered. "Riedel would punch and kick us for little or no reason and two of the men had had enough. Blythin and Adam Bromley lodged an official complaint to Engelskircher. I think it was the spring of 1943 and they went to Engelskircher's office. I tried to tell them that the commandant wouldn't listen and sure enough, after twenty minutes they both walked into our small restroom area in the old sawmill. Bromley said that Engelskircher hadn't listened to what they'd had to say, took Riedel's side and accused them of refusing to work. Blythin and Bromley said that they hadn't refused to work; they just refused to work with Riedel. Adam Bromley was a tough Glaswegian; he said he would have Riedel for breakfast if it hadn't meant a bullet to the back of the neck."

Mania said she didn't know why Mr Bromley would want to eat Riedel for breakfast.

I had to laugh. "It's an English expression, Mania, it means Riedel wouldn't have stood a chance if he and Riedel had decided to fight."

"I see."

"And this is what I was explaining: certain men took advantage of the situation; they were brutal to some of the prisoners because they knew the prisoners couldn't fight back."

"They were cowards," she said.

I nodded. "Engelskircher was the same, always aggressive, always ready with a fist or a kick, but on this occasion much, much worse."

167

"He followed the men into the restroom?"

"Yes, he came in with Riedel and Engelskircher took off his belt that held his pistol holster. If I remember right, he demanded that they get to work. They said they were happy to work but not with Riedel. Engelskircher launched himself at Bromley, hitting him around the head with the belt and the gun. He fell to the floor and Engelskircher kept hitting him, kicking him in the stomach repeatedly. Eventually, Bromley staggered to his feet and Engelskircher kicked him out of the door. He turned his attention to David Blythin, told him he would be next if he didn't get to work immediately."

I'll never forget David's face that day, a mixture of Welsh determination and pride. He was going to stick to his guns. I knew it wasn't going to end well.

"And he shot him?"

I shook my head. "Not straight away, he started to hit Blythin with the belt, he caught him a few times and I noticed a trickle of blood on the side of his face. David snapped, he threw a punch at Engelskircher and caught him on the top of the shoulder. Engelskircher flew into a fury and eventually, they both fell to the floor. In a flash, Engelskircher pulled his pistol from the holster and jammed it into the side of David's face."

I paused. I was aware that my bottom lip was trembling... it was all coming back to me, as fresh today as it had been all of those years ago.

Mania reached across the table and stroked the back of my hand. "Mr West... "

I looked down at the table, at the now empty vodka glass.

"I thought it was just a threat, Mania, I thought that would be the end of it... but... no, he pulled the trigger."

Mania clasped her hand over her face as she tightened her grip on my hand.

We could do nothing but watch and keep quiet. It was a feeling of pure helplessness, knowing that if we'd intervened in any way, we'd... "

Mania knew. I didn't need to finish the story.

I had been standing just yards away. In the small, confined space, the noise was deafening, and I noticed David's body go limp. I knew then he was dead. I wiped something from my shirt, blood, small fragments of bone and grey matter. As I sank to my knees, I noticed that there wasn't much left of the back of David's head and a large pool of blood spread slowly onto the floor behind him.

I lifted my head. "Engelskircher executed my friend in cold blood, in the restroom of Ostholz Sawmills. I'll never forget David's face and his lifeless corpse."

The nightmares continue to this day. There were tears in Mania's eyes, and in mine too.

Chapter 31

JOHN THE BASTARD

The night wasn't over, despite the late hour. I had shed a tear relaying the story about David Blythin, yet dare I say it, I felt glad that I had. I had read somewhere, I can't think where, that unhappiness cannot lie in a man's soul when it is wet with tears. It made perfect sense.

I told Mania about Blythin's funeral. She was surprised as I described the camp procession. I had a recollection that even Engelskircher had taken part in the ceremony but wasn't one hundred percent sure. I wondered if that had been part of some bizarre nightmare. A photograph... yes... I'm sure I'd seen a photograph at some point, the coffin being carried by the prisoners. Mears was there, I think, he was our camp man of confidence at that time, and right there at the front, holding the bloody coffin, a pallbearer, some bastard in a Nazi uniform. The indignity of it all, the coffin carried by the executioners.

Mania's soft voice brought me back from my thoughts. "But there was a proper funeral procession in the camp?"

"There was."

"But surely you are imagining it."

I wasn't. Mania had heard all about the Nazi cruelty, their lack of respect for prisoners and the vision of a respectful funeral was totally alien to her. There had been no funerals for the Russians, her fellow countrymen or the Palestinians. I wish I could have found the photograph and shown her. As she looked across the darkened table into my eyes, I could see that she thought it was an old man's fantasy.

I found myself telling Mania more pleasant stories, the more I told her the more came back to me and the names were dropping from my lips. I could still see the faces of those young men in their prime. I recalled Terry Downs and his brother; Terry loved to box.

"Can you imagine the poor mother, Mania? Both of her sons captured, she would have received two telegrams telling her that her boys were missing in action."

Geoff and I had discussed those missing in action telegrams on the flight into Warsaw. It was a little hope for a mother to hang onto if they didn't end with 'presumed dead.' God knows what went through their minds as they opened the envelope the telegram boy had delivered.

Damn! I couldn't remember Terry's brother's name. I do remember when the Red Cross sent boxing gloves and a length of rope to construct a ring, Terry couldn't wait to mark it out and his brother helped him construct the four wooden posts that they cemented into the ground. Poor Terry, he was never happier than when he was knocking hell out of a fellow prisoner, and then afterwards, they'd be best mates again. A boxer's bond he called it.

"His bond with his brother was stronger than anything I'd ever seen; they simply couldn't bear to be parted and one day, Engelskircher announced that they were working different shifts. Terry's brother wasn't going to have it and deliberately poured boiling water onto his hand."

"What a silly thing to do."

"It probably was, he thought he'd be excused a couple of days sick leave and then he'd be put on the same shift as his brother again. But it didn't work; instead, they sent him to the main camp at Lamsdorf. He never returned to the mine."

There were a lot of self-inflicted injuries at the camp, mostly from men who couldn't face that dark descent into the shaft. It was hard to tell what was self-inflicted and what wasn't. Taffy Worth lost a finger or two I remember, and another chap stuck his hand into a rubber belt. I think he was looking for a slight friction burn that would excuse him from work for a few days. Bloody hell, his arm got stuck and at one point I thought the machine was going to rip his arm off. I was first on the scene. There was no such thing as an emergency stop in those days. Even if there had been, nobody would have heard above the racket down there. Between the two of us, we managed to drag his arm out before the belt took a real hold. Poor bugger had every inch of skin peeled from his arm, he was like a skinned rabbit from his wrist to his elbow and he broke four fingers. They sent him back to the Lamsdorf hospital; he was away nearly three weeks before he returned. I told Mania how George also lost the tip of his finger, he had

171

caught it in a loop of wire and it ripped the end off like a knife cutting through butter.

"And they didn't sew it back on?" she asked.

I had to laugh. "No, Mania. They threw it away for the rats to eat and bandaged it back up. He got a few days off work but was back down the mine the following week."

Mania shook her head. "The poor man. No hospital then?"

"No, it had to be something fairly serious before the Germans considered a hospital visit. The Russians, they never went to hospital, they just let those poor men die."

Mania's face took on an expression that I hadn't seen before. I couldn't quite describe the look as she started to speak.

"There was a hospital just north of here called Lubliniec. It would have been called Loben in those days."

My blood turned to ice.

"Have you heard of it, Mr West, they sent some of the British POWs there?"

"Yes, Mania, I'd heard about Loben. It was a psychiatric unit and they sent a few of our Lamsdorf boys there."

"Yes," she whispered quietly. "To be honest, Mr West, they were lucky to have come out of there alive. The Germans sent Dr Ernest Buchalik to run the hospital. He wasn't a doctor; he was a monster, a mass murderer."

"I know, Mania," I said, "He ran the Nazi E-Aktion programme at Loben."

"You've heard of it too?"

"I studied it after the war. The murder of disabled and mentally ill children. Euthanasia."

I'll never forget the day I read that report. It was like something out of an Edgar Allan Poe horror novel; it was beyond the realms of human comprehension. It must have been the late fifties, early sixties when the documentation found its way to the World Psychiatric Association. The whole world knew of course, but until you see the evidence it's almost as if there is a part of you that doesn't want to believe it's true. For me, the evidence was reading the secret order that Hitler had given to the Chief Reich Doctor.

I reached into my trusty leather satchel. "Give me a second. I think you should read it. I was at the Psychiatrists Association's Meeting where this was all revealed."

I rummaged around. My notes were quite well organised, several exercise books compiled by now. Loose papers and many photographs.

I located it. "Here it is; the exact words that Hitler wrote with his own hand."

I handed the piece of paper across to Mania and she read.

'There are three objectives to implement: the implementation of the idea of purity of race, striving to reduce unnecessary state expenditure on people who are unable to work and must be supported, and increase hospital facilities for the needs of the war, by removing creatures unworthy of life.'

Mania looked up in a rage. "That man, that horrible, evil bastard. How dare he call them that, how dare he assume the role of God. Creatures unworthy of life. Creatures."

Mania was right. Hitler played God and he answered to no one.

It was late 1939 when he decided to implement these objectives in the territory of Poland. He gave the secret order to ensure them 'death by grace'. Death by grace. How could he possibly have worded it like that? The poor mites were poisoned, they died in agony, where was the grace in that?

I remember reading the report for a second time. I read the doctor's names and somehow that hit home harder. I had long since known that Hitler was an evil madman, hell-bent on genocide and world control. But doctors?

Dr Buchalik was an entirely mediocre doctor but thrived under the new Nazi regime because he shared all their prejudices. He was well known for his hostility towards the Poles. They brought in children from Silesia, Zagłębie and Saxony. Their parents were told they were going to a sanatorium that would have long-term health benefits. Many of the parents were pleased to send their sons and daughters away. It was a tough time for everyone and feeding and looking after handicapped children in wartime wasn't easy. Little did they know that most would never return, they were packing them off to a sanatorium of death.

I recalled one of our Lamsdorf boys who returned from Loben around mid-1942. He told me that the hospital was full of loony kids. I believed that he must be mistaken. It turned out that his observation was spot on.

Initially, the children were placed in what was called Department A, run by a female doctor, Elisabeth Hecker. A female doctor... that made it much worse. Did she not have an ounce of maternal instinct in her body? How did she manage to sleep at night?

"There were stories about experimentation," Mania said.

"Yes," I nodded in agreement. "The children were all observed at first, their fate depended on Dr Hecker. If she considered the children to be minimally handicapped, some were referred to a correctional facility. That's where the experimentation would take place. God knows what sort of methods they used but, nevertheless, some lucky ones were returned to their parents.

"And the rest of them, Mr West?"

"I think you know what happened to the rest, Mania. They were deprived of their lives."

"They were gassed?"

"Oh good God, no. The Nazis weren't stupid, these were Aryan children. They were given increased doses of luminal or veronal, a kind of sleeping pill or anaesthetic. But they even experimented with this, playing with the level of doses. A lot of the children simply vomited the drugs back up, some even got used to it, but they'd increase the levels and watch the poor children stagger around like zombies. They'd keep some of the poor mites in that state for days, but they'd start to fall ill, get a fever and some bled and frothed from their mouths. Eventually, they succumbed."

"And then what, Mr West?"

"And then they covered the deaths up, they faked the cause of death. They reported to the authorities and the children's parents that they'd died from pneumonia, influenza, and cardiovascular diseases. Dr Buchalik would sign the death certificates. Who was going to argue with the eminent doctor?"

Mania was quiet for some time.

Psychiatric abuse of the patient. It's been going on for hundreds of years. Once a patient has been officially diagnosed a lunatic, everyone looks the other way. Mania made a comment about those dark days being in the past.

"Oh no, Mania," I said. "This abuse is still going on, even now. Two years ago, we ejected the USSR from our Psychiatry Association because they are still sending perfectly sane people to mental institutions."

"But why? How can they do that?"

"It's politics. Think about it. The General Secretary of the USSR must be obeyed, you can't disagree with him. But some people do, they've broken no laws so they can't be sent to prison in case the trial collapses."

"But the authorities want them out of the way."

"Exactly. And what could be a better solution than manipulating psychiatrists like me to certify them insane? No trial, no sentence, nothing! Locked up indefinitely."

"The perfect solution."

Chapter 32

INTERPRETER

As the night progressed, we inevitably drifted back to Engelskircher.

It wasn't that Mania had a morbid fascination with him, I believe she wanted to hear about his eventual demise. When she had heard what he did to my friend and the other prisoners he'd executed in cold blood, she was furious. He had murdered the Palestinians who had escaped, but there were rumours of many more killings and he had beat people up for little or no reason.

"There was another incident."

"Tell me," Mania said as she leaned forward, set her elbows on the table, and rested her chin on her clenched fists.

"I wasn't there of course; it took place in another part of the forest where the men worked in the wood camp. There was a British Sergeant, a man called Bill Bailey. He was having a break in their little hut; he said that Engelskircher had been in a foul mood, clearly hungover from the night before and smelling heavily of drink."

I think many of Engelskircher's most violent outbursts were because of alcohol. He clearly couldn't cope with his responsibilities. He was yet another mediocre individual before the war, over-promoted by the Nazi thugs to a position of power. He just didn't know where to draw the line. I dare say Engelskircher even became desensitised. He was so drunk at times he forgot what camp he was in, everything descending into a blurry haze.

"Sergeant Bailey said he burst into the hut screaming at everyone 'Raus, Raus, Raus,' slurring his words. The boys got to their feet immediately and stumbled out of the hut into the forest to begin work. As they assembled outside, they heard a shot from inside the hut. Bailey noticed that one of the Palestinians was missing. When Bailey questioned Engelskircher, he said the man had resisted and he'd shot him. Bailey was livid, said he was going to report him, but the problem was that nobody had witnessed the incident. Engelskircher drew his weapon and pointed it at the men. He told them that if they didn't get to work immediately there'd be another shooting.

The men worked for the rest of the afternoon and the Palestinian never appeared. When Bill went back to the rest hut at the end of his shift, there was a small pool of blood but no body. He felt compelled to report the missing man to the officers in charge of the guardroom. Unfortunately for Bailey, Engelskircher was also in the guardroom when he arrived. Nevertheless, he mentioned to one of the officers that a man was missing and said that he'd last saw him alone in the rest hut with Engelskircher.

Engelskircher turned casually to the guards and told them that he'd seen the man making his way into the forest alone. Because he hadn't returned, Engelskircher assumed that he must have escaped. Bailey wasn't having it and told the guards that the last time he'd seen the man was when he'd been alone in the restroom with Engelskircher.

Engelskircher jumped up from his chair, pulled his gun out, and told him to clear off, that the man had definitely escaped and how dare he question his word. When the sergeant went back to the restroom the following day, the blood had been scrubbed from the floor. They never did find the poor man's body."

I told Mania that the man was a sadist; there was no other word to describe him. Some of the things he did were beyond comprehension to us.

"The Red Cross came to inspect the huts one day and because they were all wooden, insisted that fire hoses had to be available and working for safety reasons. The day before they arrived, Engelskircher had one of the hoses connected up. It was winter, bitterly cold. Engelskircher announced he was going to test the hose for those good old boys in the Red Cross. There was no glass in our windows and Engelskircher took the head of the hose up to the open window and switched it on. He stood for more than five minutes and deliberately soaked every single mattress and the blankets with the ice-cold water. He screeched like a laughing hyena. I swear it was the craziest thing I'd ever seen.

The Red Cross team arrived the following day and Engelskircher proudly switched on the hose and demonstrated that it was in perfect working order. I'll never forget the nights we spent together, all huddled in a group, bloody freezing, the blankets were frozen stiff. Nobody slept a wink for three or four days until everything dried out."

I watched many men go mad in my time in Lamsdorf and the work camp, but Engelskircher was by far the maddest of the lot.

"And was he ever punished?" Mania asked.

"I don't know. I just remember that he wasn't there at the end of the war. There were rumours that a prisoner shot him. More likely he was killed by the Russians."

Mania smiled. "I hope so."

I couldn't help warming to this little Polish girl, yet there was a bitterness in her that I wanted to try to change. Could I make her understand that, although I had witnessed these events and the Germans had taken away five years of my life, I tried not to be bitter? If I was, I don't think I would have been able to function properly afterwards.

That thought made me remember Mary O'Leary, still detained in a Mental Hospital in Somerset. What damage had the war years done to her? Sadly, she hadn't adjusted back into civilian life. She'd turned to alcohol and snapped during what was clearly a sexual attack. But why had no one spoken up for her? Why were her records made secret, why weren't allowances made? She'd been locked up for the best part of forty years, most of that time in psychiatric hospitals. It wasn't clear to me that she had any evidence of a psychiatric disorder. I made my mind up that I needed to get Mary rehabilitated. With intensive day centre support, there was no reason why it couldn't happen. I'd make it happen.

This time it was me who reached for Mania's hand. "Don't be hostile, Mania, bitterness eats away at the soul, it festers inside you and will eventually destroy you if you let it. We must all learn to move on, to forgive and forget."

She stood up from the table abruptly and glared at me like I was her worst enemy. "I will never forgive them, I will never forgive the German people," she said, raising her voice.

I told her to sit down, to calm down. I said the German people had nothing to do with what went on in the camps but she threw it back in my face.

"They stood back and did nothing," she said. "They are as bad as the worst Nazi; don't tell me they didn't know what was happening in the slave labour camps all over Germany. Don't tell me that they didn't know what their great leader was doing to my people, don't tell me because I won't believe it."

She lectured me.

"The Nazis came for the communists and the trade unionists, and the people did nothing. They came for the disabled and the Gypsies, still they did nothing. By the time they came for the Jews, there was nobody left to stop them," she ranted.

I sat and listened. I let her get it all out and, believe me, she did. This little girl was going to get a big part in my story.

I didn't speak for a full five minutes and then when she eventually quietened down...

"They put me in Engelskircher's office. To work with him."

"I don't understand."

"You remember I mentioned Norman Gibbs?"

"Yes."

"Well, he was the camp interpreter or Dolmetscher. Poor Gibbs, for four nerve-wracking years, he had to work alongside that maniac, Engelskircher. Then one day, around the time we started hearing rumours about the D-Day landings, I saw them having a disagreement. I didn't even know what it was about, but Engelskircher was furious. Gibbs, as usual, was doing his best to keep the situation calm. I didn't know what to do. I remembered Blythin... his execution... those memories came flooding back and I was convinced Engelskircher was about to reach for his gun again."

"But he didn't?"

"No. Instead, Gibbs was dismissed and the next day he was nowhere to be seen. They had sent him to another coal mine. Engelskircher told me that, with immediate effect, I was to take over as the official camp Dolmetscher."

Mania smiled. "Oh dear."

Oh dear indeed. Despite never having to go down that awful pit again, I'd been given the worst job in the world, a middleman between my mates and that trigger-happy sadist.

"Tell me what happened," Mania said.

"Well... "

The reality is that nothing happened. Almost immediately upon being appointed, another argument broke out between a prisoner and John the Bastard, right there in his office. The fact that he hadn't shot Gibbs made some of the prisoners think that Engelskircher had softened. That wasn't the case. I could read the cunning commandant like a book. The reports filtering back from the front were becoming more and more positive for the

Allies, and Engelskircher must have seen that too. If he had any sense he would have tried to moderate his behaviour just to save his skin but the truth was that he never changed a bit. The Red Army could have been walking in through the front door and if Engelskircher was drunk, he still would have shot the prisoners.

"Mr West... "

"... yes Mania. Give me a minute."

The memories of my time in Engelskircher's office were returning. Within just a few days I had studied his makeup and knew him better than his own mother. He had no compassion, only interested in where his next bottle was coming from. I managed to get a hold of a bottle of schnapps and that became the diffuser. I told him it was a gift from the prisoners because they respected him so much. The silly bastard fell for it hook, line and sinker. I hid the bottle away in his office, told him that it would be his emergency reserve.

"Some of the prisoners were getting too bloody brave for their own good. They'd blatantly refuse to work for Engelskircher and there'd be arguments in his office. I'd have to mediate a solution to the stalemate."

Mania frowned, shook her head, "I don't know what you mean."

"Well... I remember on one occasion, one of the prisoners complained that he'd injured his wrist and couldn't complete his shift. He asked Engelskircher for a week off. Engelskircher was livid, said he was behind on the quotas and the Germans would discipline him. I stood in the middle translating. The prisoner spoke in English and Engelskircher in German, neither understood a single word the other was saying.

The prisoner called Engelskircher a heartless bastard, said he wouldn't work another single minute. Engelskircher asked me what he'd said. I told him in German that the prisoner had visited the doctor who had declared that he should be granted a week off labour."

"You lied?"

"Through my teeth, Mania," I grinned. "The man hadn't even seen the doctor, but he was clearly in some discomfort, his wrist all swollen."

"And what did the commandant say?"

"He reluctantly allowed him three days. I turned to the prisoner and told him that Herr Engelskircher had been very generous, and he could have his week off. The prisoner smiled, even leaned forward and shook Engelskircher's hand and thanked him."

Mania and I burst out laughing together.

"The commandant said he would go and see the doctor to confirm."

"On no!" Mania said, "you'd be found out."

I shook my head. "No, because I had a secret weapon in that bottle of schnapps. I persuaded Engelskircher that a couple of glasses in front of the coal stove in his office was a far better idea than trudging the half-mile in the snow to the doctor's office on the other side of the camp."

"But you gave the prisoner a week off, not three days, wouldn't Herr Engelskircher know?"

"No chance, he didn't know what day of the week it was because he was drunk most of the time. The prisoner got his week off and Engelskircher spent most of the days toasting himself in front of the fire."

Mania nodded. "You are a clever man, Mr West."

Clever. I'm not so sure. To me, it was a built-in instinct of survival, or Überleben to use the German word.

I began to gauge Engelskircher's moods, to know when he was sometimes ready to compromise, the days where I could ask him for a little more food for the workers, and the days when he wouldn't budge on anything. But most of the time I just made sure the men were kept out of his way. I made sure he didn't overindulge, that's when he would be at his most dangerous. I hid those bottles all over the place.

Chapter 33

MY LONG MARCH

It was almost two o'clock in the morning when Elwira appeared. She looked concerned as she joined us at the table. She understood nothing but listened carefully, studying her daughter intently and then casting glances in my direction.

She spoke in Polish, Mania turned to me and said, "My mother remembers seeing columns of British soldiers trudging through the snow at the end of the war before the Russians came. She would have been a child. She asked me if you were there, could that have been you?"

I nodded. I realised that I had made very few notes on the Long March of 1945. I suppose it was a period of my war that I wasn't yet ready to confront.

I said to Mania, "We'd heard rumours about evacuating the camp for a couple of days. In the end, it was all done in a mad hurry after the night shift had finished. One minute the men were digging coal, the next we were told to collect our belongings and get ready to march. I remember the exact day we left, 23rd January 1945. It was bitterly cold. Engelskircher had left the office a few days previously, I wasn't told where he had gone. We never saw him again. I remember realising that we had made no provisions as far as food or shelter was concerned. I was tasked with translating the guards' instructions to the men. It was clear they didn't have any idea what we were doing. I remember looking into the bewildered faces of the guards, they were herding us to nowhere in particular. During those first few days, we were all marched long and hard, twenty miles a day through deep snow. Anyone who didn't keep up was left to freeze in the nearest ditch."

I paused as Mania turned towards her mother and recounted the story. Elwira listened and nodded intermittently with rapt attention. Hearing it

182

retold in Mania's delightful Polish with all its inflections made it feel safe to go on. Despite the late hour, I felt, for the first time, I could tell my story to an interested audience. Somehow the pauses for translation made my story feel truthful and valid.

I went on, "It was chaos, brutal chaos. There must have been about twenty work camps evacuated round here: hundreds of prisoners marching in columns, three or four men abreast. I'd say there were more than three thousand men. We were marched through Hindenburg and on to Gliwice."

I heard Mania translate those place names as Zabrze and Gliwice. The name Hindenburg, with its German connotations, had been changed completely. Elwira nodded in understanding.

"The guards' only concern was the Russians, about to cross the border into the Fatherland, and what they would do. We could hear their guns constantly."

"Did they know it was over at that point?" asked Mania.

I nodded slowly. "Yes… they did, we all did."

Elwira spoke again in Polish and Mania translated.

"My mother asks, you weren't told where you were going?"

"Never."

There was more rapid-fire conversation in Polish between Mania and her mother. She turned to me and said, "Mother asks if you know the route you took, where did you end up?"

"After the first day's marching, I made a break for it, Mania. I hid in a graveyard in Gliwice. I thought I could wait there until the Russians came and I could turn myself in to them." Mania looked at me admiringly, her hero surrogate grandfather again.

"But, I got arrested by a German Feldwebel. He pointed his gun at me and said 'come on soldier, time to join your friends.' I'd had about two hours of freedom in five years. Trust my luck to get caught, but at least I'm alive to tell the tale I suppose. Your father was kind enough to stop while I visited that graveyard on our way to Lamsdorf yesterday."

I went on, "By February, it was still extremely cold, but the snow was starting to turn into wet slush. Our boot uppers were soaking wet and, after walking all day, our feet were sore. The temptation was to take our boots off at night. The problem was that the boots wouldn't go back on again. Our feet were swollen and the boot uppers froze like plywood, the leather laces snapped. We soon learned we had to sleep with boots on, if possible under straw to make it possible to endure the numbness. I decided to keep my boots on the entire time."

I looked down on my brown leather brogues. My feet carry the scars of those blisters to this day. I paused while the story was converted into the music of spoken Polish.

"Mania, we were walking in the opposite direction from our route into captivity and that helped to keep us going. And it really helped psychologically when we crossed the border into Czechoslovakia. The locals were much more friendly there, even the guards seemed to relax slightly. Some of the men kept diaries of the places we walked through, but I didn't keep any notes. A lot of the towns and villages had the signs removed. I just kept my head down and walked, trying my best to keep in step. After about five hundred miles, I do remember one place, Marienbad, a spa town in Czechoslovakia. It was stunningly beautiful there. I must have made a mental note to remember this place, and it was here I felt reconnected with the natural world that me and my friend Jack had always loved. I remember feeling the temptation to fall out, to risk being shot, just to lie down on the meadow and enjoy the sensation of spring emerging. There were fruit trees along the sides of the roads in wonderful displays of blossom."

I thought to myself, *Yes that's a place Geoff and I could visit, perhaps next year.*

"Around the beginning of April, we had crossed the border back into Germany. Now we were in Bavaria, very different to the Silesia we'd left two months previously. There were mountains in the distance, we were marching through forests and fields. The farms were still being worked, there were cows and chickens and more food to scavenge.

We started to hear heavy artillery in the distance. I overheard whispered conversations between the guards, I could tell it was all over. 'Deutschland ist Kaput' one of them said. One day some American planes flew around us before moving off to strafe some targets nearby, they returned to do a victory roll above us."

Mania translated to her mother, and I smiled as she used her outstretched hand to simulate an aeroplane rolling over the kitchen table.

"At last, I met the Americans somewhere in Bavaria. It was General Patton's Army. I waved in their direction, but to my horror one of the GIs knelt on the ground, lifted his rifle and fired two shots in my direction. I could feel my heart pounding as I realised it could be all over at the very last moment. Luckily for me, he was a rotten shot. After a few more POWs emerged, the GIs took a closer look at our rabble and realised we were British."

I took a deep breath.

Finally, I had recounted the story for the first time to anyone, not on a psychiatrist's couch but right here in my taxi driver's flat. It was the early hours of a winter's morning in communist Poland. I laughed at the ridiculousness of the situation.

It slowly sank in after forty years. I was so damn scared. There was no end destination for that darned March. The Germans had been playing for time, running away and using us as their human shields. I felt a knot in my stomach as I thought of all those pointless deaths, men who had survived five years of hell only to fall at the very last hurdle. We thought we had starved in the camps, thought that food was scarce. It was nothing compared to what we endured on those long miles through Silesia, Czechoslovakia and then southern Germany. Night after night for three months we expected at least a barn and the equipment to boil up a pot or start a warm fire. Sometimes there was nothing. We raided beet fields and scavenged for root vegetables in fields long abandoned. Occasionally, we struck lucky and came across a field of potatoes. The Germans watched on as we scrambled and scraped on our hands and knees in the frozen ground. At the point of a gun, we were forced to hand over the lion's share of what we had found.

I can't remember now whether I ended the war angry, relieved, or perhaps just shell-shocked. I know I was hungry. I'd completed an IS9 Liberation questionnaire on 30th April 1945. I handed it in to the soldiers processing us in Brussels. It reflected anger for sure. In the box entitled,

'Have you any other matter of any kind you wish to bring to notice?'

I had written,

'Being thoroughly familiar with German methods of extracting the last ounce of work from POWs in the coal mines of Silesia, I wish to draw attention to the slave methods used against us, inadequate food and refusal to replace worn-out boots or clothing.'

Now I realise I had blocked it all out, I hadn't told my wife, my children, Geoff, anybody. I remembered that when we got home the official advice for us returning POWs was, 'Least said, soonest mended.'

I'd read accounts from other POWs, I thought they had exaggerated, used a bit of poetic license to enhance their stories. Now I knew differently. I looked at Elwira's tear-streaked face as Mania finished recounting my story to her. Surely, I had been to Hell and back?

Chapter 34

TRAGEDY AT MIECHOWICE

There was another short dialogue between Mania and Elwira. Mania drew breath, turned to me and asked, "My mother says maybe you British were lucky to escape the Russian Army. Did you hear what happened at Miechowice when the Russians arrived?"

I tried to pronounce it. I got it wrong, it was quite a mouthful.

Mania smiled. "Your Polish pronunciation is terrible, Mr West."

She said something to her mother and they both laughed.

"You've never heard of Miechowice?"

I shook my head.

"Miechowice is a place with a, how do you say in English, a terrible past? It's just a few kilometres from your work camp. My mother lived there and still won't talk about it. We Polish people aren't allowed to mention it now, the only memorials around here are for fallen 'heroes' of the Red Army." Mania said ironically.

She hesitated and added, "Ah, we now live in The Recovered Territories. Previously this was part of Germany and when the Nazis came to power they renamed the area Mechal — you would have known it as Mechal, Mr West, and before that the Germans called it Miechowitz."

Mania talked about what she called The Miechowice Tragedy.

"It was the end of January 1945. I don't need to tell you about January 1945. You know that this area was in chaos and the Red Army was closing in. The Red Army Generals had told their soldiers that the towns of Beuthen and Mechal were their foothold into Germany. Here, they had finally crossed the border into Germany."

I had a sense of foreboding. I knew exactly what was coming; the Soviets were hell-bent on revenge.

"The German troops dug in, they were determined to stop them and most of the civilians were evacuated." She turned and looked at me. "Most, but not all, because a lot of the Silesian civilians looked upon the Soviets as their liberators."

I didn't know this story and so I started scribbling notes in my exercise book. I could certainly remember the gunfire behind our column as we set off on the March, trudging through the snow towards the west. Little did I know what was taking place a few miles behind us.

She told me the First Ukrainian Front moved towards the town. Civilians were forced to dig anti-tank ditches.

"Towards the end of January, the Red Army entered the outskirts of the town. The battle for Miechowice commenced. The German troops were overrun, but it took nearly three days to defeat them. By that point, the Russians, who had severely underestimated the German resistance, had suffered hundreds of casualties. They were in no mood for forgiveness. When they entered the village, they were like a pack of bloodthirsty animals. They treated the town as if they had just marched into Berlin. They listened to nobody, not even those civilians who offered handshakes or drinks and waved the Silesian and Polish flags."

Mania frowned and took a deep breath, she looked like she was composing herself. I said nothing.

"In the eyes of the Red Army, they were all Germans. Did they really think these soldiers had any compassion; did they think they would show them any mercy? Of course not, they tortured, raped and murdered for four days. And when they'd slaked their bloodthirst and lust, they burned the houses and shops to the ground."

She added that the Red Army killed nearly four hundred civilians.

"They started to execute teenage boys and the elderly, marching them out of their houses into the snow, most of the boys were barefoot. They raped and killed mothers and daughters, the Red Army Officers just stood and watched. They singled out a priest who was trying to comfort the families and made an example of him. Father Frenzel was tortured and humiliated in the town square. Mr West, he was barely alive when they took him into the woods of Stolarzowice and executed him."

Mania went onto to tell me about the mass deportations. She lowered her voice in case we were overheard by our secret police friends outside.

"After the massacre, the Soviet NKVD rounded up Silesians to work for the USSR. Men aged fourteen to sixty, women aged fifteen to fifty-two.

Germans or Poles, it didn't matter to them. They were loaded onto railway wagons and sent east. They were sent to work in Soviet coal mines, maybe sixty thousand men and women. Now, we're not allowed to speak about this, Mr West. And the tragedy for our family was that my grandfather must have been one of them. The grandfather I never had, Mr West. After the Russians arrived at Miechowice, my mother never saw him again."

I stood up from the table and walked around to where Mania sat. I pulled up a chair, sat beside her and put my arms around her. I looked over to where Elwira sat. She was crying. There was a connection, I was sure.

Chapter 35

REFUGEES

I'd slept for no more than three hours.

Mania woke me and I wandered through to the kitchen following the smell of cooking. Mania was already sitting at the table; I flopped into the empty chair.

"Well, Mr West," she said, "you don't look so good today."

I realised it was my last day in Silesia. I wanted to put the record straight.

"I feel so sorry to have blundered into your grandfather's story last night, Mania. I feel a bit guilty; I've been talking about myself all the time. I hope your mother will forgive me for dredging it all up. Now I understand how much the Polish people suffered after the war."

I felt genuinely grateful to Antoni and his family. I added, "Geoff and I want to thank you all from the bottom of our hearts. For me, there's one final part of the jigsaw. After the war I received a letter from Frau Adelheid Spaniol, the mine manager's wife from the E72 camp. After his trial, she had written to the War Crimes tribunal pleading for clemency and I think she was asking for my help. Not that I gave her any." I added as I reached into my satchel.

I read out part of her letter, which was neatly handwritten in ink and in German. It was dated April 1948.

"She says that her family 'were expelled from the east' and she says they 'have lost all their property and all their savings because of the currency reform'. What does this mean, Mania?"

I hadn't read this letter since it was sent to my solicitor unexpectedly in 1948. I made a mental note to look up all the trial paperwork when I got home.

Mania told me that, after the war, millions of Germans living in the area were forced to migrate into the new, much-reduced German homeland. Most of Upper Silesia was incorporated into Poland as a result of the Potsdam Agreement. Churchill, Truman, and Stalin had effectively moved the Polish border with East Germany westwards to the River Oder, while the USSR gobbled up the eastern provinces. Germans weren't welcome in the Recovered Territory. Thirty thousand German towns and villages were renamed, German monuments and buildings were destroyed. The old capital of Upper Silesia, Breslau, was renamed Wrocław. Some of the refugees ended up in the GDR, those who had family connections made it into the new West Germany. Wherever they ended up, their property was confiscated by the Polish state.

Mania explained that Spaniol's savings would have been in Reichsmarks, which were replaced by the West German Deutsche Mark in 1948 at a rate of ten to one.

I paused as I realised that I'd been completely unaware of the plight of the German Silesians after the war. It had hardly been mentioned in the newspapers back home.

I'd never quite understood the politics of Upper Silesia. During my spell in captivity here I recalled how it was often difficult to work out where the civilians' loyalties lay, Poland or Germany. Sometimes they seemed interchangeable. After the Great War, in the aftermath of the Kaiser's defeat, they'd held a referendum in which the locals voted to remain in Germany by a large majority. In 1945 everything had changed.

I loaded my overnight bag into Antoni's taxi wishing I'd brought some warmer clothes. As Antoni started the engine, I leaned over the front seat. "Take us to Katowice," I said. "It's time to go."

Mania looked disappointed but it was time, I had reached the end of the line. It was a strange feeling as we drove away. The weather was changing, there seemed to be a strong wind buffeting Antoni's car as the clouds parted and the sky began to clear.

We drove out of Pyskowice. We made an unplanned stop after a few miles and Antoni met another shady-looking man to purchase two jerry cans full of petrol. Antoni was full of beans this morning and chatted to his associate for some time. It must have been all the money in his pocket. Mania casually slipped into the conversation the previous evening that I had paid him more than he normally earns in a month.

As we drove through Bytom, I got my last view of those bloody winding towers. I was leaving many of my demons behind here in Silesia but I was leaving many memories too. I knew I wouldn't be coming back. That saddened me a little. My friends, those men, the football teams. A band of brothers bound together with a desperation to survive.

I remember an Aussie who had never seen snow in his life and wouldn't join in the snowball fights that we loved so much. There were a few Kiwis too, a big rivalry developed between them and the Aussies whenever we played football or rugby. And there were some strange happenings too.

There was a nice woman who ran the canteen. Everyone liked her and she did her best to make sure we were fed, always going the extra mile to push a few potatoes or an onion or two into the cabbage water that they served up and called soup. At the beginning of my captivity, she told us that she had a teenage son, an only child, and it was clear she doted on him. During the fourth year at the mine, she called me over one day. She was beaming from ear to ear, said her son was in the military now. She had a photo of him, a few of the other prisoners congregated around her as she reached into her pocket. When she pulled out the photograph her son was dressed in an SS uniform. Our attitude towards her changed from that day.

There was Bryn Jones who wore heavy glasses; the lenses were like jam jar bottoms. There were others whose names I had long forgotten. The musicians of our E72 orchestra, Bisset the violinist who had lifted our souls on that Christmas day, a boy on the harmonica and a Scotsman who was a wizard with the accordion.

All good chaps. I wondered what had happened to them all and why we had never attempted to arrange a reunion.

"What are you thinking about?"

It was Mania, leaning over the back of her seat staring into my eyes. Over the noise of the engine and crashing suspension I replied, "What?"

"You are very deep in thought, Mr West."

I was. "I'm sorry, Mania, yes you are right, I was thinking. I was thinking about my friends."

"The men who died here?"

I shook my head. "Not necessarily, the honest answer is that I don't know what happened to them. We were split up on the March, in groups of no more than a couple of hundred. Hopefully, they all made it home alive."

The snow was coming down heavily as I continued. "I've suppressed a lot of memories about that March. I don't know who I walked with, who made it and who died."

"That's awful," she said.

More names burst into my mind. Men like Dobbin, an Australian medic, Butterworth, Kitchener and Harry Leek, the tinsmith who once made a ladle for the soup. The journey dragged. I wanted it to be over, I wanted one last night in that comfortable hotel in Warsaw.

Mania was still asking questions.

"But surely there were regimental reunions back home, POW get-togethers?"

"And why would I want to go, Mania?" I said. "Why would I want to go and talk about friends I had lost, about the brutality of it all?"

"But you... "

"Could have what, Mania, compared old shrapnel wounds, the scars where a guard had taken the skin off a prisoner's back with a rifle butt?"

"I... "

The poor girl had no words. She didn't know. She was thinking along the same lines as the well-meaning people back home afterwards. It's all over now, you can get on with life. Just put it all behind you. 'Least said, soonest mended' again. If only it were that easy.

I took it better than most. I had always prided myself on my strength of mind, but there were others who couldn't cope. They were thrown into a system that had never heard of post-traumatic depression. I didn't go to any reunions because I didn't want to know how many hadn't made it. Thankfully, my best mate, Jack Portas, had also survived the war, but I couldn't bring myself to take a trip to the Lake District with him. I had been forced to walk more miles than I ever wanted to walk in my life, walking for pleasure had lost its appeal. The Nazis had taken away one of my great loves. I had never walked up another fell since.

Mania never said another word. My fault. Not the way I would have wanted our trip to end.

The car windows were covered in condensation as we approached the city of Katowice. Ten minutes later, Antoni told us we were pulling into the station car park. As he opened the door, a blast of icy air sucked into the car, which made me take an involuntary gasp for breath. Antoni was making his way to the boot and Mania crept gingerly out of her seat and stood by my door. We both knew it was the final goodbye. As I stepped out of the car she came forward and fell into my arms. She said what an honour it had been to meet me. She handed me a slip of paper with her address and asked if I would write to her.

"Of course, Mania," I said without any conviction. "Of course I will."

There was a gentleman's handshake with Antoni. I reached into my pocket and handed him an envelope.

"This is for your family Antoni, look after them. You should be very proud."

He tucked it into his back pocket smiling. He had the good manners not to open it in front of me. Antoni insisted on taking a photo of me and Mania standing next to his pride and joy, the trusty Polenz. He said he would send it on to me once it was developed.

As goodbyes went, it was short and sweet, just the way I like them.

The next train to Warsaw was in just over fifty minutes. That gave us time to look around the station concourse. I walked into the newsagent where there was a small stand of postcards. There was a limited selection, a picture of a grand church, another of an aeroplane on the runway at Warsaw airport and, bizarrely, the Polish national football team. I picked three of them up. I smiled to myself. Wouldn't my son and daughters just love a postcard from dear old Dad on his travels?

On second thoughts…

I replaced two of them, kept the one of the church, and took out my biro. I scrawled Mrs Knight's address on the right-hand side and then penned just a couple of lines.

Weather is here wish you were fine.
It was a little standing joke between us. And below.
On my way back to Warsaw, speak soon, can't wait to tell you all about it.

The journey back to Warsaw was uneventful. I think Geoff dozed most of the way. We walked back to the hotel. It was bitter cold as we walked down a street as wide as a Parisian Boulevard. A mass of frozen air whistled relentlessly in our faces. It was a sheer joy to walk into the heated lobby of the hotel; the staff recognised me and greeted me like a long-lost friend. In truth, I think they were worried I might get arrested and never return. We were in time for dinner, just… and as I took my seat in the grand restaurant, I turned the tables on Geoff before he could breathe another word of our trip to Silesia.

I commanded of him, "Now then, brother, I've spilled an awful lot of beans; it's time for you to tell me what really happened in India."

Chapter 36

DOOLALLY

It was May 1945 when I returned to England, fresh from a Long March that would permeate my waking hours and haunt me with nightmares for the rest of my life. I was seriously underweight, withdrawn, and though I hate to admit it, suffering from anxiety and possibly a little paranoia. I still couldn't believe that we had won the war in Europe and the Germans had surrendered. Unlike many of my friends, I had survived.

Incredibly, those fine chaps from the army informed me that my 140 Artillery Regiment, cut in half by the losses at Cassel, had been disbanded in 1944. Apparently though, an offshoot of the regiment was still on active service in Burma. "Never mind," they said, "you're being posted to a new regiment, 203 Field Regiment, Royal Artillery." I was given six weeks' leave. I was to build myself up for the Japanese onslaught and that after that I'd probably be heading to Burma.

The British Government were determined to participate in Operation Downfall, the Allied invasion of Japan. Returning POWs were going to have to be part of it, the army didn't have sufficient manpower without us. Once again, there were many in authority who thought we hadn't done our bit, lazing around in the Polish countryside for the last few years. The fact that the average POW had lost half his body weight appeared to have been overlooked.

Well, that wasn't going to happen. Not me, I wasn't going to be leaving British soil for a very long time. Even if I did, it would be my choice, not at the behest of a faceless suit in Whitehall. I didn't tell them that of course, but I knew a lot more about my body and my mind than they did. Six weeks just wouldn't cut it.

A couple of weeks after my posting I was granted official leave and returned home to my parents in Cheam. Within a couple of days, I felt like a cuckoo in my parents' nest. I had changed so much that it didn't feel right sleeping in what seemed like a child's bedroom. It certainly didn't feel right using the toilet inside the house; thankfully we still had an outside privy where I could spend time alone. I felt surges of uncontrollable anger. My parents had changed too. Five years of wartime stress and the terror of the recent V1 and V2 attacks had left them neurotic wrecks. It wasn't the happy time I'd spent all those years dreaming about. The bomb damage from the Blitz wasn't as bad as the guards had made out, but it was still shocking to see the destruction all around my parents' house. My bedroom still had blackout blinds and tape across the glass.

I had written letters to the Belgian girl I had met in Brussels on the way home. The RAF had dropped us there for processing prior to our return home. Her English probably wasn't good enough to understand my letters. For some reason, in a surge of euphoria associated with my new freedom, I had asked her to marry me in broken French. To my amazement, she had said she would. Of course, I hadn't admitted to my parents that I was engaged to be married on top of everything else.

I longed to see my young brother, Geoff. It had been five long years and he was just a boy when I had left home in 1940. To my dismay, I was told that he was in training with his Royal Engineers unit and wasn't due any home leave for several weeks. While I was determined to stay put, Mum and Dad said Geoff was exactly the opposite, an army officer cadet at the time and keen as mustard to get on with his posting to India at the end of July.

A couple of weeks after I returned home, we had a short note from Geoff saying he'd be home for a few days prior to his ship leaving from Liverpool at the end of July. It had been confirmed, he was heading for India. Their ship would sail down through the Mediterranean, the Suez Canal, the Gulf of Aden, into the Arabian Sea and onto Bombay.

It was a man who walked through the door that day, the first time I had set eyes on him for five years. I could tell he was shocked at how I looked, a stranger to the big brother to whom he had said farewell in 1940. I had been in the prime of my life when I had last seen him, just before my twentieth birthday, and weighing in at over eleven stone. The prison camp diet and the Long March had taken away five of those stones. I had weighed just over six stone when I had signed my liberation questionnaire on 30th April 1945 in a holding camp in Brussels. Thankfully, I had gained twenty pounds since then, but now my kid brother was a bit taller and far better built than I.

Geoff said he wished he could spend more time with me. I gripped both his hands. I told him that our time would come, and it wouldn't be far away.

"Geoff, when you're home, we'll take the ferry into France and the world will be our oyster. I'll buy a nice car and we'll stay in the finest hotels."

"Really?"

"Yes."

I explained how the army would be paying me a significant amount of back pay.

"They haven't paid me a shilling for five years."

Geoff's eyes lit up.

"So, you do your bit, Geoff, and sort those bloody Japs out and before we know it, we'll be heading across the Channel."

"You promise, brother?"

"I do, Geoff. I promise, we'll make that trip, don't you worry about that."

I remembered that conversation with Geoff like it was yesterday.

We chatted over dinner in Warsaw. He told me he hadn't recognised me at first and had been surprised when we sat down to dinner. Mum had followed the advice in the leaflets the War Office had sent out to returning POW's families and only given me a child-size portion of mince pie and potatoes.

"We had to take it easy, Geoff," I said. "Our stomachs had shrunk to half the normal size and for want of a better word had to be stretched, gradually."

Geoff said his journey to Bombay had been exhilarating, he had loved every moment, particularly the way the temperature increased day by day, a few degrees at a time. He said that his trip through the Suez Canal to Bombay had been marvellous and that it was surely the greatest engineering task ever carried out in the history of mankind.

"From Bombay, we were taken to a holding camp called Deolali." Geoff laughed. "It's where the expression 'going Doolally' comes from."

"You're kidding me?"

"No," he said, shaking his head. "The troops were sometimes left there months at a time, and it's said many of them went crazy, a combination of the searing heat and sheer boredom."

"I remember your first letter home, Geoff."

"You do?"

"Yes. I've still got it in my satchel. It was dated the twenty-third of August 1945 and it came through our letterbox in the first week of September. I remember the postman had even knocked on our front door, he had been more excited than Mum because he knew you well. The letter said it had been a smooth, though uncomfortable journey and that the heat had been almost unbearable for about a week when you'd arrived in India. It rained hard every day, you said it had rained like you had never seen it rain before, but after the first week it cooled down somewhat. You'd mentioned the filth and squalor, thousands of the natives crammed into small huts and tents made from sacking.

But halfway through the letter, it bucked up, you told us about the first bananas you had seen for five years and the abundance of nuts, raisins, peaches and pears. You wrote about the shop camp, which was also well-stocked, how there were barbers, shoemakers, and even a man who mended watches. There were two cinemas, a games room, a reading and writing room, and a canteen. You described the canteen as the dirtiest little street café you had ever seen and mentioned that there were ceiling fans above the little brown waiters, who served the food."

"You mentioned VJ Day in that very first letter, Geoff."

"I did, yes."

"You were one lucky bastard."

Geoff nodded and smiled. We all wanted the war in the east to come to an end, especially me. I had experienced it all, death and destruction, the starvation of my captivity, and I had seen men lose their minds. The last thing I wanted was for my kid brother to experience any of that. Even though that first letter was quite upbeat, I wondered if the words flowing from his pen would have been so positive if he had been told he was on his way to Burma to fight the Japanese. And worse, what if he had suffered the same fate as me and been captured? There were stories filtering back home of how evil the Japanese soldiers were, how time in a German POW camp was a walk in the park compared to what the Far East boys had been through.

"You'd written, 'You can imagine the elation caused by the Japanese surrender and I've no doubt you are pretty thankful too.' "

The bombs…

It was 15th August when Japan officially surrendered. I'd ventured out to a cinema to watch the formal surrender on 2nd September 1945. I remembered the ceremony taking place on the battleship, USS Missouri, in Tokyo Bay. The Americans had deliberately lined up the biggest bloody Marines they could find and they towered over the Japanese dignitaries.

The bombs…

There was no glory for the victors, in my opinion, no famous battle on some archipelago in the Pacific or the storming of a major city. The Americans had detonated two nuclear weapons over the Japanese cities of Hiroshima and Nagasaki during the first and second week of August 1945. It was estimated that two hundred thousand people were killed, most of them vaporised within seconds. The majority of the dead were civilians.

The civilians again.

Those bombs.

"It had to be done, Eric," he said.

I looked up. I nodded, though wasn't so sure I agreed with him. It wasn't a time to argue, our time together was ending.

Geoff's first letters made lovely reading, especially because we all knew that the fighting had come to an end. His letters were reminiscent of a well-respected travel writer, full of atmosphere and descriptions. There were a few small photographs too.

The letters arrived in tiny Royal Engineers Postal Section airmail envelopes. Geoff was happy in the sunshine learning to build roads and bridges with his mates. It was all a far cry from what I'd been through. There were pictures of him driving diggers with a smile from ear to ear. There was an interesting picture of him at the controls of a steam train called Sapper on the Nigrili Mountain railway line to Ooty. Ever since he had been a small child, he'd loved steam trains and here he was driving one, living out his childhood fantasy.

I gazed at him across the table.

"Tell me what happened when they posted you to Roorkee," I said.

He sat up in his seat stiffly. Suddenly his handsome smile disappeared.

"What happened there? Geoff… tell me."

Chapter 37

SEV

"I loved India," Geoff said. "It was like a big boys' adventure camp. Apart from the heat — that could be unbearable. Remember I'd never been outside England before. Although the journey there was a little rough, I was with my pals. We felt we could take on the world. We were seeing things we had never seen before, animals that we had only seen in picture books. If I'm honest, growing up in wartime England was dull. I was trapped at home with Mum and Dad, we weren't allowed to travel anywhere and everything was rationed."

Geoff told me about the Dasara Parade, a five-kilometre-long procession starting from the Mysore Palace.

"It was an elephant procession, three beautiful elephants right in the centre of the parade, all decorated in beautiful, coloured silks and headdresses. The middle elephant carried a covered platform with a man inside waving to the crowds. I think he was the Maharajah. The parade finished at a place where they worshipped a huge, decorated tree. I took some photographs that I sent home to Mum and Dad, there was one of me and Sev standing either side of the Mysore State Elephant."

"Who was Sev?" I asked.

"My school mate, Halford Severn, we were very close, we went everywhere together, our army number was only one digit different."

Geoff used words like tropical and exotic, words I had never heard him use before. He said that it was an explosion of colour out there and the experience of a lifetime for a young lad from the grey streets of London, especially after the bombed-out ruins of the Blitz.

"It was a different world, Eric, full of brown people with nothing, not two pennies to rub together, but they were happy and full of smiles. They were friendly towards us and were keen to show us their culture, share their spicy curries with us."

He laughed.

"Did you like the curries?"

"I did. Not at first, but like the heat, the taste grew on you. After the parade, we watched the torchlight procession in the dark. Sev and I found a little street bar where they sold ice-cold beer. We sat with our shirts off, covered in sweat, but it was pleasant enough and we got quite merry, caught up in the euphoria of everything we'd witnessed that day. The locals kept handing us little spicy snacks, pastries and the like. We didn't know what the hell we were eating but we didn't care."

I sat and listened to Geoff for some time. He clearly loved his time in Bangalore, Mysore, and Ooty.

"What was there not to like, Eric," he continued. "I had an idea what you had been through, it must have been hell even though you didn't tell me much... "

I hadn't. Geoff was right. He knew about the battle at Cassel and a few facts about my captivity, but during those few brief weeks together I was weak and withdrawn. I certainly wasn't ready to share my troubles with my kid brother. He was off to fight his own war.

"... and then it all changed. Why did they bloody well have to send me up to that hell hole?"

"Roorkee?"

"Yes. To me, it was the worst place in India. It was like being transported into a different country."

The journey had been a nightmare, my brother explained.

"It took five bloody days to get there, five days in the back of an army truck in that heat. Honestly, there were some days I thought I was going to die."

Geoff said that he had left Sev behind. All of Geoff's Royal Engineer gang had been lucky enough to stay on in Bangalore. Geoff had been separated, probably because his surname was at the end of the alphabet. He had travelled north with nine strangers. It was June 1946, the height of the Indian summer.

"We slept most of the way, the heat drained us and there was nothing we could do about it. At nights they billeted us in small camps, one night we slept in tents in the middle of nowhere and were bitten to bits by insects and mosquitos. It was a nightmare, one hundred and ten degrees and not even a breath of wind."

I recalled my own nightmare journey in the cattle truck trains on the way to Lamsdorf. I wasn't sure if Geoff 's journey was comparable.

I watched him as he gave me more details of his journey and worked out that even if he had landed in paradise, he had already begun to hate Roorkee before he had even arrived. He couldn't understand the reason why the British Army had sent him there without the lads he had trained with. The war was over.

What was the point? he had thought.

"The last few hours before we arrived in Roorkee, it rained continuously. It was grey, miserable and yet ridiculously hot at the same time. As we drove through the city streets they were congested with people on bicycles and rickshaws, small children begging by the side of the road."

Geoff was beginning to paint a bleak picture. He said that there was nothing to look forward to other than meeting up with Sev on his first leave opportunity.

"But even that was nigh on impossible. We had looked at the map before I had set off and said we could all plan a trip to Indore or Jalgaon which looked about halfway, but it was still more than two and a half days away by road."

Poor Geoff, he really did look cheesed off about it all. I mentioned his girlfriend at the time, Brenda Gibbs.

"Was there no home leave arranged? A man has certain needs."

I grinned, I knew how fond of Brenda he was, she was in the Land Army and, although I never met her, Geoff boasted that she was a fine girl, maybe his first proper love.

He looked up. "That was all I had, Eric, bloody letters from Brenda. After I arrived in Roorkee and asked about home leave I was informed it could be as long as two years."

"Bloody hell!" I exclaimed.

He looked over the top of his glass. There was a sorrowful look on his face.

"It turned out you weren't the only prisoner in our family, Eric."

"That first letter from Brenda, she told me to come home soon."

"She was missing you?"

"She was. I didn't have the heart to tell my darling how long I'd be away at first, but eventually, I had to spill the beans."

"And what was her reaction?"

Geoff let out a sigh, a deep heart-wrenching sigh as he looked down at the table, staring at nothing in particular. He reached for his glass and took a drink.

"She changed, Eric," he whispered. "Reading between the lines she'd definitely changed."

There wasn't much conversation to come out of Geoff after that disclosure about Brenda.

The short trip to the airport didn't seem to cheer Geoff up. It was strange; it was as if he couldn't draw himself away from India. A cloud had descended over him, and I was finding it hard to make even the slightest conversation with him.

The flight home was considerably smoother. I concentrated on writing up some of my notes for my book. I closed my eyes at one point. My brother's sad face filled my mind. I'd asked the question about what really happened in India many times but wasn't really getting a satisfactory answer. His letters home gave more away than he had during our conversations over the last few days.

I had wanted this trip to Poland to be a healing exercise for me but, more than that, I wanted to know my brother again. That's why I had wanted him to be with me. Alas, as I went over my notes, spread out on the tray table and the empty seat next to me, I realised just how little I knew him.

I reached into the folder of my wallet and pulled out his photographs from India for the hundredth time. They were small, two-inch square, but expertly developed so you could almost feel you were there, particularly the railway pictures. It dawned on me that there were no pictures of his two months in Roorkee. Not one. Strange. He had his camera with him; I knew that for a fact. He never let that camera out of his sight. As I returned them into the folder, I pulled out a handkerchief and wiped a tear from my eye.

At the airport, it was time to bid Geoff goodbye. I tried to talk to him, but I knew I would never get to the bottom of what had happened in India. As he disappeared, I waited for my taxi driver to pick me up.

The taxi arrived twenty minutes after I'd walked through the arrivals gate.

"Good time, Mr West?" he asked.

"It was different," I said, "but definitely worth doing."

"Good," he said. "I'm glad to hear it."

204

I spent the journey home deep in my thoughts. I'd taken the opportunity to write up some of my notes on the journey home. The trial, why hadn't I gone to Hamburg?

I'd also been thinking a lot about Mary O'Leary since our last meeting. I knew nothing at all about the secret operations in France and Germany at the end of the war; I set myself the task of investigating the SOE and SAARF. So far, I could find practically nothing about the SAARF organisation; it seemed to be a truly secret part of wartime history. I knew that Mary had been a wireless operator tracking the desperate forced marches across Europe, one of which I was participating in. Once I'd got things clear in my mind and studied this untold history, I'd make another appointment and go and see her.

A week or two, that's all it would take. A week or two to get this sorted and I'd be back in business.

Chapter 38

THE TRIAL

I felt guilty. I remember that I had agreed to attend the war crime trial at first, but then chose not to. Maybe it was the thought of going back there, to the enemy's territory. After all, I had only been home two years.

I had been asked to prepare statements by the War Crimes Tribunal. They had obviously read through the IS9 questionnaires from our E72 mob, the forms that Mary O'Leary used to collate before she joined the SAARF. They had decided to pursue the numerous war criminals from our camp.

They had given it the official title 'The Beuthen Case. Alleged Mistreatment of POWs at the Hohenzollern Coal Mine'. There was a separate investigation about the murders of David Blythin and the two Palestinian boys, Eliahu Krauze and Dov-Berl Eisenberg. Arthur Engelskircher and Fritz Pantke were given high priority on the Allied wanted list for those crimes.

The British had a unit appropriately called 'Haystack' that was combing through the prisoners in Allied hands for the men we had highlighted. But Engelskircher had disappeared. My heart had skipped a beat at the thought that they might catch him, but they genuinely couldn't find any trace of him. I did my best to help with his description and home address. I'd been his translator after all, I knew him inside out.

'Five foot ten inches tall, blotchy complexion, age about forty years, sometimes wore horn-rimmed glasses' I had written.

I mentioned he had been moved to command the Russian R77 work camp just before we were evacuated from E72. That seems to have been the last anyone saw of him. As his translator, I may have been the last British soldier to see him alive. There were rumours he had been captured and then killed by the Red Army.

To find Hans Shuster, the Haystack unit flew to Vienna after a tip-off but, in the end, that trail went cold too. They found Fritz Pantke, however, and charged him as an accomplice to the murder of the two Palestinian boys.

But here was chubby old Gerhard Konstantin Spaniol, a middle-aged civilian with a paunch. In 1945, the fact that he was so well built must have made him easy to find. By then, most of the population of Europe was near starvation. Spaniol had been captured by the Allies in the town of Seesen in Saxony on 1st July 1945. He was there with his wife Adelheid and their three daughters. They didn't say how the entire family had escaped the Red Army then made it to the British sector from Beuthen. The British were detaining him in the old Stalag IXB concentration camp at Fallingbostel.

I was very relieved that, at last, justice of sorts would be done. I felt proud of our British legal system, how it contrasted with the anarchy and disregard for any form of human rights in Nazi Germany. I appointed my dad's solicitors in Cheam. Their services were provided completely free of charge. That was one of several examples of how being a returned POW was opening doors that had previously been entirely closed for me. I had to sign my statements in front of a Commissioner for Oaths. I'd sworn an affidavit about the murder of poor David Blythin, and they told me to be ready to attend the trial if they ever caught Engelskircher.

My affidavit about Spaniol was only a couple of paragraphs long. I'd said he was a civilian, a mining engineer, responsible for maintaining coal output, which had been closely monitored by the Nazi authorities. Sure enough, his office at the mine was adjacent to Engelskircher's but I had said, in my opinion, he was neither a war criminal nor the main cause of our troubles. Later on, I saw the statements Sergeant William Mears, Sapper Glyn Davis, Private Sydney Line, a New Zealander, and Private James Catleugh had submitted to the court, which each ran to two or three pages.

I was so pleased to see Sergeant Mears had survived his Long March and had got home in one piece. I remembered Mears and me fighting together at Cassel, and our struggles at the coal mine. I'd last seen him in 1944 when he was our Man of Confidence and before he left to go to another camp. Engelskircher had regarded him as a troublemaker and had had him removed on a trumped-up charge. I contemplated contacting Mears, but we were warned that witnesses were 'frozen' and weren't supposed to collude. I thought he'd be proud of me now that I'd been promoted to Staff Sergeant.

The events recorded in the four soldiers' statements didn't tally with my recollection. I'd felt they attributed some of Engelskircher's beatings to Spaniol. But I was worried I would be asked under cross-examination to contradict the camp's Man of Confidence, a man senior to me in my old regiment.

It wouldn't look good if us Kriegies started disagreeing with each other in open court. Some of the facts might be wrong but Spaniol may have to fend for himself, I thought.

The trial was listed for five days starting on 7th September 1947. By then Spaniol had been detained at Fallingbostel for over a year. They'd sent my solicitor all the court paperwork. I was to be flown from London to Hamburg as his defence witness, given a military escort to the Hotel Reichshof in Hamburg where I was to stay 'frozen' in strict quarantine without talking to any of the other trial participants. To enforce everything, the hotel and court rooms would be guarded by the scary military policemen that I remembered from my liberation with their white webbing, white pistol holsters and red-topped caps.

Hamburg at the time was a city in ruins. The RAF had comprehensively destroyed most of its important buildings. However, the five-storey, stone-built building known at the Curiohaus on the Rothenbaumhaussee had remained virtually unscathed. Built in 1911, the Curiohaus had been an important focal point before the war for the intellectuals and decadent artists that the Nazis later persecuted. The War Crimes court had taken over the building and it was here that many of the important British sector war crime trials were held.

The Ravensbrück concentration camp guards, Gestapo agents who had murdered the Great Escapers from Stalag Luft III and the perpetrators of the 1940 Les Paradis massacre, had all been tried at the Curiohaus. The judges had handed down over one hundred death sentences to a total of just over five hundred war criminals.

It was a case of 'vengeance, a dish best served cold' for sure.

I'd had a fortnight of sleepless nights. My nightmares were happening virtually every night without fail. Should I go to Hamburg, contradict my brothers in arms and spend energy defending an admitted Nazi or should I just refuse to attend? I knew that Sergeant Mears and Sapper Davis were attending as prosecution witnesses. In the end, I took the path of least resistance and told them I had other commitments. It was a white lie. The telegram still sits in my file of trial paperwork. It read:

'Ref. 010/186 of 27092 War Crimes. Beuthen case.
RESTRICTED.
WEST refuses to attend as defence witness for SPANIOL.'

Afterwards, they'd sent my solicitor the trial transcript. I hadn't really looked at it at the time. The President of the Court was a Royal Artillery Officer, Lieutenant Colonel G.A. Glindenning. Prosecuting for the Crown was a civilian barrister, Mr T.G. Field-Fisher. They'd flown Mr Field-Fisher in from London especially for the case.

Defending Spaniol was a Hamburg lawyer called Dr Rudolf Herzog. Herzog had managed to find a couple of mine officials, Hans Behrens and Eduard Battel, as well as Richard, one of the Hoppe brothers, to testify on Spaniol's behalf. My name 'Mr West' was at the end of Herzog's list of defence witnesses. It made my blood go cold to see it amongst all those Nazis.

Spaniol's defence team were in a hopeless position; it was their word against the affidavits of four British and New Zealand POW survivors, with Mears and Davis testifying in person. And no one could deny that E72 was an evil, badly run and inhumane camp. Spaniol didn't stand a chance. The judge had heard enough and summed up his thoughts in a report dated 24th November 1947:

'The Deputy Judge Headquarters, British Army of the Rhine
Military Court (War Crimes) Trial
Beuthen Case. Gerhard Konstantin SPANIOL

The accused was charged with committing a war crime between May 1941 and March 1944, when an official at the Hohenzollern mine near Beuthen in violation of the law and was concerned in the ill-treatment of British prisoners of war.
The accused pleaded not guilty. He was found guilty and imprisoned for seven years.
There was evidence before the court both verbal and documentary of severe ill-treatment by the accused personally and by guards under his orders.

The ill-treatment in some cases amounted to the infliction of grievous bodily harm.

There was one instance where a prisoner of war, who was obviously unfit, was forced to work in the mine and died as a result.

The accused, who gave evidence on his own behalf, denied these allegations and contended that he was in fact only a civilian technical expert and had no say in the control of the prisoners. He also denied the individual incidents spoken of by the prosecution witnesses.

In my opinion there was ample evidence on which the court could find him guilty of the offence as charged and in view of the brutal assaults which were described by some of the witnesses, I do not think that a sentence of seven years imprisonment is unduly severe.

The proceedings are in order for confirmation.

The accused has petitioned against the finding and sentence. I have examined his petition and find therein no grounds for advising any interfere with either finding or sentence.'

And so it was. Spaniol had been sentenced to seven years imprisonment; his appeal was dismissed. He was sent to Werl prison near Dortmund, along with many hardened Nazis. Looking at it all these years later I could see Spaniol had taken the rap for Engelskircher and some of the guards' behaviour. But these were hard times. If the Red Army had caught him there wouldn't be any question of a trial, at best he'd have been deported to the Urals to work in a Soviet mine, at worst he'd have been shot dead, his wife and daughters raped and then murdered.

Fritz Pantke's trial followed shortly afterwards. He had been accused of participating in the murder of the two Palestinian boys at Schomberg. Pantke was acquitted — he hadn't pulled the trigger. It was Arthur Engelskircher they were after.

Chapter 39

JOY

I couldn't keep dwelling on the past. The new year 1948 was fast approaching and Joy and I had set a date for our wedding in February. We'd met at Kingston Polytechnic; we both needed an extra academic year to finish off our 'A' levels. My studies had been interrupted by a degree of idleness in my final school year and then, of course, I'd been conscripted into the artillery. The rest, as they said, was history.

Joy's schooling had been disrupted by the London Blitz and then later by the V-bomb campaign. She'd gone to live with her aunt's family in Leeds until the war was over. As it turned out, her family home in Morden was only two or three miles away from mine in Cheam.

We were both busy with our studies to get into medical school and were enrolled in the same class. Joy had a natural vivaciousness and charm. She was always the brightest in our class and, unlike me, seemed able to answer all the questions. *I can't have this!* I had thought and so I had asked her out for a date.

Her name 'Joy' was exactly right. It was unalloyed joy that she brought into my life, and from time to time if I needed to talk seriously, she would listen patiently. She never judged me. Over the next few months and years, I'd told her little details about my army life, my time as a POW, my Long March and the experience of trying to untangle all those German boys from Nazi ideology. My Mum and Dad were both having a mental health crisis of their own at the time. But with Joy's help I was, at last, looking forwards; we had a lot of fun. All around us, London was slowly being rebuilt, there was optimism in the air. Although they were getting much better, sometimes without any pattern, my nightmares would occur.

I had secured an interview at the medical school of St Thomas' Hospital in London. The hospital had only just returned to its pre-war site on the south bank of the River Thames. After several direct hits during the Blitz, it had been evacuated to Hydestyle near Godalming.

I had sent them a testimonial from Lieutenant Colonel Mantle, my commanding officer at POW camp 167 in Leicester. I unearthed it recently while searching through my wartime papers. It read:

> 'Eric West was a POW for 5 years. He was promoted to S/Sgt Interpreter in which capacity he has given complete satisfaction having shown himself able to cope with both the linguistic and administrative sides of his work. He has also made good use of facilities available to fit himself for his proposed career in medicine for which he appears to be excellently suited.'

As I sat in the waiting room, I looked at all the fresh-faced, well-spoken young men. They were mainly teenagers, just out of school; there were only a few older war veterans like me and even fewer women. Most of them seemed to have family connections to medicine and had been privately educated. Here I was, a humble staff sergeant, the twenty-eight-year-old son of a pipe factory manager with no medical connections at all and with a very ordinary education. As soon as the interview panel called me in, however, once again the magic spell of being an ex-POW was cast.

They thumbed through my application papers and the first question asked was, "Mr West, do you agree there's much too much academic emphasis in medicine these days?" and the second, "Don't you agree that we should be helping working-class lads up the ladder now?"

The panel seemed to be willing me to say something, anything that wasn't too foolish, to which they would nod their approval vigorously. After about fifteen minutes, the chairman (I didn't realise at the time he was the eminent physiologist Professor McSwiney) stood up and reached across the desk to shake my hand.

He said, "We'd be delighted to offer you a place at this medical school, Mr West, and we do hope you'll accept."

From that moment on I became the most loyal Thomas' man there ever was. I was determined to repay their faith in me. I knew, provided I kept myself together and passed the exams, that they'd given me the chance of my lifetime. It meant I could aspire to become an equal to the officer types.

Brave men like Odling, Clarke and MacDougall, to whom I felt I owed so much.

If only they could see me now, I'd thought.

It was time for me to get respectable, after all, I would need to fit in with the St Thomas' crowd. There was a saying in medical circles,

'You can always tell a Thomas' man, but you can never tell him anything!'

Dad donated me one of his tweed jackets and Mum altered my demob trousers, so they fitted me properly. I had never smoked, even when in the POW camp, but I remember buying a pipe and some tobacco to help cultivate the look. It never worked, the smoke tasted foul, and the damn thing kept going out.

With a combination of my army back pay and some help from Mum and Dad, Joy and I bought our first house together in Tooting, about five miles south of the hospital. We were a newly married couple and savoured every moment. We didn't have much money to spare and so we used to visit museums or sit in the public gallery at the Old Bailey for free entertainment and warmth in the winter. We buzzed around London together on my 250cc single-cylinder BSA motorbike, with Joy riding pillion. It was probably less powerful than my lawnmower today but, to us, it represented our new freedom. Unfortunately, one day I misjudged the sharp corner at Tooting Bec Road and lost control of the bike. Joy and I ended up rolling onto the pavement, both of us thankfully uninjured. After that, I was on my own on that blessed bike.

In amongst all these papers, I recently uncovered my graduation photograph from St Thomas' dated 1955. There were thirty proud, optimistic faces in that photograph. Big Ben and the Houses of Parliament were in the background. There was only one young lady in our graduation class of 1955 and I couldn't remember her name.

Meanwhile, Joy had managed to secure a place at Leeds Medical School. It meant we were going to spend the first years of our married life in different cities. But it was a start. A leap into the unknown perhaps. The beginning of our thirty-two-year adventure together.

Chapter 40

WITNESS

The letter had come out of the blue. It was marked *Private and Confidential* and addressed to my solicitor. The solicitor said it would be best to take no action, not to reply in case that prejudiced any future appeal. It was neatly written in blue ink and was entirely in German. My German skills have become rusty, but with the help of my dictionary I managed to make what I think is a reasonably accurate interpretation. It read:

'Dusseldorf, April 1948
Dear Herr Eric West,

Please forgive me for writing this letter, but I do not know where else to turn. I ask for clemency for my husband because it has been proved that he was not responsible for the prisoners' welfare, but only for repairing and new building by order of the Bergwerksdirektor. Accommodation and food were the concern of the Camp.

My husband always assured me that he never beat a prisoner and I believe him, and I hope you do too. I was sorry you weren't able to attend my husband's trial in Hamburg, but I realise it would have been upsetting for you. But I hope you, as camp translator, understood that he would never prevail to such an action. If there were differences between army and prisoners, he, as a civilian, had no authority to interfere. The reports of the Red Cross, Geneva never mention ill-treatment by civilians but by the camp and some of the guards, who were removed at that time.

In the case my husband has offended against law I ask to consider the following:

1) Compared with the sentences now passed, this sentence of seven years imprisonment without counting the internment of one and a quarter years at Fallingbostel is a very hard one.

2) The internment and the imprisonment of nearly two years at Werl prison so far has completely ruined my husband physically and mentally.

Having lost our home and all our property and our son-in-law, who has not yet returned from Russian captivity, we have met with much hardship. We hoped, having happily escaped from the Russians, to start anew to live working quietly, and owing to democratic help, we could find a new home. How great a disappointment and trouble we had to suffer instead. Our breadwinner was taken away from us and we were left in distress and misery. I have been sick for years and have one child at school-age; she cannot understand that her dear father shall be away from her for such a long time.

My husband will perfectly perish behind jail walls as I realised during my first visit after the currency reform on 13th April 1949. For nearly three years he is away from us; and in the meantime, the energetic man who liked work has changed into a sick old man who is now totally unfit for a miner's work. He loved the wonderful but dangerous trade of a miner and for thirty years he worked with all his energy and knowledge to satisfy his chief.

Isn't it a positive point that in his department no British prisoner was killed by accident? And what didn't he do to give the prisoners every possible facility, when in 1942 he took over the labour in the camp? He was not allowed to act from his own will. If anything did not go on in the right way, you cannot blame a subordinate, like my husband. Therefore, I earnestly request you to help me ask the British authorities to exercise clemency and to release my sick husband, father of three children. Do not let an efficient and reliable man perish behind jail's walls.

You know my husband only joined the Nazi party in 1933 to keep his job at the mine. He is a catholic and came to see Hitler's terrors early in the war but only dared say things to me. Do please help set free our breadwinner so that our distress, misery, sorrow and grief may be mitigated.

I trust to your justice and generosity and should be very grateful, indeed, if you would help me with my sincere request. I hope not to have made a fruitless request.

Yours respectfully

(signed) Frau Adelheid Spaniol'

I remember reading the letter and wondering whether I should submit something to the War Crimes tribunal but in the end, I decided not to. I knew Frau Spaniol had a point; her husband hadn't been a saint but probably wasn't the perpetrator of a lot of the crimes. Casting my mind back though, I couldn't remember ever seeing her or her daughters in the camp.

How could she know all that went on? I thought to myself.

My solicitor was advised that most of the 'lower grade' war criminals, which seemed to mean the ones that hadn't been executed, were going to be released early in any event. The world had moved on from Nazi war crimes. They were yesterday's news; concern was switching to the Soviet threat in the east.

And so, I put Spaniol to the back of my mind until 1951 when another set of official correspondence arrived, this time from The War Crimes Tribunal. Their letter included a copy of the official notification of Spaniol's early release which read:

'To the Governor of WERL Prison or any other Penal Establishment in which the undermentioned may now or hereafter be lawfully confined

WHEREAS one Gerhard SPANIOL was convicted of a War Crime by a Military Court sitting at Hamburg and sentenced to seven years imprisonment with effect from 10th September 1947 by Judgment dated 10th September 1947 and was committed to Werl Prison

On the instructions of His Majesty's Government in the United Kingdom I HEREBY ORDER that the said Gerhard SPANIOL be released forthwith by you the Governor of the Prison unless otherwise lawfully detained.

AND that for so doing this Order shall be sufficient warrant.

Dated this 21st day of December 1951.

M.E. BATHURST, Legal Adviser'

I heard no more from Frau Spaniol. Her pleas had obviously been successful in the end. Later, I learned that the Nazi war criminals released from Werl prison had received compensation, provided they could prove they were German citizens that had been imprisoned by a 'foreign power' because of their military service. A condition for receiving payment was the submission of an 'Unbedenklichkeitsbescheinigung.' That translated to a clearance certificate, which seems to have been issued to almost all of them.

Compensation! Clearance certificates! Remembering it now, it still seems incredible, the magnanimity of us British. On the one hand, I felt proud of our country, but on the other hand, I couldn't help feeling a moment's sorrow for David Blythin, the Palestinians and countless others in the camp and on that damned Long March. Where were our clearance certificates? Would we ever receive an early release?

Chapter 41

SHADY LANE

It was damned annoying. I'd really wanted a couple of weeks studying, reading and writing up my notes. Here I was partially retired and yet, just like my National Health Service days, I still felt pulled in multiple directions. My employers wanted their pound of flesh and they had telephoned me to say that my services were required once again. At first, I thought it might be Mary O'Leary but no, this was a different case altogether, a middle-aged man who'd been under Mental Health Section for nearly twenty years, and this time in Bedfordshire.

I'd been doing these Mental Health Act visits for several months now and to be honest, they felt a bit of a two-edged sword. I could make a day out of them, but sometimes the travelling was a bit irksome. I'd taken a lot from the visits to Mary, and I believed she had also benefitted immensely, but the others... well... definitely in the take it or leave it category. I'd far rather spend an afternoon sitting by a lake with my fishing rod or making a start on my allotment.

Somehow or other I had to find my way to Bedford, but I didn't fancy driving up through central London to find the M1 motorway. I could claim travel expenses and so, for this trip, I decided to use public transport for the first time ever.

My initial idea was to take the train from Cheam Station to Victoria and then use the underground for the first time in what... twenty years, to get to St Pancras Station and catch the train to Bedford.

I was up early in the morning, but it was over breakfast that the doubts started to creep in. It wasn't exactly a panic attack, but I was aware of a slight tremble and a sheen of sweat on my top lip when I pictured myself descending one of those huge escalators deep into the bowels of central London.

The suburban train was the journey I used to undertake when I was working at St Thomas' on the days when it was too cold to ride my motorbike, all those years ago. Even then it wasn't so pleasant and I'd have flashbacks of the mine, dropping like a stone in that rickety cage that looked like it was going to fall to bits at any minute.

Those crowded trains too. It would be rush hour by the time I hit Victoria, they'd be packed in like sardines, bodies pushing against me. Desperate memories, the Germans knew exactly how to cram us in like sardines. Men died...

Now, forty years later. Could I face up to that again?

No.

I rang the number stuck on the fridge with one of those hideous souvenir magnets someone had brought me from a holiday.

"Hello. Yes. To St Pancras and it's on business so I'll need a receipt. Thank you. One hour please."

My taxi was on time. A charming Pakistani gentleman lifted my bag into the boot and talked enthusiastically the whole way, no doubt grateful for a decent morning's pay as we crawled at no more than walking pace through Tooting, Battersea and Lambeth. The taxi meter was ticking away merrily. I glanced inside my wallet to see if I would have enough cash to settle the bill when we finally got there.

St Pancras Station was a dirty old place, the Victorian station building was encased in diesel and coal dust. The roof looked like it was living on borrowed time, about to collapse at any minute. My chest tightened as I lifted a handkerchief to my face in a vain attempt to block out those bloody diesel fumes. There's definitely something to be said for steam trains. The pigeons seemed to like it though; scores of them were flying about inside the old canopy. There was pigeon crap everywhere. What a bloody disgrace, why had they let this grand old station go to rack and ruin? Hell, even a good clean would make a big difference. I had read that John Betjeman had got involved with the campaign to reform the elegant old station.

I waited in the queue at the grand, wooden ticket office. The young lady who handed me my ticket also gave me a British Rail route guide. The pamphlet informed me that after Bedford, the train called at Market Harborough and finally terminated at Leicester. Leicester, my goodness, I spent a year of my life up there. I realised I'd not been back to Leicester since 1946.

219

It was the 7th September 1945, and I was twenty-six years of age. I weighed just over eight stone, having put on two stone since being repatriated. I had avoided India and the fighting that had still raged on in the Far East as late as August that year. The Japanese had formally surrendered just a couple of weeks before I landed in Leicester. The stark reality was that I hadn't been fit enough to make the journey out to India and anyway one of the officers had discovered that I spoke fluent German. To use his words, 'We have a mission for you Lance Bombardier West.'

They said that they would promote me to Staff Sergeant and transfer me to the RAOC (Royal Army Ordnance Corps) for 'clerical work'. Who was I to complain?

I was to become a poacher-turned-gamekeeper. My new base was to be POW Camp 167 at Shady Lane, Stoughton, Leicester. My mission was to help the officers to identify any hard-line Nazis and prepare the remainder for rehabilitation prior to their return to Germany. It was an interesting period of my life that would eventually convince me that, whatever the difficulty, a career in medicine was where my civilian destiny lay.

It was a pleasant day and the short journey passed quite quickly. A taxi took me to Bedford hospital and I chatted with the staff for an hour before I was told that the patient wasn't fit enough to see me. He'd come down with a fever a nurse said, although I suspected the real reason was that he just didn't want to see me. They had tried to persuade him all morning, he wasn't having any of it.

I had a small bite of lunch in the hospital canteen and then they called me a taxi. I arrived back at the station just before two o'clock.

"What a waste of a day," I mumbled to myself. Or was it?

On a whim, I checked with the ticket office. A chap informed me that there was a train to Leicester at 14.21.

"It's a forty-seven-minute journey," he said. "The train is on time."

"I'll take a ticket," I said and handed over the fare.

There were several taxis outside of the station at Leicester and I climbed into one. The taxi driver looked a little disappointed when I told him Shady Lane, Stoughton and I understood why when he pulled into a layby just fifteen minutes up the road.

I felt a little guilty as I realised he was hoping for a far longer ride so I gave him a five-pound note and told him to keep the change. He perked up a little and handed me his card, told me that he was available for the return journey.

"What is it you're looking for anyway?" he barked as I clambered out of the car. "It's just a park, the riding stables were closed down years ago."

"Errr... nothing," I said.

The man was in his early thirties, probably didn't know the history of the place.

"Just a bit of fresh air and a walk. It's too early to head back into London; I wanted to avoid the rush hour."

"A wise move," he said. "I'm on duty until eight so just you give me a call." He pointed over the road at a partially hidden public telephone box. "There you are, over there, don't get lost."

I waved him off as I tucked his card into my jacket pocket. I took a deep breath and walked into what a large sign told me was an Arboretum, belonging to and maintained by the City of Leicester. The sign read that it was a recreational, botanical, wildlife, and historical area with over five hundred species of native trees and shrubs and a sown wildflower grassland.

Impressive, I thought.

Where were the Nissan huts and the remains of the buildings I had called home for twelve months?

There was nothing, not a scrap of any remains or evidence that the area was once home to nearly two thousand German POWs. I felt I had wasted my time, I expected something, maybe even a small museum like the one I'd visited in Łambinowice.

I wandered through the parkland for around thirty minutes before I spotted somebody walking their dog. I don't know what prompted me to speak to him, but I did. He looked a lot younger than me, late forties at the most.

"Excuse me, young man, do you live around here?"

"Yes, I do. Born and bred, sir."

"Do you ever recall buildings standing here, old buildings which were used in the second world war?"

"I certainly do. They were demolished in the late seventies I think, trouble with the squatters."

"I see, so I have the right place then?"

"You do. But there's absolutely nothing left of them if that's what you were looking for."

He studied me a little curiously.

"Were you here during the war?"

221

"Just after, I looked after the German POWs."

The young man's face lit up. "You did?"

"Yes."

"My God, my dad had two of those POWs working for us during the war."

"He did?"

"Yes, we have a farm, they were appointed as labourers, nice chaps he said, although I can barely remember them. They helped with the harvest, picked the fruit and Dad said one of them even taught me to ride my bike."

I was frozen in time at what this young man was telling me. While the German POWs were teaching our children to ride bikes and picking strawberries, we were toiling in mines, starved half to death and forced to march for hundreds of miles in the depths of winter. They weren't starving that was for sure, not if they were picking fruit and working the fields.

"We had them one year for Christmas dinner," he continued. "It was after the war, 1946 or 1947, I was about six or seven I think but I remember it well. We had a goose and all the trimmings, well as much as we could muster given the rationing. Mum managed to bake a Christmas pudding; she really pushed the boat out that year, she even gave them a present each."

I shook my head. Christmas bloody dinner and presents. I was speechless.

"Why don't you come and see Dad? He'll tell you more about them."

The man's words brought me back from my thoughts.

"Sorry?"

"Our farm." He pointed. "Just through that gate and a five-minute walk up the track."

I wasn't going to pass on an opportunity like that. Within just ten minutes I was sitting in his beautiful farmhouse kitchen looking at the weather-beaten face of a farmer holding a hot cup of tea and some homemade biscuits. He introduced himself as Walter Hannon. Mr Hannon proudly boasted he was eighty-two years old, but still worked the farm every day. I spent nearly an hour with him as he pulled out photographs from the thirties, forties, and fifties, mostly of his farm of which he was clearly proud. Eventually, he found a photo from the heart of the camp and then, finally, several pictures of the German prisoners. One caught my eye, a tall blond chap, standing with young Barry and his bike.

I recognise that one, I thought to myself.

But was my mind playing tricks? It was forty years ago, and there was no way I could recall his name.

"I think I remember him," I said.

"You do."

The old man's eyes lit up.

"Helmut was with us for three years, a lovely boy, a good worker." He pointed to his son. "He taught Barry how to ride his bike. Such patience he had with the wee lad."

Barry smiled.

Should I tell them he would have been a Nazi when I first met him? I thought to myself.

No. Why shatter their illusion of him?

There were several groups that the prisoners could be boxed into. One of the groups that formed were the older men, those who wanted to see out their time in England and get back home to their families as quickly as possible. There was no talk of war, what they had been up to or any mention of the fighting They never asked for anything or gave us any trouble. Then there was Category C mob, mainly youngsters who were still fiercely patriotic, who couldn't accept that they'd lost the war. Nazis believers to a man. That lot would have been back fighting at the drop of a hat, just as soon as someone had put a Karabiner rifle in their hands.

The camp authorities rigged up a cinema a few months after I arrived. It seated fifty men comfortably. The officers had interviewed most of the prisoners by then, with me translating. We asked them the specific questions that the War Office had compiled in a long list. The Nazis held nothing back, still defiant, still believing that Hitler's policies had been just. They believed fervently that the progression of the Aryan race and world domination had merely been halted temporarily. Some of them were convinced that it was just a setback, that normal service would be resumed.

We showed them the devastation of their cities in that hut with a cinema screen while they sat in silence. We showed them aerial film of a broken Berlin and the firestorm of Hamburg.

The men had known nothing of what happened to cities like Hamburg or Dresden, they had been hundreds of miles away from home. Quite naturally their Ministry of Propaganda conveniently overlooked the attacks. We showed them the footage of frozen dead Germans at Stalingrad.

I believe we turned most of the prisoners away from Nazism. They came to realise that pictures and film footage don't lie, that the Nazis weren't invincible after all. One man ran screaming from the hut as he recognised his local church in Hamburg and the burning buildings that surrounded it.

We held what was termed as Jewish Week, towards the end of the year in 1945. We stuck posters up outside the building entitled, 'The Annihilation of the Jewish Race.'

By now my German was flawless.

Die Vernichtung der Jüdischen Rasse

I don't know what they expected to see as the hard-core ones trooped into the cinema, full of smiles. All I do know is that they didn't troop out full of smiles afterwards. We locked the doors for three hours, made them watch as we showed them the footage that the American liberators had shot at Dachau. The Yanks had expected to find no more than an abandoned training facility for SS forces. Instead, they found cattle trucks and train cars filled with badly decomposed human remains and thousands of near dead, walking skeletons, some so weak that they could not even stand to greet their liberators. They found mass graves and crematoria. It was all filmed.

As one American commentator had said at the time, "So that nobody can ever deny this has taken place."

We showed them the Red Army film reels from Auschwitz. The Germans had left in such a hurry there had been no time to bury the freshly dead, more than six hundred corpses were scattered around the accommodation huts, victims of the last few days of Nazi terror. There were just seven thousand emaciated prisoners left in Auschwitz, the rest had been deemed fit enough to embark on a death march. We all watched as the Soviet cameraman moved around the camp, filming old men and women barely able to walk. There was one poignant moment where Russian soldiers held up piles of baby clothes that had been stripped from the infants prior to execution. They filmed the thousands of discarded shoes, wire-rimmed spectacles, and piles of clothes twenty feet high.

I stood at the front of the cinema and translated the commentary into German; at times I struggled to hold it together. I'll never forget some of the faces of those young men as it slowly sank in exactly what they had been a part of.

"Helmut still sends us a card every year."

The farmer was holding out what I presumed was that year's Christmas Card. I took it. A typical German snowy market scene, traders wrapped up against the cold, trading their wares to happy fräuleins. I looked inside, a brief two-line Christmas greeting written in basic English. At the bottom of the card, in the right-hand corner, was Helmut's address.

I couldn't believe my eyes. Helmut's surname, Steinborn and his hometown, Meppen in Lower Saxony. I opened my mouth and looked at the farmer.

"When did you last see Helmut?"

"In 1948," he said without hesitation. "When he left for home."

"Have you spoken by telephone?"

"No, I don't suppose he even has one."

"He has."

It was the farmer's turn to look surprised. He turned to his son and then back to me.

"How do you know?"

"Because I would have translated for him here after the war and then, by chance, I met him in northern France a few months ago."

The farmer sank into his seat as his legs buckled and his mouth fell open.

We telephoned Helmut five minutes later. He picked up on the fourth ring.

"Helmut?"

"Ja."

"Helmut, it's me, Eric West, I met you in Cassel a while back."

"Ah yes, the Britisher, I remember you well," he said. "You were waiting for your brother but he didn't show up?"

"Helmut, there's someone I want you to speak to."

"Ja?"

"I'm at what's left of Camp 167 in Stoughton, Leicester."

Silence.

"This is Staff Sergeant Eric West handing you over to farmer Walter Hannon."

Walter spoke to Helmut for a good ten minutes before handing him over to Barry, the boy he'd helped ride his bike for the first time. Watching the farmer's eyes as he spoke to the man he'd last seen forty years ago was a sheer joy. His eyes were all glazed over as he leaned forward to shake my hand and thank me. We both listened to the conversation between Barry and Helmut as I waited patiently for my turn.

At last, Barry handed over the phone.

"He wants to speak to the Staff Sergeant."

I took the phone from him.

"Helmut, *wie geht es dir*, how are you?"

"I am well, that was truly a big surprise."

"For me too."

"I remember Walter well, he must be a very old man, how is he?"

"He is well. I hope I look like him when I'm his age, he still works the farm every day."

"And you are truly there, at the old camp?"

"I am, but it's no longer a camp. There are no huts, no buildings."

"What does it look like?" Helmut asked.

"It's nice, Helmut. It's pretty; wide-open spaces, trees and flowers. Listen, I'm virtually retired now and have some time on my hands. Why don't you come and see for yourself, why don't you come and meet Walter and Barry?"

I told Helmut about my trip to Poland, how it had helped me close a book on my life and get me started on another. He said he understood, and he described that déjà vu moment in Cassel. He said he had happy memories from Camp 167, just before we said goodbye he apologised and then thanked me.

"You don't need to apologise," I said, "and why do you need to thank me? You were our prisoner."

"You know why, Eric, you really helped me; you made me see what they did to us."

I handed the phone back to Walter for a final goodbye and found myself thinking back to those Pathe newsreels.

They had listened to us after all. Maybe that year of my life wasn't wasted.

Chapter 42

BRAINWASHED

Helmut drove from Meppen to Rotterdam, where he caught the passenger ferry to Hull. As arranged, I met him at Hull docks. He embraced me. It seemed strange and I was a little uncomfortable. He was brimming with excitement, told me how wonderful it was to see me again now that he knew exactly who I was.

"Look at us, two veterans of the last war," he said.

Then he added in German, "Wir waren auch Überlebende." I knew this meant 'we were survivors too'.

There was a passing comment or two when he realised that I was driving a Mercedes.

"You can't live without our fine engineering, Staff Sergeant West." He grinned.

It was the third time he had called me that. It was time to nip it in the bud, as well-intentioned as it was.

"And you can stop calling me that, Herr Steinborn, or I will put you on a charge and you'll find yourself cleaning out the toilet block."

Helmut fell back in his seat and laughed like a hyena as he slapped me hard on the thigh nearly causing me to lose control of the wheel.

"Agreed, Eric," he said, "no more names from the war."

It wasn't the nicest of days as we drove through the city centre and out towards Hessle. There were dove grey skies overhead; heavy rain clouds and a fine drizzle falling. The Humber Bridge loomed up in front of us and I couldn't help myself.

"That, my friend," I said as I pointed, "is true British engineering."

Helmut was genuinely impressed as he looked up to the bridge and across the expanse of the dirty Humber estuary. 204He let out a long whistle as we swung around in a big U-turn and headed for the ramp to the bridge.

"We are going to cross it?" he asked.

"Yes. We are heading south, just a couple of hours and we'll be there."

I had booked a couple of rooms in a small hotel listed in my AA book and less than a mile from Shady Lane. We'd stay a couple of nights and then I had promised to take Helmut across to the Lake District. I wanted to show him some of those fells I'd walked with Jack Portas back in the day. My walking days were well behind me, but there was something about that corner of England that made me feel good.

We had exchanged pleasantries and small talk for about thirty minutes when it dawned on me how little I knew about the old German prisoner who sat beside me. Indeed, Helmut appeared to know a lot more about me than I knew about him. I probed gently, realising how difficult it had been for me to talk about my own wartime experiences.

"Tell me about where you live, Helmut, have you always lived there or was it somewhere they resettled you after the war?"

"No," he said, shaking his head. "I've lived in Lower Saxony all my life. Meppen is the largest town in that area. We are only about twenty kilometres from the Dutch border. It has a little POW history itself, a little like your Shady Lane."

"It has?"

"Yes, I'm from the Emsland area, there were a lot of Stalags nearby during the war."

What an irony, I thought.

I remembered my nightmare forced march into Emsland in the scorching heat of June 1940. What I remembered most was the terrible thirst. If anything, the thirst was worse than the hunger that I had felt in the forced marches in the freezing winter of 1945. By then I was a seasoned Kriegie but in 1940 I was much younger and this was my first encounter with the enemy.

The Belgians had put water buckets out for us and the guards laughed as they kicked them out of our reach. My first POW camp was Stalag VIB at Versen, a place I never want to see again. I remembered it was flat, featureless and marshy. There were mosquitos and flies, I had to contend with painful insect bites and sunburn as well as the sheer terror of arriving at a POW camp. My buddy, Eric Johnson, from F Troop was with me at Versen but otherwise, I didn't know any of the other men there. Frankly, I was just a terrified twenty-one-year-old longing to be home with Mum and Dad.

I told Helmut I knew Emsland, that I'd been there before, I had marched right through Holland and crossed the German border in searing heat. In truth, all I could remember were the darn mosquitos. He looked a little sheepish. That march hadn't been pleasant; we hadn't been treated very well. He probably knew that.

Helmut changed the subject as he casually told me about serving in Rommel's Afrika Korps in 1942-43. I recalled that we had a lot of the Afrika Korps at Shady Lane. He was flown in a Junkers Ju-52 from Italy to an airbase on the Tunisian Algerian border and when he got there, he was promoted to the rank of Gefreiter, a private first class.

"Our supplies of food and particularly water, were inadequate."

Tell me about it, I thought to myself.

"It was hot and dirty, Eric, we rarely washed and there were no showers. I remember those damned flies, we had to wear nets over our faces and, although it was so hot during the day, the nights were freezing."

His memory was good. He told me all about Operation Morgenluft.

"It was February 1943, Rommel wanted to push the Americans from Gafsa and advance north to Kasserine in Tunisia. It was a disaster, we were routed, slaughtered like lambs, and many taken prisoners by the Americans."

"About a quarter of a million of your chaps were taken prisoner, Helmut."

"Yes, but I wasn't counting."

Helmut roared with laughter at his little joke. I recognised that quirky, black sense of humour I'd witnessed so much during the darkest times when men with little or no hope forced themselves to find something funny amidst the impossible situation they found themselves in.

"Those of us who had escaped hid out in the desert for several weeks and then we marched for many days, to a small beach. I think it was in Algeria although I can't be sure. An inflatable dinghy picked us up and took us to a German warship in the Mediterranean. While we had been given a bloody nose, at least we lived to fight another day."

I happened to glance away from the road ahead of me. Helmut was no longer laughing as his thoughts drifted back to those times.

"I'd never experienced thirst like it. It was so hot. Even though I had a half bottle of water left, it wasn't enough." He gripped my arm. "Men died,

Eric. Men died on that march into Algeria. Some were wounded and died from their injuries, but most died of thirst. We tried to help those who fell behind but after a few days we were just looking out for ourselves. We left the men who couldn't keep up and it was so hot we knew we had sentenced them to death. Many had lost their water bottles, they had nothing. You can't imagine it, Eric."

"I can, Helmut. Believe me, I can."

It was still early afternoon as we pulled up outside the hotel, just a short walk from the Shady Lane Arboretum. We checked in and they showed us to our rooms, across the corridor from each other. Helmut was hungry, we had a cup of coffee and a sandwich in the hotel lobby and then it was time to go.

"Are you ready, my friend?"

"Ja."

As we approached the entrance to the Arboretum, I wondered if I had perhaps brought Helmut here under false pretences. After all, there was nothing remaining of the camp he would remember, it would be nothing like my visit to Łambinowice. We walked through the gated area. A big blue sign read, Welcome to Shady Lane Arboretum. There was a picture of a small boy flying a kite, someone walking a dog, a young man on a bike, and for some reason, what looked like a sketch of Big Ben. There was nothing that mentioned that the site had once been a POW camp during the war.

And yet, as I gazed across at Helmut, he looked far from disappointed as he stood and looked around. He was smiling. Not the sort of reaction I was expecting.

"What is it?" I asked.

He held out a hand and swept it from side to side.

"I remember, Eric. There's nothing here but I remember it well."

I went into my bag and pulled out the plans that Walter had given me. Just before I'd left the farm, he'd asked Barry to bring a box from upstairs in the loft. Walter explained that the Americans had originally purchased the land to use as barracks and built the huts and outbuildings, but they had never been used. They had transferred the land to the Ministry of Defence sometime in 1943 and it became a POW camp at the beginning of 1944. He handed me the plans together with a few photos he had taken during the German prisoner occupation. He said that if I ever managed to persuade

Helmut to come over to England, at least I would have something to show him.

Thankfully, the rain had stopped and I spread the A1 sheet onto a park bench after I had wiped it down. I reached into the side pocket of my bag and pulled out the photographs of the old huts and laid them out. Helmut took a deep breath. He looked down at the park bench and then cast his eyes up ahead at the large expanse of green grass.

"It's difficult to believe, Eric, but yes, this is where we were." He pointed at a lone tree in the distance. "Over there, that's where my hut was, that's where I spent nearly three years of my life."

"Where were you captured?" I asked.

"Not far from what the Americans called Omaha Beach."

"On D-Day?"

"The day after," he replied. "I'll never forget D-Day, those aeroplanes, the tanks, the thousands of troops that poured into Normandy. I turned to my friend, and I said we were finished. He nodded his head, agreed with me and then we ran like hell. We were hiding in a ditch when the Americans caught up with us. We thought they would kill us, but they were okay I suppose. That night we were taken to a big field outside a small town. There were thousands of us, and they gave us all a bowl of stew. It tasted fantastic because we hadn't eaten for three days."

"You know, Eric, when we met at Cassel, my wife and I were returning from a little pilgrimage I made to Normandy, behind Omaha beach, my first visit since 1944."

"Ah, it makes perfect sense, we were two men on the same mission. Two veterans of the last war, as you say," I replied. "And when did you come here?"

Helmut shook his head. "I'm not sure exactly. There were rumours. Some said they were going to take us out to sea and sink the boat, others said we were sailing to America."

He turned to me. "I was frightened, Eric, I was just a boy."

Helmut stared straight ahead for a few moments. I thought it best to let him continue when he was ready.

"After a couple of hours, I knew they weren't going to sink us. We sailed through the night, the conditions were quite calm but the boat wasn't very sea-tight. By the time we docked at Liverpool we were all wet, cold, hungry and miserable. They fed us again at Liverpool and I sensed we were going to be alright. I was never going to admit it to my fellow soldiers, but I was pleased that we had been caught. I was relieved. I sensed that a part of the madness was over."

I listened quietly as Helmut told me how they had been taken by train to a racecourse for a few months where they were processed. They had slept in tents and then been moved to different parts of the country, some taken to Scotland and Wales, at least half were sent to America. I told Helmut that because his surname began with a letter in the second half of the alphabet, he'd been allocated to a British camp.

"Those prisoners with surnames A to M were sent to America, that was the deal, it was as simple as that."

"And I ended up here, Eric, and I met you."

"Yes, but I wasn't here in 1944, I was still in bloody Poland at that time."

I told Helmut about the forced marching, repatriation, and then my ill health and how I'd just avoided the fighting in the Far East. I told him I only weighed six stone when I returned home.

Helmut hung his head, didn't speak for a long time, shaking his head occasionally. Eventually, he spoke to me, "I know you weren't here at the beginning. When did you arrive, Eric?"

"The summer of 1945. They'd found out I spoke German and needed translators."

"It makes sense."

We studied the pictures a little while longer and then refolded the plans. I put them in my bag as we set off to walk the Arboretum. We walked slowly. We took in the quiet, peaceful atmosphere, there were few people about. I noticed some sort of shiny plaque embedded into a wooden post.

Helmut noticed it at the same time as I did. "What's that over there?"

I shrugged my shoulders; I hadn't noticed it the last time I'd visited.

We stood over it and I read the name out loud. "It's a memorial to Sophie Hermann."

"She sounds German," Helmut said.

"Jewish I would think."

"How do you know, is that what it says?"

"No, but it says that she was murdered by Hitler, so I'm taking a wild guess."

Helmut didn't respond.

We'd been walking for fifteen minutes when I eventually came straight out with it.

"You were a Nazi, weren't you, Helmut?"

He stopped suddenly and turned to face me. The colour drained from his face.

"You remember?"

"I do."

Before I could say anything, Helmut walked away from me. He turned around.

"Follow me, Eric. I will explain how much you helped me."

It was some minutes before he spoke again.

"We were machines, Eric, once an order was given there were no questions asked. It had been like that since school. In the history lessons we had learnt about Hitler and Goebbels and Goring, the great Nazis the teacher called them. We celebrated the National Socialist Party. You don't realise how bad things had become in Germany and how quickly things seemed to improve after they came to power.

We didn't realise that we were living under a dictatorship. My father had no option but to become a member of the party. The postman, the policeman, the baker, the town hall clerk, everybody had to join otherwise they were looked down on and persecuted. Men who refused lost their jobs; they were kicked out of their homes."

He stopped. I noticed he was trembling as he looked at me again.

"And it's true. Yes, I was a Nazi, the hairs stood up on the back of my neck when Hitler spoke on the radio."

"You had already been categorised by the time I arrived at Shady Lane," I said. "The prisoners were given a colour, white, grey or black, depending on their views. You were a black Helmut, strong pro-Nazi, your file read. We were frightened to send you lot home after the war, we feared it might start all over again."

Helmut stamped his foot on the earth.

"Here," he said, "do you remember what was here, Eric?"

"Yes, I do."

"It was what we called the lichtspielhaus."

"The picture palace."

"That's right, Eric. It was around the time when you arrived at the camp that the lichtspielhaus opened. I remember you presented the film footage with the British Officers and there were question and answer sessions afterwards. We didn't want to see those films because we didn't want to believe them. But as a youngster, I'd witnessed some cruel treatment in a

POW camp at home in Meppen. I saw an old man being beaten up by two guards. I wondered what on earth he'd done. It was after the footage shot at Belsen, you showed us, where the Americans marched one thousand Germans from a nearby village… errm… "

"Weimar."

"That's right. Weimar. You stood there afterwards while some of my countrymen shouted that it was a big hoax, American propaganda they said. And you stood there quietly. You were dignified and can you remember what you said?"

I nodded my head just once. I remembered it like it was yesterday.

"You said, 'Don't believe the Americans, don't believe the British or the Russians or the French.' You told us to look into the eyes of the villagers from Weimar, you told us to look into their eyes and look at the tears rolling down their cheeks, disgust and shame were written across every single face and then you played the film again."

"You're right, I did."

"Nobody left the lichtspielhaus, we stayed, and we watched. One or two men vomited where they sat, but we watched the tears and we stared into the faces of our mothers and sisters and a few old men. We knew what their eyes had seen, the stench of death that their nostrils had picked up, the sounds from the dying they'd heard with their own ears. We knew then that it was no hoax."

Helmut grabbed my arm; there were tears in his eyes.

"They fooled us, Eric, they fooled us all. I thought back to my Jewish schoolmates who just disappeared one day, and we didn't even ask the question. We stood back and did nothing."

I felt for Helmut as he stood on the ground where he had been held prisoner for more than three long years. He composed himself as I handed him a hankie and he dabbed at his eyes. He said that he'd been treated fairly by the guards and the British civilians had been kind and generous. Leicester had taught him something. He told me that he'd like to meet Walter and Barry again.

I pointed to the gate where Barry had walked me through some weeks back.

"Let's go," I said. "They live through that gate."

Chapter 43

WELCOME BACK

As I opened the gate and beckoned Helmut through, he continued to speak.

"Nobody stopped the Nazi party, for that, I hold up my hands and plead guilty. My parents too, while they didn't embrace the party ideals, they too did nothing."

"Nobody did," I told him. "They were all guilty of doing nothing. The judges, the politicians, the journalists."

"And the Church Eric, the Church ministers were standing in their pulpits every Sunday and their lips were sealed. As a teenager in the mid-thirties, I still went to chapel with my parents. I overheard a conversation one Sunday where my mother questioned what the Nazi party were doing to the Jews. She asked him why the Church says nothing; she told my father that Jesus was a Jew so why do they hate the Jews so much?"

I closed the gate and fastened the latch to the post with a piece of rope.

"They turned a blind eye, Eric, and all the while good German citizens, who attended church regularly, waited. They waited for condemnation, they waited for guidance, they waited for the organisation that stood for everything good to come out and tell them that what the Nazis were doing was an affront against God."

As we approached the front door of the farm cottage, Helmut stopped and gripped me by the arm.

"And I waited too Eric. I waited for someone… anyone, to tell me that it was wrong to be a Nazi." He shook his head. "But nobody did. Instead, my teachers encouraged me to join the Hitler Youth. They gave us smart uniforms, real leather boots and fed us the finest meat. We marched to songs that made us feel proud. And once in the Hitler Youth, they had us. There were lectures on genetics and inferior people. One day, they told us how bad the Versailles Treaty was, how the whole of Europe had conspired against us. We Germans were undefeated, it was an armistice. The French, and to a lesser extent you British, were attempting to ensure we could never become a threat by keeping us poor. Our Fuhrer was going to make the nation great again."

I knocked on the door and we waited for an answer.

I didn't quite know what to say to Helmut. He had been as much a victim of the war as I was, as Mary was, as Geoff was. None of us had wanted to pick up guns, shoot strangers and throw grenades at each other.

I glanced across at Helmut as we heard footsteps approaching. It was Barry who opened the door. I watched Helmut crumble as he set eyes on the fully grown man whom, forty years previously, he had taught to ride a bicycle. Walter walked over and they hugged each other like brothers as Walter too fought back his tears.

Well, well, well, I thought to myself. *The former Nazi and the man who had happily used German POWs as free labour for his farm work.*

We talked for hours. Helmut's grasp of English progressively got better the more he listened and spoke. Helmut praised me up on more than one occasion; he kept telling Walter and Barry how I had saved him. He also told the farmer and his son that their kindness and generosity had also changed his outlook of the world.

I asked Walter about the plaque to Sophie Hermann we had noticed at the remains of the camp. He told us that it was a plaque that had been placed by a local paediatrician and public health doctor, who lived in the area. She had managed to leave Germany to train in medicine in Switzerland during the war. It was a memorial to her mother who had been murdered in the 1943 Berlin round-up of Jews.

There was a moment of uncomfortable silence yet again as Helmut lowered his head to the table.

As it grew dark, Barry brought out some beers and we toasted each other's health. He put some ham, cheese and fresh bread on the table. We sat until midnight. I placed an arm around Helmut who by that point was getting a little drunk.

"It's time to get you home my friend."

"Ja," he said as he raised himself to his feet. He looked a little unsteady.

"Do you think you could get us a taxi?" I asked Barry.

"I'll run you back," he said as he grinned in the direction of Helmut. "He'll never make it to the hotel otherwise."

Chapter 44

MEIN KAMPF

The following morning, it was time to head over to the Lake District for a day and a night before the drive back to Hull to get Helmut home again.

We lifted his two small bags into the Mercedes and set off. It was a nice day. The county of Leicestershire was looking spectacular as we drove out of the city. The morning sky looked magnificent with reds, oranges and yellows mixing in with the greys and dark blues of the remainder of the night sky. We had driven no more than about twenty minutes. I think we were both overawed with what had happened over the last few days.

"Helmut," I said. "There's something I'm going to tell you that I haven't told anyone else. I think you'll understand."

"Tell me, Eric."

"Towards the end of my time here in Leicester, I started to feel very low. The camp was emptying as you boys were heading home; I had more time on my hands. There was no one to talk to anymore. What to do with myself was one question but at the same time I had received some bad news from home."

I was ready to tell Helmut about that terrible time, but he looked a little surprised and, dare I say, sad too. I didn't know a thing about his family, what they'd been through, if they'd been bombed, how many had died.

"I'd briefly met a Belgian girl just after VE Day in 1945. Would you believe we bloody well got engaged Helmut?"

"Ja?"

"Yes. It didn't work out; of course we'd dived in too quickly. But it was the end of the war, the Allies had won, and we all floated along on a tide of euphoria. Suddenly, the world was a better place. And do you want a laugh, Helmut?"

"Yes, Eric, tell me, make me laugh."

We'd got engaged and neither of us understood what the other was saying. How I managed to propose to her I'll never know."

Helmut sat in the passenger seat and chortled to himself as he pictured the scenario.

"And I was all skin and bones. What the hell was she thinking of saying 'yes' to a skeleton who couldn't speak her language?"

Helmut laughed again, slapped me hard on the thigh and I nearly lost control of the car for the second time. His laugh was infectious, I burst out laughing too.

"But I wasn't laughing back then, Helmut, I think I really did love her, and with the bad news from home, I suppose I sank into a depression. Thankfully one of the officers picked up on the fact I wasn't right and suggested a visit to our Civilian Rehabilitation Unit. We had CRUs all over the country, run by army psychiatrists."

"Like you, Eric."

"Yes. They sent me to Lilford Hall, which I guess is about twenty-five miles away, near Oundle. It was a rather grand stately home and going there felt like a weight had been lifted from my shoulders. To be honest, the hours I was spending watching over German ex-soldiers like you were beginning to get to me. And I liked the army doctor who sat and listened to me. He was probably the first person I had actually told how I was feeling."

And although at first, I was sceptical, he seemed to understand me immediately. He said he had seen it all before and reassured me that what I was feeling was normal for returning POWs and exactly what they'd expect to happen."

"I understand, Eric, I went through many of these emotions myself."

"I questioned the psychiatrist why it had taken so long for the depression to sink in. He said a delayed reaction was completely normal. It would generally take some other drama to trigger things off. I told him about the nightmares I had been having, including one where I drop down the mine in the cage in total darkness. He said that they might never go away but would get less frequent over time."

I told Helmut I had realised then that psychiatry was the career for me. And yet it was an impossible dream. Was that even a part of my depression? I was a mere Staff Sergeant; would they accept me into Medical School? It seemed that it was normally the preserve of the officers, those were the chaps who followed in the medical profession.

Men like me went into clerical work, like I was doing before I had joined up.

"Anyway, Helmut, I liked Oundle so much that, many years later, we put my son down to go to school there."

I had brought Helmut the scenic way; I was keen to show off how beautiful my country was. He took it all in, sometimes pointing at something particularly picturesque. We were now driving through the Yorkshire Dales and heading towards Kendall and Shap, one of the highest roads in England. We drove slowly through Kirby Stephen, a beautiful little village, and then the high fells of the Lake District came into view.

Helmut pointed. "And that is Scotland in the distance?"

"No," I said, "but it's very like Scotland, mountains, lakes and buckets full of rain."

"Ja, I see the black clouds." Helmut turned to me and with a built-in intuition said, "This place is special to you, Eric, isn't it?"

"It is."

"And this is why you wanted to show me?"

I nodded. "It was my adventure playground before the war; we climbed those big hills for fun, me and my pal Jack Portas."

"Jack... ja... you mention him a lot I think."

"Yes, Jack escaped with his regiment at Dunkirk. They were fighting alongside us until they reached the Belgian border in retreat. His regiment headed to Courtrai, while ours headed south to Tournai. He was a grand lad was Jack, got promoted to sergeant and was even mentioned-in-dispatches."

Helmut threw me a confused look. "Mentioned in dispatches, what does that mean?"

"Ah well, when you are mentioned in dispatches it's a great honour."

"Like a medal?"

"Sort of, only no medal is awarded."

"I see."

"Jack's mention was for bravery in northwest Germany 1944-45, when he was in Montgomery's Army liberating your part of Northern Germany. We were great friends and were highly annoyed that you bloody Germans split us up."

"I'm sorry about that, Eric."

I laughed. "I'm only joking, I don't suppose you had any part in it, Helmut."

"I didn't."

"After the war in Europe ended, we were told that we weren't finished and that the Japanese would have to be defeated next. We were together in June if I remember right, the Ministry of Defence still determined to get us fighting again but the atom bombs were dropped and the invasion never happened."

I had a melancholy moment of reflection. Jack's face was firmly etched into my mind even though I'd not set eyes on him for more than twenty years. We never fulfilled the friendship that should have been. While I was a POW in Germany, Jack married his childhood sweetheart during the war, coincidentally called Mary, and of course, I was a single chap. Quite naturally he spent most of his time with Mary and his new daughter after the war. It wasn't until the early 1960s that we began to see each other again. It hadn't lasted long. Just as we were beginning to re-form our friendship, he made the announcement he was heading to pastures new.

Helmut interrupted my thoughts. "And your grand friend, Eric, is he still alive?"

"Yes, yes, he is still alive, but he emigrated to Western Australia in the 1960s. He's set up a civil engineering business in Perth. I haven't seen him since, but we stay in touch by letter. He is doing very well but unfortunately… " I pointed at the mountains which we were approaching and continued, "we'll never get to walk those hills again."

Helmut spoke, "Then you and I must walk them."

I looked at him. "Are you serious? We are both old men."

"Ja, ja, but we are very fit old men, Überlebende. Survivors of the last war don't forget."

I had never thought about Helmut wanting to wander up the fells but suddenly the idea appealed.

"We can toast the good health to your Australian friend."

"We can; we'll buy a bottle of schnapps in town."

I told Helmut that we had named my son John after Jack Portas.

"I was going to call him Geoff initially, after my brother, but some of the family suggested that wasn't suitable."

The weather was appalling as we drove carefully over the Shap Pass and down into Penrith. I swear the rain was falling sideways and I could feel the car drifting all over the road in the wind. We made it safely down into Keswick and I found the small bed and breakfast I had booked on Stanger Street, the first road on the left as we drove into town. Memories of those great times with Jack came flooding back. The God I didn't believe in seemed to have a habit of removing the best friends from my life.

After we had checked in, we went for a stroll around Keswick. I took Helmut to a real English pub for a pint of bitter. I was pleased that we sat in a quiet corner and that there weren't many people in. Helmut spoke about guilt and the Holocaust. Once again, he told me that I had helped to save his life. I told him he was exaggerating. Helmut gripped my wrist with his right hand.

"Eric, you changed my mind, made me see that it was for real. I came and I questioned you. At times I was very rude, told you I didn't believe what the British were saying, that the Holocaust had never taken place."

"And what did I say?"

"Not a lot, Eric. You listened. You let me do most of the talking."

A psychiatrist in the making, I thought to myself.

"And then you gave it to me."

I remembered the day well. Young Helmut thought I had taken leave of my senses.

"A copy of Mein Kampf."

I couldn't help but smile. Helmut remembered.

I had managed to get a German copy of Hitler's Mein Kampf from the camp library. It was controversial as the authorities had effectively banned the book. I had read it while I was working with my hard-core Nazis. I realised it was the only tool I needed. Now I could read German, I could see it was an obvious rant and it was so poorly written. I'd figured that it would save me a lot of work.

"Ha, and then the book!" Helmut slapped a hand hard onto his knee. "You gave me the book and told me to read it. I couldn't believe it and ran back to my hut where my fellow Nazis were. I showed them what you had given me. Some of them were delighted. They drew lots to see who would get the book after I'd finished it."

"You read in it two days, didn't you?"

"You remember?"

"I do."

"At first, I revelled in the book; those first few chapters outlined Hitler's world view and his plans for a resurgent Germany. An undefeated country devastated by the unjust Armistice."

I knew what was coming next.

241

I prompted Helmut. "And then my friend, what did you read after that?"

Helmut shook his head. He looked like he was struggling for words.

"I... I read about an evil man consumed with hatred, about his hatred towards the Jewish people. He was very explicit about what we should do with the Jews; I couldn't believe what I was reading. You were right Eric, it was all falling into place with every page I turned. My eyes were full as I read that Hitler wanted to annihilate the Jews and I understood that it was all true. I was no longer proud to be a Nazi."

I placed my hand over Helmut's. "You were never a real Nazi, Helmut."

"No?"

"Of course not."

"And why do you say that, Eric?"

"Because we knew you. You were a man who could love your fellow human beings. Even in the field of battle."

Helmut didn't speak for some time as his eyes glassed over.

"Thank you, Eric," he said as he walked slowly towards the bar.

Chapter 45

LATRIGG FELL

The following day we kept our promise to each other and walked up towards the summit of Latrigg Fell. It wasn't far from the hotel.

The old legs and lungs managed just fine. We took our time and were rewarded at the top with a beautiful view across Keswick and Derwentwater. I picked out Cat Bells and I think Helvellyn, fells that Jack Portas and I had scaled fifty years previously. I sat on the bench with my German friend, wishing fleetingly that I had been there with Jack.

"Your country is truly beautiful, Eric," Helmut said. "I can see why you brought me here."

It was a fine dry day and I reached into my knapsack and pulled out the bottle of schnapps and the two glasses I had temporarily borrowed from the hotel. We toasted absent friends. We toasted peace in Europe and our families who survived and those that didn't.

We talked about our wives. Helmut said that his wife had been his rock; he said he had woken her many times in the middle of the night as he'd wake up screaming from a nightmare.

"I've been in the same dream," I said. "Everybody talks about how tough the war was but nobody ever talks about how tough it was afterwards."

Helmut grunted in agreement.

"We brought our troubles home with us, didn't we?"

"We did, Eric."

"I don't think it was easy for my wife and my children. Looking back, there were many things that I wish I could have changed. I was married in 1947, Helmut. It was probably too soon. When I made my wedding day speech, I said something to that effect."

Helmut turned to me. "You did? What did you say?"

I slapped Helmut's back. "My wife teased me about what I said for many years."

"And what did you say."

"You won't believe it, Helmut, I said to the guests, 'Well... this is going to be difficult, but Joy and I are going to make a go of this.'"

Helmut looked shocked and covered his mouth with his hand as he started to giggle.

"And it was difficult, Helmut, we brought back a lot of bad memories."

"Ja, we did."

"No one had ever heard of post-traumatic stress back then. They called it shell shock. Bloody shell shock, can you believe it?"

Helmut tried to pour me another schnapps, but I told him I had to drive. He took a large mouthful straight from the bottle. We gazed out of the hill in silence before I told him we had to get going.

"Come on, Helmut, we need to get you on this night ferry."

I stood. Extended a hand down to him and pulled him up.

We made our way back down, dropped into the hotel and picked up our bags. I settled the bill. My treat. Helmut wasn't happy, but I insisted.

"You're a guest in my country," I said. "I pick up the tab."

He was already planning the return trip to Lower Saxony as we walked out to the car, insisting that he would return the favour.

In just over four hours we pulled into the ferry terminal in Hull. We were ready to say our goodbyes. I'd miss Helmut, he had been a fine companion. Once again, he enveloped me in a tight bear hug, even planting a kiss on my cheek. I refrained from telling him that it wasn't the 'British way'. I'd let it go. Just this once.

Strangely enough, I waited in the car park for nearly an hour, until the ferry pulled out of the port. I think I saw Helmut standing up on the top deck waving, though I couldn't be sure.

I watched as the huge boat sailed out into a grey North Sea under a similar coloured sky.

Goodbye, dear friend, I whispered under my breath before I turned up my coat collar and walked back to the car.

Chapter 46

THE REPORT

I had spent some time on the report. I had asked Mrs Knight to read it over and she made numerous corrections, sometimes retyping several paragraphs and pages but, eventually, it was ready.

I sent copies to all the relevant departments; I was pleased that it was clear and concise. I had used enough medical jargon to convince those that needed convincing that Mary O'Leary was neither a risk to society nor suffering from a psychiatric disorder. In my view, she was ready and able to be re-integrated into society. I left out my sentiment that the country owed it to her too, I didn't think that had a place in a purely medical report.

My meeting was with Mary at the end of the week. I wondered how she would react.

"Something's wrong," she said as she sat at the table and looked at me.

I didn't think I was acting any different, but she had sensed something in me. Nervousness, fear, perhaps a mixture of both.

"There's nothing wrong," I said. "Nothing at all, it's just… "

"Tell me, Doctor, what is it?"

Where to start?

"Well. I did a lot of thinking and I've looked through your case notes from start to finish."

"That must have been exciting," she said sarcastically.

"The thing is Mary… I don't think it's right that you should be locked up in here for the foreseeable future."

She flopped back in her seat.

I continued. "As you know, you are sectioned under the Mental Health Act but, if an independent psychiatrist decides that a patient does not justify a Mental Health Section and compiles a report stating the reasons why then, generally speaking, his recommendations are adhered to. It's not

245

always the case of course, but ninety-nine percent of the time his report is generally acted upon and the process begins immediately."

I looked at Mary.

Concern. But did I also see a slight twitch at the side of her lips or was that my imagination?

It took her a minute to speak. She caught the attention of a nurse and asked for two cups of tea. The nurse came and went, the teacups were placed on the table and Mary took a big gulp. Then she spoke.

"I see."

"Don't worry, Mary, we won't throw you out onto the streets with a sleeping bag. You'll be moved to a day centre at first. You can go out for walks or shopping trips. You'll be accompanied at first but then, and only then, when you feel confident enough you can go out on your own."

Mary drank from the cup. Looked up. "And I'll sleep at the day centre?"

"Yes, you'll have your own room. You can stay there as long as you need. In time, it may take a year or two, you'll be moved to a small flat with a warden, someone you can turn to for help, someone you can trust. A year or two down the line you may want more independence, perhaps a flat of your own, who knows."

Mary was tapping her foot on the floor. That was something I'd never seen before. I knew what she was thinking.

She took a long drink of tea. "I'll have to leave here?"

"Yes."

Mary looked slowly around the room, out into the gardens through the window, tried to take another mouthful of tea that wasn't there. Her cup had been drained.

"It's up to you, Mary, they'll run at your pace. It's first things first; they'll take it a step at a time."

"I'm scared," she whispered like a small child. "I... I... "

"I know how you feel."

"You do?"

"Yes, I can read your thoughts like a book. It's not ideal to be locked up here you're thinking, but it's the only thing you know."

I recalled my own thoughts as we set off on that Long March in January 1945.

"You have felt like this, Dr West?"

"Yes, I have."

246

She grimaced. "The March."

It wasn't a question. She knew. She was there.

"We didn't know where we were going or if we would ever make it," I said. "I remember taking a glance over my shoulder as we set off down the road and a bit of me wanted to stay behind, even in E72. It was familiar territory, with a familiar routine." I reached for her hand. "That's exactly how you're feeling right now, isn't it?"

"Yes."

"You are setting off on your own Long March, Mary. Believe me; the world has changed out there. It's not the same place you'd remember, and it might frighten you at first."

"Were you scared on the March, Dr West?"

"Yes. I was bloody well petrified."

Mary rose slowly from her seat and walked over to the window. She looked outside for some time. Her head swept right to left several times and then she looked up into the sky. I left her with her thoughts, tried hard not to interrupt. It was raining, she eased a finger up to the windowpane and followed a raindrop as gravity pulled it towards the sill.

She turned around. "I am ready, Dr West. I am happy for you to start writing your report."

"It's written, Mary. It has been written. In fact, I've had a reply, they have agreed with my suggestion. You are no longer sectioned under the Mental Health Act. You are leaving here at the end of the month."

Chapter 47

ABSENT FRIENDS

The centre was back in my hometown, in Sutton, Surrey. In a way, even though she hadn't been there for a generation, Mary felt that she was going back to her roots. Her roots, sadly, weren't full of fond memories. A little over fifteen miles away was Smithfield, where the German V2 rocket attack on 8th March 1945 had changed her life. Wasn't the world an unfair place? After all she had gone through during the war when victory was in sight, someone somewhere, some greater power than her, saw fit to take away the only stable influence in her life.

Her mother was her soul mate, her best friend, her confidant, especially since her father had left. She hadn't grieved properly. Not really. Everything took its toll after the war. She'd lost her father and then her mother, many of her colleagues and friends too. She had witnessed the madness of the final days of the war in Germany. She had been pushed into a place from where there was no escape. She had never visited her mother's headstone at the cemetery. She had found it hard to come to terms that there was very little of her mother found, certainly no body to bury. That would be her first trip out, arranged with the staff; a psychiatric nurse called Carol had agreed to accompany her.

South London had changed beyond all recognition. The traffic was the biggest change and the streets looked neglected and crummy, with too much glass and chrome. What had happened?

And yet she liked the feeling, the hustle and bustle, the busybodies rushing around. People paying no attention to her. That suited her fine. Anonymity.

She also found herself talking quite easily with Carol. She was the listening type, just like Dr West.

She owed so much to, Dr West.

Carol parked her car in the cemetery car park in Kingston Road near Wimbledon Common. The short drive seemed to have taken forever, the traffic lights, roundabouts, pedestrian crossings, one-way streets. Everything seemed like obstructions, designed purposely to slow the traffic up. She couldn't help thinking that they could have walked there quicker.

"In your own time Mary," Carol said. "Your mum's headstone is here somewhere."

They climbed out of the car and Carol pressed a button on her key fob that automatically locked the central locking system to the doors. Clever stuff. Mary smiled.

My God, I've been away for such a long time, she thought to herself.

It took them some time to find her mother's plot as they didn't have a plan of the headstones; they just knew that it was situated in the northern part of the cemetery, the area where the plots were so much smaller as they only contained a small urn with the ashes of the deceased. Ideally, her mother would have wanted to be buried but, with no body to bury, it had resulted in a formal Catholic service and then an official headstone in the cemetery.

She had vague memories of visiting the graveyard as a teenager, an aunt had died in childbirth, she had come with her mum. A real grave, a body six feet below. Something to grieve, not just dust and fresh air.

They walked and checked the stones, eventually after fifteen minutes of searching, they found it. It was non-descript, the letters were worn, the grass around the headstone uncared for and weeds were sprouting up after the recent rain.

Be still and know that I am with God.
Roslin O'Leary
12 December 1901 – 8 March 1945

There was no mention of the violence that took Mary's mother's life.

Mary laid the bunch of flowers in front of the headstone.

"Sorry, Mum," she whispered to herself. "Sorry it's taken me so long."

On the way back to Sutton and as arranged, Mary enrolled in the local library. That would be her next trip out. She surprised herself when she realised that she couldn't wait. She visited the library accompanied by Carol just once when they'd had a quick look around. The second time she

249

decided she wanted to do it alone. The library was just two hundred yards from the centre in Sutton. Carol walked her to the entrance; made sure she had her library card and pointed to a small café opposite.

"I'll be in there if you suffer any sort of panic attack."

"I'll be fine," Mary said.

Poor Carol. Mary thought perhaps she should tell her what she had faced up to during the war years. A bespectacled middle-aged librarian was hardly going to cause her any real concern.

She had forgotten just how wonderful a library was. The smell of fresh paperback pages mixed with old tomes was intoxicating, almost like a drug. The wall-to-wall carpet was dated, but thick and earthy, cleverly designed for soundproofing with polite notices asking the customers to respect the silence.

She wandered around the shelves for some time, familiarising herself with the reference books. There was a coffee percolator, an honesty box and small individual desks scattered in every nook and cranny. There was a small lounge area with half a dozen two-seater sofas scattered around a huge, oak table. A notice read:

Please talk quietly and only when necessary.

She was in no hurry. She walked over to the percolator and poured herself a cup, put a coin in the box then ambled over to one of the empty desks.

Mary recalled that day when the doctor had eased back in his chair and his eyes looked up to the ceiling. He was remembering all his old friends and comrades. As he mentioned the names of Odling, MacDougall, Clarke, Milton and a few others she had asked him where they were now and if they had survived. He told her bluntly that he didn't have a clue.

It was time to find the answers to Dr West's questions. He had said that, rightly or wrongly, he had never wanted to go to POW or regiment reunions. He was doing his best to put those years behind him and yet he had said he now regretted not knowing what had happened to them all.

She recalled Dr West describing his excitement finding a newspaper article about just one of his officers. While he was a medical student at St Thomas' Hospital in 1950, by chance, Dennis Clarke had appeared in his local newspaper, the Sutton and Cheam Herald.

The article had said that a one-armed Major Dennis Clarke was running as the Liberal Party's Parliamentary Candidate for Carshalton. Well, he had obviously survived, promoted to Major Clarke and the article portrayed him as somewhat of a war hero. He had escaped at Dunkirk but had lost his arm during the desert war. Mary remembered Dr West laughing and saying that he was a better soldier than he was an MP. The newspaper said he had lost his deposit.

Mary had asked if the doctor had ever gone to see Clarke or voted for him at the election. He went quiet.

'No,' he had told her.

Then he smiled and said that it was good to know he had survived, that he had rebuilt his life again.

Tracing Clarke's life was relatively easy as the library had an archive of bound Daily Express newspapers dating back to the twenties. Clarke was the journalist who had been in Vienna in the years before the outbreak of the war. She found several articles he had written from Vienna about disappearing Jews. In March 1939, he'd written a prophetic piece analysing the German economy and what the Czechoslovakian invasion would have brought the Nazis in stolen Czech gold and currency. At the time, Clarke had written that the German economy was hopelessly in debt and virtually on its knees. He wrote that stolen Czechoslovakian gold was the key that opened the door to the coming conflict.

She found an article describing his injury that occurred in March 1943. He was fighting in Tunisia alongside Basil Strachan, another 140 Regiment Dunkirk veteran. The army medics had operated on him virtually on the spot and saved his life.

The Express archives from 1950 onwards were in a new binder. Here, there was little to find. Mary was on the point of stopping her search until she found a brief obituary notice in the Daily Express dated June 1955. She winced as she read, 'Famous journalist, Major Dennis Clarke, has died in Westminster at the age of forty-three years after a long battle with illness.'

Mary took out her notepad and made some more notes.

An old schoolmaster had once told her, "If you're looking for answers, you'll find everything you need to know in a library."

She had put his theory to the test.

Chapter 48

NEEDLE IN A HAYSTACK

The very first book Mary borrowed was 'Saturday at MI9' by Airey Neave. Sadly Neave, a Member of Parliament, great wartime hero and Colditz escaper, had been the victim of a different conflict just seven years ago. The Irish National Liberation Army had blown up his car outside the Houses of Parliament.

She needed to know more about the organisation she once worked with. It gave her an insight into the story of the underground escape lines in occupied Europe. There was a very good reason she wanted to know more about those escape lines. When she had been with MI9 she recalled several men who had passed through a very specific escape line department. By the end of the war, they had managed to bring nearly four thousand men and women safely back onto British soil.

It may have been a coincidence, but Mary could now vaguely recall a young, artillery man from the Dunkirk battles who had been debriefed at MI9. The question was whether it was one and the same man. She had never met him, but the whole department had been talking about his legendary escapes. The young lad was apparently a shy, unassuming type of boy, but his reputation went before him. He'd been captured outside Dunkirk and had escaped from a stationary train and went on the run. If she remembered correctly, he escaped a second, then a third time and miraculously a fourth time where he had managed to smuggle himself on a boat bound for Africa. The Nazis and Vichy French just couldn't keep hold of this man. Now Mary wondered, could this have been the same gunner that Dr West had mentioned during one of their first meetings? If memory served her right, Dr West had mentioned that Gunner Martin had been the driver for one of his commanding officers, Major Milton.

She read the whole book. She drew a blank; there was no mention of a Gunner Martin anywhere. She took out three books on MI9 specifically. She wasn't giving up. More blanks. After she returned the books, the librarian engaged in conversation with her, albeit in a whisper. Mary explained that she had worked in MI9 during the war and was looking for specific information relating to soldiers who had served with a London Territorial Regiment.

"And do you have their names, dear?"

"Yes."

"And you want to know what happened to them?"

"Yes. I'm not a relative but we were connected."

"Okay," the librarian said, "let me help you."

She walked out from behind her desk area, placed a little sign on the desk which read, 'Back in ten minutes' and asked Mary to follow her.

As she walked away, Mary followed on behind wondering which bookshelf she was guiding her to. As they reached a door the librarian turned, took out a key.

"I reckon you could read two dozen books connected to MI9 and not find what you are looking for."

As the librarian inserted the key in the lock and turned it, she spoke again, "This is the microfiche room, or as I call it, the archive grotto. This is where you will find what you are looking for."

Mary had heard of microfilm, but never seen or used it. There had been a flurry of activity towards the end of the war to preserve records, and she'd been vaguely aware of the term. The librarian explained that libraries started using microfilm in the early sixties, along with banks and post offices, local government and even schools.

"I've been here twenty-five years love; I can remember when we first started using it. We were trained on how to use it as a storage medium."

She took Mary to one of four machines sitting on a desk on the far side of the room.

"Sit," she beckoned.

Mary took a seat and the librarian pushed a button on the side of the machine. The screen in front of her flickered into life.

"Now dear, I'm going to show you something."

There were two envelopes on the desk adjacent to the machine.

"Lazy buggers won't put things away," she said. "Never mind, this will do for what I'm about to explain."

She opened one of the envelopes, fished inside, and pulled out a dozen large pieces of microfilm. She held them to the light and screwed up her eyes, straining to read the larger writing at the bottom.

"Righto! This is the London Evening Standard from 1964."

Mary pulled a confused look.

"I'm not joking," the librarian said, "this is every single copy of the newspaper that particular year."

She slipped a piece of film onto the glass surface and rotated a large ball at the bottom of the machine.

"Here we are, this is August 1964."

Mary focussed on a headline. A house fire in Hackney, a mother and two small children perished in a blaze that was thought to have been started deliberately.

The librarian took Mary through a demonstration and then let her have a go. She picked it up within a minute or two.

"Just scroll through the editions until you find the day you are looking for," she said.

She then walked Mary around the room, explaining how the archive system worked. Each large shelf represented a year. There were newspaper records; The Sunday People, Daily Telegraph and News of the World, births, marriages and deaths, even specific magazines dating back to the 1920s.

"And of course, there are the publications that will interest you; records from the Ministry of Defence, the War Office and even some Military Intelligence information that is now in the public domain. After a certain time has passed, all those records are made available to the public and some poor bugger has to copy them."

"Somebody copies them?"

"Yes, I served my apprenticeship and spent six months in the department. It was soul-destroying at times and yet some days were fairly interesting if you stumbled on a good story or some gossip."

"So, everything is copied and put onto microfilm?"

"Well dear, not everything, but within reason, yes."

Mary stopped and looked around the room. Tens of thousands of boxes, fifty or sixty years of information. Perhaps somewhere, all the information she needed to build up a record of what had happened to the men of 140 Regiment.

The librarian said she could go into the room anytime she wanted, it was open to the public from 9 am to 5 pm, she just had to sign in and she would be given the key.

Chapter 49

A BREAKTHROUGH

Mary returned the following day at nine o'clock sharp. She felt at home as the librarian looked up and greeted her with nothing more than a smile and a nod. Mary poured herself a coffee and took it to an empty desk. Such a simple pleasure, being able to pour yourself a coffee and sit where you want without someone watching over you.

The library was full of young students; last-minute research for a morning exam or a lecture. The occasional whisper but apart from that a pleasant stillness, a calm. The silence itself was a little unnerving; it wasn't something she'd been used to over the last forty years. It was ghostly... eerie.

As she got to the bottom of her cup, the librarian ambled over to her desk. She said nothing but placed a key on the desk. She had somehow sensed that Mary was going to take her research seriously.

She had made two pages of notes, bullet points of exactly what she was going to look for first. It shouldn't be so difficult and although she didn't expect to find what she wanted straight away, she told herself that in time she would be able to streamline her searches, familiarise herself with the strategic relevance of the thousands of boxes in the archive room. It was challenging and reminded her of the days filled with frustration during her wartime decryption work.

She spent the next three days pulling the heavy boxes from the shelves, sorting through the cardboard files and placing sheets of transparent microfilm onto the projection screen. The concentration levels were high, the strain on her eyes intense.

She found nothing on Gunner John Martin. She tried everything, even different spellings of the name, Jon, Martyn, and trolled through dozens of files. She checked births, marriages, and deaths, a pointless exercise as there were literally thousands of John Martins. Even the army's active service records threw up nearly three hundred John Martins and gave nothing more than a rank, number and whether they had survived the war or been killed in action.

It was while she was lying in bed several days later that the breakthrough came. She was half sleeping, half awake, and at first she thought it may have been a dream. But no, definitely not a dream. She was wide awake now; looking at the bedside clock she saw 06:15. The doctor had said something about John Martin being a farm boy, somewhere down south. Devon. Yes, that was it, John Martin had been a farm boy in Devon, born and bred the doctor had said.

As she walked the wet, early morning streets a few hours later she wondered what Sutton library held in their archive department relating to newspapers from Devon, but more importantly how far they went back.

It took her three hours. She found what she was looking for in an obscure Devon publication from August 1944 referring to an incident at Sword Beach on D-Day, the Allied landings in Normandy. No wonder she couldn't find him, he wasn't called John Martin, he was called William John Henry Martin. This was him, without a doubt; the newspaper article referred to 140 Regiment and that Martin had been a driver.

Mary spent the rest of the day researching everything that had happened to Martin during the war. What a story the man had; she couldn't believe that she had been in the same room as him at one point.

She was back bright and early the next morning and the day after too. Her second home. And only when she felt that she had found everything held on Gunner William John Henry Martin, did she strike a red line through the bottom of the last page in her exercise book. It was time to move on. Major Milton was next on the list and she already had a head start on where to look.

Dr West was due to visit at the end of the month. She'd have everything ready for him.

Chapter 50

REPORTING FOR DUTY

It was always going to be a daunting prospect, moving from a lock-and-key controlled environment to the sort of place where you could come and go as you pleased. Mary was still very much under supervision and observation but, by all accounts, she was thriving in her new home. She was interacting quite normally with the staff and other residents. During her free time, she had apparently set up camp in Sutton library.

She'd make it, I had every confidence in her and a library was the perfect place to keep her brain ticking over. She had the right sort of distractions, a project to keep her focussed and to give her a sense of achievement. Mary had a new mission.

In my experience, these moves only benefitted the patient if they grasped the opportunity with both hands and immersed themselves in a new hobby, some sort of community service or even a job. Those who sat around and looked out of the window all day wondering what time their next meal would be placed in front of them generally couldn't cope with the change. Many of them ended up back where they started, or worse.

But not Mary. As soon as I walked into the common room lounge, I noticed something in her eyes, something that I had never seen before. Her eyes were bright and alive; I knew she had something important to tell me. She told me about the library, how she had settled in so well and that her supervising warden and the staff were 'nice and easy to talk to.'

Who would have believed it? Mary the mute, I thought.

She thanked me several times for my report and how good it felt to know that she was no longer looked upon as a nutter. Her words, not mine.

She told me that the world had changed but that she was taking it all in and progressing slowly but surely, she'd cope just fine. She was talking like a bloody psychiatrist!

We talked for a while and then Mary decided it was coffee time. She disappeared and then brought me a cup of coffee that she'd made in the communal kitchen.

"Gunner Martin," she said.

Surprised that she had even remembered about him and even more surprised that she had brought him up, I looked over the rim of my cup.

"What about him?"

"Gunner William John Martin."

"Yes," I nodded. "Major Milton's driver. I haven't seen him since Cassel."

"I want to tell you what happened to him."

I leaned forward in my seat, placed my cup on the table. She started speaking. From the outset, I was absolutely engrossed.

"Gunner Martin was captured on the thirtieth of May 1940 along with your commander, Major Edward Milton."

"That's right," I said. "Unfortunately, Milton was badly injured, I believe he died from his wounds, but I never knew what happened to John Martin. He was captured you say?"

"Yes, during the breakout from Cassel he was in a small section in a house surrounded by German tanks. They did their best to hold out but as you know, you lot were abandoned at Cassel."

"Tell me about it."

"He was captured and according to his MI9 debrief notes, he was part of a long column marched through northern France to Cambrai. The conditions in Cambrai were not good, it was hot, there was little water and next to no food."

"Wait a minute," I interjected. "Martin was with you in MI9. But why?"

Mary raised an eyebrow. "Well, Dr West, if you stop interrupting, I'll tell you why."

Suitably admonished, I buttoned my lip.

"At Cambrai, the prisoners were herded into the village square; they were kept there, out in the open perhaps for a couple of days and nights. They didn't know what was going to happen to them, some had whispered that they were going to be executed."

The great uncertainty. I knew the feeling well.

"Early in the morning, the prisoners set off in long columns surrounded by German guards. Some of the columns were two hundred strong, others five hundred. Martin's column marched for most of the day and was eventually put on a train. It moved out slowly under cover of darkness and they stopped at a place called Hirson, near the Belgium border. Martin said that as night closed in again, the German guards were as restless as the prisoners. Through a slit in the side of the truck, he noticed that many of them were pulling out rolled blankets and trying to get some sleep. Martin took his chance. Despite the threat of a bullet in the back, he managed to slide one of the doors open a few inches, enough to slip through and disappear into the darkness. When daylight came, he stole some civilian clothing from a washing line and discarded his army uniform in a forest. He was confident he could survive, after all, he was a country boy, he was used to living off the land."

I notice Mary's expression had changed. "There's a 'but' isn't there?"

"You have a second sense, Dr West. Yes, you are right. Two days after he had escaped from the train, he was re-captured and handed over to the authorities. He was detained in a camp close by with three hundred other Frenchmen. Gunner Martin lasted five weeks and then he was off again."

"Transported to another camp?" I questioned.

"No, the bugger escaped yet again."

"No way... how?"

"Well, we aren't sure. All Gunner Martin said was that he was always on the lookout for an opportunity, a lazy guard, a weakness in a fence. He was patient and studied everything, constantly weighing things up. Anyway, he was off again and this time he managed to stay free for three weeks. He made his way south; northern France was crawling with Germans, and he'd heard from other prisoners about escape lines operating in the Vichy controlled south. He made it through Reims and swam the River Marne but ran into a German patrol near Epernay. He hadn't quite made it one hundred miles."

I shook my head in disbelief.

"And then he escaped again."

"What?"

"Yes, he scrambled over a high wall and this time he covered a lot more miles. We're not sure how long it took him as obviously he was a bit vague with dates, but Epernay to Marseille... "

"He made it to Marseille!"

"From Epernay to Marseille, yes, nearly five hundred miles."

"Good God!"

"Yes, he walked most of the way keeping off the main roads, walking through the forests and meadows, over the hills. He passed through Troyes, Auxerre, Clamercy and Limoges. Again, he lived off the land, stole food from farms. He gave MI9 good intelligence of a Nazi training camp for Hitler youth, he had spotted what he thought was around one thousand young boys at an aerodrome. There was also a munition dump there. He crossed the line of demarcation a few miles from Nevers but, unfortunately, he ran into the Vichy authorities in Marseille and they handed him over to the police. We believe he was held in an internment camp in Fort Saint Jean and then guess what?"

Mary looked at me as a slight grin crossed her face.

"You're not going to tell me he escaped again?"

"That's right, this man's story would make an incredible book, although no one would believe it."

"I'm not surprised; they must have known he was a prolific escapee. My God, they should have shackled him to a stone wall."

We took a short break. Mary told me there was still a lot more to tell me about Gunner Martin and his face was ingrained in my mind from that last time I ever saw him. He was roughly my age so, hopefully, Mary was going to tell me he made it back home.

We had coffee in the small kitchen area; I couldn't wait to get back in the main lounge so that Mary could finish her story. Her research was impeccable. She told me all about the archive room in Sutton library and the days she had spent with the boxes of microfiche film.

"They only managed to hold Martin for ten days," Mary said, "then he was off again, he said he lived on stolen fruit.

He hid out near the docks waiting for an opportunity to get on a boat. The Germans were looking for him; he knew he had to get away from the French mainland. He climbed on board a boat bound for Oran in Algeria and hid out under a lifeboat cover.

The poor gunner wasn't to know at the time, but Oran was then also under the control of the Vichy French government. He was arrested almost straight away and sent to a civilian prison where the conditions were extremely harsh.

But there wasn't a prison or a prison camp in the world that was going to hold this man."

"I don't believe it."

"Yes. And this time he made it onto another boat bound for Casablanca and eventually he got lucky."

I rocked back in my seat like an excited schoolboy. "Keep going."

"He made it to the American Consul, Dr West, and relayed his incredible tale. He wanted only one thing, to get back onto British soil and re-join whatever was left of your regiment so he could fight Germans again. The Americans got him onto a Portuguese boat bound for the Straits of Gibraltar and there he joined up with a Royal Navy vessel."

"My goodness... incredible... truly incredible."

"He arrived back in England on... " Mary consulted her notes, "the 14th December 1940."

"Well I never, seven months on the run. And a home run too. That makes my feeble escape effort at Gliwice look like a bit of a damp squib."

What an extraordinary story. I sat for some time staring into space, trying to comprehend what I had just been told. Gunner Martin had escaped five times. Why hadn't they made a film about him?

"This story is better than the Great Escape film."

I looked at Mary. She seemed reluctant to continue and yet there had to be more, a conclusion.

"And then what happened, Mary, did he join up with the regiment, did he go back to Woolwich?"

"He did, Doctor," Mary nodded. "William John Martin reported back to 140 Regiment's depot almost as soon as he could, before Christmas 1940."

"Splendid."

"And he was recommended for a Distinguished Conduct Medal by one Lieutenant Colonel Graham Brooks. He received his award for bravery and initiative in March 1941."

Mary had her head in her notes again. "We're not sure exactly why, but for some reason, soon after his DCM award, it appears that Gunner Martin transferred to the 50th Mechanical Equipment Company, the Royal Engineers."

That was a bit of a puzzle right enough. Why would he do that? Probably not enough of our lads left, perhaps Martin had a particular skill the Royal Engineers were looking for. On reflection, the transfer made sense as I remembered that Martin seemed good with all things mechanical.

"Finish the story," I said to Mary, "tell me what happened to him, is he still alive? I'd love to meet up with him and shake his bloody hand if nothing else."

And then Mary dropped the bombshell and my whole world seemed to cave in.

"Dr West, I'm afraid Sapper Martin was killed on Sword Beach during the D-Day landings. He was twenty-six years of age."

Chapter 51

CEDRIC ODLING

I'd never find out how long Mary's research took. I had no idea how many hours she spent each day. All I knew was the information the staff from her day centre gave me. She was in Sutton library most days for many hours. Sometimes she returned for lunch and went back in the afternoons.

Gunner Martin. What a crying shame, where was the justice in life? Don't anyone try and convince me that there is a God up there somewhere, because that gunner's end was a bloody tragedy. He had been blown up on the beach, a mortar shell they thought. Mary had shown me his grave registration report; he had been buried in a Commonwealth War Grave at Saint Andrew's Churchyard in the tiny hamlet of Aveton-Gifford. His grave was next to his parents, who had both post-deceased him, and near to the family's home in Devon.

She then handed me his own accounts of his escapes.

It was quite sobering seeing it all written down, albeit probably typed out by some bod in MI9. His own words. My goodness, they touched me so much.

The Major, Major Milton, after giving the order to surrender, he'd passed away. I recalled vaguely at Lamsdorf someone saying Major Milton never made it but, throughout my captivity, I didn't know for sure. It wasn't until some years later that I found out. He had been buried at Saint Omer in France. I now regretted that I hadn't taken the time, when I drove past that cemetery with Geoff, to look for his grave and pay my respects.

Edward Milton had given his life for the regiment and his country. He had fought in the Great War, as most of my officers had done, survived that carnage and then, just over twenty years later, he'd joined up again. This time around, he hadn't been so lucky.

How many of my old friends were left? How many had made it in civilian life without a breakdown? How many were lucky enough to have had a successful career, even made it to retirement like me?

Mary glanced at me, a pencil tapping against her teeth, clearly itching to tell me more.

"There's another man who escaped."

"Who?" I asked.

"The Peruvian Scotsman, Captain MacDougall. I found an account from a Captain Hood. He wrote that he had shared a tin of bully beef with him in the small hours of the thirtieth of May near Winnezeele. Then the drama started. As you know, the Germans were all over the place by that time. It sounds as if MacDougall got detached and joined a group of around forty Royal Engineers from the 100th Monmouth Regiment. They marched for some hours in a gradual left-hand circle. They nearly made it to Dunkirk, but the Germans had been tracking them. As they crossed the road they were shot up by Panzer tanks. MacDougall, a Major Whitehead and a Sapper called Bate were the only three to escape that ambush."

"Well, I never. That news never filtered back to us in the camps."

"The Captain, Whitehead and Bate were on the run together for two months. He never made it back to Blighty though."

Two months, I thought to myself, that was an awfully long time to avoid capture in enemy territory. As if pre-empting my thoughts, Mary spoke.

"They were helped by the French of course, but would also have to live off the land, stealing from farms, catching rabbits, that sort of thing."

"But their luck eventually ran out?"

"Yes. We don't know the exact circumstances, but I've found another account that the three men were captured near a place called Forges-les-Eaux, just north of Rouen on twenty fourth of July 1940."

I knew that place; Rouen was about one hundred miles to the southwest of Cassel.

Mary turned a page in her notebook. "Captain MacDougall was also mentioned in dispatches, in December 1945 after recommendation by the British Secret Service, MI9."

"Let me guess," I said to Mary.

"Go on," she said.

"I would suppose it was something to do with his communications from the POW camps."

"Yes," Mary announced with a grin. "The War Office said that his communications were 'by secret means', I think we both know what that means."

"Anything else?" I asked.

"No, his wartime service is still something of a mystery; I wasn't able to find out anything else. All I know is that he had married in 1935 and then remarried again in 1967. I can't find anything else about him, but I believe he's still alive because I can't find any death notices or obituaries. I'd think if someone like Captain MacDougall had passed away, someone would have written an obituary somewhere."

Mary had pulled out a fresh jotter, it appeared that Captain MacDougall and Gunner Martin had taken up a full notepad. This one was altogether much thinner, not anywhere near as many words.

Mary opened proceedings with a smile. "Colonel Odling survived the war, Dr West."

I was engulfed with a warm feeling. This was somehow going to be a better story, not as exciting, but with a nicer ending. I sensed it. Mary told me what I already knew. Cedric Odling was injured in one of the regiment's northerly gun troop positions at Mont des Recollets. She read out the date, "Cassel, the twenty-eighth of May 1940."

"He was in a bad way, we knew they had to get him some specialist medical help otherwise he would die," I said. Mary looked over the top of her glasses. "I was with him, Mary. We took the colonel up the hill to the Field Hospital in Cassel. It was a hopeless position we were in. Germans were everywhere. At one point I thought we weren't going to make it. We managed to get him in the vehicle. He was a brave man."

"So Odling owes his life to you then, Eric?"

"He was deteriorating fast, so I suppose that decision was taken out of my hands, but yes, I'd like to think I did my bit and I stayed with him right until we got him there. But there was a twist in the story."

"In what way."

"Well, Jerry was closing in and we knew we had to get out of there. They were getting nearer and nearer to the field hospital which was in the town square. Shells and those pesky mortars were landing quite close. Of course, Jerry wouldn't have known it was a field hospital, as far as they were concerned it could have been our HQ."

Mary sat silently and listened intently as I continued.

"Our officers made an incredibly tough but brave decision which ultimately saved more than a hundred lives." I felt a lump in my throat. "We... we had to abandon them."

Mary's hand covered her mouth. "Gosh."

"If we'd stayed where we were and fought the Germans, they would have blown the place to bits, along with the wounded and the injured. They'd be sitting ducks, men who'd lost legs and arms, how were they going to run? One of the officers, I can't remember who, came and told us what they had decided.

'They'll all be killed,' someone said.

The officer shook his head, said calmly that if we drew fire away from the hospital and they raised the white flag of surrender, they'd be prisoners but, hopefully, would be taken to German hospitals and at least had a chance of survival. He then told us that the medics had agreed to stay behind to care for the badly injured."

"My God, they volunteered knowing that the Germans would be coming for them too?"

"Yes."

"That they'd become POWs."

"Or killed," I said as I shrugged my shoulders. "Nobody knew what was going to happen and there had already been stories of Germans massacring prisoners. Oh yes, we all knew about the Geneva Convention and how POWs should be treated, but in the heat of the battles going on around Dunkirk, those rules were getting ripped up."

I remember looking back at the old Flemish building in the town square of Cassel and thinking about those poor boys awaiting their fate. And those bloody medics, my God they should have all been awarded a medal. A selfless sacrifice.

"But the plan worked, Mary, those boys all survived. The medics were taken prisoner of course, but the injured were transferred to German hospitals. Colonel Odling was among them, the Germans took care of him."

Mary spoke, "Colonel Odling spent three years as a prisoner in Oflag IX."

"Only three years?" I asked.

"Yes. At the beginning of November 1943, he was repatriated to England via Sweden under the Red Cross scheme."

"Because of his injuries?"

"Yes, he walked with a stick; the Germans knew he would never fight again. There was an agreement between the Allies that they would send the badly injured prisoners home. It made sense, it meant that they wouldn't need to feed and shelter them."

I sat back and took it all in. Mary was a good storyteller. It was fascinating.

"But the Nazis had made a mistake with Cedric Odling because, on his return to England, he was debriefed and then transferred to SHAEF."

"Right, the Supreme Headquarters Allied Expeditionary Force"

"Yes, in Grosvenor Square, London. He helped plan the D-Day Landings, Dr West."

Well I never… the Germans had released him thinking he was of no use anymore and he helped plot their ultimate downfall. I looked at Mary and a simple eye movement and a sweep of the hand begged her to continue.

"I don't know if you ever knew but, before the war, Cedric was a marble merchant for a family business. They were producers of memorials and gravestones; at the time it was one of the largest stone businesses in Europe. Cedric was the chairman, they had depots in London, Hull, Liverpool, Glasgow, Plymouth, Bristol and Dublin and even one in Italy."

I had no idea.

"After the war, he picked up his chairmanship again; I don't suppose the millions of dead in Europe over the course of the war did the business any harm. He retired in the mid-1960s."

My heart started to beat a little faster, could it be that our old commanding officer was still alive? He must be nearly ninety by now, perhaps more.

I dared to ask the question, "And is he still alive?"

I detected a slight smile.

"Tell me, Mary, please."

"Yes, he's still alive. I've tracked him down. He's very old and infirm; he's in a nursing home in Sussex."

I flopped back in my seat. My head tilted back, and I took in some air. Would it be possible to see him, would he remember me?

"He's all alone, Doctor, no family, it appeared he never married."

"Of course he never married, we knew he never would, it wasn't his thing. Oh, we all knew, the entire regiment knew. Of course, at the time homosexuality was frowned upon, but we never made a big thing of it. I guess it was a sign of respect, it showed how much we all thought of the colonel. None of us would have dreamt of turning him in; it would have meant prison with hard labour. That was the real bond between the officers and us."

"I've called the nursing home," Mary said, bringing me back from my thoughts.

"You have?"

"Yes. The manageress said he rarely gets any visitors, and she thinks it would be a great idea if you wanted to travel down to see him."

"Of course, yes, of course, I'd love to see him."

I surprised myself with my spontaneous reaction. That wasn't like me, nor was it like me to even consider a reunion. I had spent forty-five years avoiding them like the plague. Why was this one so different? I'd never seen or even spoken to my old CO since we'd thrown him into the back of a vehicle all those years ago. Would he remember me? Perhaps he was senile, perhaps even dementia? There was only one way to find out.

I asked Mary and she gave me the telephone number of the nursing home and the name of the manageress. Ms Turner.

"Excuse me for a minute," I said as I stood.

I walked over to the main office and asked permission to use the telephone. A short time later I was speaking to the manageress. I explained who I was; she told me she recalled the conversation with Mary.

"Any time you like, Dr West," she said. "He's very frail but bright as a button. I'll tell him you are coming, I'm sure he'll remember you."

It was all arranged for the following week, a Wednesday afternoon, after Cedric's post-lunch nap. The manageress said it would be a good time to talk, he was always lively after his lunchtime nap, not so good in the mornings.

On the day of the visit, I was up bright and early.

I had a light breakfast, shaved carefully and put on my best suit. I even splashed a little of the expensive aftershave that Mouse bought for me at Christmas time. I had to make an effort for my old CO. It was only right.

I couldn't wait to see him, I wondered what he would say when he knew I was a doctor. Proud, I should think. Yes… he'd be proud that one of his mere gunners had managed to become a doctor. Proud and pleased as punch.

As I was leaving the house, I was so nervous about meeting him that I realised I'd forgotten my car keys and had to go back into the house.

"Damn!" Just as I located them in the fruit bowl in the kitchen, the telephone rang in the hallway.

I looked at my watch. I still had plenty of time to answer it.

"Hello, Dr West," the caller stated.

"Yes, speaking."

"Good morning, Dr West, it's Stephanie Turner, the manageress of the care home in Sussex."

"Oh yes, Ms Turner, I'm just about to leave, is everything okay?"

"No, doctor, I'm very sorry but Mr Odling was taken to Haywards Heath Hospital during the night."

"Oh dear, I'm sorry. So, today's visit is cancelled then?" There was a noted silence at the other end of the phone. "Ms Turner, should we reschedule for next week?"

"I'm sorry, Dr West, I'm afraid I have some bad news."

Chapter 52

IN DUNKIRK'S GRIM DAYS

It took me the best part of a week to get over the news that within just a few hours of our rendezvous, my commanding officer had slipped quietly away in his sleep.

I felt cheated. I was distraught, so much so that I cancelled my next couple of meetings with Mary. I knew she had more to tell me but, quite frankly, I wasn't sure I really wanted to know. Realistically, how many of my mates had made it to retirement? I moped around the house for a while but eventually pulled myself around and drove over to Sutton. I met Mary for lunch at a small tearoom on the high street.

After our first cup of tea and while we waited for lunch, Mary was straight on the case again.

"I found a letter from a Brigadier Somerset; he was commander at Cassel when you were there. Do you remember him?"

"Yes, of course I do, I met him briefly when we took Colonel Odling to the field hospital. What's this about a letter?"

"He wrote to the Daily Telegraph in 1948. It appears he wasn't very happy about Churchill's war memoirs."

"In what way?"

Mary quoted directly from the letter. Somerset was referring to the battle for Dunkirk.

"Mr Churchill had written, 'After the loss of Boulogne and Calais, only the remains of the port of Dunkirk and the open beaches next to the Belgian frontier were in our hands.'"

"What, he wrote that?"

"Apparently, yes. But I never read his war memoirs."

"Me neither."

"Well, the brigadier must have read the bloody memoirs and it prompted him to write to the Telegraph. It was his brigade that held the sector from Cassel to Hazebrouck. Reading between the lines, he was incensed. He said how they were attacked by the Germans on... "

"Twenty-seventh of May."

I'd finished Mary's sentence for her. The date was etched onto a part of my brain that would not allow me to forget.

"That's right. Twenty-seventh of May," Mary said. "The brigadier said they were surrounded. He made a serious accusation that he did not know that the BEF were on the retreat and heading for the Dunkirk beaches. He said that you lot at Cassel were expecting a counterattack by the British to relieve you."

"We were," I said. "We didn't appreciate the BEF were cutting and running, and nobody bothered to tell us. Our boys fought like lions, men and officers together and we held out until the evening of the twenty-ninth. There were so many killed. The Germans dropped leaflets telling us to surrender, they read: 'Your generals are gone' but we didn't believe them."

Mary was nodding. She read out the final part of Somerset's letter verbatim.

"'I feel it is fair neither to myself nor the troops under my command to let this stand pass from mind, especially as so many gave their lives, and most of the remainder of us spent five years in captivity. Incidentally, by holding on at Cassel we not only deprived the Germans of one of the main roads to Dunkirk but enabled many British detached units and individuals to reach the bridgehead. All these facts appear to have utterly escaped the notice of the authorities at the time owing to the indescribable confusion, and I feel that an opportunity has now been afforded me of bringing them to light.'"

Well, I never. Even after so long, our officers continued to fight our corner.

"It had been Churchill's 'we shall fight them on the beaches' speech in which he'd referred to the root, core and brain of the British Army who had been stranded at Dunkirk. Everyone knew that the BEF were about to be massacred or captured. But not us, not Brigadier Somerset and the men under his command. We fought for our country, we fought for liberty and by blocking the roads we had stalled the German attack."

Mary chewed on a sandwich while I rambled on about how let down we felt after we found out the truth, many years later.

She cleared her mouth and spoke, "So, I guess your old battalion doesn't think a lot of Winston Churchill, he seems to have conveniently forgotten about your heroic stand. My God, doctor, there were over three hundred thousand men rescued from the beaches at Dunkirk, that's a war-changing number of troops."

I held up a hand. "You're right, but I won't have a word said about Churchill."

"And why not?"

"Because nobody wanted the bloody job of Prime Minister in the first place. Don't forget Churchill had only been PM for a couple of weeks at that point."

Mary said she hadn't realised.

But Mary was right. The BEF were in disarray. Hitler held every ace in the pack and the pressure on Parliament was immense. So many wanted to sue for peace. It was no secret, in early 1940 that Hitler was trying to seal a deal with Britain. He was quite happy to run amok on mainland Europe. He made it clear that he wanted some sort of treaty with Britain, that if we left him alone, he'd leave our Empire alone.

I turned to Mary. "There were so many MPs at the time that pushed for a peace pact with Hitler. Most of them, I'm sad to say, were Conservative."

Here I was, a supporter of our Prime Minister, Margaret Thatcher, sitting in a tearoom discussing wartime politics and feeling, for the first time in forty years, a sensation of anger about the Tory MPs who had failed to support us in France. The truth was that they had never properly supported Churchill in the early part of the war. There were a few brave exceptions, like Major Ronald Cartland, the Conservative MP who fought alongside us and died out there in Cassel.

It was no surprise we servicemen voted Labour en-masse in 1945, I thought to myself.

"There were all of those men scrambling for the beaches, the Luftwaffe were bombing and strafing the roads and the beaches around Dunkirk, the Wehrmacht in northern France were poised too. Meanwhile, some of our politicians wanted to start talks with Nazi Germany, mediated by that Italian idiot Mussolini. The bargaining tool was all those trapped men; by

273

all accounts, Hitler was ready to let them go for a peace pact. That's an awful lot of men with families back home, unthinkable pressure on Churchill and, in the background, cabinet shenanigans from Lord Halifax and others pushing for peace."

I could see the cogs of Mary's brain running wild. She had no idea of the politics involved at that time. Neither did I. It wasn't until decades later when cabinet papers were released into the public domain, was it known just how close we came to putting pen to paper with the Nazis.

"Some historians say that week, the last week of May 1940, was the most important week in history. Because if Great Britain had signed a pact with Germany, knowing what we know now, they would have won the war and the Nazis were hell-bent on world domination and genocide."

Mary sat in silence, shaking her head from side to side. "It's unthinkable."

"However, that didn't happen, because news filtered back to the cabinet that more and more troops were making it safely back to the beaches, the evacuation was underway and that 'a mob' were actually keeping the Nazi ground forces occupied."

"Your mob, doctor," Mary smiled.

I puffed out my chest with pride. "Yes Mary, our bloody mob." I continued. "The Luftwaffe was somewhat hampered by bad weather, the low cloud and of course most of the evacuation was happening in the dark. But even then, the cabinet were so close to throwing in the towel. However, military intelligence filtered through about Cassel holding out. Churchill wondered if it were possible to buy a little more time and with the help of a flotilla of small boats, get our boys back so that they could live to fight another day."

"Amazing," said Mary. "I didn't know about any of this." Mary held up the letter. "And Churchill conveniently forgot about 'your mob' in his memoirs?"

"He did. Now can you see why the brigadier was so cheesed off?"

Mary handed me the letter.

I read it quietly several times, then looked up. "Don't tell me the brigadier is still alive?

Mary nodded softly. "He's ninety-two years old."

I walked with Mary back to the centre. It was a beautiful sunny afternoon. It was fitting; my heart was filled with warmth.

I had no real desire to make any attempt to go and visit the brigadier. There were several reasons. The man wouldn't probably recall me for one, he commanded over a thousand men and I had only met him once, briefly, in the heat of battle when he had a hundred other things to think about. Although I was now a consultant, I would always feel a mere conscripted man and him, my superior.

Nor did I want to tempt fate. Cedric Odling's death had upset me. I had never believed in a God in any shape or form, but if there was an entity up there, he had a cruel sense of humour in taking away Cedric, the day I was due to meet up with him. We had fought the Nazi scourge of evil together and both survived, albeit affected in different ways.

But we had overcome. I had lost five years of my life, Cedric Odling a year or so less. I had been treated like a subhuman at times. I think the officers fared slightly better. I had been starved, beaten, degraded, subjected to unimaginable brutality and mental torture. Cedric had walked that walk with me, and the evil regime had left him permanently disabled.

And Somerset had suffered too. Somerset had also spent five years as a POW, so why would I want to bring it all up again? Why would I want to sit with an old man and make him relive all of those horrors? Let's be honest, it's all we had in common. It simply wasn't fair to put a ninety-two-year-old man through that all over again.

As we turned into the gates of the building, Mary was strangely quiet, and I knew why. I stopped at the entrance and turned to her.

"I won't come in, Mary, if that's all right."

"Of course, doctor."

"I would like to thank you for everything you've done for me."

She let out a little laugh.

"Surely it's the other way round," she said.

"I suppose we've helped each other, Mary. You've brought me closure on some terrible times. Oh yes, Geoff helped of course, he was by my side every step of the way."

Since the war had ended, my life had been a series of closing doors, facing up to my demons and in a way, exorcising them. The ghosts were in my head, and they were never far away, especially in those first few decades after the war. I had to live with the nightmares. Some were particularly bad; some working weeks were a haze. How I got through those years of study and passed all those exams, I'll never know.

I threw myself into my work and that helped. 'Batten down the hatches' was the expression I often said quietly to myself. There wasn't much more I could do, because if I hadn't battened down the hatches the only other alternative was to give up on life and throw in the towel. I battened down a lot of hatches over the years. I'd battened down the hatches again when I'd lost Joy at such a young age, just over six years ago. It felt like yesterday.

There was no choice really. I convinced myself that however much I had suffered, there were always people who were worse off than me. I always tried to take the positives out of life. In the POW camps, those poor Russian prisoners, I'd never forgotten them, desperate men, walking corpses. Even as a prisoner I counted myself lucky. Those trains full of Jewish men, women and children. The noise of desperation, the smells, the cries of young infants.

The forced marches. Even on the Long March, I was lucky. I was lucky because I was not one of those executed for being too slow or one of the men frozen to death sleeping in the snow.

I'd closed a door firmly on Cassel. The last week of May 1940, maybe it was the pivot-point of the entire war. And I was a part of it. For the first time, this bloody Kreigie could allow himself a few moments of pride.

The names of the men in my regiment would live on. That I was sure of. There had been books I'd read during the research for my own book, and men like Brigadier Nigel Somerset who would shout out loud what we had done and our sacrifice.

I opened the door and Mary stood at the entrance. I didn't want to dwell on the fact, and I certainly wouldn't mention it but Mary's research had brought about the biggest closure of all.

My life seemed to suddenly make sense and I felt unburdened, as though someone had taken a great weight off my back. She'd found heroes, the heroes that I'd fought with. Although many were dead, there were those who had made it too, those who had cocked a snook at the Nazi regime and had helped me get on with my life. Some gave me a leg up when needed.

Maybe this was why I gravitated towards a career in helping others. Hopefully, I had helped others at their worst times. At last, it seemed to make sense. I felt I had achieved some kind of resolution.

I could now tell my story, without shame, with pride even. My book was nearing completion, I was looking forward to seeing it published. It was my story of Überleben, survival. Like Bisset's precious violin from our E72 Orchestra that survived the Long March and made it back to New Zealand, somehow I'd also made it home in the end. Like that violin, I was battered but repairable. And so I'd share my story with my children, their children when they eventually came along. I was looking forward to grandchildren.

I could now tell my story, without shame, with pride even. My book was nearing completion,

Who knows, I might be able to even sit them on my knee, tell them a story about good and evil, about history, tell it in a way that might keep them interested. There were photographs too, old black and white photographs, me and Geoff, Mum and Dad. Yes, they'd like those photographs.

When they're old enough, I'll sit my grandchildren down and tell this story properly. Right from the beginning.

Chapter 53

UNINVITED GUEST

It was a hot sunny weekend and it occurred to me that I couldn't put this off any longer.

Health wise I was feeling okay, though I'd lost an awful lot of weight. Hopefully, after the operation, I could build myself up again.

"Cancer isn't the death sentence it once was," they kept telling me. They all said that. doctors, nurses, my family, friends and acquaintances, even some of my ex-colleagues. That might well be true, but I wasn't the normal run-of-the-mill patient. I had a medical background and when the surgeon had told me the prognosis, Dukes D carcinoma of caecum with liver secondaries. I didn't have to dive into a medical textbook to know what that meant.

It meant six months, perhaps a year or two at the most.

But I was grateful for that time, remembering my good friends who had died in Flanders, behind barbed wire in Poland, in the fields and by the side of the roads in Czechoslovakia and Germany. It had been tough; it had tested every fibre of my being.

How had I got through it all, I wondered to myself. *Maybe fighting cancer will be easy by comparison.*

The truth is, I struggled initially and some of those experiences never left me. But with Joy's help that terrible bitterness and anger I once knew started to evaporate. I could even see some of the funny side. Joy and I had raised a wonderful family and we'd live on through them whether they liked it or not.

Mrs Knight was there. We were having tea in the garden. My notes, notebooks, research material, and photos were spread out on the table. There were half a dozen maps, or rather sections of maps, two of which were Cassel and the surrounding area and a photocopied A5 map of India.

And of course, there was all the material by my feet, two full foolscap box files.

I had made a start on my biography some time ago, but like most writers, the discipline to sit down and write every day, if only for a few hours, had proven more difficult than I ever imagined. Mouse had tried her best to push me, she knew most of my story and urged me ever onwards. She said it was a story worth telling and she was happy to type it up for me. We'd sat for hours, me dictating notes, sometimes she just talked me through a particular episode, and she was the one who took the notes. She opened her small suitcase on wheels. She had that grin on her face as she reached in and pulled out a bundle of A4 sheets.

"Wow!" I said. "My book?"

"Yes," she said.

"There must be a hundred pages."

"There's one hundred and sixteen actually," she said.

"And you've typed it all up?

"Yes. Most of it anyway. But remember, Eric, I'm a typist, it didn't take so long." She let out a deliberate sigh. "What's taking so long, Eric, is your side of the operation. You procrastinate; get yourself too tied up in the research, unnecessary facts about tank types, and the length of a German aircraft wing. You fly off on a tangent when all I'm trying to do is to bring you back to what needs to go into the book."

I had to laugh. The Mouse was spot on. The truth was that I enjoyed all that side of things. It interested me greatly; it was my hobby, in a way, and it was far more enjoyable than hour upon hour of boring writing, bringing back the memories that sometimes I had no wish to recall. But I had a surprise for her. I'd been busy.

Just as I was about to hand her two more completed notebooks, the French window in the sitting room slammed shut. That meant only one thing. Someone had opened the door at the front of the house causing a vacuum.

"Are you expecting someone?" Mrs Knight asked.

"No."

Mouse looked decidedly uncomfortable as my son breezed into the garden with a big smile on his face.

"My son, John. He sometimes does this if he's in the area," I said.

I stood up to welcome the man Mrs Knight had last seen when he was an eleven-year-old boy.

"John," I said, "this is Hilda Knight, my secretary." I turned to Mouse, "Mou… Mrs Knight, this is my son John."

John stepped forward. "Mrs Knight, pleased to meet you, I've heard all about you, pleased to have met you at last."

Mouse smiled innocently. "Ahh but we've met before, John. You were just a little boy, your father brought you into the office and I showed you the tropical fish tank."

There was a spark of memory recall in John's face.

"Do you remember, John?" I asked.

"Vaguely," he said. "I remember the fish, but sorry, Mrs Knight, not so much you."

He squirmed. Always the honest one. That was John.

"That's okay," she said. "I expect the tropical fish were a whole lot more colourful than a dowdy old secretary. Your father was explaining to you that we had the tropical fish in the waiting room so that the patients would relax before their appointments."

He turned to me. "And did it work?"

"Yes. I believe it did."

I invited John to join us at the table. I said I'd make some more tea, but I could see my female friend was decidedly uncomfortable in John's presence.

"I must be off," she said after no more than five minutes.

I sighed. She'd just arrived. We'd hardly got started and now I had to come clean to John that finally, after all these years, I was about to tell my story.

I had a plan. I'd ignore Mrs Knight's last sentence; pretend I hadn't heard her. Should anything happen to me, she'd need someone to help her with this monumental task. We'd need readers and editors; a publisher would need to be found. I'm sure that if we could somehow get John interested, he'd be willing to help, perhaps he could even take a little of the writing on board.

"What's all this, Dad," he said, taking a seat at the table. "And this bloody great case on the grass, what's this?" He pointed to the dozen, red Silvine exercise books on the table. "And this, Dad. Are you writing a bloody book or something?"

Barely a second passed. It felt like an eternity.

"My God, you are, aren't you? You're writing a book, that's why Mrs Knight is here, isn't it? She's helping you with it."

Mrs Knight slid the one hundred and sixteen pages of A4 across into the middle of the table.

"He is. This is what he has written thus far, I typed it up for him and I'm sure he wouldn't mind you looking."

"Not before me," I jumped in.

And just like that, the ice was broken and to my great delight, there was a sparkle in my son's eyes.

"Why you cunning old bugger," he chortled. "You never said anything."

"No, I didn't."

"Why not, I would have helped you; it must be an enormous undertaking."

"Well, I wasn't sure you'd be interested in all that boring stuff from the war."

"It's about the war, your time as a prisoner?"

"Yes, most of it anyway."

Even as I spoke with John and filled him in on some of the content, I could see Mrs Knight making to leave. She twitched and fidgeted and eventually sprang to her feet.

"I'll see you soon, Eric," she said as she tidied a few things away and slipped some bits and pieces into her handbag. "You make sure you've read what I've typed up and I want another notebook from you next week."

"My God, Dad, how long is this bloody book?" John said.

My chest puffed out proudly as I lifted the pile of notebooks. "I believe there are nearly one hundred thousand words in here."

My son was stunned into silence.

Mrs Knight was in the starting blocks, itching for the signal. She tapped me on the shoulder, I had no option but to stand politely and bid her goodbye. I could see that she was obviously contemplating the usual farewell kiss but decided against it. Instead, she shook my hand gently. She said goodbye to John and before I was aware, the Mouse was scuttling across the garden into the house.

John's gaze followed her as she left.

"What a nice lady," he announced.

"She always was. She's been such a rock over the years."

"Dad, Mum's been gone nearly six years, it's okay to have a lady friend you know."

I nodded but didn't answer. I feared the problem lay with Mrs Knight. But John was right, and it was his way of saying that it was more than acceptable.

But John's head was already in the open case.

"My goodness, what's all this?"

Over the years I'd accumulated hundreds of photographs, some family, many of my old regiment but also random photos of POW camps and the forced marches. There were photos of the old E72 winding tower and another at Gliwice. There were photos of prisoners playing football and rugby, pictures of concerts on stage, and frozen bodies in the snow from that winter of 1945.

John had pulled out an old address book.

"Were these wartime friends of yours?" He flicked the pages. "Helmut from Germany, Jan from Watou, Celina from Łambinowice, Antoni and Mania from Katowice. My goodness, Dad, have you kept in touch with these people?"

"Some," I said. "Helmut was a German POW in England, I met him in Cassel, it was a pure fluke that it turned out we had been together in Leicester, at Shady Lane POW camp."

John flopped back in his seat. "Well I never, Dad, you're a bit of a dark horse. Tell me about him?"

He was genuinely interested. I looked into his eyes while he waited for me to answer him. I knew at that moment that I'd move heaven and earth to get the book finished as quickly as I could. We spoke for an hour or so. I told him there were so many details that I had forgotten about and joked that he would have to wait for the book.

"And what will you call it?" he said.

Mrs Knight and I hadn't got to that stage, hadn't even found an editor.

"The Psychiatrist," he announced. "By Eric West."

Before I could answer him, he was delving into another box file.

He pulled out a photograph of my brother. "And who is this chap?" he said.

"Come on, John, surely you've seen that photo before, that's your Uncle Geoffrey."

"Don't think so," he said. "I don't think I've ever seen these photos before."

Another photo of Geoff, a 1930s black and white family photo of the three West boys.

"I was twelve here, Geoff would have been about seven. That's him in the middle."

John studied the picture for some time. I could see that he was getting quite emotional.

"I wish I'd met him, Dad," he said. "He looks such a fun bloke, but... "

"Not now, son," I said.

Those memories from so long ago were still so raw. I picked up one of the notebooks.

"You can read all about him in here," I said with a smile disguising the tear that had formed in the corner of my eye."

"I will, Dad," he said. "I can't wait."

Chapter 54

DELEGATION

It was the day of the operation and John arrived at seven-thirty to collect me. The operation was scheduled for mid-morning, nothing more specific than that, and I had to be at the hospital by eight-thirty. They told me that I'd be in overnight and depending on how I recovered, I would probably be allowed home in two or three days. Knowing Joy wouldn't be there to look after me, I'd booked myself into a local nursing home to convalesce.

John was fussing over me. Have you got this, have you got that?

"I'm a doctor," I told him, "I know what I need to go into hospital."

"Sorry, Dad."

"Anyway," I said, "sit down; I need to talk to you."

I lifted the crate onto the kitchen table. "Remember this?"

"Yes, Dad, of course I do."

"Right," I said, "there's everything in here to go forward and get the book published."

John looked at me as if I was mad.

"If anything should happen to me, John, Mrs Knight will need some help."

He wafted a hand in front of me. "Don't be daft, Dad, you'll probably outlive me."

"I know the risks, John," I said firmly, "and this is important to me now. The full manuscript is in there. It's finished, one hundred and ten thousand words but I think it will need polishing up. The photos are in there too. I think it should have a few photos, maybe some pencil sketches at the beginning of a few of the chapters. Your sister is a great artist, perhaps she could help?"

John looked stunned. "I never realised how serious you were to tell your story."

"I wasn't, John, I never wanted to, but those trips to Flanders and Poland, well… things changed. It was when I started to take a few research notes that it dawned on me that perhaps someone might want to read about what we went through. So, I made more notes and started to pull a couple of chapters together. I gave them to Mrs Knight. She said they were very good. Interesting."

John looked up, smiled and repeated, "I can't wait to read it, Dad."

"That's good," I said. I slid the crate across the table. "Because this is your responsibility now. I'm placing you in charge of the operation. I'm delegating." I grinned.

"You sound like a brigadier in the army. Are you sure this book hasn't transported you back to 1945?"

"Stand to attention when I speak to you!" I barked back at him.

John was on his feet straight away. He stood stiff straight. Saluted.

"To the regiment and the pineapple."

We laughed like we hadn't laughed for years.

We had a cup of tea before we left. We put the world to rights. We talked about Cassel and Poland and books, and how the hell we would go about finding a publisher. John assured me that he would make sure it happened.

And as I looked into his eyes, and studied the lines on his face, I knew he wouldn't let me down.

Chapter 55

VISITOR

I woke up to find myself being turned by a nurse. She was prim and proper, very gentle but at the same time, efficient in her starched uniform.

"Thank God for that," I said, "I thought I might have died."

She laughed.

"No, Dr West, you're very much alive and kicking."

I didn't feel very much alive and kicking. I felt like I had been rolled over on hard tarmac by a fleet of buses.

The room was spinning; I was in a morphine-induced haze.

I closed my eyes again. More pain, this time in both temples. I may have slept for a while and then woke with a start.

I had momentarily forgotten that I was in hospital. I remember panicking, shapes and forms came into focus, it was dark, those smells. I thought I'd overslept in a barn somewhere in Czechoslovakia. Voices. I didn't understand the words at first. German voices? Was I about to be kicked or hit with a rifle butt? The rifle was prodding my shoulder. But gentle, oh so gentle.

Not a German guard, not a rifle or a jackboot. A nurse. A pretty nurse. A brunette, I think. The words becoming clearer. Not German, English, a west country accent.

"You have a visitor, Dr West."

I opened my eyes. He blurred into focus. A familiar face.

"It's good to see you," I said.

He gripped my hand. Squeezed tight. My brother. Fading in and out, a bright light behind him, more of a silhouette. My mouth was dry, I summoned the energy to speak.

"Do you remember that cemetery we visited at Winnezeele?"

"What cemetery, where on earth is Winnezeele?"

"Flanders, it's in Flanders."

"I've never been to Flanders."

"Of course you have, we went together, the boys' road trip."

He shook his head. "No, Dad. I haven't been to Flanders."

Dad?

"John...?"

This bloody morphine.

The nurse fluffed up my pillow. She returned to her notes at the foot of my bed.

I could see it now, a different tone of voice, darker hair. He looked a little like Geoff as I recalled.

"Of course," I said to John. "You weren't there."

"No, Dad."

I turned my head. A sharp pain shot across the back of my skull.

"It was you, Geoff, wasn't it?"

Geoff nodded silently.

"Who are you talking to, Dad?" John asked. "Try and focus on me. I'm here right in front of you."

I looked at John and then back to Geoff.

The nurse stepped forward again.

"It's cold in here now."

She looked over to the window and then to John. Have you opened the window?"

"No, nurse."

I closed my eyes again. It was all too much. What was Geoff doing there anyway?

I spoke in a whisper, my eyes still closed. "Geoff, come a little closer. Remember the lady in Flanders, the lady who was trying to find her son?"

"It's quite normal," a female voice whispered softly. "It's the drugs wearing off."

"My bedside cabinet, Geoff, my notes," I said. "I have them with me, in the cabinet. Please get them for me."

"I'll get them, Dad."

I heard movement beside me, the click of the latch. The squeak of the hinges as the door groaned open. The rustle of paper.

I opened my eyes. "Pass them to me."

John opened the cabinet and reached inside. He took out the book on the top and handed it to me.

I opened the book, pointed at the title page. The Collected Works of Rudyard Kipling.

"Her name was Helen Turrell, her son was called Michael. Remember? She pretended Michael was her nephew," I said.

"I haven't a clue what you are talking about, Dad," John said. "Who are you talking to, Dad, you're not looking at me?"

"Your Uncle Geoff, I'm talking to your Uncle Geoff." I said.

"There's nobody there, Dad. I'm here with the nurse, there's just the two of us."

"Geoff," I repeated, "right beside you."

"Dad," John said. "Uncle Geoff died soon after the war."

I smiled. The two men looked like twins. They could be brothers.

"He took his own life in India, Dad. Remember?"

Geoff smiled at me. He was still with me. He would always be with me. I closed my eyes again.

John spoke with the nurse quietly. She said something about hallucinating, that many people waking up after anaesthesia saw Jesus Christ or the ghosts of their dead relatives.

The brain is a complex thing.

EPILOGUE

Sue sat with John in the living room of his father's lounge. He had decided to bring his sister in on the task at hand.

"So, he's looking for a publisher. That won't be as easy as he thinks."

"You think it's good enough to be published, John?" she asked. "I mean, he never mentioned a dickie bird about his war years. What the hell is there to say?"

John lifted the lid on one of the box files. "You need to have a look at some of this stuff. To be honest I can't explain some of it." He reached in and pulled out a photo. Modern. In colour. "I mean look at this, who is this young girl?"

He handed the photo to Sue.

"Mm… "

"Recognise her?"

"No. She looks Eastern European, it's fairly recent I'd say." Sue turned the photograph. "'Mania, Bytom,' it says."

"So, who is she?" John questioned.

A wicked grin pulled across Sue's face. "You don't suppose Dad was a naughty boy out there in Poland during the war. I've read that there were dozens of prisoners with Polish or Czech girlfriends, a lot of children with a little British blood in them." She held up the photograph and studied it again. "This young girl could be a long-lost relation of ours, Dad's granddaughter."

She handed the photo back to her brother.

"I can't see it, no West family features on that face. You're right Sue, maybe just someone he met when he went to Poland."

John reached back into another of the box files. He handed his sister a pile of exercise books with Eric's spidery handwriting.

"These look fairly random but they're not. Mrs Knight has typed most of it up."

John stood. He walked over to a table by the TV. There was a rucksack. He opened it, pulled out three packages wrapped in brown paper and walked back to the sofa.

"There are three copies of his book." He handed one to her. "We all need to read it through, take notes and then compare those notes. It will have to be rewritten, I'm happy to do that."

"You're bloody serious about all this aren't you, John?"

"I am. He's put a lot of work into it."

John handed her another piece of paper. An old document. "Here, look at this."

Sue took it and started to read.

"My God, it's an official War Office letter to our grandfather about Uncle Geoff. He must have been so desperate. I remember Dad telling us that he'd stabbed himself in the heart. Something to do with the unbearable heat, he was homesick, and his girlfriend had found someone new I think."

The letter was headed 'The War Office, London SW1' and dated 19th February 1947.

Sir,

I am directed to refer to War Office letter addressed to your son, Mr E.D.West, of 2nd October 1946 and previous correspondence addressed to Mrs West on the subject of the death of your son, 2/Lieutenant Geoffrey West, Royal Engineers, on 24th September last and to say that further information has now reached the War Office regarding the manner in which your son met his death.

Your son was transferred from Roorkee to the Hospital at Lucknow and then to the British Military Hospital, Delhi, on 19th August 1946 for treatment by psychotherapy for anxiety state symptoms and had made considerable improvement in his mental condition, particularly so during the last two weeks; he had become more cheerful and more sociable, but it was noted that his principal symptom – a fear of responsibility remained to some degree. He was not placed at any time under any special restrictions and up to the date of his death, there was nothing to indicate to those responsible for his care that his condition had deteriorated. It is feared that on the morning of 24th September 1946 he experienced a sudden discharge of emotional tension and, while his mind was so disturbed, he inflicted the injuries from which he died subsequently although immediate treatment by a surgical specialist was applied and every proper and necessary step was taken in an attempt to save his life.

I am again to express the deep sympathy of the Army Council in your sad bereavement.

I am, sir,

Your obedient Servant,

W. Macfarlane

Sue wiped at the corner of her eye. "It's making me come all over with emotion."

John took the document, slipped it back into the envelope, and returned it to the box file. "You know, Sue, when I was with Dad after he came round from the operation, he was calling me Geoff, he was convinced that Geoff was with us in that room."

"Drugs brother, that's the power of drugs."

"Perhaps," John nodded, "but he also said something quite strange."

"Go on."

"Well... he started talking about a place in France called Winnezeele. He thought I was Geoff, he said that we'd both been out there in Flanders. I don't suppose he was on drugs at the time."

"The mind is a complex place, brother, who knows what the hell was going on inside his head."

John's head was back in the file. "I found this War Grave certificate, Geoff was buried in Delhi Military Cemetery in 1946. He'd been transferred to Delhi from a place called Roorkee. Anyway, I'd never heard of Winnezeele until I found this." He handed his sister a sheet of A4. "It's the last page of the Kipling short story, 'The Gardener,' he's pencilled in 'Winnezeele Cemetery visit, 1985'. It sends a shiver up my spine, Sue."

Sue read:

... She climbed a few wooden-faced earthen steps and then met the entire crowded level of the thing in one held breath. She did not know Hagenzeele Third counted twenty-one thousand dead already. All she saw was a merciless sea of black crosses, bearing little strips of stamped tin at all angles across their faces. She could distinguish no order or arrangement in their mass; nothing but a waist-high wilderness as of weeds stricken dead, rushing at her. She went forward, moved to the left and the right hopelessly, wondering by what guidance she should ever come to her own. A great distance away there was a line of whiteness. It proved to be a block of some two or three hundred graves whose headstones had already been set, whose flowers planted out, and whose new-sown grass showed green. Here she could see clear-cut letters at the ends of the rows, referring to her slip, realized that it was not here she must look.

A man knelt behind a line of headstones — evidently a gardener, for he was firming a young plant in the soft earth. She went towards him, her paper in her hand. He rose at her approach and without prelude or salutation asked, 'Who are you looking for?'

'Lieutenant Michael Turrell — my nephew,' said Helen slowly and word for word, as she had many thousands of times in her life.

The man lifted his eyes and looked at her with infinite compassion before he turned from the fresh-sown grass toward the naked black crosses.

'Come with me,' he said, 'and I will show you where your son lies.'

When Helen left the cemetery, she turned for a last look. In the distance she saw the man bending over his young plants; and she went away, supposing him to be the gardener.

THE END

Made in United States
North Haven, CT
31 August 2023

40978429R00189